THE PRALAYA PROPHECY

Advance praise for the book

'Intriguing and engrossing, *The Pralaya Prophecy* is climate fiction at its most compelling. Seamlessly weaving mystical auguries with scientific truths, this oracular book crackles with suspense, excitement and a deep, piercing wisdom.' – **Namita Gokhale**, Winner of the Sahitya Akademi Award, *Things to Leave Behind*

Select praise for *The Climate Solution*

'I have great pleasure in recommending warmly the book, *The Climate Solution*, for widespread use in developing a strategy for meeting our climate-change crisis.' – **M.S. Swaminathan**, Father of India's Green Revolution, and recipient of the Padma Vibhushan

'Mridula Ramesh's pragmatic ideas of pushing individual initiative and climate-resilient start-ups to solve this problem offer an original roadmap to policymakers as well as the people of India for years to come. A must read.' – **Suresh Prabhu**, Minister of Commerce & Industry and Civil Aviation, Government of India

'*The Climate Solution* takes on a difficult task and delivers well.' – ***The Hindu***

'[T]imely and important…Communicating science, and encouraging us to care about somewhat distant problems is no simple task, and Ramesh does an impressive job of both.' – *Scroll.in*

'[T]hought-provoking…it impels the reader to think about what he/she can do to help the cause.' – *The Hindu BusinessLine*

Select praise for *Watershed*

'Fascinating and lucid…' – **Montek Singh Ahluwalia**, former Deputy Chairman, Planning Commission of India, and recipient of the Padma Vibhushan

'This is compelling material. A must-read.' – **Anand Mahindra**, Chairman, Mahindra and Mahindra

'*Watershed* reveals in clear, gripping language how close to the abyss we have come…' – **Rajendra Singh**, the 'Water Man of India'

'In *Watershed*, Mridula Ramesh lucidly and masterfully explains the science behind India's hydrology…' – **J. Srinivasan**, distinguished scientist, Indian Institute of Science

'The definitive book on water…' – **Rohini Nilekani**, founder–chairperson, Arghyam, and water philanthropist

'[A] riveting book…' – **Mahesh Rangarajan**, Professor of History and Environmental Studies, Ashoka University

'[A] must-read…' – ***The Book Review***

'It is everything about water that one should know.' – ***Business Standard***

'[I]nsightful and thought-provoking.' – ***The Tribune***

'[S]imple and engaging...The book takes on all the trajectories related to water…seamlessly and seemingly effortlessly to make the reader understand how the various strands weave and come together to shape India's water destiny.' – ***The Hindu BusinessLine***

'Ramesh, however, makes it [water] dance in a myriad way to her narrative.' – ***The Week***

THE PRALAYA PROPHECY

MRIDULA RAMESH

First published in 2026 by Hachette India
(Registered name: Hachette Book Publishing India Pvt. Ltd)
An Hachette UK company
www.hachetteindia.com

1

Section divider illustration from Dafont
('Snake Mix' by Woodcutter)

Print ISBN 978-93-5731-398-8
eBook ISBN 978-93-5731-793-1

Hachette Book Publishing India Pvt. Ltd
4th & 5th Floors, Corporate Centre,
Plot No. 94, Sector 44, Gurugram 122003, India

Typeset in Adobe Garamond Pro 11.5/15.5 by R. Ajith Kumar, New Delhi

Printed and bound in India
by Manipal Technologies Limited

For all those who wander and seek

DISCLAIMER

All names, characters, organizations, incidents, dialogues and locations – whether historical, mythological, political, religious or contemporary – are either imagined or used creatively within a fictional narrative. Any resemblance to any person or persons (living or dead), or to real events, scripture, places or institutions, is either entirely coincidental or creative and not real.

References to any religious, historical, mythological, scientific or cultural figures and episodes, places, texts, doctrines, and practices appear only to enrich the narrative fabric of the story; they are interpretative and purely fictional, and no claim of accuracy is made or implied, nor is any portrayal intended to challenge, demean or criticize any religion, ideology, belief system or political position. Quotations, verses – wherever included – are illustrative not authoritative references.

This book does not purport to offer scholarly perspectives in any domain, including religion, mythology, spiritual practices, astrology, history, temple architecture, anthropology, meteorology, sociology, philosophy, political science or cultural studies. The author repudiates any and all liability and claims arising from interpretations or actions based on this fictional narrative, and readers are advised to treat all content as imaginative and fictional and to exercise discretion in drawing conclusions. The author cannot be held liable or responsible to any person or persons or organizations with

Contents

1

The Signs

THE OLD MAN WOKE WITH A START. PEACEFUL SLEEP WAS hard to come by these days. But even so, this particular image had been real. So real. So vivid, stirring old, almost forgotten memories. He got off his wooden cot, ignoring the ache in his knees, and hobbled over to the earthen pot, kept covered with a plate to keep out insects and snakes. He dipped a tumbler in, and splashed some water on his face. More awake now, he grabbed an *angavastram*, tossed it around his thin shoulders, and left the house.

'It couldn't be,' he mumbled to himself, his heart leaping at the thought of his little granddaughter curled asleep back in the house. 'Not yet.'

The walk to the temple didn't take long. Opening the creaky temple door didn't rouse the sleeping guard. He noted with annoyance that the cameras were not working. At any other time, he would have woken the guard and given him a piece of his mind, but today his need to get to the cupboard was too great. Anxiety overcame annoyance, and he kept walking. He shuffled past the pathway, the guardian, the tank. He made his customary bow to the sanctum, but that was not his destination today; it was the chamber below it. The chamber that was always kept locked and closed and only opened once a year by the auditors to check on the jewels. He took the key from the ring he wore around his waist, opened the lock with shaking fingers, and entered the chamber. As he flipped the switch, his eyes narrowed, and he flinched as the tube lights erupted into a blinding blue-white blaze. He closed the door behind him and climbed gingerly down the steep stone steps, knowing that if he fell, his body would not be discovered for a long while, perhaps not until the next accounting exercise. He was not interested in the splendourous jewels – the ones about which so many newspapers around the world had speculated – but in a tiny cupboard, almost a secret room really, set to the side, intentionally kept in the dark, meant to be forgotten. But every young boy in the old man's family learned of it – and its contents – when they turned fifteen.

As he knelt in front of the cupboard, he pressed a small knob that opened the first door. Then, he crawled in and slid his key into the keyhole of the inner door. His knees blazed with pain. He whimpered and cursed as he closed the outer door behind him – he knew the inner door would not open until he did so. Then, he turned the key and opened the doors. He took out the manuscript from the back of the lowest shelf, holding a torch awkwardly between his neck and shoulders. He unwrapped the thread and carefully turned the Palmyra pages that were on the verge of falling apart due to age. In the back of his mind, he noted that the planets were in position: Jupiter, Venus, Mars, and the serpent node Rahu together in the house of the Sun. Mars had just moved the previous day. How had he missed that? A hollow feeling settled in his stomach as he turned to the page he wanted. One by one, he reviewed the necessary conditions. The social conditions had been met quite a while ago. The physical signs had become unmistakable in the past ten years, with the last one coming to pass just the prior month. The fools kept talking about how angering the gods had caused the floods. The gods were not involved.

How had he missed all of this, he asked himself again. He could have told his family; he could have told someone important – maybe the local councillor. Even amid his terror, his ever-present enjoyment of the ridiculous asserted itself. The picture of the corrupt councillor listening to him, let alone believing him, was ludicrous enough to bring out a crooked grin.

He shook himself and checked the manifestation of the special signs. The planetary condition was fulfilled. The others? The Three? The Saviour? Could anyone save them all anymore? In his desperation to find hope – any hope – he paid no heed to the unfamiliar pain spreading through his left arm. When would the Three come together? What did he need to do? He wanted to hit the authors of the book. It was all so obscure.

He began sweating profusely and wiped the sweat from his eyes to keep reading. Did anyone else know of the prophecy? He needed to tell someone, even if only the drunken heap lying on the floor of his home.

The pain was moving up his arm, and he felt lightheaded. 'No. Not now,' he said, realizing what was happening to him. He grabbed the book and tried to stand up. His knees flared in pain, and he screamed. His last thought as the darkness claimed him was of his granddaughter.

Far away, in a small temple in the mountains, the bells began to toll.

2

The Loss

IT'S HARD TO LOSE SOMEONE. IT'S EVEN HARDER WHEN that person is your only hand to hold, your only lap to curl up on. Her grandfather was missing. They had sent teams to look for him, but nothing had turned up for months. And now the temple's baton had to pass to her grand-uncle. Lakshmi was silent as strange men and women patted her head, walked around, ate, and left. The hum of activity lasted several days. She missed her grandfather's smile in the morning. His parchment-skinned, veiny hand holding hers while walking to the temple for evening prayers. Sitting with her during her homework later. And his snores at night. Her father didn't snore. But then, her father didn't do much of anything. He was a silent figure of a man, one who looked lost in a house that felt empty, quiet, hollow.

Her father looked at her. He had never really looked at her before.

She turned away and went to school.

3

Rajan

RAJAN DIDN'T QUITE KNOW WHAT TO DO.

His young daughter was a stranger. A stranger with sad, scornful eyes. A familiar, disdainful stranger. He had checked out of life so many years ago, disappearing into the numbness that liquor offered to those who could not bear life's load. Coming back, with his father gone, and being responsible for a young daughter was proving overwhelming. The bottle beckoned. He ignored it.

A long time ago, too long, he remembered his uncle insisting that he be sent to the *Patashala* like others his age. 'What is he going to achieve with studying numbers?' His gentle father had seen the light dying in his son's eyes but was unable to stand up to his brother's arguments. So, Rajan went to the Patashala. Years passed. Monotonous years. Where the focus was on rote memorisation, not understanding. The only time there was a glimpse of what might have been was during the pilgrimage he took with his father after his *upanayana*. But that was a brief spark in an ocean of grey. His natural intuition pushed him to ask probing questions into the truths briefly alluded to in concise verses, but his teachers dismissed his questions. And over the years, he stopped asking them, and his intuition quietened with disappointment. A few years later, he was married – he wasn't consulted, and yet, the deed was done. At nineteen, his bride, Radha, was on the older side. Not a classical beauty. But kind. And funny. He never knew softness until their marriage. Nor friendship. Nor the luxury of shared, secret laughter. She understood his frustration with being *just* a priest. The unpleasantness that creeps in when constantly chafing against one's leash. They shared many joys. The joy of togetherness, of humour and of understanding. Then came the joy of expectation. Of planned futures.

But all those joys were torn asunder by the clumsy hands of the poorly trained, uninterested doctor at Radha's delivery, leaving just a mewling baby and a wrenching hole in Rajan's heart. A hole he tried to fill by slipping into numb intoxication.

4

The Key

THE PAST TWO WEEKS HAD BEEN DISTURBINGLY CLEAR. He could remember every detail. The buzz of activity in the house and in the temple. The chanting. The smoke. And his daughter. *His* daughter. He'd hated her for taking away his wife. But now, he couldn't help but admire her. He saw the way she was shaken by the news of her grandfather's disappearance, but also how she pulled herself together.

He looked at her. And away. She had Radha's eyes. But without Radha's warmth, and with his uncle's disdain.

'Can I walk you to school?' he asked.

'I can manage.' This was said without looking at him.

He turned away, hurt. There was no welcoming numbness. On the contrary, an unfamiliar, uncomfortably clear mind holding one question: where was his father? He'd gone missing six months ago. He could not have travelled far, not at his age, with his knees. They had done the necessary rites so that his uncle could get his father's job at the temple. The other Brahmins wouldn't have dreamt of giving the hereditary job to him, the prodigal son. Not so much his alcoholism as his barely concealed contempt for them would have stuck in their gullets.

So, where was his father?

He didn't have a clear answer, so he swept up what remained of his breakfast and went to his father's desk in their house. It was small, with pictures of various gods stuck beneath the glass top. The desktop itself was spotless, much like his father's mind, with its only occupants being his father's diary and the almanac.

He picked up the diary. But respect, along with the innate reluctance to be privy to another man's innermost thoughts, made him put it down again. That left the almanac. He picked it up and began idly flipping the pages. On a whim, he looked at the position on the day his father had disappeared. Astrology had been the one thing that had brought father and son together. Not so much in angst-ridden questions but in a cool appreciation of how planetary positions appeared to indicate shifts in the direction of one's life. The indifference vanished. The three planets and a node in the house of the Sun. But that meant…

Rajan had always been known for his photographic memory. His mind leapt to the book in the cupboard in the chamber in the temple. Worry and excitement made for uncomfortable bedfellows in his chest. Could his father have seen something? Possibly. Were the other signs in place? Had his father taken the book and gone away to find the others or the Three?

A scene from several years ago came into his mind. Lakshmi, a toddler at the time, was nervously huddled on the floor of the hall filled with cupboards, shelves and a large bed. It was raining. His father was begging him to think of her, of him, of his talents. He was saying something about two of the social conditions and one physical sign being met and how each member of their family had to stand up and perform. He remembered his own anger. His rage. He remembered violently throwing away a round clasp with a key. Lakshmi had begun to cry. He also remembered slamming the door shut and walking away.

He needed that key.

Rajan's house was not a large one, but one with infinite hiding places. Rooms led into smaller rooms. Cupboards everywhere and an endless number of unswept corners. Rajan began to clean. His uncle would have said it was beneath his dignity. That only added to his need for something to work off both the worry and the excitement. He tackled the books first. They were all over the room – on tables, on windowsills, under cots, under cupboards. He picked them up and brought them all to his father's study. Many a time, a rare jewel of a book would surface, and he would have to fight hard against sinking onto the floor and entering into its pleasures. By the time Rajan was finished, lunchtime had come and gone. Chellamma, the maid, had, out of habit, not called him for lunch, but had left it covered in the kitchen.

Then he moved on to the odd bits of paper. Going through those took longer, as one of them could be holding the key to his father's disappearance. Wedding invitations printed on glossy pink and yellow paper, temple functions, old calendars, a few letters. Nothing of import. He pushed them all into a battered green bag and stood up, sweating. Chellamma had come in and stood there, staring at him. He smiled at her, his old smile. She smiled back. His smile was hard to resist.

'How are you, Chellamma?' he asked. 'Where do you keep the broom?'

'Have you started drinking again?' she asked and instantly regretted it, as the smile was wiped from his face. 'Please forgive me. It's just that it was such an odd request.'

'I need to find something. Something that might help find my father. It's somewhere in the house. I just don't know where.'

Chellamma edged closer, suspicious. Then, relieved that there was no tell-tale smell coming from his mouth, she got the brooms and the dustpan out of their storage bin. 'Let me sweep, sir. It's not your place.'

'You have two brooms, Chellamma. And I'm in a hurry,' he said, gently taking one from her. They started to sweep, bending and reaching into every corner they could. Several indignant cockroaches came rushing out and, surprisingly, only one mouse. Finally, Chellamma called out, 'Sir, sir. Come here. There is something stuck under this bed. I can't reach it!'

He ran to her and bent to peek under the bed – one of those old, large, heavy wooden cots. There were two boxes under it and stuck beneath the edge of one was a metallic circular clasp. Sweating, he bent down, and ducked under the bed, trying to reach the key with his broom. But he couldn't quite reach it. He pulled out – too quickly. Ouch! He sat up rubbing his head.

'Chellamma! Chellamma! I'm home.'

It was Lakshmi. The child had come home. She came in and saw the usually cluttered and dusty house clean, and as she walked further into the hall, she saw her father sitting on the floor, rubbing his head, with a broom lying next to him and Chellamma standing over him. Curiosity overcame resentment.

'What are you doing?' she asked.

'We're looking for a key. It's stuck under the bed, and we can't reach it,' said Rajan.

'I can go in,' she said and darted under the bed.

'Stop. Stop. Don't go in. You might get stuck, and we'll never be able to get you out,' said Chellamma.

Rajan didn't know what to say. He just sat there watching his daughter scramble under the bed. Finally, with just her feet sticking out, Lakshmi's muffled voice cried out, 'I got it. But I can't seem to slide out.'

'Wait. Don't lift your head,' said Rajan. 'I'll pull you out.' He clasped her ankles and began to pull her out. 'Don't lift your head. Are you hurt?'

'No, I'm okay,' said Lakshmi. And soon she was out.

Father and daughter smiled at each other. The same smile. Crooked, toothy, with crinkled eyes. And then Rajan looked at the key. The key that every boy in the family learned of at the age of 15.

'Lakshmi, please wait here. I think I may know what happened to your grandfather. I'm going to see if I can find out more about what happened that day. I'll be back soon.'

'Take me with you,' Lakshmi asked.

'No. Stay with Chellamma. I'll come back as soon as I can,' he replied and left the house.

Walking fast, Rajan reached the temple in no time. The temple doors were open, and he hurried in. Old habit and an older fondness made him bow towards the sanctum, and once more to the Narasimha – the half-lion, half-man incarnation of Vishnu – shrine next to it. He turned and made his way towards the chamber, nervousness growing in his mind. His hands were shaking as he slipped the key into the lock and turned it.

Talk went on in the village for weeks. The story of how the missing priest's body was found in the locked chamber below the sanctum.

'He must have wanted to steal the jewels, and God punished him.'

'Not Varadan sir. He was a good man.'

'The spirit of the chamber attacked him.'

'The spirit has awakened.'

'Are any of the jewels missing?'

'When did he die? How did he die?'

In the end, there was an investigation. The auditors were called in. The CBI came and passed their probing eyes over the riches. The conclusion was splashed across all the local dailies: the jewels were untouched; the old man had died of a heart attack. But no one had noticed that the small cupboard set in the side of the chamber was now lighter by one book.

5

The Book

THE BOOK WAS RAJAN'S CONSTANT COMPANION OVER THE next few weeks. He would wake up with the book by his side. He read it through the day after Lakshmi had left for school, putting it down only when he heard her voice in the evening. And after she slept, the book was again in his hands.

Rajan was a tall man with a good physique, but sloth and alcohol had left their mark on a once-athletic body. As the mind grew keen again, the body strove to keep pace. It started with a walk in the morning and then another in the evening with Lakshmi through the temple.

The temple was large, faced east with several entrances, each with a *gopuram* on top. One entered into a long passageway flanked by tall pillars, which opened into a courtyard built around the temple pond. The same pond that was believed to have given *moksha* to devotees over the centuries. On one side of the courtyard lay a sacred grove, while on the other was a shrine dedicated to the very unusual female guardian deity of the temple. She was a fierce guardian, and most hurried past her with a quick bowed head and a salutation. Beyond that lay the *garbha griha.*

Rajan always felt a brief frisson pass through him as he stood in the sanctum. Like a receptor vibrating to a different resonance. Then, Lakshmi and he visited the other shrines in the temple, some with hundreds of stories associated with them, while others were merely statues on a pillar smeared with vermillion and turmeric, with a small mud diya lit in front. The whole walk would take a little more than an hour and always left Rajan feeling lighter than when he entered.

Back home, he and Lakshmi sat down for their evening meal and spent time hesitantly getting acquainted before Lakshmi went to bed.

Then the book came out, and Rajan sat at his father's desk poring over it.

It was long – about a foot or so – made of several hardened palm leaves with holes along one end, tied together with a string. The cover itself was made of aged wood covered with what had once been a painting but was now merely some daubs of fading paint.

The book had twelve chapters. The first was essentially verses from the Isha Upanishad, saying that liberation lies not in rejection of the world, but in seeing the eternal presence within everything. One of the verses that Lakshmi loved hearing her grandfather sing was

Om Purnamadah Purnamidam Purnat Purnamudachyate
Purnasya Purnamadaya Purnameva Vashishyate
Om Shanti, Shanti, Shanti

(Brahman, or the Divine, is complete; the material world is complete. From completeness or fullness comes fullness, and when fullness is taken away from fullness, only fullness remains. Peace. Peace. Peace.)

The second chapter was a *bhashyam*, or an explanation, of the first, and spoke of the nature of the world – how it was knit together with the Universal Soul and how all souls were connected – and of *dharma* – acting in consonance with your being and the being of the world, in the full understanding that the same divine pervaded all. The next two chapters explained how balance was maintained when all walked the path of dharma and what would happen if people behaved in an *adharmic* way. The fifth chapter explained the three social conditions that would act as harbingers of the breakdown of the world – the drivers of the disease, as it were. The next chapter described in detail the physical signs that would ensue when the world tipped into imbalance; it spoke of specific changes in land, air and water – of frozen forests burning, of rains changing, of ice turning to water, of flooding and famine – and contained a couplet from the sage Sattaimuni that was Rajan's favourite verse in the book, which linked the external changes to what happened within one's body.

Andatthil ullathe pindam, Pindatthil ullathe andam
Andamum pindamum ondre Arinthuthaan paarkkum pothe

(What is in the universe, exists within us. What is within us, is reflected in the universe. We must realize that they are both one.)

The chapter suggested that the working of the body mirrored that of the universe. When balance was maintained in the body and the mind, the universe remained balanced, but when the body/mind became imbalanced – consumed by greed or distorted by fear, for example – the universe tipped into imbalance. When the universe tipped into imbalance, calamity followed, just as when the *dosha*s were out of whack, disease ensued.

Rajan's father had spoken about this to Rajan many times. 'We are not hapless bystanders, Raju, remember that. As within, so without. An ocean in a drop, and the drop becomes the ocean.'

The seventh chapter described the temples Rajan's family visited on pilgrimage. Rajan clearly remembered how he and his father had visited each of them after Rajan's upanayana, in a pattern that had remained constant over the centuries.

The eighth chapter was written in code, placing a test that ensured only a few could understand the special signs. The key from the eighth opened up the last chapters that explained what the reader could do to prepare.

Rajan leaned back and let out a breath he wasn't aware he had been holding. Seeing those verses, written centuries ago, spelling out how shifts in social order were really harbingers of an approaching Armageddon shook him to the core. He felt the bottle beckon. The burning in the throat. He clenched his hands, trying to will that thought, that yearning away. And then he heard his father's voice in his mind, 'As within, so without. We are not hapless bystanders.'

'What are you doing, *Appa*?'

Lakshmi's voice broke into Rajan's reverie, startling him. The child had woken up and found her father missing. She had seen a light burning in her grandfather's study and followed it to find her father sitting at his father's desk with an old book. He looked as if the world were about to end.

'What? Nothing…'

'You've never lied to me, Appa. What's that book? Where is it from? I've never seen it.'

Rajan stared at his daughter. Doubts chased one another like rats in his head. Finally, he said, 'It's a book that has been passed down for generations in our family.'

'Why haven't I seen it before?' asked Lakshmi.

'It's part of a tradition where the boys learn of it after their upanayana at fifteen,' he said gently.

Lakshmi's face fell. 'Oh.'

Rajan looked at his daughter again and made his decision.

'You're not fifteen yet. But we can start studying it together.'

Lakshmi beamed.

'What is it about?'

Interlude

THE BUOYS IN THE WESTERN PACIFIC, JUST NORTH OF Papua New Guinea, were behaving strangely. Data from the instruments that recorded wind speed and direction was signalling an unwelcome shift: the winds had reversed course.It could be nothing, the man at the helm of one of the world's most important meteorological institutions told himself. They'd just come off an El Niño the previous year – surely it would be a few years before another one. True, there had been back-to-back El Niños before, but those were rare. Best to wait a few days before jumping to conclusions. The next morning in Australia, divers from tourist boats reported that the tips of corals were bleaching. The captain frowned. Each season it was getting harder to find vibrant reefs to show the visitors. A week later, as the data from the buoys came in, the signs were unequivocal: it was indeed a westerly wind burst. The winds had turned. The models showed mixed projections, and the Climate Prediction Centre issued a cautious 'El Niño Watch'. But in his gut, the man felt a cold, hard knot of dread – this did not look good.

6

The Dissolution

PRALAYA.

The time of dissolution. Every age is but a day in the life of Brahma, the creator. As he closes his eyes and night falls, one age comes to an end and the world is deluged before being born again, and the cycle continues.

'Why is the book on Pralaya, Appa?' asked Lakshmi. 'And why are you reading it now? Is it coming nearer? *Thaatha* told me we have already had three ages, and we are in our fourth, Kali. Chellamma keeps saying: *Kali muthipocchu* (Kali has ripened).'

Rajan looked at his daughter again. He could see more curiosity than fear on her face. He said to her, 'The book talks of what we can expect to see in society before Pralaya occurs. It says that society would change in three important ways before Pralaya starts to manifest.'

'What are you saying, Appa?' Lakshmi asked. 'Are you trying to say that we cause Pralaya?'

He admired her quickness.

'That's what the book appears to suggest, Lakshmi. And on reading it closely, I am beginning to understand how it would come about.

'The first condition is met when the material or human world takes too much space. When humans cease to see themselves as part *of* Nature and think of themselves *above* Nature. Apart *from* Nature.' He saw a look of bewilderment on her face, paused and tried to explain it better.

'Look around you. Even when you were a baby there was some greenery around us. You remember the *Puliyamaram Eri*? The lake where the pelicans used to come every winter?'

'The one that has now become a shopping complex?' replied Lakshmi, comprehension dawning on her face.

'Yes. Because we think our needs matter more, we step up and take over parts of the world which used to belong to other forms of life. Humans are taking up too much space on the planet – we are disrupting its balance. Even in a small town like this, we are taking up too much space. And now, Nature is fighting back.'

He stopped, catching the worried look on her face, but then steeled himself to continue.

'Lakshmi, in our family, the upanayana was always conducted a little later than it was in other families. The thought was that perhaps the boys would be more grown up and better equipped to handle the things this book has to say. I don't know if I am doing the right thing by telling you now, but I didn't want to lie to you. And it's important that you know.'

She said nothing. He was too unused to children to know what to do. He wished his father were there.

'Lakshmi, it's late. Shall we go to sleep?'

'I can't sleep.'

'Come, I'll lie down with you…I can tell you a story.'

Father and daughter left the study and went to lie down. He knew she was upset, but he was too awkward and too sensitive to take any action that might make it worse.

'What about the story?' asked Lakshmi in the darkness.

'Which one do you want?'

'Actually, do you know the song Thaatha used to sing to me? "*Kurai Ondrum Illai*"? Can you sing me that?'

Rajan hesitated. He knew that song very well. Radha used to sing it every night when she was pregnant. 'We are so lucky, Rajanna. What more could we possibly ask for?'

'I don't know. Why not a story?'

'No, Appa. Chellamma told me you have a nice voice. I want to hear that song.'

He was silent.

'Please?'

He cleared his throat. '*Kurai ondrum illai, marai moorthy kanna.*'

The song was about Krishna, and how his love was enough – a lilting love song, from the devotee to the Lord, working its way through haunting scales.

Rajan's voice was a little scrappy from disuse but low and soothing in the dark. By the time he came to the end of the song, Lakshmi was asleep, and surprisingly, he felt better.

7

The School

MORNING CAME. THE ROOSTER'S CALL PIERCED THROUGH the silence as the rays of the sun glided through the windows just as they always did. Rajan woke up and shook Lakshmi. The morning routine proceeded like it always did. Bathe. Dress. Prayers. Breakfast. A little too studiously so.

While they were walking to school, Lakshmi asked, 'Are we going to die, Appa?'

He had expected this question, but that made it no easier to answer. He found that he didn't know what to say. Looking at her, he knew he had to say something. She would not let this slide. 'The book is not clear on when the timing of the Pralaya will be. The signs are important. Sometime after the manifestation of the social, physical and special signs, Pralaya will commence. But the language appears to suggest that we may be able to do something.'

'Will it be like the Matsya avatar, Appa?' asked Lakshmi, referring to the story of how Lord Vishnu in the avatar, or form, of a fish had saved a small section of humanity from a great deluge.

'Perhaps, Lakshmi. I'm not sure. I probably should not be talking to you so openly, but to tell you the truth, you are the only one I can talk to, so I need to. This is too important.'

Despite the gravity of the situation, Lakshmi felt buoyant. She was part of the solution now, not a hapless bystander. Rajan, for his part, felt proud. What a girl! She was frightened – only a fool would not be. But she was intelligent and curious, and she was continuing her questions despite her fear.

'So, what is the second social sign?' asked Lakshmi.

Rajan chanted:

'Brothers living side by side
On wealthy lands,
But chasms of wealth them do divide
Creating warring bands.'

'Is it about wealth then?' asked Lakshmi.

'I think it means more people will live closer together than ever before. And while we will be wealthier as a whole than at any time in the past, there will be great inequality. Some will be very wealthy, while others very poor,' answered Rajan. 'You see, sometimes, if you don't know what you are missing, you don't really miss it. But if someone else has it, and flaunts it, then you realize you don't have it, and you are constantly reminded of something that you don't have.

It chafes against your skin like a jute rope. And you would do anything to catch up, especially if your children lacked something other children had.'

'I don't have a mother.'

Rajan felt his world stop spinning. He began to tremble.

'But I have you now.'

He bent down and lifted his daughter into his arms and hugged her until she was his entire reality. It was not common for fathers to hug their daughters in their town, less so in the middle of a road. But Rajan didn't care.

Lakshmi rushed into her school just as the gates were beginning to close. The old, sadistic watchman, who loved closing the door a few seconds early just to see children fidget and perhaps extract a small bribe, was surprised. Lakshmi was a model student who was never late, although she had been cutting it fine of late.

Lakshmi slid into her classroom – a small, old room with sloping roofs, large windows and walls painted with white distemper, filled with wooden benches standing behind long, polished tables. One corner of the roof was missing a few tiles, and during the rainy season, a bucket caught the leaking rain. There was a single, rickety fan that did little to cool the room but was enough to meet the school's regulations.

She was glad she wasn't late. She liked her class teacher.

Miss Ganesan was super smart, not too strict with some rules, and encouraged her students to question her. Unlike the other teachers in the school, Miss Ganesan was dressed in her usual long kurta over pants and had her long hair tied up in a ponytail.

Swati Ganesan looked at Lakshmi with a casualness she didn't feel. She felt worried about the child. Naturally, the child was shaken by her grandfather's passing. She had heard some rumours about the father – by all accounts, a worthless drunkard. Then, a few weeks ago, Lakshmi had appeared to perk up, with a new bloom permeating her face. But then, in the last week, she began looking wan and worried. She answered readily enough when questioned, but at other times, she looked...almost distraught. As though the weight of the world rested on her thin shoulders.

The day passed quickly. One class followed the next, and soon, the last bell rang, signifying the end of the day. As Lakshmi packed her bags and got ready to leave, she saw Miss Ganesan standing before her.

'Lakshmi, I want to meet your father.'

'Why, Ma'am? Have I done something wrong?'

'No, not at all. I would just like to meet him and speak to him.'

Teacher and student left the classroom and walked down the alley to where several parents were waiting for their children.

In the crowd, Rajan loomed head and shoulders above the others. Wearing a simple blue shirt and black trousers, he was scanning the oncoming students for his daughter. He saw her, looking a little anxious, walking beside a tall woman. When they reached him, Lakshmi said, 'Appa, this is Miss Ganesan, my class teacher. She wanted to meet you. Miss Ganesan, this is my father.'

Swati Ganesan saw a tall man with thoughtful eyes tinged with anxiety looking down at her. He didn't look drunk.

'Hello, sir. I wanted to meet you and tell you what a pleasure it is to have Lakshmi in my class.'

Rajan beamed. Lakshmi blushed.

'I'm so happy. Is there…is there anything she needs help with?'

Swati smiled. 'Well, I hear her Tamil is not so good. But that you should take up with her Tamil teacher.'

The crooked smile appeared.

Swati responded to his smile; it was hard not to. She turned to Lakshmi and said, 'I need to show your report card to your father but, unfortunately, I've left my bag in the classroom. Could you please get it for me?'

As Lakshmi rushed away, Swati turned to face Rajan. The smile was gone.

'What has been worrying Lakshmi so much this past week? You may think this is none of my business, but I'm fond of Lakshmi. The child looks distraught when she thinks no one is watching.'

Rajan started. 'What?'

Thoughts chased one another like rats in his head. He had never been very good at lying, and he found it harder than ever to lie to this blunt woman with light brown eyes.

'Something appears to have upset Lakshmi very much in the past week. I wanted to make sure that she is being cared for properly.'

She unsettled him. He didn't know what to say. 'It's been a difficult time…' he started.

'I can understand. Which is why I am asking if you need any help. You see, Lakshmi appeared devastated when her grandfather disappeared. But then she appeared to become better after he…after his body was found. But then, in the past week, she has been looking distraught.'

Rajan stood staring at his feet, not knowing what to say.

Suddenly, there was a loud explosion. They both jumped.

Rajan's heart squeezed. 'Lakshmi?'

He ran into the school, only to see Lakshmi running out with her teacher's bag in her hands.

Everywhere, people were rooted to the spot, and then children began to scream. There was a large spire of smoke rising from the direction of the temple. From near their home.

More screams. More smoke.

'What was that, Appa?'

'I'm not sure. Let's give your teacher her bag and go.'

Lakshmi paused and turned to her teacher. 'Ma'am? Will you be okay? Do you need any help?'

Swati was touched. In some ways, her life had not been easy. And here was this girl, a child already suffering, reaching out to help. She reached out and squeezed Lakshmi's hand in gratitude, and said, 'I'll be all right, my dear. You go on with your father.'

Rajan felt a little ashamed. He had not thought to offer help. Belatedly he asked, 'Where is your house? Perhaps we can walk you there.'

'That's okay. I'm meeting someone two streets down. We can walk together until then.'

The three of them began to walk out of the school and into the town, where they saw hundreds of people running towards them. The sound of an ambulance siren pierced the air, and they saw fire engines rush past. Rajan saw the shopkeeper, from whom they bought their provisions, running towards them.

'Sir, please stop. What's going on?'

'The devils. May they be cursed – they've bombed the temple!'

Rajan slumped down on the road. It was not possible. The temple had stood there for more than a thousand years. Some said it had always been there. He felt the tug for the numbness so strongly that he wanted to drop everything and sink into it.

'Appa, get up. Appa. Come on, Appa.'

Swati knelt beside Rajan.

'Your daughter needs you now. She has no one else.'

Rajan shook himself. There was no numbness to sink into. He looked at his daughter and turned to Swati.

'Madam?' he hesitated. But his anxiety overcame his distaste for asking favours. 'Could you keep Lakshmi with you? I will come and pick her up later. Our house is in the *agraharam* very close to the temple. With this talk of bombing, I don't want Lakshmi there.'

'Of course.'

It was Lakshmi's turn to be anxious. 'Appa? Why aren't you coming with us? Why go there…?' She stopped. She realized what pulled her father back to the house. 'Be careful, Appa.'

'I will. I'll come for you very soon.'

He noted down Swati's number and address and watched them as they walked away. Rajan continued, running now, towards the temple. As he ran on, the crowd grew and the air became smokier. Soon he ran into the police cordon. Rajan recognized a constable.

'What happened?' he asked, panting.

'What a tragedy! These accursed fellows. They've bombed the temple.'

'Is the Lord okay? The chamber?'

'I'm not sure. I heard someone say that the chamber is in ashes. But I'm not sure.'

He ran, his anxiety powering him on. The smoke grew thicker and the screams shriller as he came closer to the temple. Then, he saw the main gopuram was intact. *Thank God.* He pushed through the mill of people staring vacantly at the temple with the smoke rising from it. As he neared the entrance, he couldn't push through. In desperation, he took off his shirt, hoping to pass off as a priest. He saw a familiar face, the sub-inspector, looking very harassed.

'Sir! Sir!'

'Rajan! What is it?'

'Sir, what happened? I want to go inside.'

'Are you crazy? Do you realize what has happened?'

'Sir, please. The temple is like a home to me. The Lord is my family. Please, sir, I must see, I must know. Please. Please, I beg of you.'

The inspector considered the man in front of him. The quiet man, not given to speaking or to emotion, was now giving in freely to both. Silently, he signalled for him to pass the cordon.

Rajan ducked under the ropes and ran towards the temple.

The smoke grew thicker.

Coughing, he ran down the passageway, past the tank with a quick, instinctive bow to the guardian deity and into the inner courtyard. The smoke was so thick here, he could hardly see where he was going. But through the chaos, he heard chanting.

'*Bhoota-bhavya-bhavan-naathah…*'

('Lord of all that was, is and will be.')

He recognized the verses from the *Vishnu Sahasranama,* and on hearing them, Rajan felt as though he had taken a dip in a cool, refreshing stream. The sound of the chanting led him to the sanctum. The smoke was coming from the chamber. Men were trying to douse it. The sanctum's entrance was blackened. One lamp was completely destroyed.

But the Lord was safe.

Relief overwhelmed him. He sat down next to his uncle, who was leading the chanting. His uncle stretched out a welcoming arm. Even in this chaos, there was disapproval of Rajan's black trousers, approval of his bare chest and longing for his full head of hair all blended in the glance that his uncle gave him.

Rajan began to chant. After some time, they came to the verse:

> *paritraanaaya saadhoonaam vinaashaaya cha dushhkritaam |*
> *dharma samsthaapanaarthaaya sambhavaami yuge yuge ||*

> ('For the protection of the good, for the destruction of the wicked, and for the establishment of Dharma, I am born in every age.')

Rajan felt a surge of excitement.

Was it time for Kalki to appear?

The chanting ended. They bowed to the deity and rose.

Rajan turned to his uncle. 'What happened?'

He noticed two white streams on his uncle's cheeks where tears had cleared the soot stains.

'I must have sinned. I must have sinned. May Lord Narayana have mercy on my soul.'

'*Chittappa*, don't talk nonsense. What happened?'

For a while, it appeared as though his uncle was far too overcome with emotion to speak.

By then, the water hoses had put out the worst fires, and now it was a question of what could be salvaged.

'Raju, what can I say? We opened the temple for the afternoon as we always do. We had just finished the first *arati* when there was a loud noise. I'll never forget that moment for as long as I live. My arati plate fell down, and Sridevi's* saree caught fire, which I put out with the *theertham*. I am cursed. I am cursed. Then the smoke began to come out of the side, as though from the chamber. I hugged the Lord and dared not move. To get to him, they would have to destroy me.'

'Does anyone know who did it?'

'Who knows? There are so many heathens with their greedy eyes set on the Lord's wealth.'

'But, Chittappa, if they wanted the wealth, why would they blow it up?'

His uncle had broken down into sobs, making it impossible to get any answers out of him. As Rajan looked around, he saw numb faces, faces that showed that what was inside had given up and was clinging to rigid traditions because it did not know what else to do.

There were swarms of people still trying to put out the fires and enter the chamber. The smoke was still thick.

Suddenly there was another loud sound.

---

* Another name for Goddess Lakshmi, Vishnu's consort

The wailing broke out afresh.

'Narayana! Narayana!'

'Pralaya is here…'

'Protect us, oh Lord!'

Rajan turned to the sanctum – smoke was still billowing about, but the Lord was safe. The explosion had come from outside.

He began to walk and then run towards his home. As he left the temple, he saw fresh smoke rising from his uncle's house. His anxiety deepened. He ran to his house, several houses away from his uncle's – it was still standing, smoke-free.

Rajan entered the house and rushed into his father's study and opened the drawer to the right. The book was still there. As he grabbed it, he found another book under it. An album – he opened it to find his mother's face smiling at him, and then Radha and then Lakshmi as a baby. He grabbed the book, the album, and from the top of the desk, his father's diary and the almanac. He opened the steel cabinet to the right – in there were the certificates and other documents. Their family was not wealthy, so there was very little jewellery or money – only a small, but lovely, ruby necklace and earrings that Radha had worn. Rajan reached up and gathered a small backpack that rested above the cabinet and hurriedly put everything inside: the book, his father's diary and almanac, the album, their certificates and the ruby set. He quickly packed some clothes. He put on his shirt, and on a whim, swathed an angavastram over his head and took out his father's dark glasses. He found his hands shaking as he put on the glasses. It felt like a voice inside him was telling him to hurry up and leave quietly and quickly. He had not run into Chellamma, and he hoped she had gone out to buy vegetables, although the same internal voice chided him that she was probably taking her customary afternoon nap at the far end of the house. He knew he did not have time to search for her. His heart ached, but he knew what was at stake. He used the small side door, the one that no one used, which led into the well area of their neighbour's house. He crouched through the length of that large house's unkempt garden and jumped over the wall that let him out into a quiet street, far away from the main entrance of the agraharam. He kept his head down. Had anyone asked him why he was hiding, he wouldn't have been able to give an answer; it was like a voice inside was telling him to do it. As he walked away quickly, he heard another explosion. This time, he was not surprised to see the smoke rising from his house. His heart sank as he thought of Chellamma, and he sent a silent prayer for her safety, feeling impotent and hating himself.

Keeping his head lowered, he stayed hidden among the crowd as he headed towards Swati's house. After half an hour of brisk walking, he came to the road curving into a coconut grove. He followed it and came to a gate, which an old man opened. He asked for Lakshmi, and was let in. The path inside was fringed with glorious old trees. As he walked along it, he became calmer; the explosion seemed to belong to another world, far removed from this gracious setting. Soon he came to a lovely little house: white, with a pillared veranda running all around and riotously coloured bougainvillea flowers draped over the terracotta tiled roofs. *What was an ordinary teacher doing living in a house like this?* he thought to himself.

Lakshmi was waiting anxiously by a startling blue door.

'Appa, Appa…you're back!'

She ran into her father's arms, and he hoisted her up into the air and hugged her.

'I was so worried.'

Rajan hugged his daughter one more time and set her down. He turned to see Swati come out of the house. She was wearing jeans – very unusual for a woman in these parts.

'Please come in.'

'Thank you for taking her in. I will never be able to repay you, but we will leave now.'

'What are you saying?'

'We have to go. We may be in danger, and we don't want to put you at risk.'

There was a brief silence.

Swati looked at Rajan. She could smell the soot off him. *Danger. Well, that might prove entertaining*, she thought to herself. And she liked Lakshmi. She even liked Rajan, if she was being honest with herself. *I don't have to tell them everything about myself, after all. And it would be nice not to be alone all the time.*

'Come in. Lakshmi is tired. Maybe you can too. Rest,

I mean. And then decide what you need to do. You have warned me. I accept the risk – if it indeed exists.'

The last part annoyed Rajan.

'We really should…'

'Where are we going, Appa?'

That simple question stumped Rajan; he really did not have a clue where to go. *Away. But where?*

Srirangam was an option. His mother's uncle's family was from there. Or Kancheepuram. Another uncle lived there. *But would they take them in?* He stood there, feeling remarkably foolish.

Swati's voice interrupted these thoughts. 'Stay here for as long as you need to. You are not imposing. I am asking you. Come in.'

Rajan looked at Swati. 'We could be putting you at risk.'

'Are we in danger, Appa? Why?' asked Lakshmi.

Rajan hesitated. 'Madam, I don't wish to offend you, but I need to know a little about you before I can share anything. I'm fully aware that I am in your debt and that you are being far kinder than you need to be. Again – I don't wish to offend – but why are you being kind?'

Swati was not sure how to respond. She didn't want to share the details of her life and her choices with these people, not yet. She didn't want their…judgement. She did like the fact that the man in front of her appeared genuinely uncomfortable – he didn't want to put her at risk, he did not fully trust her, but he knew he needed her help. And she was fond of Lakshmi and strangely drawn to this man. So, she aimed for a compromise.

'I'm attached to Lakshmi, and you both seem like decent people. You appear to be in trouble, and I want to help. That's really all there is to it. I don't have an ulterior motive – if that's what you are implying – although if I did, I probably wouldn't admit to it,' Swati said, smiling at the last bit. Swati had a warm smile – her eyes glinted mischievously, and her teeth flashed white and even.

Rajan couldn't help responding to it. There was something about her that made him trust her. That same inner voice that had warned him of danger earlier was quiet. And they did not have a place to go to yet.

'Thank you. It seems inadequate as a word but thank you.'

They entered the house, Rajan holding Lakshmi's hand while looking around cautiously. The first room appeared to be a sitting room with an old Tanjore painting adorning the walls. There was solid wood furniture, upholstered in silk, and a small cupboard holding bronzes. They passed it and walked into what appeared to be a corridor around a small *muttram*.

Swati turned to Rajan. 'You look a bit dishevelled. Would you like to freshen up?'

Rajan coloured up. It hadn't occurred to him how he must have appeared to her.

'Why don't you wash up?' she repeated. 'You can mull over your decision while you do so. The bathroom is over here,' she said, leading him into what appeared to be a very comfortable but stylish bedroom.

Rajan accepted her offer. But as he washed up, he thought furiously. *Who was this woman?* This house belonged to someone who was wealthy. *What was a wealthy woman doing being a teacher in a small school in a small town? Why was she helping them? Should they leave? But where would they go?*

As the cool water cascaded down his body, the smoke and fatigue fell away. Rajan only wished he could refresh his mind as easily. He dressed and walked out of the room, backpack in hand. Lakshmi and Swati were sitting at a table. He walked around the muttram to join them.

'Madam, you have been very kind, and I thank you for that. But now it is time for Lakshmi and me to leave.'

Swati stared at Rajan. She could detect the steel beneath his hesitancy. He was not going to acquiesce until he got some measure of truth.

Lakshmi looked from Swati to Rajan. She saw closure on her father's face, and trouble on Swati's. She tried to defuse the tension. 'Appa, I like Swati ma'am. Can't we stay here for a little while? Should we go immediately, Appa? Where are we going?'

Rajan took Lakshmi's hand in his. 'Lakshmi, we are in danger. I'm sorry to say that to you, but I don't know what else to say. It's not fair we put your teacher at risk as well. We have used her kindness far too much already. Come, let us thank her and go.' He turned, and reluctantly, Lakshmi rose with him.

Rajan turned to Swati. 'Thank you, Madam. I apologize for any rudeness, and I am in your debt for your care of Lakshmi.'

Lakshmi was crying as she gave Swati a big hug. The hug lasted a long, long time, neither wanting to let go.

Finally, Rajan placed his hand on Lakshmi's shoulder.

They broke apart. Swati was surprised at the depth of her fondness for Lakshmi – she would miss that child! – and realized how much she had hated being alone. But she hated the judgement that would be pronounced on her choices. So, she wiped her tears, and said: 'This is not about my safety, is it? This is about you not being sure of who I am and whether I would add to your "danger".'

Rajan flinched. He was unused to being spoken to in this way. He fell back on his dignity.

'Thank you again, Madam, for your exceeding kindness.'

'Stop it! You are the one taking Lakshmi into danger. Please don't mention my safety as a factor.' She saw the expression on his face and stopped. 'Okay, maybe it was a factor in the beginning. But the main one now is you don't trust me, isn't that it?'

Rajan rarely got angry. But he was angry now.

'I would never put Lakshmi in danger. But no, I don't trust you. You work as a teacher in a school. That salary doesn't go with this house, with your manner. We don't know who you are. And after today, I cannot let a contradiction like this pass.'

He stopped when he realized that he had raised his voice. All the blood had drained from Swati's face. Lakshmi was cowering. The old attendant who had let them into the house had entered the room and stood watching, a stony expression on his face.

'I'm sorry. I didn't mean to raise my voice. But I don't know you. Thank you again, but we must be on our way.'

He took Lakshmi's hand, grabbed his backpack and began to walk out of the house.

'Wait.'

Swati's voice reflected her reluctance – reluctance to let them go, reluctance to share her past.

'Stay. I'll tell you my story.'

8

Danny

DHANRAJ 'DANNY' SETHI FELT JOYOUS. THERE WAS NO TIME like the present. Not since the beginning of humanity. He placed his glossy black $2,500 Italian handcrafted shoes on his rosewood desk and looked through his glass wall at a world that lay, unknowingly, at his feet. Physically, he did not fit the mould of a jet-setting wild-child hedge fund czar. He was short, just under 5 feet 2 inches. He had fair skin, a hooked nose, beady black eyes, thick, coarse black hair, and a pronounced limp. But his money camouflaged these trifling faults to the merry-go-round of mistresses that shared his bed. There were whispered rumours about what went on behind those doors, of which very few were brave (or foolish) enough to speak openly.

The cause of Sethi's elation was a small room. He had finally (finally!) taken possession of it a year ago. Nested within the hallowed portals of the Central Stock Exchange, this humble room hosted servers that allowed Sethi's staff to execute trades a few milliseconds earlier than his competitors.

Welcome to the world of high-frequency trading.

In modern markets, computers with inhuman reaction times had come to dominate equity trading. While the public cherished an image of men holding slips of paper and screaming prices at one another, modern trading had done away with all of that; trades were now executed on computers where an advantage of a few milliseconds – a timespan a hundred times faster than a blink of an eye – translated to billions in profits. Brokers, tasked and trusted with executing a client's orders, thrived in this world of milliseconds and grey legality. When a large client, call it Muco, wanted to buy 1,00,000 shares of company ABC, it called its broker and asked them to buy the shares at ₹1,500 +/– ₹2 per share. Now 1,00,000 was a large quantity, and when an order like that hit the market, the market moved. The broker placed an initial order to buy 1,000 shares at ₹1,500. Then things became interesting. When other operators learned about such a large order coming in, clever programs, or algorithms, tried to take advantage. Faster brokers – those whose systems were co-located within an exchange, or who had faster servers – rushed in and bought ABC shares for ₹1,500.5, ₹1,501 or even ₹1,501.5. Now, Muco's broker told their client that the ABC share price had climbed to ₹1,502 and bought the remaining shares at that rate from those who front-ran the order. The early bird did indeed get the worm.

In the past year alone, Sethi had made more money than he had in the past ten years combined. Risk-free.

Sethi managed his billions well. The steady stream of income from trading was ploughed carefully into real estate, stocks of global companies, art and philanthropy. The last was most important. By carefully throwing scraps at the vociferous defenders of the poor, he could buy their gratitude and their reputation. Many organizations recognized his money for what it was and turned it down. Some philanthropists turned away, put off by the stench of his sharp dealings. But too many succumbed. He sat on the board of one entity with prime real estate in the capital and was on first-name terms with the heads of a half-dozen more. He was a regular at the right kind of parties, and any political donations or leanings were invisible to the public eye. Truth be told, Sethi truly subscribed to the golden investment principle, 'Diversify to lower risks', especially in politics. So, he paid all the parties and called no one his 'enemy'. This helped when his client wanted to build a tower over a neighbourhood lake or lower building costs by dumping rubble in a river. Not too much. Not too often. But just enough. What others called 'corruption', he called the 'Democracy Tax' – the tax that allowed the rapacious to work the system. The papers, for the most part, kept quiet – some because the advertisement revenues from the full-page glossy ads were too sweet to turn down; most because, these days, there was no dearth of bad news to fill the front pages.

In glittering rooms within gated buildings, Sethi met with other men and women who were like him. Predators. Sleek, powerful, ruthless. Some philosophers believed man had given up his predatory instincts when civilization and enlightenment dawned. In truth, the hunters sheathed their claws in electronic gloves as their appetites and ambitions grew. Individuals were no longer worthy prey. Countries and entire industries were more interesting. The masses were beguiled by reels on social media, by influencers touting the latest 'must-have' trend and soon, they were building their own house of cards – an entire metaverse in which one could create one's own reality with no harsh tones or dissenting facts to bother one.

And in those rooms, the powers-that-be decided energy prices would fall in 2025. The same few who made money on the way up, made money on the way down. A quick war, to make even more money from the chaos, because why not? The bogeyman created by harassed parents in ancient times never really went away. Humanity was wired to be fearful – that's how it survived for so long. Such an intrinsic hole would always need to be filled. Only now it was filled with rather boring words like 'slow growth' and 'inflation'. Why innovate when one could lobby to protect oneself from competition? There were so many bogeymen that could be paraded before decision-makers with crowded agendas and short attention spans: 'Companies will fail! They will move to another country, taking thousands of jobs with them! If you tax us, how will we innovate?' All the while, the very same companies would invest in technology that eliminated jobs – ten or twenty or a thousand at a time. Or bought small companies with threatening innovations and smothered them quietly. Death by a thousand paper cuts was so much harder to fend off.

Sethi and his tribe understood the importance of stories, of public hangings, of highlighting what the already-hurting stood to lose. They understood the powerful bogeyman of the 'other'. They paralysed the masses with a diet of fear, of doubt, of seemingly infinite choices, while they deftly steered the system to their own profit. These Sowers of Chaos – master storytellers to the last man, gifted psychologists, tenacious street fighters – came into full force when a threat appeared on the horizon. The tobacco industry used their services until it became too clear to the dullest mind that coating the delicate passages of one's lungs with tar and mutagenic substances did, in fact, cause the cells to change and die.

But the tobacco industry was not dying. It was selling more cigarettes than ever, mainly in poorer countries with regulation that was cheaper to influence. Only now, tobacco had become passé. The merchants needed a fresh challenge. And they found it. The fossil fuel industry, seeing an emergent threat on the horizon, engaged the very effective and expensive services of merchants to cast as much doubt as possible on the fact that the Earth has been warming faster of late. First, they said the Earth was not warming. Then, when the warming was apparent to all, they said the warming was driven by natural causes. Then they cast aspersions on the leading scientists. Then they said poorer countries were getting a free ride. They said anything to distract customers from the truth that balance was needed, respect for nature and the space for all beings was needed, that one needed to connect with others rather than retreat into a metaversal shell. They peddled a seductive vision – 'No change in philosophy needed, tech would solve all.'

Investors, many indifferent to anything but profit, found that some of the technologies created fresh opportunities, fresh markets. For Sethi, this was just money begging to be made. So, he betted. First on solar, with suitable guarantees of profits from governments, of course. Then, with burnished credentials as a bona fide climate hero, there were other, quieter bets taken – on a plantation in Indonesia where rainforests larger than a city were cleared to make way for palm oil plantations. Palm oil went into so many things – shampoo, snacks for children, medicine, even dog food. Activists fighting to protect rainforests washed their hair with a product that led to the forests being cut down. They protested on phones powered by batteries made with metals dug out from rocks by children working with their bare hands. Sethi, of course, knew this, and the truth made him smile.

He was smiling when his phone rang. He started. Very few had this number. Even fewer used it. Fully alert, he took the call. A mechatronic voice spoke:

'Tonight.'

He found his hand shaking as he put down his phone.

9

The Story

SWATI LOOKED STRAIGHT INTO RAJAN'S EYES WITHOUT flinching.

'Let us eat. Let Lakshmi sleep. I'll tell you my story, and if you doubt any part of it, you can leave.'

Rajan looked at the woman before him. Independent. Shrewd. Helpful. It seemed churlish to refuse. His inner voice, the one that had always guided him well, told him he could trust her. But still, he held back.

'Please understand. This is more than about us.'

'Shh. I understand. Come. Sit. Eat.'

Lakshmi ran to hug Swati. Swati hugged her and bent to kiss her head, and looked up to see Rajan watching her, a troubled look on his face. There was a sincerity about him, and a...depth. He was no fool, but he was not exploitative. So different from most people she had met. She led them to the dining table. Rajan and Lakshmi were unused to eating at a table and were a little uncomfortable at first. Dinner was simple but delicious. By the time the *thayir saadam* came, Lakshmi was yawning.

'Bed, Lakṣhmi,' said Swati. 'Come, I'll show you the way. You can't sleep in your uniform; I'll give you something of mine that might work as a nightdress.'

Swati walked to another room and came out holding a large T-shirt with a big dog wearing a T-shirt and a hat on it. Lakshmi smiled when she saw it.

A little later, Rajan came out of the bedroom. 'Lakshmi has fallen asleep, Madam. I'm sorry I raised my voice. I can't thank you enough for what you have done for us.' He hesitated and then continued, 'There has been a lot of destruction today. I can't take any chances. Please forgive me.'

'Come sit down. Can I get you something to drink? Water? Or something harder?'

Rajan was stupefied. He didn't pretend not to understand.

'Just water, Madam. Thank you.'

Swati poured herself a glass of white wine and him some water and came to the table. She sat down, indicating that Rajan should sit down beside her.

Slowly sipping the wine, she began to speak.

'I come from Madurai but grew up in the US. I studied there, worked there. I was in love with a man there. We were together for several years. I was happy. My parents were, at first, completely against the relationship. He was not Indian, and they felt he had an unsavoury reputation. They thought he was using me.'

She stopped.

'Naturally, I defended the man I loved. I told my parents that they were wrong, prejudiced. I stopped talking to them. My father said he would disown me if I continued with him, that he would not watch me fall victim to my own blindness. I ignored him. I was earning well; I didn't need their money. I had a man who loved me. I thought I didn't need their love.'

She stopped again. The glass was now empty. She walked to the counter to pour herself another glass.

'More water? Or something else?'

Rajan felt such a longing.

'I can't. I don't know if I'd be able to stop.'

She came back and sat down.

'A year later, he quit his job. He said they didn't appreciate him and that he wanted to try writing, to express himself. I always thought he was very creative, so I supported his decision. I earned enough that money was not an issue. Then he joined a college course. He sent me the bill via an email that said: "Take care of it." I didn't like his tone but decided not to make an issue of it and "took care of it". After that there were times when he was never at home. When I asked him about it, he would just say the course load was too heavy.'

Rajan had said nothing until now and continued to remain silent.

Swati stared at a painting on the wall. 'Then one day, about two years ago, I came home early. It had been a difficult week, and I wanted some comfort. As I opened the door, there was music playing and a strange, almost acrid, odour in the air. I had a premonition, but I chided myself for being paranoid. The door to our bedroom was slightly ajar, and…'

Swati stopped. She drained her glass and set it down on the table with a shaking hand.

'The next few weeks were a blur. He told me it was my fault, that I was not womanly enough. I asked him to move out. He refused. I actually had to get a court order to get him to move. In all this turmoil, my performance at work suffered, and I was given a friendly warning. A week later, I got a call from India, from my cousin. My father had had a heart attack. It was not serious. But it was a heart attack.'

Swati finally looked at Rajan.

'It seemed like a sign. I quit my job and returned to India. To my home. I called my house from the airport to let them know, and when I landed, a car was waiting, but neither of my parents was there to receive me. This was unusual because normally they would have been there. I put their absence down to my father's illness. When I entered the house, I went to my father's sitting room. I was shocked. My father had aged. My mother had aged. There were creases around their eyes that had not been there a couple of years ago. My mother rose to hug me. But as I turned to my father, he said, "I thought you said you didn't need us. Why have you come then?"

'I felt I had swallowed acid. I hugged my mother and

walked out. I could hear my mother shouting, begging me to come back, asking my father to call me back, but neither of us heeded her.

'I asked Thangam to put my suitcases back into the car and called my cousin. I spent the night in his house. This is also my cousin's house – he often spends time here and is friends with someone involved with the local school. I asked for a job and stayed in this house. That was two years ago. And I have been here since.'

Rajan had not taken his eyes off Swati's face during this entire recital. He knew one thing: this story was true.

'Will you stay?' she asked.

'Do you really want us to? I really don't want to put you at risk.'

'I accept the risk, if there is any.'

Rajan was annoyed. The 'ifs' got under his skin.

'Yes, the risk is real! A temple was bombed. Untold treasure has been destroyed. My uncle's house was bombed. My house was bombed. I don't know how many people in my family are dead. I don't know if the people behind this know that Lakshmi and I are still alive.'

He paused. He was breathing rapidly and realized that he had raised his voice again. He forced himself to calm down before continuing, 'I'm sorry, but the risk is real – there is someone who wants us dead. A kind of person who bombs temples. Who wants to destroy the knowledge we hold. If you really want us to stay, you should understand this.'

Swati had stiffened when Rajan had raised his voice. But

something about this hesitant man and his simple apology moved her. She simply said, 'I have opened up and told you my story. Now it's your turn. Tell me yours.'

Rajan saw no way out, so he told her. About Radha. About his father. He said more to her than he had to anyone else. She listened but said nothing. He got up to refill his water. He told her about the book, about how his family had always believed that they held the power to restore balance. He told her about the signs. He stared at the table while talking. Every time he looked up, he saw the unwavering light brown eyes looking directly at him.

Finally, he stopped.

'So, you think that Pralaya is here?' Swati tried her best to keep the scepticism out of her voice.

'I know it's hard to believe,' Rajan said. 'This book has been in our family for centuries. The description of the signs is exact. The social conditions have been met in the past thirty years. The physical signs are now manifesting: ice turning to water, the heat and the fires, the continual flooding and the drought. Without changing how we live, there is no chance of reversal. The first special sign is now manifesting.'

'You don't mean the planets.' The scepticism was now out in the open.

'Yes, the planets,' Rajan said.

'Oh, come on! You really believe that some planet somewhere influences our life. That our lives are preordained somehow.'

'Not preordained. I'm not sure how exactly it works, but I have found an uncanny correlation between what the charts indicate and what actually happens.'

'You look nothing like the kooky internet psychics in the US. Tells you that appearances can be deceptive.'

Her tone and face left no room for misinterpretation. Rajan was angry. He'd had enough.

'Why don't we check your chart? Let me tell you a few things about your life.'

'Nice try. I've already told you my life story. There's nothing left to predict.'

'Let me try anyway.'

'Okay. It's a bet. If you lose…'

Rajan was feeling slightly nervous. What he had seen of Swati led him to believe she would not be easy on him if he lost.

Perhaps she saw the nervousness on his face, because she laughed and said, 'Loser pays ₹1.'

'I need your time, date and place of birth and some paper and a pencil,' Rajan said, his shoulders sagging with relief at being let off so lightly. Soon, almanac in hand, he was preparing her chart.

But the emerging chart didn't make sense. As per the time, Swati should have been short. She should not be as straightforward as she was and she should have had a limp, or at least shuffled a little. The chart in front of him did not tally with the woman sitting next to him.

He looked up. 'Are you certain of your time of birth?'

'Yes, of course. 10.35 a.m.'

'I'm not so sure. It doesn't tally with what I can see.'

'You mean your idiot-astrology doesn't really work, even by your own estimation?'

'No, I think you have the time wrong. It looks as though you were born in the night; 10.35 p.m. fits much better.'

'Are you telling me when I was born?'

'Is there a way to check?'

Swati picked up her phone.

Rajan looked shocked. The evening had passed, and a quick look at his watch showed that the time was past 11. Who could she be calling at this time?

'Amma? How are you?'

Swati's mother's voice sounded happy but tired at the other end. 'How are you, *Kanna*? Why so late? Are you okay?'

'I'm fine, Ma. How are your knees now?'

'Better, Kanna. The new *thailam* appears to be working well.'

'Amma, I need to confirm my time of birth. It's 10.35, right?'

'Your time of birth? Now? Are you okay, Swati?'

'Yes, Ma, I'm fine. I'm sitting with someone who claims to know astrology. But they say I was born at night, but I was born in the day, right?'

'Kanna, you were born in the night. There was a mistake in the birth certificate that we never got corrected.'

Rajan smiled at the change in Swati's face.

His smile broadened when he heard her mother's next sentence.

'Kanna, ask the astrologer when you will get married.'

Swati's cheeks reddened. She knew Rajan had heard her mother's request.

'I'll call you back.'

'Please ask, Swati. It's important. You're getting older—'

'Bye, Ma,' and she put down the phone.

Swati turned to Rajan to see him struggling to suppress a smile.

'So?'

'So.'

'Shall we look at your chart?'

Despite herself, Swati was interested.

Rajan drew her chart. It was a large square containing twelve smaller squares all along its inside edges. There was a diagonal drawn across one of the squares and letters in some of the squares.

'Astrology divides our life, our persona, into 12 parts, called houses. The first house, called the *Lagna*, provides the vantage point from which the entire horoscope is read. A person's Lagna changes every two hours. So, when you said you were born in the morning, this would've been your Lagna,' he said, pointing to one square. 'However, this did not tally with what I see. Whereas this,' he continued, pointing to another square at the opposite end, 'tallies much better.

'The Lagna represents you, your personality, your appearance. The lord of the Lagna determines the tenor of your life. How strong he is, who aspects him, determines the quality of your life. Yes, I know this sounds fatalistic, but I don't see it that way. Within the broad brushstrokes, I do believe there is scope for human choice. My father used to ask: "Who chose the Lagna? Perhaps it was us, from a different plane."

'The second house represents speech and wealth. Your lord of speech is Mars. It says you will be direct – forcefully and perhaps hurtfully so. But see here, Jupiter is placed in a direct aspect. Jupiter is a benefic, and moreover, he is strong in your horoscope.'

'Slow down. I can't follow you.'

'Your speech would be forceful but tempered with wisdom, because of Jupiter's aspect. But in this chart, Jupiter represents career – your karma – so perhaps you spoke for a living.'

'I was a lawyer…'

Rajan was now mesmerised. This was a stupendous chart. Her Mars, the Moon and Mercury were all placed in their own houses and powerful even in the *Amsam*. Her 7th house contained Saturn and Rahu, or the serpent node, in it, perhaps explaining the turbulent relationship. Her Venus was in the 5th house. Could be tricky…

He moved on to calculating her *Dashas*, or the periods into which one's life was divided. Each Dasha was ruled by a planet, and a change in Dasha usually signified a change in one's life path. Swati had finished her Moon Dasha two years ago. She had begun her Mars Dasha. Given the position of Mars as lord of the 2nd and 9th houses, the chart indicated that this was an important time in her life. Maybe even a pivotal time.

'Hello?'

Swati's voice broke his concentration, and he looked up.

For the first time in their interaction, Swati felt shy. Here was a man she had just met, and she was sitting with him late at night, alone. She had told him her life's story, and he was looking at her as though he saw more than he was letting on.

'You have an engrossing chart.'

Not quite the line she was hoping for.

'So? Will my mother's prayers be answered? Will I finally get married?'

'The house of relationships is a little troubled, and Saturn being there indicates a late marriage. But the lord of the 7th is powerful, so I would say, yes. Maybe in about a year?'

'And what will he be like?'

'He—'

'Appa?'

They both started. Lakshmi had come out, rubbing her eyes.

'I'm coming, *chellam.*'

Swati got up. 'One second. You can't sleep in that. I think my uncle left behind something that might fit you.' A minute later, she came out with a kurta pajama that Rajan took gratefully.

'Thank you. Good night.'

'Good night.'

10

The Raised Hand

THAT NIGHT, SETHI CLOSED THE DRAPES OF HIS STUDY AND sat down at his desk, which had once belonged to some royal. He ran his fingers along the surface, enjoying the smoothness of the ebony with an ivory inlay along the edges. The thick, grey silk drapes blocked out the sun, but their lustre winked in the reflected light from the chandelier. Despite the plushness of his surroundings, Sethi found himself feeling unsettled, and he took a sip of the whisky he had poured for that very purpose. As the sting of the cold liquid hit his throat, he felt himself calming down.

He opened his computer, donned his mask and logged into a VPN, and then into the special software that existed only for the members – unhackable. They had funded several top hackers to find vulnerabilities. None had succeeded. Then, two of the hackers met with grisly ends. The others learnt to keep their mouths shut.

He was not the first to arrive for the meeting, even

though he was five minutes early. Almost everyone else was already there – eleven men and two women – people who rarely waited on anyone or anything, were waiting. All were masked and silent. The leader, known only by a gold cowl, logged on four minutes after Sethi, and after confirming all were present, cleared his throat and spoke in an electronically camouflaged voice.

'Good evening. I have encouraging news to share. Our agents report that they appear to have neutralized our enemy. The chamber was destroyed as well as the houses of the priests. They have gone through the village and there is no sign of anyone from the family. Our agent believes the family was killed – charred remains were found in both houses. We will not, of course, rest and will remain vigilant, but for now, all traces of that family have been erased.'

Quiet applause greeted his statement.

The leader continued. 'We can now begin the second part of our campaign. We have all been buying land in the American Midwest and Canada for many years now. This is the time to double down. Our military friends in the Middle East and elsewhere have indicated that trouble will continue, keeping rates elevated for some time to come.'

There was greater applause at this one. Each one of them had 'shorted' the market and stood to profit when financial markets fell, as well they would, if interest rates remained high. With the current developments, they were each adding handsomely to their already large fortunes.

'Our next tasks are clear: Publicly speak about the global threats to the world – AI. Talk of job losses while always hinting that if we don't do it, someone else will. Talk of climate change. Sow fear. Sow pessimism. Some of you say that the problem is unsolvable. Some of you blame. The last is key: the more people fight, the better we do.'

A hand went up – a rare thing in their meetings.

'Yes?' asked the leader.

'I agree with everything you say and will obey. But my children were aghast at the floods in Pakistan last year, where over a thousand children died. Children. They asked me why our companies weren't helping more. They told me that we have more wealth than we can spend in ten lifetimes, so why can't we help them? So many are suffering—'

Silence fell.

And then the man who had spoken up disappeared from the screen.

No other hands went up.

'We all have our tasks,' continued the leader. 'You will receive a call for our next convening.'

Sethi logged off. He dialled a number, and after an hour, his doorbell rang. He opened to find a beautiful young woman standing with her eyes tied shut and plugs in her ears. Smiling, he pulled her in. An hour later, he dialled the number again and stepped into the shower. When he came out, the woman was gone, and he was feeling relaxed yet raring to go. He opened his phone to check the news. Rakesh Dutta, an Indian billionaire with interests in pharmaceuticals and real estate, had fallen from one of his buildings. Had his been the raised hand?

Calm gone, he poured himself another glass of whisky.

11

The Feet of the Goddess

LAKSHMI WOKE UP. SHE SAW THE LIGHT FILTERING IN through blue curtains woven with bamboo sticks. At first, she was confused about where she was, but then she remembered. Her father was sleeping beside her. She was wearing Swati ma'am's T-shirt. Everything was new. Different.

She went outside and saw the old man, who had served them dinner, sweeping. When he noticed her, he went away wordlessly and returned with a glass of hot milk and some biscuits. She was finishing up the biscuits when Swati walked in.

'Good morning, Lakshmi. Sit down, you're not in class – you don't need to jump up when I enter the room. Did you sleep well?'

'Yes, Ma'am. Thank you.'

Just then Rajan walked out. His brow cleared when he saw Lakshmi.

'Good morning,' he mumbled a bit self-consciously to Swati.

'Good morning.'

The old retainer came out just then with two steaming cups of filter coffee in old-fashioned stainless steel *dabara*s. The coffee was excellent. The birds were chirping. They sat in the muttram while the morning sun streamed in lazily. Sipping her coffee slowly, Swati asked, 'So, shall we look at the book?'

The sleepiness vanished, replaced by a taut tension. The awareness of being pursued – hunted even – returned. Rajan sputtered, and the hot coffee spilled over his legs. Lakshmi dropped her plate.

Swati was a touch rueful at the reaction her question had provoked.

'I'm sorry, I didn't mean to startle you. From what you told me last night, it sounded urgent.'

Father and daughter still looked shaken. Swati persisted. If the fate of the world lay in balance, they needed to get real. Fast.

'Is there something your father,' nodding at Rajan, 'your grandfather,' smiling at Lakshmi, 'said about this? Typically, these are oral traditions passed from father to son in families.'

The last of Rajan's sleepiness disappeared with that. Lakshmi smiled.

'What? What is it?' asked Swati, smiling herself, responding to the two crooked smiles.

'My father said…'

'Thaatha said...'

'Go on, Lakshmi...'

'Thaatha said that there was a pilgrimage every father took his son on when the son turned fifteen – just after his upanayana. He said he would take me too when I turned fifteen. He said we would visit temples and go to specific places there. He said it was very important. Appa, did Thaatha take you?'

Rajan was almost glowing with excitement.

'Yes, he did, and I think I know where we need to go next.'

Swati laughed. 'Well, that was quick. And where do we need to go?'

Rajan paused. 'We?'

'Yes, we. You're not leaving me behind.' Personally, Swati still had her doubts about their story. But two years in the village school had reduced her to tears of boredom. She needed this.

'This is the most excitement I've ever had. And you can't keep calling me "Madam". Call me Swati.'

Rajan blushed and said, 'Um...you really helped us along, but—'

'You can't leave me behind now—'

'The risk is significant. There may be others like the ones who attacked the temple today—'

'And I'm an adult who said I'm willing to accept it. This is getting annoying.'

'Appa, please let Swati ma'am join us. Look at how easily she got us started.'

'Um...'

Swati had had enough.

'Get out.'

Rajan stared.

'If you are worried about the risk, leave Lakshmi here and get out. But it's not the risk, is it? You don't trust me. I've shared my house with you. I've shared my life's story with you. You still doubt me? Then get out.'

Rajan had stiffened in anger. He opened his mouth, ready to lash out and take Lakshmi with him and rush out of the house. Then he noticed the old attendant had entered the room and was watching him. Something about the man calmed him down.

He realized that Swati was right. She had been open. And her chart – she was not a liar, or deceitful.

'I'm sorry.' The words were hard to say.

'Let me get the book.'

Rajan fetched the book and placed it on the dining table. Swati saw a collection of a hundred or so palm leaves, each about a foot long, tied together within a wooden cover. Rajan unwrapped the string and opened the book, laying the leaves flat on the table.

'What language is this?' asked Swati.

'It's Grantham, Ma'am,' answered Lakshmi. 'Every child in our family is taught to read and write it. I never understood why until now.'

Swati touched the palm leaf...dry and a little crumbly. The possible fate of the world resting on crumbly dried leaves. Not a comforting thought.

'We should photocopy this. We can't keep handling the book. The paint is already fading. The leaves might crumble. We can't afford that.'

'Good idea, Madam. But where would we do that? If we walk into a copy shop with this book, won't people be suspicious?'

'I have a copier in my study here. We can do it now.'

There was a small printer in the corner of the room. Rajan took the book and spread it open. Swati moved to help him, while Lakshmi perched on the table.

As the machine started to do its work, Swati asked, 'So where are we headed?'

Rajan paused and then, seeing the frown crease Swati's forehead, hurriedly said, 'Madurai.'

'What?' shouted Swati. 'I can't go to Madurai.'

'I know you are from there,' continued Rajan, frowning a little on seeing the shock on her face. 'But that is where we have to go. Our first stop on our pilgrimage was to a small temple outside Madurai – set into a mountain…'

'You can't mean Narasingam?' interrupted Swati.

'Yes, you know it?'

'I spent every Sunday for three years visiting that temple. It used to be abandoned – almost. Quiet. Peaceful. Yet powerful.'

Lakshmi clapped her hands.

'It's meant to be, Appa. Swati ma'am is meant to come with us.'

Rajan said nothing.

Swati smiled. 'I don't know about "meant", Lakshmi, but I am coming, even though the last place I want to go to is Madurai. This is the most exciting thing that has happened to me.'

Turning to Rajan, she asked, 'What are we looking for at this temple?'

Rajan was staring at the copier. The old book was almost falling apart. Swati tenderly placed each plate, shut the machine, tapped a button, waited and repeated the process. It was almost meditative. Then he felt a hand on his forearm, jerking him out of his reverie.

'What are we looking for at this temple?' asked Swati.

Rajan frowned. He wasn't comfortable sharing so much with someone who was still somewhat a stranger. But he found he couldn't lie to her, and she did not seem the type to back down.

'The sanctum sanctorum is set into the mountain. The part of the mountain that is enclosed by the temple is covered in Grantham script. Appa used to pray to the Lord and then come and sit on the left side and lean against the mountain. Before sitting, I remember him kneeling and praying to a carving within the script on the mountain. Then he made me do it too.'

'Too bad you guys didn't carry a camera with you. You could have photographed the place.'

'What is special about it, Appa?' asked Lakshmi.

'It's a carving of Narasimha and Bhoomi Devi. Which is odd in itself.'

'Why?' asked Swati.

'Because Bhoomi Devi never appears in any story with Narasimha. She appears with Varaha, but never with Narasimha.'

The hum of the photocopying machine continued. Lakshmi started idly flicking through the copies. Then something caught her eye, and she began to tremble with excitement.

'Appa?' Seeing Rajan lost in his reveries, she repeated herself, a little more loudly, 'Appa?'

Rajan turned towards his daughter. 'What is it, Lakshmi?'

'Appa, there is a verse here about Narasimha with Bhoomi Devi…

'The path to follow will stand revealed
On the eighteenth day of the Karthikai month,
As Surya's rays illumine Ela's tender feet,
Held tenderly in a lion's paw'

'Isn't "Ela" another name for Bhoomi Devi?'

Rajan almost snatched the paper out of his daughter's hands. Could it be? Could this be it? Then another thought came…what was the date today? 5 October. The eighteenth day of the *Karthikai* stood fifty-four days away.

The air stood still and the hair on Rajan's arm stood up. He felt a charge pass through him.

This was the time.

Pralaya was beginning.

The purpose of his family, over the generations, had

fallen upon him – the eternal disappointment, the drunk. He smiled at the irony. Then fear rose up in his throat as he thought of his daughter and the explosions in the temple and his house. They were so fragile, so infinitesimally small against the forces of chaos they intended to battle. Any hope lay in a book written in code and in repeated rituals carried through a family. His father had spoken of the challenge when he had taken Rajan on the pilgrimage. 'We cannot say which one of us will be called forth, Raju. We can only prepare and pray. But whoever is called, the Lord will be there. Don't worry.' He smiled, squeezing the hand of his fifteen-year-old son, who looked frightened out of his wits. Rajan missed his father so much.

'Appa?'

'Rajan?'

This was the first time Swati had called Rajan by his name. That broke the spell. He shook himself.

'We need to be at Narasingam, in about fifty-four days from now.' He paused – thinking about when the sun's rays were likely to hit the carving – before continuing, 'The temple faces northwest, as does the carving of Bhoomi Devi and Narasimha. We need to be there first thing in the morning, as the sun's rays hit the Goddess's feet.'

Fifty-four days.

Fifty-four days.

There was a date. And now they needed a plan.

12

Thangam

THANGAM WAS HIS NAME. GOLD. WITHIN AND WITHOUT. He had been with Swati's family far longer than he cared to remember. He still remembered the day they'd met: Swati, a little baby swaddled in a white cloth and smiling toothlessly at a strong young man with big teeth. The years had taken away the smooth skin but had left the strength within the sinews and wrinkles of his spirit. It had almost broken his heart when Swati went away from Madurai. She was *his* child – his one and only dear. He had left then to see what life had to offer. Years later, he'd come back when he found out she was returning to India. But she had come back and left almost immediately – sobbing. He had driven her to her cousin's house that night. He would not willingly let her out of his sight again.

He looked up to see Swati standing in front of him.

'I need your help.'

It was instinct. She did not know why. She just knew that if she asked him, he would know what to do.

Swati knew Thangam had hidden depths. That night, two years ago, when she had sat sobbing in the car, he had suggested that she call her cousin. When they were at her cousin's place, he had suggested she take up a job in a quiet place to get away from it all. She had heard that Thangam had gone away. There had been speculation. Something about him being a smuggler. Something more. All whispers but no facts.

'I need your help.'

He saw only the swaddled baby with big brown eyes in place of the tall woman standing before him.

'They are in danger…we are in danger. I…' she sighed. 'We need to be in Madurai in fifty-four days, and we…we need to stay hidden, I think. Only I don't have the faintest idea of how to do it…'

Thangam was not a man given to speaking much. He listened intently as Swati haltingly laid out the contours of their problem. He didn't like it. He would have preferred to keep her safe. But, deep within, he realized that this was not a battle to sit out. He also knew that she was set on it. She would not back down. So, he sighed and told her what to do.

Swati needed to go to school. She could not stay away. That might arouse suspicion. Rajan and Lakshmi needed new identities. After all, if someone had traced everyone in their family, the logical decision was to have died in the fire and risen, phoenix-like, in a different avatar. The only hurdle was the paperwork.

'They need new identities. Let him grow a beard. And we can cut the child's hair.'

'But the identity cards…' interrupted Swati.

'We can take the photos for those after the changes have been made. I will need to leave for a couple of days. I will need some money. Will you be all right?'

Swati sagged with relief.

'Yes. No problem. I will be fine.'

They waited for Rajan's beard to grow. Every morning, Lakshmi would wake up and look at her father's face as the morning sunlight trickled in through the curtains. First came the stubble. Rajan had mixed feelings when the stubble came in peppery – when had the grey come in? His hair was still black, but why was his chin greying?

The years had passed him by. A lonely youth. Then a brilliant spark that burnt out so quickly. Then a long, long, long haze. And here he was…middle-aged? *Old?*

'Come, Appa, we need to watch TV.'

Lakshmi's voice broke the uncomfortable reverie.

The identity they chose to assume was of a 'modern' Indian family. (Why? Rajan had asked. On the off chance that you need to interact with people, no one connects you to this part of the country and to a traditional priest's family, Thangam had replied.) For that, the accents needed to change. The lingo needed to change. The books read needed to change. The TV shows watched needed to be different.

The other plan was to try and memorize the book – Lakshmi finding the phrase in time had been a lucky break. Swati and Thangam both believed that the harder one worked, the luckier they became. Thus, the plan was to religiously memorize the book, to ensure that the associations became easier.

When Swati came back in the evenings, she read the translation Lakshmi wrote for her. There was too little time to teach her Grantham. Translation was the best option.

When Thangam returned a few days later, he took Rajan aside.

'*Thambi*, please don't mistake me. Swati is my life. I think your daughter is yours. You need to protect them.'

Rajan looked at Thangam. He knew so little about these people but something about this quiet, old man inspired trust. *What was he getting at anyway?* he asked himself.

The old man continued.

'You need to be stronger. Physically. You need to be alert. More watchful. *Paapa* didn't tell me much, but it looks like the destruction in the temple has something to do with the people hunting you. There are several types of villains, but it takes a special type to bomb a place considered holy by so many. It tells me these people will stop at nothing. And if they are after you, you need to be more ready than you are now.'

The old man was very politely telling him that he, Rajan, was a puny weakling. *Good to know.*

'If you let me, there are things I can teach you.'

13

The Routine

THEY FELL INTO A ROUTINE.

Mornings began early. Swati took classes in language and culture for Rajan and Lakshmi. She was pleased with Lakshmi's progress – within a month, the child's accent was urban upper class. She knew the shows. The jokes. The fads.

Rajan however…

She could have screamed in frustration. His 't's' remained thick. He extended vowels he didn't need to, and shortened others unnecessarily. He knew the background. Undergrad abroad. Math major. Banker with a hedge fund located in the middle of nowhere. He knew the lingo. He had memorized the tiniest details of his story. But he stuck to his accent almost petulantly.

Finally, after four weeks, Swati had had enough.

'Do you want to put Lakshmi in danger?' she said, looking him straight in the eyes.

There was silence.

'Because that's what you're doing. In the places we are visiting, you will be talking – booking tickets, asking for directions. People weigh others almost instantly by accent. And your accent does not fit with the rest of the story.'

More silence.

'The people who are after us are no fools. In fact, the more I think about it, the more scared I am. But you…you don't seem scared enough. And that could put Lakshmi at risk.'

She finally had his attention.

'I don't think it is ability blocking you. I think it's pride. No, I think it's some form of misguided vanity.'

Rajan's nostrils flared. He was just about to say something cutting when Thangam spoke up quietly.

'Thambi, why are you not changing the accent? All the risks we have taken will be for nothing if this part sticks out, *pa*. Are you worried that you will become a good-for-nothing just because of the accent? No, Thambi. Worth lies within and will stay that way.'

'Okay, you win.' He smiled at Swati's surprise when the words came out exactly right – just the faintest slur of an American accent. Through his cultural training, Rajan began to get a handle on the nuances of Swati's world. What mattered, what was admired, and what would give them away – the wrong hairstyle, extra oil in the hair. He began to understand why Swati was so insistent on the accent. It would have been a dead giveaway.

His training with Thangam began after Swati left.

Thangam began with a set of exercises that strengthened the core. They worked outside. The weather was hot, hotter than it should have been that time of year. On the first day, Rajan lasted all of ten minutes before falling flat on the sand.

The next day, Thangam insisted they resume their training despite Rajan's protesting muscles. That day, he could only last for ten minutes again.

By the seventh day, just as his muscles began protesting a little less, Thangam got him running. To build his stamina, he said. A few days passed. One afternoon, after Rajan had collapsed, Thangam, who had run behind him, came up and said, 'Get up, Thambi. The world has not ended.'

'I'm not sure about that,' whispered Rajan.

'Come, come. You've made excellent progress. You may yet save the world.'

This was so sly, so unexpected, that Rajan's eyes flew open. Then, Thangam began awareness training. It was the ability to remain completely in the present and be aware of one's surroundings. It was like the meditation his father taught him – just directed outward rather than within.

The two men drew closer. Almost imperceptibly, the younger man began to lean a little, just a little, emotionally on the older man. Nothing was said. No confidences were exchanged. But there was the merest suggestion of a bond.

Thangam trained Lakshmi to build up her strength and

flexibility. He was far more patient and gentler with her. By tacit understanding, they had begun helping Thangam with the chores – Lakshmi loved the garden, in particular. Swati helped with the meals, while Rajan pitched in with the rest. And in the evening, when Swati came home, he trained her too. It was pouring in the evenings ferociously, so they worked inside the house.

'I'm tired!'

'Paapa, you cannot hold up the rest of us.'

'Just one coffee, and then I have to memorize the book. Use me where I'm good.'

'Yes, Paapa. But still…'

He could never be strict with her. But Rajan had no such problem.

'Do you want to put Lakshmi in danger?'

He'd never appreciated how sweet petty revenge could be.

Swati's eyes smouldered.

'Thangam is tired. He's been training us and doing the heavy lifting with cleaning the house and cooking. I've had time to rest. I can teach you.'

Swati's breathing rate had increased.

Okay. He'd pushed her enough. He stopped smiling and said, 'Jokes apart, you know you need to do this. At least some of it. Yes, I know you're tired. Lakshmi and I are more beholden to you than either of us can say. I have no right to ask you, but you will put us in danger, sure as hell, if you don't shape up.'

Perhaps it was the slang that did the trick, or perhaps it was the real note of sincerity in Rajan's voice, but Swati smiled and nodded. But she still hated exercising. Even as she got better, she hated it. But bit by bit, she grew stronger.

By the end of November, Rajan's beard had grown in, lush and thick. His face was thinner, and his body was wiry and strong.

But then came the time to cut Lakshmi's hair. She was crying as Rajan stroked her long, lustrous hair, so like Radha's. Swati stood at the door. 'I'm sorry. It's time. Thangam has to take the photo and leave in half an hour.' She hesitated and then approached the crying child and knelt in front of her.

'Lakshmi, I'm so sorry, but we have to do this. Your hair will grow back. Please, Kanna. I'm sorry, but we have to do this,' she said, stroking Lakshmi's back.

Rajan had his cheek cradling Lakshmi's head.

'Come, Kanna,' repeated Swati.

Finally, Lakshmi disentangled herself from her father's arm and took Swati's hand.

They went to the bathroom, and Lakshmi sat on the chair as Swati picked up the scissors.

In ten minutes, there was a pile of hair on the floor, and a crying boy sitting on the chair wearing a dress.

14

Madurai

RAJAN WAS AJAY KUMAR, SWATI BECAME HIS WIFE, Sunita Kumar, and Lakshmi became Arya Kumar. Rajan kept looking at the picture staring back at him – a lean face with a peppery beard, a mop of thick, black hair, and brown eyes framed in professorial glasses. He had a driving licence from New York state, a Maltese passport and several credit cards. He lived in a place called Rochester on 108 Clearborne Drive.

Swati and he had rehearsed his story until he could recite it backwards in his sleep.

'Do we really need this?' Rajan asked Swati and Thangam.

'We don't know how far or for how long we have to travel,' the old man answered. 'We don't know who will be watching. We don't know who we will need favours from. This identity protects your origins from chance discoveries. We need to sever any link to your village. We may – and probably will – need other disguises, but the bedrock will be an identity very different from what you have now. That's why we need this.'

Rajan relented. Lakshmi, or Arya, as he would have to learn to think of her, was all excited about her passport, her new backpack and the other unfamiliar trappings of her new identity. Rajan could not help but smile at his daughter's happy face. But it lasted only for a moment. The realization of the reality of why they were doing this, and the very real danger they all were in, soon wiped the smile off.

In an hour, the house was locked, and the group was in the car as the sun was setting. Thangam was driving, with Swati seated in the back. Rajan was crouched on the floor beneath the front seat, with a blanket and a basket placed on his back. Lakshmi was seated on the floor of the back seat also swathed in a blanket with pillows on top. To a casual observer, it would seem like Swati was taking one of her usual outstation trips.

An hour and a half later, Rajan could feel his legs beginning to throb with a cramp and his neck ache.

'Can I come out now?' he whispered to Thangam.

'No, Thambi. We have just passed Sattur. In half an hour more, when it is dark and we are in a less crowded place, you can come out.'

The thirty minutes passed slowly. The stars had come out along with a sliver of a moon. Lakshmi pushed aside the pillows and sheets and sat on the seat next to Swati, stretching her hands and legs.

It took a little longer for Rajan to uncoil himself. 'Is this a good idea?' he asked Swati, referring to their plan of going to her cousin's house.

'Do you have a better one?' Swati retorted.

The silence that answered her was eloquent. Thangam smiled his tight smile, and the car sped through the night.

'What if he tells on us – even by accident?'

'He has never betrayed me. He may be a little...eccentric, but I trust him with my life.'

'We are trusting him with more than our lives.'

More silence followed Rajan's pronouncement. Lakshmi had her nose pressed against the window. She had never travelled outside her little village, and this was all so very different from anything she had experienced. So many vehicles. So much noise. Such speed!

In an hour, the lights began to grow more clustered as they approached Madurai.

'Get under again, Thambi. You too, *Kutti*.'

Rajan scrambled under the basket and draped the bedsheet again. Lakshmi sank to the floor.

The car turned off the highway and entered Madurai. They passed by small huts, neon lights, loudspeakers blaring the latest Tamil hits. They came to a bridge over an almost-dry river, and in the distance, the four large gopurams of the Meenakshi Amman Temple rose, marked out by lights in a black sky. Swati bowed to the temple – seeing it gave her new strength.

The car turned off the crowded streets into a leafy neighbourhood where the houses stood further apart. Soon, it pulled up to a large house and stopped in front of a closed gate. Thangam got out in a flash before the household help, Selvam, could come too close.

'It's Swati-amma,' he told Selvam and opened the gate. The car pulled into a portico and stopped. Swati got out and went into the house, while Thangam stood guard over the car. The house had a lovely veranda with a deep brick-red flooring of handmade and hand-polished *Attangudi* tiles. A teak swing hung at one end of the veranda with a cluster of plants around it. The living room was lit by exquisite Italian glass chandeliers hanging from a high ceiling. Tanjore paintings and modern art could be seen peeking from behind overflowing bookshelves, while fabulous bronzes jostled for space with a pair of charming Dresden porcelain dancers on a shelf by the sofa. The room was a curious mixture of luxury and slovenliness – both putting up a good fight, and neither conceding defeat.

'Arjun? Arjun, where are you?' called Swati, going from room to room in search of her cousin. She finally found him in his study at the end of a corridor. As she opened the door, the stench of cigar smoke hit her, as did the sound of Bach's *Wachet auf.* The man who lay back on the black leather sofa was very short, very thin but for a proud belly, with straggly curly hair that came to his shoulders. He had a book in his hands, a half-empty glass of red wine stood on the table next to him. He looked up in annoyance when he heard the door fling open.

'What the—Swati, my darling, how are you?' Arjun's surprise turned into delight when he saw his favourite cousin. He got up and pulled her into a deep hug.

Interlude

SEVERAL WEEKS HAD PASSED SINCE THE WESTERLY WIND burst. And the chatter in the climate channels that mattered was frantic.

The man's mind was elsewhere, as he poured himself his fourth coffee of the morning. Why are you so worried, his wife, who had never bothered about the details of his work, asked. He looked at her and then around the living room of their suburban home. Their house was so ordinary, so calm, so far away from what was happening thousands of miles away.

Usually, he explained, strong Trade Winds blow from east to west across the tropical Pacific Ocean, pushing the warm water on the surface towards Asia and Australia to form something we call the Western Pacific Warm Pool. This warm pool causes the depth of warm water, or what we call the thermocline, to be deep in the west and shallow in the east of the ocean. Because it is so shallow in the east, deep, nutrient-rich cold water comes up to the surface. We call this upwelling. His wife listened, interested but not anxious. He sighed and continued. What happened a few weeks ago was that the winds in the western Pacific changed course and began blowing from west to east. This removed the atmospheric brake holding the warm water in the west and allowed the warm water to move eastward towards Peru.

I'm a little confused, his wife said. Isn't Peru to the west of pretty much everything?

He smiled and answered, we call the Pacific Ocean next to Peru, 'East', while that next to Australia, 'West'.

His wife rolled her eyes.

He gave a weak smile and continued. Anyway, this eastward push of warm water stops the upwelling, which causes the waters off the coast of Peru to warm considerably. This has happened and has weakened the Trade Winds further. And in one part of the Pacific Ocean, the part that matters, the waters are warmer than we've ever seen them.

Is that why Australia's forests are burning?

He nodded.

Will it go away?

It should, eventually…hopefully. But what calamities the world will face before it does, I can't say.

15

The Cousin

EMERGING FROM THE HUG, ARJUN LOOKED AT HIS favourite cousin – the one who had made his childhood bearable in a town too parochial for his tastes. She was much the same – with slightly leaner cheeks, perhaps. Swati had always had a little roundness to her. But that had now disappeared, and there was an anxiety on her face, like she was really spooked by something. And his Swati did not scare easily. That sobered him up.

'What's troubling you, Swati?' he asked bluntly.

Swati clung to her cousin. This smoke-filled room, with its books and nooks where God only knew what existed, seemed so removed from Rajan and Lakshmi and the book. How wonderful it would be to sink into it and never leave.

She sighed.

'I need your help, Arjun.'

'Anything, always.'

'You may regret it.'

'I may regret so many things, and I may not. But I will not refuse you.' He waited, and when she still hesitated, he asked again, with a touch of irritation, 'What is it, Swati?'

'The world is ending, and I am with a man and his child who hold the only key to saving it.'

There was silence and then Arjun burst out laughing.

'I knew if you stayed long enough in that village that you would join a cult…Oh Swati, Swati. The world is not ending – it's going to hell, slowly and in style. And no one can save it. Come, have a drink,' he said, taking out a glass from a desk, wiping it with his T-shirt before pouring wine into it.

Swati took the glass from him and sipped. She had expected this.

'I'm not in a cult, Arjun. You should know me better than that. I know it is hard to believe, but I've never lied to you. What I am saying is true. There are dangerous people chasing us. I know it sounds mad…' She stopped seeing Arjun's incredulity written plainly on his face. 'I'm not mad. Look at me. I'm the same person. The same person who always had their head on straight. It took me a while to believe what I am asking you. But we don't have time, and I feel awful about putting you at risk, by bringing you into it, but this is really important. I'm sorry but I need you to believe me, and I don't know what else to say.'

The laughter slowly disappeared from Arjun's face and the eyes behind the thick glasses grew keen. Swati had never lied to him. That was one of the laws that he knew he could rely on. But saving the world…

'C'mon, Swati. I know you've never lied to me, true, but this seems fantastical. That's the whole thing with cults. They convince you that whatever bullshit they feed you is the truth. But the world is not ending soon. Look outside…it's the changing climate that will get us – but slowly,' Arjun said.

'It *is* somewhat about climate change, but it goes deeper… think of it as the philosophy behind climate change. That's what has brought us to a tipping point now, and we don't have much time left,' said Swati, in a rush.

Arjun was taken aback. Climate change was his speciality. And philosophy was at the heart of it. *Sure, the world was going to hell,* he thought to himself. *But months? Impossible!* But Swati never lied. He resolved to listen more to her story before deciding.

And he loved her – she was his family, his only family. And she looked like she was in trouble again. Bad trouble, from what he could make out. The book he was reading was pretentious twaddle. And adventure appeared to be beckoning. He didn't need to believe their story to join them. But before he committed, there was one more question to ask.

'Where is Thangam in all this?'

The old man would rather let the world burn than let any danger come to his little chick or let her jump headfirst into cultish rubbish.

'In the hall with my friends. I wasn't sure how you…how you were placed…I wanted to talk to you first.'

Thangam's presence was a good sign.

'Okay, Swati. I'll help you. Come. Let me welcome my guests properly.'

Swati's face broke out into a big smile, and she hugged her ragged cousin.

'One more thing…'

'What is it now?'

'Send Selvam away…a man and his child are hiding in the car. No one should know that they came with me…we need to break the trail of whoever is following them.'

'And how am I supposed to manage without Selvam?'

'You can, for once…the bloody world could be ending… we will all pitch in.'

'You know how painful you are now? I was so immersed in pointless deep intellectualism, and you want me to get my fingers dirty by converting theory to practice!'

Swati smiled. This was Arjun's way. He would gripe and complain but would do what needed to be done.

'Thank you, cuz.'

Arjun called his favourite restaurant and ordered food. He then walked out, shouting for Selvam. When the man came running, Arjun told him that a friend from America was coming to stay, and since there was no food in the house, to pick some up for them.

Thangam watched Selvam leave the house, waited for five minutes and then opened the car doors to let Rajan and Lakshmi enter the house. Rajan could barely walk – being cramped up for so long had tested even his newly limber muscles – and he hobbled into the house.

Arjun saw a tall, bespectacled man with a full head of hair and a salt-and-pepper beard limp into the hall with a thin boy who clung to him. Thangam, surprisingly, walked and stood behind the boy protectively.

Does the old man have a new chick now? wondered Arjun silently as he smiled and went forward.

'Welcome, welcome. I'm Arjun. Can I offer you anything?'

Rajan stuttered, surprise and discomfort throwing him into his own language. '*Mannikka*…um…so sorry to bother you…I told Swati that we should try a hotel, or at least call ahead, but she brushed me aside,' making a quick recovery, he continued, 'I feel quite uncomfortable about pushing into your home.'

Arjun waved him aside, pretending not to notice the initial faux pas.

'Not at all. Actually, you're doing me a favour – I was getting so bored. Interesting as I am, there is only so much of myself I can take.'

Lakshmi gave a nervous giggle, and Arjun swooped down on her.

'I am Arjun, and what is your name, young man?'

'Arya,' she answered. 'Arya Kumar.'

Rajan stretched out his hand.

'I'm Ajay Kumar, Arya's dad. It's really very kind of you, we're very grateful.'

Swati silently applauded the angle of his arm, the accent and the assumed confidence. Meeting Arjun was the first test, and Rajan – barring his initial faux pas – was doing well.

'Please don't thank me again, I might get bored and turn you out!' laughed Arjun.

Swati showed Lakshmi the powder room. It had been a long journey and the child's bladder must have been bursting. Thangam carried their luggage into the rooms upstairs, leaving Rajan and Arjun alone. As they walked to Arjun's study, the men sized each other up.

Rajan was tired. His joints were aching – *middle-aged, with no youth to speak of,* he thought to himself – and he was hungry. Fear – of what was unfolding, and of trusting their fates to a man who appeared a weak and privileged dilettante – made him cranky and inclined to quarrel.

Arjun, on the other hand, was fascinated. *Who was this man who had won over Swati (no fool) and Thangam (born suspicious)?* he asked himself. *What was this 'Save the World' quest that they were on?* The world couldn't be saved. The so-called green warriors were essentially rearranging the deck chairs on the Titanic. They spoke in conferences of how they would cut their emissions by 2050, while the floods and droughts raged on. He had tried, once upon a time, to work in the field. He knew he lacked the patience to persuade and build coalitions. He was mercurial and impatient, expecting everyone to understand the logic of his arguments. 'You need to be more of a people-person,' his cousin had said, but he'd considered that to be beneath him. And so, when he'd run into enough hypocrisy and shallow talk, he had retreated into his books and music. And into his retreat, came this.

'So…' said Arjun at last, when it was clear that the other man was not going to talk.

'What has Swati told you?' asked Rajan, somewhat belligerently.

'Easy, fellow. She told me the world was ending. And you held the key to stopping it somehow. Naturally, I found it hard to believe, but Swati has always been straight with me, and Thangam trusts you.'

'That's not quite right but let that be. Has she told you about the risk you'd be running by agreeing to help us?'

'She hinted at it.'

'And you're okay with that?' Privately, Rajan was oddly pleased with his grasp of slang at a moment like this.

'Once I was concerned about the world. About how society had frayed, and how we were tipping out of balance. But I found that I couldn't do anything about it. That didn't stop me from caring. And you carry a message of hope… Also, I've never said no to Swati.'

'But you don't believe her…believe us.'

Swati and Lakshmi entered the room just then. They looked at the two men and felt the clear tension emanating from Rajan. Lakshmi's face crumpled up with worry, while Swati thought to herself – *it was just like Rajan to be difficult.*

Before she could say anything, Thangam surprised them

all by speaking up. No one had noticed the old man enter the room.

'Thambi,' he said to Rajan. 'Arjun-thambi is a little strange, but I trust him with all my heart. Once he accepts something, he will stick with it. You have enough battles ahead; don't add to them with battles of the mind.'

'You're making me blush, Thangam,' said Arjun.

Lakshmi looked at her father, hoping he would calm down.

Thangam's unexpected entrance and words jolted Rajan, and he realized he was being an idiot. Here were three people saying and showing repeatedly that they were willing to accept the risks and help, and he was being churlish and rude.

'I'm very sorry, please forgive me. You're all trying to help, and I'm being rude.'

Everyone's shoulders slumped in relief.

'Before we all burst into tears, let's eat. If that lazy fellow has got the food,' said Arjun, leading them to the dining room.

16

The Growing Band

AFTER DINNER, RAJAN WENT TO PUT LAKSHMI TO BED, while Swati and Arjun went back into his study. Closing the door, Arjun turned to his cousin and asked, 'Does Ajay, or whatever his name is, know that you have a weakness for glasses and beards?'

Swati blushed and threw a cushion at her laughing and unrepentant cousin. 'Don't be an ass,' she said, accepting the glass he handed to her.

'His name is Rajan. He comes from a family of priests in the village. Arya is actually his daughter, Lakshmi.'

Arjun sipped slowly and looked at his cousin. She looked happy and fit – a far cry from the blubbering mess she was two years ago. And yet she said the world was ending.

'So?'

'So.'

'Are you going to tell me more about what this is about?'

Swati hesitated. It was not her secret. Just then there was a knock on the door.

'Come in,' said Arjun.

Rajan walked in. He saw a messy room with squashy sofas, books on every surface. On a table stood a beautiful bronze sculpture of Mahavishnu, with more books stacked around him. A desk was piled with empty snack bowls and bottles. He had not yet seen that the room was a pretty exact replica of Arjun's mind. Messy, eclectic, brilliant.

'I'm sorry, am I interrupting?'

'No, not at all,' said Arjun, rising. 'What is your favourite poison?'

'Water,' Rajan smiled.

'You're not serious.'

'But I am.'

'I don't have that here.'

Swati interrupted, growing impatient with this word-fencing between the men.

'Arjun was asking what this is about,' she said bluntly.

Rajan was uncomfortable – he barely knew Swati's cousin. But why whinge about that now, when they had taken the plunge and crossed the Rubicon. *No point in dithering further*, he told himself. He took a deep breath, and said, 'Everyone can see the world has changed very fast, very quickly. Yes, there have been terrible famines and wars in the past where millions have died, but this time seems different. It's as though the fundamental character of the planet itself is changing. That the planet is tipping over.'

'Couldn't agree with you more,' Arjun acknowledged.

'And this happens because of how society is changing – how people are relating to each other, or not. Communities are splintering and man is becoming an island, surrounded by electronic seas.' As he said this, Rajan saw Arjun looking at him gravely and intently. There was not a trace of a mocking smile on his face.

Gaining confidence, he continued, 'In my family, we have always believed when there are a set of signs – physical, social and astrological – Pralaya, or the world's end, is at hand. Some of those conditions have now been met. For example, the third social sign speaks of an intelligence rooted in *maya*, that has no *atma* to guide it to the *paramatma*.'

Arjun's eyes widened, as his brilliant mind began making the connections. He said, 'Something like AI. Where there is a semblance of intelligence or wisdom but no thirst to unite with the divine. Where the world is completely artificial and people immerse themselves…in this metaverse.'

Rajan smiled. 'So, you *do* understand. My family has been given a book that suggests a way to stop or help with this. We've always believed that the practices we have followed through the centuries and something within the book will help bring back balance to the world. But some of the text is in code. The book contains a set of clues that can help crack this code and know how we can act. The time to solve the first clue is day after tomorrow, early in the morning, at Narasingam.'

Arjun was quiet, while his mind tried to process all this information. All his life, he had relied on his brain, and his brain was overwhelmed. Going by data alone – and data had always been his god – what Rajan was saying didn't hold water. But something deep inside him was whispering that this was it. This was right. *Perhaps he should listen*, he told himself. After all, listening only to his brain had left him lonely, bitter and bored in Madurai. And Rajan's take on the philosophical underpinning of the crisis was spot-on.

What was the worst that could happen? He drew a deep breath.

'Tomorrow, let's visit the Meenakshi Amman Temple in the morning, and the Nayak Palace in the afternoon. Selvam would think it very odd if Narasingam was the only temple you visited. Let's poke around some forgotten corners. After that, we can come back and plan our next steps.'

Rajan smiled – his mischievous yet shy, crooked smile. Arjun gave him a tight grin in return. Swati let out a breath. Their band was growing.

17

The Dugong

THE FACTORIES HAD BEEN SET UP TOO CLOSE TO ONE OF THE world's most fragile environments – a coral reef that had once supported schools of colourful fish and the gentle dugong. The British saw the broken coral as useful building material. Indeed, a colonial seaside bungalow was built entirely of coral – a good way to save costs and make something sturdy. The architect and the contractor were applauded. But few understood or appreciated the real value of the coral reefs and associated mangroves, in keeping the coast safe and livelihoods protected.

As more and more people stopped living off the land, their appreciation for the reefs faded, and when the coal plants came up, no one protested. After all, new jobs were created, and the company set up a foundation – the chairman's daughter with a Hollywood starlet in tow – to study and protect the dugongs. It was slickly done. The starlet drew the local intelligentsia. A wildlife 'expert' spoke of the gentle dugong and how more funds were needed to study this mysterious creature (true). And how the company would be making the largest grant ever to study this creature (also true).

Watching this on the TV in his office, the chairman snickered. That grant was less than a fortnight's profitability from the plant. No one spoke much about the waste or the hot, ejected cooling water that entered the seas quietly – invisible, but deadly. He had played this game before. The windmill fields that operated not far from his factory produced power only when the wind blew. That happened for only a few months, whereas people needed power year-round. Coal was the answer, and the newer plants were more profitable when they ran using imported coal. To save on transportation costs, plants needed to be set up on the coast, which had the added advantage of using seawater to cool the plant. The plants needed fresh water too, and the factories quietly signed agreements to procure that – along with agreements to sell the power once it was produced. The whole scheme was so profitable that, one after the other, coal plants came up. The banks lined up to finance these schemes, without understanding that the district where these plants came up did not get much rain – and that the environmental clearances for some of the plants were not quite up to the mark.

One of his competitors had invested in a desalination plant to make his factory water-neutral and spent more money on treating the fly ash responsibly. But for the chairman, the fees paid to the starlet and local media made for a better investment. The local population, mesmerized by their screens, failed to see how their mangroves and corals were weakened by factories that were blasé about their compliance. Their children no longer went to the sea or worked the land; they wanted office jobs in front of a screen. As their connection to the land disappeared, so too did their awareness of its suffering.

18

The Temple

EARLY NEXT MORNING, THE GROUP WAS DROPPED OFF by Selvam at the temple. Lakshmi was excited to be visiting the temple she had heard so much about. The first hall contained pillars with carved figurines – dedicated to the *Ashtashakti*s – welcoming the visitors. This opened up into a larger hall, the ceiling soaring and being held up by giant pillars. The air was fresh, and light coursed in from high ventilators along the pathways. Towards the end of the hall stood an elephant with a mahout. Swati made her way towards the elephant, which seemed to know her. 'Yes, my baby, I'll feed you,' cooed Swati. 'How is she?' she asked the mahout.

'Good day, Madam. She is getting better. The doctor has said she can't eat her favourite *kadalai mittai*, but we give her watermelon.' By this time the elephant had slobbered all over Swati, trying to fish out whether she was carrying her sweets. 'Yes, Kanna, I'll feed you. Parvati!' she admonished, as the elephant pulled her hand roughly.

After feeding the elephant, the group walked on and soon came to a large square tank, surrounded by the majestic gopurams on all sides. This was the tank where Indra had bathed to cleanse himself of the sin of killing his friend through deceit. It was a hot day and standing in the cool air around the tank provided some welcome relief. Then they were in line to see the goddess. There was not much of a crowd that day, and within ten minutes, they could see her. Short, dark (one of her names was 'Shyamala' or the dark one), and emanating endless power and grace, Meenakshi drove all thoughts away from the minds of the group. Swati found tears pouring down her face as she folded her hands. Meenakshi. Mother. Her kindness was palpable. After seeing the goddess, they went around her shrine. Arjun stopped them within a few feet. Built into the wall was a small female statue with the words '*Iccha Shakti*' inscribed below her – representing the power of our desires. He turned to Lakshmi. 'Don't negate your desires. Acknowledging and understanding them can help us unleash their power and is the first step towards true knowledge'.

They walked a little more, and right behind the sanctum stood another statue. 'This is *Kriya Shakti*, or the power of action. Desire alone is not sufficient, you have to act,' said Arjun.

'Sufficient for what, Arjun Uncle?' asked Lakshmi.

Arjun smiled and looked at Rajan. Rajan felt pride blossom in his chest. It was not just parental pride. Lakshmi was truly special. 'Sufficient to know oneself. One's true self.

The more we peel back the layers, the more we discover the gem within. One of the mantras of Tibetan Buddhism is: '*Om Mani Padma Hum*' – meaning 'Praise be to the gem at the heart of the lotus'. By this time, they had come to the next statue.

'*Jnana Shakti*. The power of knowledge. There is a verse in the Brihadaranyaka Upanishad that says: "You are what your deepest desire is." When your only desire is union with the infinite, you will achieve that illumination. This *prakaram* is a physical representation of that verse. Having it around Meenakshi simply says that grace is what makes that travel on the path possible.'

They exited the shrine and soon walked past the large Ganesha, who – if legend was to be believed – was found when an old Nayak chieftain was digging a tank. Then they prayed to Shiva, marvelled at the magnificent sculptures and left. After lunch, Swati suggested they drive to Alagar Kovil, an ancient temple dedicated to Vishnu. The Lord was considered the beautiful one, and whoever stood before him momentarily forgot themselves – lost in his splendourous smile. But Thangam objected. Alagar Kovil, as Rajan had shared, was on the pilgrimage route of his family. Swati said he was being too cautious, but Thangam insisted. So, they visited the Nayak Palace and called it a day.

Back in the house, they introduced the book to Arjun. 'It's a collection of palm leaves, Uncle,' started Lakshmi, 'written in the Grantham script. There are twelve chapters in all – the first part speaks of walking the path of the soul, then there are chapters on how society has changed and what signs show that it has reached a breaking point, and chapters on the physical world and signs to show that the planet is tipping over. Those signs have now appeared. And Pralaya will follow unless we do something.'

'And what is that "something"?' asked Arjun.

'We are trying to figure it out, Uncle,' said Lakshmi. 'Our family has always taken a pilgrimage, and it seems like some of the clues relate to that. And something that can help restore balance is hidden in the chapters written in code. So even if the book were to fall into the wrong hands, they cannot decipher it.'

'Hmmm. And the first stop is Narasingam.'

'We think so, Uncle.'

'Ajay, if you don't mind, can I see this book? I know Grantham reasonably well. And it would help me get up to speed.'

19

The Lion and the Goddess

THE NEXT MORNING, BEFORE THE CRACK OF DAWN, THEY arrived at Narasingam. Thangam had hired a cheap taxi – one of those ubiquitous small, slightly dented and scuffed white cars. The old man also told them that the driver of the taxi was indisposed and that all of them would have to wear caps that covered their faces. It was a mark of trust that the others did not question him further on this. He himself drove, wearing a muffler and glasses, while the others stayed crouched down, invisible to the outside world. He parked close to the temple, behind a shop. Signalling the others to stay down, Thangam asked them to wait, saying he would be back in less than ten minutes. Rajan groaned but said nothing, while Arjun showed no restraint. 'Why?' he asked.

'There will be cameras around. I will disable them.'

He disappeared like a shadow in the dark. He reappeared ten minutes later.

'I've taken care of the cameras, but the temple appears to be shut.'

They got out of the car and stretched. The small temple was dimly lit by one or two tube lights, while the giant rock rose up behind it. 'That's not possible!' exclaimed Swati. 'The temple opens at 4 a.m.!' As she looked around, the reason why the temple was shut became apparent. 'Tccha! They are renovating,' said Swati, pointing to the bamboo trusses put up around the temple.

Rajan and Lakshmi looked at each other – worried. They needed to get in, and the minutes were ticking away. Swati thought for a minute. There could be a way to get in through the side. She led everyone to a sprawling water tank outside the temple, filled with lotuses, and signalled them to walk along the edge of the tank until they came to the mountain face.

In the dark, Lakshmi could not make out how high the rock was. A single rock, shaped like a resting elephant – 90 metres high and over 3 kilometres long – was majestic during the day. But in the dark, with only lamplight shining on it, it seemed endless. Thangam began to scramble up the rock before jumping onto the low wall around the temple. Once he was over, he asked the others to wait until he returned, which he did in a few minutes. Then the rest of the group crawled up the mountain and jumped onto the shallow platform that lay on the other side. As they walked up the steps into the temple's antechamber, they found the entrance closed and padlocked.

Once again, Thangam stepped forward. He drew a small needle from his pocket and inserted it into the hole in the lock, fiddling with care until a satisfying click sounded. They opened the door and crept inside.

It was almost pitch dark within the temple – there was a faint lamplight emanating from the sanctum, but that did not light up the rest of the space. Arjun and Swati switched on the torches they were carrying, and the group made their way gingerly to the sanctum. They bowed to the deity within – a gentle man-lion, believed to have arisen naturally, seated in meditation, radiating wisdom and kindness.

Then, they stepped down to the mountain face, which formed the walls of the antechamber before the sanctum. The rock itself was covered with inscriptions in Grantham. Rajan remembered the trip with his father, made in what now seemed a different lifetime. He had been happy to get away from the stifling life at home. His father seemed more carefree and affectionate in their travels – cracking jokes and gently introducing his young son to the wonders of the world. Breaking out of his reverie, Rajan knelt at a spot to the left of the doorway leading into the sanctum, about halfway down from the ceiling. When the others gathered around him, they could see the carving of Narasimha and Bhoomi Devi with several lines of inscriptions below it. Arjun shone a flashlight onto the lines, revealing a list of temple names.

'This is it. Now we wait for the sun to rise – that should be in less than an hour.' Lakshmi sat down next to her father while Swati wandered around the temple she had once thought she knew like the back of her hand. On a whim, she began filming.

After a couple of minutes, she exclaimed. 'Ra…Ajay!'

Rajan turned around and looked to where Swati was pointing. The temple faced north-west, but the chamber they sat in had a ventilator with three slots to let sunlight in from the east. They saw what Swati was pointing at – a thatched covering over the bamboo scaffolding. If it let any sunlight in at all, the rays would be diffused. Panicking, Rajan turned to Arjun and Thangam and said tersely, 'Tear it down – now. Hurry.'

Wordlessly, the two men left. Thangam reached out from behind his back and brought out an *aruval* – a deadly looking scimitar common to these parts. They noticed a scaffolding they had missed in the darkness earlier and clambered up. Thangam began hacking away at the covering while Arjun tried pulling it away. They worked furiously, but their haste made noise, and soon, they could hear raised voices in the distance.

They heard the main gate open, then footsteps and men shouting. Rajan stayed put but made Lakshmi move back against the wall with Swati. Two men came running inside.

'Who the hell are you? How did you get in?' they shouted, grabbing Rajan by the scruff of his neck and trying to pull him away. He pushed them back and felt his new muscles respond. One man went flying. Then, Thangam's training kicked in. 'Use their strength,' the old man had instructed. 'Calm down and look for opportunities.'

He noticed both men were wearing loosely draped lungis. He reached down and tugged. One man began shouting in embarrassment. The other got up and ran towards Rajan, shouting.

Out of the corner of his eye, Rajan noticed that the predawn glow had started to appear. Desperation added an edge to his strength. He swung hard at the man's solar plexus, and the fellow went down. A red sliver was now visible on the horizon. Thangam and Arjun were pulling off the last bit of thatch, and the unimpeded sunbeams began hitting the wall. But the second man seemed to have decided that security was more important than modesty. He came at Rajan in his underwear. The first man had also gotten up, and together they circled Rajan. He tried pushing them away but was unable to. The sliver of sunlight grew larger, and the sun began to rise. Arjun and Thangam came running up and charged at the men.

Rajan used the distraction to pull away and turn towards the wall. But the light was shining near the bottom of the wall – well below the carving of Bhoomi Devi's feet.

He slumped down. They'd missed! Generations of efforts ruined by a thatched roof and two ignorant goons. All fight went out of him, and he bowed before the statue, stung by defeat. Arjun came running up to him. Thangam had pressed the pressure spot on the necks of both men, and they lay stretched out, cold.

'What's wrong?' Arjun asked Rajan, shaking his shoulder.

'We missed it…we missed it. The light has risen too high.

I don't know where the next stop is,' Rajan muttered. To his embarrassment, he felt tears running down his cheeks.

Arjun went pale. Thangam stood wordlessly – the old man had seen enough to know they had missed their goal. He looked around for Swati and found her standing next to the wall, arm around Lakshmi and…smiling.

She came forward. 'It's okay…' she told Rajan.

Rajan was still hunched down. Swati shook his shoulder and pulled him up. 'Look, I recorded the sunrise on my camera.' She played the video, and sure enough, Rajan saw the rays shine slowly on Ela's feet – three rays trickling in through three precisely engineered openings. Slowly they began to move closer together before converging over one word. A temple that every Vaishnavite knew by heart.

Srirangam.

Rajan hugged her. Swati was taken aback. For a moment, he just held her, the relief so overwhelming he could not speak. Arjun smiled. Thangam's face turned stonier than usual. Lakshmi giggled. That sound broke the two apart. Rajan was blushing, but his hands remained on Swati's shoulders.

'Thank you. I know I've been difficult. I'm sorry. Without you, it would have all been for nothing. My life would have been a waste. You saved us. You saved the world. I'll never doubt you again.'

Now, it was Swati's turn to blush. She looked into the

brown eyes of this hesitant, earnest, awkward man in front of her and felt something stir inside. Before she could say anything, Lakshmi rushed forward and hugged her. 'Swati ma'am…you're a superstar!'

'Quite the saviour, Swati. You should wear a cape,' quipped Arjun.

Thangam just beamed. His chick was the swan he always knew she would be.

'Come, those idiots will wake up soon. I need to do one last thing before we leave.' Saying that, he broke into the sanctum.

Rajan was shocked, but he had learned to trust the old man.

Thangam prostrated himself before the Lord, muttering. He then stood up, shook himself as though steeling himself to commit a terrible act, and reached gently to pick up the necklace from the idol's neck.

Lakshmi gasped. But Thangam ignored her and carried the necklace to the cupboard kept to the side and opened it. It was stuffed with old cloths, pots of water, wicks, half-empty cans of oils, and all manner of ephemera. It was clear no one had cleaned it in years. He took the necklace gently and placed it at the back of the cupboard, underneath the multitude of detritus. He bowed to the Lord again, sighed, and locked the sanctum.

As they left the temple, he bowed again to the Lord – this time, as though asking for forgiveness.

20

The Dugong – Part 2

THE PRESS BOX WAS FULL. THE CAMERAS WERE HELD AT the ready. The PR maven was a suave older woman, whose minions were rushing about looking important. The maven smiled. The conference was just tinsel. The heavy lifting had been shouldered by the prime slots booked on the TV outlets and the more discreet favours handed out.

The older woman signalled her minions to quieten the press. A hush fell over the auditorium, and then, on cue, applause broke out as two people stepped up to the podium. One was the starlet, a blonde dressed in a colourful saree; the other, the chairman of one of the coal factories.

'We are here to herald the dawn of a new era,' the maven shouted to the crowd. 'Clean Coal!' She paused, waiting for the applause from the planted audience.

In reality, the company she worked for was probably the dirtiest of the cluster along that patch of the coast. Some of the others had tried to clean up their fly ash, make their plants more efficient and reduce their water footprint. But that wasn't the chairman's style. He liked the flash and the lure of quick cash before trying to find a sucker to buy his company (along with its liabilities) and reemerge in a new avatar.

None of that was visible on the white, green and blue stage. The event was marketed as 'net zero waste' and had a negative carbon footprint. Every visitor was given a charming goodie bag with handcrafted sustainable soaps made by tribal artisans.

On stage, the starlet simpered for the cameras. The chairman stepped up, a hidden smile playing on his face. 'We have a huge surprise to share – our company has been nominated as one of the top 100 sustainability champions for this year!'

The crowd began to cheer. Dramatic music played along with green and blue strobing lights.

Then three women jumped up and began screaming, 'What about the dugongs? What about the reserve? What about the eleven lives lost?' The press cameras swivelled towards them. They liked the advertisement revenues, but they loved sensationalism.

The chairman glared at his lackey, who looked to the PR diva. This should have been managed. The PR maven took the mic.

'The company funds the Dugong Foundation, which leads the largest research and resilience work into the dugongs. Without this research and work, we will not be able to protect these gentle creatures from the climate crisis. The warming waters are destroying their food, fishermen need to be incentivized to protect them, and the foundation is studying how to replenish their food stocks and work with fishing communities. The company is also supporting fifty livelihoods around the reserve to help protect it and the communities that depend on it. We believe in being a responsible planetary citizen. Thank you for raising these questions. Yes, sir…' she said, looking to another man dressed in a kurta, with a ponytail, stubble and a slouchy air.

'Why not move the plant outside India?'

'In this era of geopolitical uncertainty, energy self-sufficiency is critical. This plant is central to that. And the dugongs would lose any funding they get today. Plus, we create more than a thousand jobs that would be lost if we moved away.'

The chairman smiled. The PR woman was expensive, but worth it.

21

The Path and the Key

THANGAM DROVE FAST – AWAY FROM NARASINGAM, AWAY from Madurai – on a narrow country road. After half an hour or so, they came to a small copse of trees in the middle of empty fields, into which Thangam turned the car. Out came the costumes that the old man had managed to stash in the boot. Rajan, to whom this was all completely new, was amazed at his meticulousness and foresight.

'Why do we need these costumes, Thaatha?' asked Lakshmi.

'I had hoped we could slip in and out without a fuss,' said Thangam. 'But we broke in, and there was a fight. That is out of the ordinary, and will stand out, especially to someone who has their eyes open.'

As he handed out their disguises, Rajan felt ashamed. Lakshmi and he would have died by now if it hadn't been for the others. This level of planning was beyond him.

His reverie was broken by Arjun asking him if he was

actually going to put on his disguise – turban, lungi and vest, the same as Arjun's. The others were in burqas.

Thangam, Swati and Lakshmi walked a few kilometres to the north, caught a bus and left for Madurai, while Rajan and Arjun walked south and caught another bus half an hour later. By design, Thangam's party reached first. He asked Swati and Lakshmi to wait by the bus stand while he went to the house and packed off Selvam for the night. Swati and Lakshmi joined him soon, and peeled off their burqas in relief once they were inside the house – it had been hot outside – far hotter than was normal for that time of year. An hour later, Arjun and Rajan arrived.

There was a sense of accomplishment in the group. They had cracked the first clue. They knew where to go next. Rajan and Arjun were eager to jump into the book for clues on Srirangam, but Thangam asked them to wait.

'Look at it fresh, Thambi,' the old man said. 'First impressions matter. If your first impression is fogged up by tiredness, your tired mind will lead us down the wrong path.'

The rest of the day passed quietly.

Rajan thought he was too wired to sleep, but the relief of knowing where to go next made him sleep soundly. A few hours later, he began tossing about in his bed. Ever since he'd stopped drinking, his dreams had become far more vivid. That night, he dreamt of a forest. A forest made of hundreds of trees, no two alike, each gleaming in a different shade of green. He was looking at the forest from above –

almost as though he was flying. No, that wasn't right. There were clouds in the forest. It was cold, but he was happy.

The next morning, when he came out of his room, he saw Arjun and Swati talking, steaming cups in their hands. Rajan picked up Swati's video camera and began going over the video again and again, trying to see if anything else was highlighted by the sunlight. But nothing else was, which meant the book and his memories of his pilgrimage alone held the clues of where to go in Srirangam, and when.

'Did your father take you to any particular shrines in the temple?' asked Swati, as though she was reading his thoughts.

'We covered the major shrines. But we also spent a lot of time at the Ramanuja,* Dhanvantari and Narasimha shrines.'

'Narasimha after Narasimha. Could that be the key?' asked Arjun.

Lakshmi had come in by then, and a rumble from her tummy made Swati say, 'Breakfast, everyone. Now.'

Over breakfast, with Selvam present, conversation was strained. Rajan could see that his daughter was clearly bursting to say something but was restraining herself with difficulty. After breakfast, they retired to Arjun's study, where Lakshmi barely waited for the door to be shut behind them as she blurted out, 'I remember one *shloka* about Srirangam in the book, Appa.'

'Which one, La—Arya?'

---

* Ramanuja is considered one of the greatest saints in Vaishnavism. His samadhi is a shrine within the Srirangam.

'Yes, "Larya", which one?' asked Arjun sarcastically.

Swati grimaced. 'We need to be consistent, Arjun.'

She saw Rajan looking grim – he had found the shloka Lakshmi had indicated.

'What is it?'

'The shloka Arya refers to speaks of being in two places at once.'

Lakshmi began chanting:

'In the temple on an island in a freshwater sea
Where the Great Lord sleeps on his ocean
In the shrine, where the Lord rises from the ocean
Is the place to be
When the moon fills the sky
As the Sun moves north
The path shall be revealed by the lord of the night sky
But the key, oh the key, dear reader
The lord of the twilight controls
The power of the night sky lord proves helpless
Beneath the twilight lord's clawed toes.'

Swati looked puzzled, and Lakshmi began to explain. 'There is only one temple located on an island in fresh water, Ma'am, and that's Srirangam on the Kaveri. "When the Sun moves north" refers to Uttarayan, and the moon filling the sky is Pournami, or the full moon day. So clearly, we need to be at Srirangam on the Pournami after 15 January.'

'That's great,' said Arjun, and then, looking at Rajan's frown, he added, 'Isn't it?'

'Yes,' said Rajan, almost impatiently. 'And the lord who rises from the ocean is Dhanvantari and the moon beams may show us our next step.'

'So, what's the problem?' asked Swati.

'What worries me is the bit about the key. That's new – and separate.'

'And sounds important,' chimed in Lakshmi.

'"Lord of twilight"' could refer to Narasimha,' said Arjun. 'He manifested and killed Hiranyakashipu in twilight. That would also fit with "clawed toes."'

'But what is the key? What does it refer to? Do we have to be there at twilight? Or at moonlight? How can we be at two places at once?' Rajan mused, frowning. 'There is more about Srirangam in the book. I thought it was just background information, and didn't memorise it, nor did I ask Lakshmi to. We'll need to go through it closely now. That holds the key,' he said, smiling at his own weak pun.

They spent the rest of the day reading the book and resting. They had cracked the first clue, and they knew where and when they had to be next and had plenty of time to get there. Driving to Srirangam from Madurai would take less than two hours.

Later that evening, Swati went to visit her mother. Arjun and she had argued about that. But Swati's line had been a clincher: 'There's no telling whether we'll return from the path we are on. I want to see her.'

'Don't make it sound like a farewell,' said Arjun, giving up.

Thangam drove her home in Arjun's car.

She entered her own home and sat in the living room like a guest, while the maid went to see if Madam was available.

In a few minutes, her mother came hobbling into the room.

Why is she hobbling? Why is she looking so tired? Swati asked herself.

Swati's mother hugged her, tears rolling down her cheeks. 'You've lost weight, Kanna, and you've tanned so much!' she said as she let go, stepping back and stroking her daughter's cheek.

Some things never change, thought Swati. There was something oddly reassuring about that.

'I love you, Amma. I missed you.'

'What will you eat? We have a new cook – he makes the most delicious *badusha*,' her mother said, signalling the attendant to get some for her daughter.

On a whim, Swati clung to her mother. It was warm, soft and comforting. A world away from the reality she left behind. She, who had always sought excitement, found that real danger was uncomfortable – and involved a little too much sacrifice. For a moment, she wanted to sink into her mother's embrace, forget the last couple of months had ever happened, and walk a new path.

'So…you have come home!'

Mother and daughter broke apart. Swati's father had entered the room.

'I knew you couldn't manage on your own. Come to ask us for money and a home?'

'Stop it!' cried Swati's mother. 'Our daughter is here. Isn't that enough?'

'I have no daughter. Your daughter has come to my home. I'm merely observing that.'

Swati's desire for the other path died an infant death.

'I love you, Amma. I just wanted to see you. I'm leaving.'

'Wait, Kanna. Your father doesn't mean it,' her mother almost wept. Turning to her husband, she said, 'Please ask her to stay. We haven't seen her in so long.'

'I have nothing to say,' her husband replied.

Swati hugged her mother long and hard, tears rolling down her cheeks. Her heart ached. Ached at her father's words. Ached at leaving her mother. Ached because she did not know if she would ever see her again.

'Bye, Amma.'

The badusha arrived, but Swati had left.

Back at Arjun's house, Swati ran upstairs. Blinded by tears, she did not look up and bumped into Rajan.

'Wait. What happened?' he said, recoiling and holding onto her to keep them both from falling.

'Nothing. Let me go.'

'Don't cry. I can't—'

'Let me go.'

Rajan let his hands fall from her shoulders. Swati sidestepped him and ran up the stairs to her room.

There was a knock on the door.

'Leave me alone.'

'Swati, let me in.'

'Please. Leave me alone.'

'Swati. Please. I can't bear…please don't cry.'

She opened the door. Rajan stepped into the room. Swati stood there, her face splotchy and tear-stained. There was such infinite tenderness in his gaze. Such concern.

Swati walked into his chest and broke down.

Awkwardly, Rajan put his arms around her. One hand hesitantly reached up to her curls and began stroking her hair. Her tears began to slow, then ceased. When she looked up, he wiped the wetness from her cheeks with his handkerchief. For a moment, they stood just so, looking at each other.

Then Swati reached up and kissed Rajan full on the mouth.

At first, he did not respond.

And then his arms tightened around her, and his mouth opened and he kissed her hungrily.

ᘐ

Later, they were seated side by side, with Rajan's arm around Swati's shoulders. He was feeling happier than he had in a long time.

Swati's smile blended mischief with shyness. 'You know, Pralaya may not be such a big deal for you,' she said.

'Why?'

'Because when Thangam finds out about us, you're dead.'

'There have been so many miracles on this journey. Maybe he will accept me.'

'Maybe. But for now, let's keep this just between us. Our secret?'

Much later, Rajan went to bed. He was smiling as he fell asleep, but he woke up with a start. He had dreamt of blood pouring in front of a giant Narasimha statue. Women were screaming.

And a young girl lay dead, just below Hiranyakashipu's leg.

22

The Huntress

SHE STRETCHED BACK AND LOOKED AT THE BACK OF HER hand. The skin glowed – *that cream was really working*, she thought. The glistening of her skin was heightened by the three-carat, nearly flawless, princess-cut diamond ring she wore. She had bought it for herself – and that made it important to her. The ring rested on a finger adorned with a French-manicured nail. No tacky acrylic stick-ons for her – that was not her style – just her own nails, painted nude with white tips.

Her clean-eating diet was helping. At forty-five, she looked fifteen years younger, with dewy skin and shiny hair. Her new personal trainer (he was charming, that one, in more ways than one) made her fitter than ever. She had easily outpaced the others on the Kilimanjaro hike last month.

She managed more money than the central banks of many countries – which her team ploughed into stocks, loans and hard assets across the world. Unlike her (in her opinion) half-witted competition, she rarely gave interviews. She did little marketing. Her numbers spoke for themselves, and clients were begging her to accept their money – whatever her fees. Some of her returns proved too good to be true – well, given that she used any means to further the success of her bets, that was to be expected.

She got up and went to change out of the chiffon saree that was her work uniform in India. She stepped into the shower, appreciating how her feet sank into the plush bathmat, and turned the dial on. The lights of the bathroom went off, except for an iridescent blue light in the shower cubicle. A lilting melody from a cello began to play, and the intensity and the colour of the lights melded with the cascading notes. Slowly, jets began spraying water from all directions, in sync with the music. The temperature of the water changed in a pattern set by the world's leading wellness experts – hot, body temperature, cool and ice-cold – with the cadence of the music and the colour of the lighting changing in sync.

Ten minutes later, she stepped out, refreshed and alert. She pulled a thick, soft towel from the rack and dried herself, smiling. Who would have thought that one day she, a bus conductor's daughter, would be drying herself with a towel worth more than her father's monthly wages? She donned a custom-cut tracksuit made from fine Pima cotton and poured herself a glass of water before turning on her laptop.

She had cut herself off from her past – her parents did not know what she did. They did not even know whether she was alive. The moment she boarded the flight out of India, she knew she had to erase her roots. Within a month of landing at her new college, she had applied for a change of identity, and then transferred to another, far more prestigious college, ditched her glasses, and moved forward with a new name, hairstyle and an invented background. Her hunger, brains and complete lack of moral compass did the rest. She landed a job at one of the most coveted firms, and after that, she did not look back or below.

That journey had brought her here, to this apartment in Bengaluru, with a rain tree enveloping her glass-sheathed study. Priceless Greek- and Gupta-era statuary – some even sourced legally – graced the room.

The room glowed from the dim lighting, and the white beeswax candles flickered within their wooden sconces. The light winked off the glowing wood but died on her spartan, unpolished granite desk. A single painting – from the Italian Renaissance – adorned a black wall beside her desk, while the wall behind it was a dark, unrelieved grey. No paintings, no books, no statuary. She had no need to impress anyone.

She slipped on her mask, logged into the special software and found nine others waiting in the room. There were still a couple of minutes for the meeting to begin. She had expected to be last, with only the leader joining after her. Oh well. The next time she would cut it a little closer. In the next minute, three more joined, and then the image of their leader – golden cowl around his shoulders – appeared.

'Good evening. I have unpleasant news to share. There was a break-in at a temple in Madurai yesterday, which our informant says was on the pilgrimage route. It could be nothing, but our informant has asked us to be vigilant. I have a list of three temples around Madurai that were on the pilgrimage. I have dispatched our agents to these three. Any suspicious behaviour, especially around the lion statues, will be acted upon. Meanwhile, we need to check the data from the CCTV cameras. C,' he said to one of the video squares on the call, 'get the footage from 3 December. Who broke in? Did they take anything? Where did they go from there? We meet in three days.'

23

The Island

THERE WAS AN EXTRA WARMTH IN RAJAN'S EYES AS HE looked at Swati – a warmth his glasses kept somewhat hidden. The last few days had been happy ones with no further dreams since that last one. This morning, as they gathered in Arjun's study, he longed to touch her, but he did not know how Thangam would react, and they could not afford to antagonize him. Swati, unconscious of his gaze, was reading through a book on Srirangam from Arjun's library.

It seemed fitting that their path led to Srirangam – the beating heart of Vaishnavism. The temple was believed to have arisen from the Ocean of Milk as a benediction to Brahma, the Creator, who was praying to Vishnu, the Preserver, with the magical *ashtakshara* mantra: 'Om Namo Narayana'. What made this temple so special, read Swati, was the deep love the deity inspired in the devotees. Brahma; Lord Rama; Vibhishana, the king of Lanka – they all fell for the deity. When Lord Rama was coronated in Ayodhya, he presented the deity to Vibhishana, who was delighted with so wonderful a prize. As Vibhishana flew back to Lanka, he grew tired and stopped on an island on the Kaveri, near a pond called Chandra Pushkarani. When he wanted to leave, he found that the deity would not budge. He threatened to end his life, when the Lord appeared and said that while he would remain on the Kaveri, he would always face south towards his devotee. To this day, the deity at Srirangam, Lord Ranganatha, unlike most idols, faces south.

Years passed. The area became thickly forested. One day, when a Chola king was hunting in the forest, he heard someone chanting hymns. He followed the voice and came upon a parrot sitting on a giant tree. He dug up the ground below the tree to find the Lord seemingly waiting for his devotee. In an act of overflowing love, he built one of the biggest temples in the world.

Literary evidence suggested that the temple was at least 2,000 years old. It was a mini city built in seven concentric rectangles centred around the shrine of Ranganatha. Apart from the main shrine, there were other important shrines in the temple. One to the Lord's consort – the universal mother. Another to his devotee, Andal. Swati was always fond of Andal's story, where the lord preferred to be bedecked with a garland containing a strand of his devotee's hair rather than with a pristine garland. Andal epitomised *bhakti yoga* – the path to salvation through love. And it was so easy to fall in love with Ranganatha, called Emperuman – literally, my God – by his devotees. There was also a shrine to Dhanvantari – the divine physician – the only one of its kind in the world. Swati began to read more closely. The 1,000-year-old shrine was located in the north side of the fourth passageway of the temple and used to host an ancient hospital. The idol itself had four hands, with the lower right hand holding a pot of *amrit*, while the lower left hand was in the *varada-hasta*, with a leech wrapped around the palm. *Yuck!* thought Swati. She'd hated the leeches that infested the forests where she and Arjun went hiking when they were younger. Arjun, on the other hand, loved to get bitten, saying he always felt better afterwards.

Somewhere in that shrine lay the clue to their next step.

What about the Narasimha? Srirangam's Narasimha shrine was called the Mettu Azhagiyasingar, or beautiful lion. The story went that the poet, Kamban, performed his version of the Ramayana, an emotion-laden love ballad, in front of this idol. When the play concluded, the lion roared in appreciation. The sanctum, which could be reached by climbing up very steep steps, contained a small bronze idol tearing apart the stomach of a smiling Hiranyakashipu with his fingernails. The funny thing was, Rajan felt, Narasimha, in the midst of his terrifying form, strangely inspired love. At his feet stood Prahalad, bowing to the lord who rescued him from his own father. Did Prahalad hold the key?

Arjun, who had been reading the photocopied version of the book, suddenly spoke up. 'There is something else about Srirangam here, in Chapter 7.' He began to chant,

'To reach Bhooloka Vaikunta's Lord,
You must step through seven chakras,
In a physical path, the shrine will lead you forward
But if it is awakening and its key you seek
You must walk through the chakras within.
As within, so without.'

'Bhooloka Vaikuntam is another name for Srirangam, isn't it? And don't many believe that the seven concentric passageways of the temple mirror the seven chakras of the *Kundalini* within our body?'

Rajan tensed up. His father had spoken about the Kundalini. Many times. How their family had been…what was it he said?

Lakshmi spoke up, 'Thaatha told me that our family has a gift of pursuing the Kundalini, Arjun Uncle. And when we reached the initiation stage, we were taught certain rituals to make it manifest.'

Swati was watching Rajan. Clearly, he knew more. 'What is it, Rajan?'

'There may be more to this in my father's journal. It is not just our family. Certain astrological patterns show whether someone can manifest the Kundalini more easily. All can to a smaller or lesser degree. But certain people, with the right practice and grace, can manifest it fully.'

Just then Thangam came in. The old man looked grim and strode forward to turn on the TV and tuned in to a local Tamil channel. The screen showed footage of Thirukoshtiyur

Temple, about an hour's journey from Madurai. It showed people milling about – clearly agitated about something. Lots of police stood around making enquiries. A father and daughter had been murdered on the temple premises that day. Their only crime was that they had been hovering around the Ugra Narasimha for several hours, praying. The TV screen showed a girl, about Lakshmi's age, lying face down below Hiranyakashipu's body, a pool of blood around her.

Rajan looked thunderstruck. 'My father took me here. We spent time praying in front of the Narasimha.' What he left unsaid was, 'I dreamt of this happening.'

Thangam spoke, 'This is no coincidence. The enemy knows about your family. They know about the pilgrimage. The news about a break-in at Narasingam has been reported, and they now think that someone may have escaped. They are randomly killing anyone who even roughly matches your description in any of the temples on your pilgrimage. These people are informed, powerful and ruthless. And they want to kill you.'

Rajan's stomach clenched with fear and gripped at his heart when he saw Lakshmi…and Swati.

Thangam looked around and, to everyone's surprise, he smiled grimly.

'Good. I need you to be scared. Only when you are genuinely frightened, it tells me that you are taking the enemy seriously. Only then, we have a sliver of a chance to succeed. Our enemy will be watching. So, we need to go where they will not look. Something that has nothing to do with your pilgrimage.'

He paused, looked around the room, and said, 'We will go to Kodaikanal.'

24

Kodaikanal

ARJUN BROUGHT OUT HIS PRIDE AND JOY – AN ENORMOUS, battered old jeep, with enough space for Rajan and Lakshmi to comfortably crouch in the back. Arjun drove, Swati sat in the front with Thangam behind her. To anyone who may have been watching, it looked like Swati and Arjun were making their usual trip to the mountains.

In a couple of hours, the jeep had climbed high into the Palani Hills. It was raining steadily, and the jeep made its way carefully through the ancient shola forests that draped the mountain slopes.

Carpeting the crevices of the southern Western Ghats, the shola was a mosaic of multi-hued evergreen trees once cradled within sweeping montane grasslands. Only now, many of the more accessible grasslands had transformed into eucalyptus plantations or farms. The shola – cool, moist, and humming with life – clung to sheltered hollows. These forests were relics of a primeval past, alive with the rustle of mosses, ferns, and orchids in the underbrush, as the sunlight dappled through a thousand shades of green in the canopy.

The rustle was broken by the Palani laughingthrush, a voice heard only in these hills. Swati saw a family of rhesus monkeys stretched out on the banking wall of the road, sunning themselves on this cold wintry day, while a shy Nilgiri langur disappeared through the tangled green bush as the jeep swung around. In the deeper shadows, was that a lion-tailed macaque in the tree there? Swati was turning her head to look for it when she saw a Malabar giant squirrel jumping from that tree, while a kaleidoscope of butterflies frolicked below.

She could see, in the distance, the grasslands glowing golden in the afternoon sun, much smaller now than in the past. In her mind's eye, she could see, far from any human habitation, the Nilgiri tahr – a kind of mountain goat that lived high in the Western Ghats – with strong legs and special little hooves, helping it climb steep, rocky cliffs where most other animals couldn't go. She and Arjun had once hiked through the shola to a deserted grassland where a small temple stood atop a hillock – the vehicle of the goddess there was the tahr.

These forests were rich in so many ways. The streams born from the shola braided together to give birth to rivers like the Vaigai, lifeblood to the plains far below. But because the economics of the modern world did not value them appropriately, they were fighting for their life. Invaders marched steadily into the grasslands – wattle, eucalyptus, lantana and pine – colonial guests threatening the delicate balance of these unique forests. Patchworks of farms gnawed away at the forest and the ragged breath of the besieged shola whispered a warning carried on the mist.

The rain was heavier now. Crouched in the back, Rajan pored through his father's journal in the dim green light that filtered through the trees. The old man's notes were meticulous on the practices needed and his experiences with the rising Kundalini shakti. Kundalini – in Sanskrit, the word meant 'coiled', signifying the energy lying in the coiled form of a snake at the base of the spine. With the right practices and some divine grace, the energy, or shakti, would rise through the body, through astral gates called chakras, and help the soul unite with the divine. The rising Kundalini shakti could, in special cases, confer powers. In his family, the Yoga-Kundalini Upanishad was mandatory learning for everyone after the upanayana. From early childhood, every child in the family was taught the breathing techniques (*prana*), yoga and its asanas, and had to eat a balanced, nutritious diet (*mitahara*) – all aimed at two things: getting the Kundalini moving and helping the body cope with its ascent. His father was guiding him even now – meticulously, kindly and wisely. Rajan closed his eyes and leaned back. For a moment, regret and sorrow overwhelmed him. If only…

Lakshmi, as though reading his mind, leaned forward and squeezed her father's hand. Rajan took her palm and pressed it to his cheek. They had to be in Srirangam by the

Pournami after Uttarayan. That was on 4 February, which gave them sixty-one days to get the *kriya* to take root. It would be tight, but it was possible.

It was raining ferociously now and they were forced to a crawl. 'The papers say that a cyclone is going to hit Chennai tomorrow,' said Arjun. 'Perhaps we should have waited until it passed.' But the rains paused, and the sun came out – a buttery yellow orb peering through the grey, overcast skies.

The jeep ploughed through the waterlogged roads and soon came to Arjun's house, where a long road from the gate with ancient trees on either side led up to the house, which was a small cabin set at the top of a hillock. The front door led into a panelled, bright living space, with a small-but-functional kitchen set to one side and a corridor leading off the other side with three bedrooms set on either side of it. The cabin opened out to a small garden – where Swati and Arjun had enjoyed many an evening gazing at a bonfire – that fell away into a sharp ravine at one end.

Arjun had called ahead and asked for his house to be cleaned. As the jeep pulled in front of the house, a smiling woman greeted them. 'Arjun-thambi, how are you? Swati-ma, nice to see you. Both of you have been coming here together for so long.' She then drew Thangam aside and spoke to him for a bit, handed over the key and left, swaying gracefully down the road.

After unloading the luggage, they waited until Thangam said it was safe and stepped into the house. Rajan hobbled in after sitting for so long, while Lakshmi skipped inside.

The air was crisp and cold, a welcome change from the hot plains, and a light mist was rising up the mountains and entering the house. Lakshmi shivered, and Swati placed a jacket over her thin shoulders. It was too big, but that couldn't be helped. Arjun gave Rajan his father's old sweater, and they all stepped out of the large glass doors onto a small lawn. There were stone benches carved into the sides, mossy with age and damp after the rains.

But the view! The house was perched on a steep cliff. Down far below lay serried cliffs clad with forests, skirting a valley that was swaddled in clouds. Slowly, the mist rose, revealing a rainbow shola that had lain hidden below. Here, they were alone. Here, the madness of the outside world fell away.

Rajan stood gazing. This was the forest from his dream.

Thangam appeared – wearing a monkey cap and a woollen vest – with steaming cups of tea. The group sat down, each sipping the warm tea gratefully, and Rajan began.

'I think we need to prepare our bodies and minds through Kundalini yoga. I have been reading my father's notes, and there appear to be three parts – breath, body and food.' Rajan looked at Thangam and continued, 'Thanks to you, most of us are somewhat fit already. But what we eat – this is problematic. Kundalini needs mitahara. "*Mita*" means moderate, and "*ahara*" means food. We need to eat plenty of raw fruits, raw and mildly cooked vegetables, whole grains, and unprocessed foods.'

Rajan paused, smiled and looked at Swati and Arjun.

'And no caffeine or alcohol.' There was a touch of smiling malice on his face.

'Forget it,' said Swati, horror dawning on her face. 'Without caffeine or alcohol, my world may as well end.'

Arjun laughed. 'Same goes for me too.'

Rajan's smile melted into a frown. 'I can teach you the breathing techniques, but without the diet, your body will neither allow nor be able to withstand the Kundalini movement.'

Swati interrupted him. 'You said it was only members of your family who had the gift. I am not from your family. So why suffer without the potential of superpowers?'

'Same goes for me,' quipped Arjun.

Lakshmi piped up.

'But, Appa, you said some horoscopes show the gift of Kundalini manifestation. If you could check their horoscopes…'

Rajan's frown cleared.

'Okay, if your horoscopes show that you have the gift, you give up alcohol. Deal?'

Swati almost cheered for Rajan's grasp of lingo at a time like this.

Arjun asked Rajan, 'What signs are you looking for?'

'The Kundalini can be thought of as a serpent or a hidden energy coiled like a serpent. So, what I will be looking for is a powerful Rahu in a horoscope because Rahu is the serpent node. But the Kundalini helps achieve union with the divine. So, I also want to see a link with Jupiter or Venus in some way.'

'Why Jupiter and Venus, Rajan?' asked Swati.

'Because they are pure benefics who can temper the power of Rahu – Venus more so than Jupiter.'

He took out Swati's horoscope. But her Rahu was not particularly strong, nor was there a link with Jupiter. His expression revealed his thoughts.

Swati smiled. 'So, I get wine and coffee over spiritual superpowers. I can live with that.'

Rajan looked up and smiled. 'You still have an excellent horoscope…' and then stopped, blushing.

He looked at Arjun. 'Can I have your time and place of birth?'

He began casting Arjun's horoscope. No one spoke but waited – watching Rajan intently.

Rajan was mesmerised. Arjun's Lagna Lord – the planet that governed his persona – was Mercury, who was in his own house, and *Vargottama* – meaning he was in his own house in several planes of the horoscope. That fitted with the mercurial, brilliant man in front of him. Mars was in the second house, like Swati's, but debilitated, meaning he spoke the facts but timidly, almost diffidently. Rahu, the serpent node, was shining exalted in his own house of Aquarius. And he was Vargottama too. He was the lord of luck, of fortune, perhaps even of destiny. Most importantly, in the 60th division, the *Shashtiamsa* – which was considered the most important chart in any horoscope – Rahu and Venus were together. Rajan felt a frisson pass through him. If anyone could get their Kundalini to ascend, it was this man.

Swati laughed when she saw the transformation on Rajan's face. 'No wine or tea for you, Arjun!'

Arjun gave a weak smile. 'Not even a tiny glass?'

Rajan smiled. 'My father used to say that the body is stressed tremendously when the Kundalini is activated. Very few could survive it. All these – the diet, the exercise, the meditation – are just to improve the chances of the body surviving. Your horoscope is made for the Kundalini to ascend. We don't have much time. And we need every bit of luck that we can get.'

Lakshmi said, 'Arjun Uncle, you can have superpowers…'

Finally, Rajan turned to Thangam. 'Please let me have your time and place of birth.'

The old man had left the room when Rajan was casting Arjun's chart and had returned holding a small yellow bag. He took out an ancient, folded paper and gave it to Rajan. Rajan unfolded it carefully. The four corners had a mixture of turmeric and vermillion smeared over them.

The old man's Lagna lord, Venus, was in his own house with the serpent node, Rahu. Rahu was exalted and Vargottama. Guru was in the 9th house, aspecting the Rahu. The old man could easily make his Kundalini ascend. Thangam smiled grimly as Rajan looked up at him. He already knew.

At that moment, it began raining again – suddenly, furiously – forcing the group indoors. Thangam quickly lit the fire, and Lakshmi and Swati curled up in front of it. Overhead, the rain beat down as though a million hammers were falling on the roof.

25

C

C – AS HE WAS CALLED IN THE GROUP – LET OUT A LONG breath and stretched back in his seat. There had been sixteen of them in the Cabal just a year ago – the most powerful people in the country – but two had disappeared – one for failing at his task and the other for asking a question. If he failed, there would be nowhere to hide.

This was not a task he could farm out, not even to his most trusted aides. It had been a long time since he'd gotten his hands dirty, but the ace computer science student from one of the world's most renowned universities felt a tingle of excitement pass through him as he nestled deeper into his seat. A long time ago – *had it really been that long?* – he had a small cult following for his ability to break into systems. He was what they called a white hat – hackers who partnered with companies to find vulnerabilities within their systems. In his heyday, he believed there was no system he could not break into. He was smart enough to keep his less white-hattish activities concealed.

He used a street map software to locate the temple the chairman had indicated. That took less than a minute. Within the temple, he located the exact coordinates of the office and fed those into another tool at his disposal. That showed him the IP addresses of all the computers in that vicinity, including one in a room that was possibly the office of the temple. At present, it was turned off, which presented a small challenge. He tried examining the network the computer was connected to, checking for points of vulnerability – the router, or maybe even the printer – where he could break in and wait in stealth until the computer was turned on.

That happened twelve hours later, when he was in the gym. Once he received the alert, he finished his workout, showered and messaged his secretary that he would not be in that day and told her to reschedule his appointments. He smiled as he thought of his secretary; they were all the same type – curvy, subservient, silent and desperate to please. She would be his reward once he got what was needed.

He headed home and logged in again. The password of the temple's office computer was laughably predictable. He scoffed and logged in. The camera software was not protected. All these people connecting more and more devices to the internet blissfully unaware that they were exposing every facet of their lives to predators, he thought. All the better for him. But when the data came in, C's smile vanished. What should have been small squares with video feeds were instead six blank squares with a broken camera icon on each of them. This could mean one or more of three things: the cameras weren't working, the network wasn't working, or the software was corrupted.

He then tried the playback option, hoping these fellows paid enough for at least a monthly playback. They hadn't – they had paid only for forty-eight hours' worth of recording, and the video feeds from that period were all blank.

Damn! He'd have to go to that blasted place to check if the cameras had any data that could be salvaged from the physical drive. It had been years since he had flown commercial, but the private jet would not provide the anonymity he needed.

He caught the last flight that day to Madurai and checked in. The next day, dressed in the casual attire of a camera repairman, he visited the temple, carrying spare cameras with him – he'd been able to note down the brand from the camera software and the quick commerce vendor had delivered three cameras to him at the airport. The clerk in the office was unaware that the cameras were not working nor that his supervisor had asked for them to be serviced.

At first, he was inclined to ask for permission to let someone in for servicing, but C hinted subtly that a clerk who had not noticed that the cameras were down just after a break-in would not be judged kindly. That settled the matter.

C went to the camera installed at the temple entrance and checked the model to see if any data could be salvaged. But it was the cheapest type, with small SD cards in the device itself – with the backup going to the recorder. So, after currying favour with the clerk by replacing three cameras (and swiping the SD cards they held), he told him that the recorder needed servicing and that he would try and have it back to him that evening.

He then invited the clerk out for tea and bought some samosas for them to share. The clerk, unused to such attention, blossomed and readily answered, with embellishment and relish, any questions his new friend posed.

Had they seen who broke in?

There were at least six ruffians – giants to the last man. They were clearly trying to rob the temple.

Was anything missing?

Yes, a diamond necklace. From the main deity – they must have been crazy ruffians to steal from here. He was a ferocious deity – everyone in the village was scared of him. Once a fellow insulted him by getting drunk and sleeping with his legs pointed towards the temple. The next day, he had a fracture, and he considered himself lucky.

C sipped the surprisingly good tea with newfound relish. Maybe that was the explanation – a simple robbery. But still, better to be sure.

Back at the hotel, he first connected the SD cards and then the recorder to his laptop and began to scan their innards. The SD cards were unreadable – they showed signs of water damage, which was not very surprising as they were exposed to the elements. The memory card within the recorder was laughably small – barely enough for forty-eight hours of video. He took out the memory card in the last hope that his scraper could get some of the earlier recorded videos, put a new one in, and returned the recorder to the temple, before catching the last flight out of Madurai. He did not like flying and this flight was particularly bumpy in the heavy rains. Late in the night, back in his apartment, he placed the SD cards and the memory card into his computer with its powerful scraping software in the hope that some remnant of the prior videos could be captured. It was past midnight by then, and he went to bed.

The next morning, he headed to his computer and found that his computer was able to salvage mere dregs – there was no way to tell whether the cameras were sabotaged or had simply stopped working.

So, it was with trepidation that he donned his mask that evening and logged into the account. He was one of the earliest – fear made him log in sooner than he had to. It was ten minutes before the leader joined. By convention, no one had spoken before then.

'Well?'

C swallowed but managed to give an unemotional and detailed account of what he had found – data unavailable, unclear whether it was erased or malfunctioning, break-in by six large men, one necklace missing.

The pause that followed seemed interminable.

Finally, the leader spoke, 'Very well. This may be nothing after all. Our agents found a father and daughter, roughly the ages of our subjects, hovering for an extraordinarily long time near the lion statue at one of the three sites. They have been eliminated. We will meet next month at the usual date.'

The meeting ended. C let out a long breath and slumped in his chair.

Interlude

HE STARED AT THE READINGS FROM THE ARGO FLOATS, autonomous, robotic instruments that measured ocean temperature and salinity. His face tightened as the data from the Indian Ocean refreshed – subsurface temperatures were climbing off the charts, while the upper layers of the Bay of Bengal were practically shimmering with heat. Satellite data showed wind speeds of the cyclone tearing past 200 kilometres an hour and still rising. This was like Michaung on steroids – the same pattern of cyclone, only supercharged by a feverish ocean.

He could not imagine what the people of Chennai were weathering. He had visited the city years ago, in the aftermath of the 2015 floods – that had been traumatic. But this? This would be a hundred times worse.

26

The Flood

IT BEGAN AS A MILD DRIZZLE AS ALL FLOODS DO. THE RAIN fell, not furiously but continuously. Pitter-patter. On and on and on. It had rained heavily the previous month and the lakes of the city were full. But then, the lakes had a far smaller holding capacity than what was shown on paper, silted up and encroached as they were. Some of them had become schools, others entire neighbourhoods. Some of them housed the giant mountains of trash that a city like Chennai generated every day.

And so, as it rained on, the water had nowhere to flow, and the water levels rose. In the lakes at first, and then in the neighbourhoods that had once been lakes. Then the winds picked up, lashing at everyone and everything. Trees fell over and electricity wires snapped. People moved to higher and higher ground, leaving behind possessions gathered after a lifetime of back-breaking work. Then occasionally – and later often – family members were abandoned as the rains picked up pace, a lake breached its walls, and the flood became a deluge. There were only so many disaster relief forces, only so many boats, only so much dry land. People moved up the floors in high-rises, as lower floors were overwhelmed. This was a flood like no other in living memory. This was Pralaya.

And still it rained. And still the winds raged. The at-first belligerent empty-noise TV debates gave way to horrified silence. There was no telling what the death toll would be. There was no finger-pointing that would make sense, unless each person pointed to themselves. The kitchens that were churning out food on the first day with the hashtag #ChennaialwaysHelps, themselves fell victim to the flood. The army was called in, but heroic soldiers found themselves overcome by the brown waters. Still, every hour, some few were rescued – small victories in a losing war. Yet, when a little girl holding a puppy was pulled out, the world cheered and social media exploded – highlighting the puppy and erasing her tears.

A day later, the winds died, and after two more days, the rains finally stopped. It took another four days for the water to recede.

Raja was a manager at the Superfresh store. He had finally made the down payment on a flat on Old Mahabalipuram Road – they had gone for a fourth-floor apartment with a partial sea view. Raja's heart was held in the often-grubby palm of his four-year-old daughter, Adya, who was best friends with Sara who lived on the first floor. When the waters began to rise, many people had moved up and come to the higher floors. Sara had not, and little Adya went down to try and get her friend to come and stay with her. Neither girl came up. Raja and his wife were found hanging a week after the floodwaters had receded, when it had become clear that Adya would never be coming up.

Rajee was a maid who washed other people's vessels and picked up other people's clothes off the floor. Her son had fallen ill the month before the flood, and she had used up all her savings and all her credit to admit him to the hospital for life-saving treatment. In the aftermath of the flood, both she and her son survived – but her creditors, along with all her possessions, did not.

Hussain-bhai and his old mother were fond of feeding the birds in their building, which was fitting since mother and son were both bird-like and gentle. His mother's pride and joy were her immaculate kitchen and the surprisingly colourful balcony garden where she coaxed the most recalcitrant flowers to bloom. The garden was so unexpected and so charming that a local news channel had even profiled it with Hussain-bhai's shyly beaming mother in the background. That balcony was an early casualty of the flood. With its demise, Hussain-bhai's mother shrank inward and grew silent. Hussain-bhai opened the doors to the masses and they flooded in with muddy feet into her kitchen. She cooked and cooked in silence for strangers until the food lasted. The sparkling white floor of the kitchen soon became brown, and Hussain-bhai's mother slowly stopped moving.

The food had run out anyway. When the waters rose and the boats came, she refused to budge and Hussain-bhai's fingers were broken as he was pried loose from her arm in the rescue.

Finally, the waters ebbed. The talking heads began talking of the next big thing, and people tried to get on with their lives. Some couldn't move on, and they joined the failures of modern life. The suicides, the depressed, the addicts.

Scientists came out with research that showed why it had rained so ferociously: the oceans were 3°C warmer than usual, too warm for this time of year. These fevered waters fed the storm's frenzy. The lakes that should have held the rainwater had become too small – one cannot fit a bucket of water into a thimble – while the canals that should have drained the rain away were clogged with solid waste, meaning the water stayed put and welled up. People complained but soon forgot.

27

The Training

THANGAM WOKE THEM UP AT FIVE WITH A FLASK OF WARM water, ever-so-gently spiced with jeera. It was still dark and cold – so high in the mountains and amidst the trees. The first day, Arjun cursed and Swati howled. But the old man was merciless. Arjun had cold water sprinkled on him when he dawdled. Swati was finessed: when she argued that she did not have a chance for her Kundalini to rise, Thangam used his most potent weapon – Lakshmi's gentle persuasions. When Swati emerged, the look of betrayal on her face brought out his rare smile. '*Manichuru,* Paapa.' (Forgive me, child.)

Later, they stood in a row outside the house. ('In the cold?' moaned Arjun.) Then they began the Surya Namaskar – the ancient salutation to the sun god. ('But it's still dark!' complained Swati.) On the first day, Arjun collapsed after two sets of the exercise, Swati after eight, Rajan after ten, while Thangam and Lakshmi stopped after twelve, just as the sun rose and the mists cleared revealing shades of emerald, jade, ochre and scarlet sparkling in the shola forest below. Birdsong – sharp and sweet – cut through the silence of the crisp morning. The cottage was miles away from the nearest road, and no honking or raucous loudspeakers broke its serene calm.

The next day, the routine continued. Arjun collapsed after a single set, his aching muscles crumbling under this brutal assault. Swati and Rajan managed eight, while Thangam and Lakshmi finished their dozen with greater ease. Later, Arjun hobbled to the dining table, wincing as he sat down.

Swati could not resist quipping, 'The fate of the world relying on Arjun's thigh muscles.'

Lakshmi giggled, which she quickly suppressed. Thangam brought out a bowl of steaming sambar, followed by a plate of soft idlis. 'Where's the *podi*?' demanded Arjun, who believed that the *milagai podi* was the main course, with the idli or the dosa acting as mere delivery mechanisms.

Rajan smiled, knowing what was coming. 'Thambi, you cannot have spices. Your body is already so weak,' said Thangam.

Arjun was silent. It was all happening too fast. And on no tangible evidence. His whole world upended. His body ached. His brain was foggy without his morning coffee. He was suffering a headache brought on by alcohol withdrawal. And now, no podi. Swati guessed some of the thoughts passing through her cousin's head. 'Yes, Arjun. It sucks. But think of me. I'm suffering everything you have to, without the lure of superpowers. At best, I'm a side act. But you, if you follow through on this, you could make your Kundalini awaken. Think of magic!'

Arjun stayed silent.

Rajan spoke up, 'I know how you feel. When I gave up alcohol, it was like taking off a security blanket and jumping into a bed of nettles. The world was too clear. Facing all the fear, all the hurt with no barrier and a headache was one of the toughest things I've gone through. The only thing I will say is that it gets better. If you can stick to this for a few more days, the longing fades.'

Arjun stayed silent. Lakshmi looked at her father in wonder. He had never spoken about his alcoholism so openly before.

'And the muscles get better too,' Rajan continued. 'Thangam found me worse than you when he started on me. We have all been through his ropes for a couple of months now. Think of this as the price you pay for the power. There is always a price. Most don't want to pay it. Or even those who do, find the price too high in the early stages and give up. This kind of power should not come easy. It is not meant for everyone. It needs discipline. A sense of withdrawal. A spirit of sacrifice. The process itself is a way of weeding out the unworthy,' Rajan paused, seeing a shift in Arjun's expression. 'My reading of your horoscope tells me you can do it. This is hard. But it will get better soon.'

No one said anything else, and the group finished breakfast and went to rest in the lawn outside as Thangam cleaned up after them. Rajan pulled Swati aside. 'It's not okay for Thangam to clean the house and train us.'

Swati shared his quandary. 'Usually, we have a woman come in to clean. Thangam told me that she told him that she has a wedding to go to and would be away for a few days. She offered to provide her sister as a replacement, but I felt she would notice Lakshmi and your presence.'

'But won't she think it odd if she was not called at all? Does she stay the whole day?'

'No, she comes in the morning after we have had breakfast, cleans, helps Thangam with the food prep and leaves after an hour or two.'

'Then how about this? When the woman returns, let her come and clean. I'll make sure our bedroom looks unused, and Lakshmi and I will hide out in the woods while she is in the house.'

Swati was unconvinced. Thangam had entered the room to clean up, and she called to him and shared Rajan's proposal. To her surprise, Thangam nodded.

'But don't hide out in the woods. You could be seen. There is a shed where the old things are kept. It's stuffy and smelly, but we can fix that. Stay there for a couple of hours, while she cleans. It's no hardship for me, but I agree with Rajan-thambi that we should stick to our usual routine as much as possible. Which reminds me, when will you and Arjun-thambi go to the club?'

'Come on, Thangam. We always go to the library in the club and then have a drink in the evening. If Arjun and

I aren't drinking, that's a sure-shot sign that something is different.'

That was a problem. Then Rajan said with his crooked smile, 'Don't kill me, but what if…if someone asked you… Arjun implies that you are on a strict diet to lose weight to try and get married and you blackmailed him into joining you?'

If looks could kill, Rajan would have died that instant. Even Thangam permitted himself a small smile before he said, 'I'm going down to the *santhai* now to buy vegetables. I'll stop at the club on the way and let it slip that you are both on a diet. That way no one will ask you.'

28

The Changing Climate

FOR A COUPLE OF WEEKS, THE GOING WAS HARD. Uncomfortably early mornings, difficult asanas, a strict diet and no caffeine or alcohol. But, slowly, Arjun's thigh muscles, under Thangam's tough love and nourishing food, grew stronger, and the stretches became easier, and then almost pleasurable. And when the inky black turned to blue and gold, there was a familiar sense of anticipation for the orange sliver to appear on the horizon.

But that morning, after two weeks, Arjun found his senses alert and awake. He could feel his muscles – not sore but alive. His brain was clear, in the absence of the usual hangover. His emotions, usually the weak link, were calm, and his senses, usually darting about like an insect caught in a light trap, were absorbed – by the crisp cold air of a Kodi winter morning, by the sunlight gently streaming into the living area, by Lakshmi's smile as she heard Swati joke, by Swati's voice and by the tang and nourishing warmth of the sambar in his mouth. He was completely absorbed by what was happening in that moment. He was present.

He had also begun to believe – how could he not after all that had happened in the past month. And with that belief came the hope – a slim tendril – that the world could actually be saved. But then, his inner sceptic asserted itself: wait for more data. He paused in this reverie when he saw Rajan frown while reading the newspaper.

'What is it?'

Rajan didn't answer immediately. The question and the absence of a reply drew the others' attention.

'Has there been another murder?' asked Swati.

Rajan looked up, almost shaking his head, as though awakening from a trance, and drew a deep breath.

'It's this flood.'

The others waited for him to continue, premonitions filling their minds.

'Two thousand confirmed dead. Ten thousand, at least, missing. These numbers are unprecedented – at least, in a single city. Velachery has vanished.'

The others listened in horrified silence.

The army had been called in, Rajan told them, and was trying to fish people out. An entire makeshift camp city had been set up in Tiruvallur to house the thousands that had been evacuated. A minister who had gone for a photo op had been lynched by a mob. After that, no leader had dared to visit.

'I'm glad that Thangam insisted we keep the TV off – at least we are spared the disaster porn,' said Arjun.

'The Centre has sanctioned ₹10,000 crores, conditional on the encroachers vacating the channels and the tank bed,' said Swati, who had taken the paper from Rajan, their fingers brushing as the paper exchanged hands. She looked up with a strange expression on her face.

'I would laugh if this wasn't tragic. Velachery Lake used to stretch over 100 hectares. Then they gave the land to government agencies and others. Others encroached on it. And now, it's a fraction of its original size. Will the government break up its own buildings? Will all these people move? Even if they do, where will they go? Give me a break. So many cases have come up on this. They just fester in the judicial system like a slow-growing cancer.'

Arjun and Lakshmi had begun to take their plates to the kitchen to wash. Arjun turned around at that and said, 'Did you know that Velachery was an ancient Chola town? There are inscriptions dating back a thousand years; it was not just a place of worship, but a bustling community of scholars. Slowly, it fell in importance, as modern Chennai came up. In the 1980s, my friends used to tell me that they never went out there alone at night – they were too scared of snakes and bandits. But when Chennai's IT sector came up on Old Mahabalipuram Road, everyone wanted to live in Velachery. It had water, it was cheap and close to work. No one cared about the lake. Earlier, the farmers considered these lakes divine. But they sold their land, and the builders and their tenants treated the leftover bits of the lake as a large dustbin. Soon people started seeing these lakes as garbage-

and-sewage-filled-nuisances that attracted stray dogs and mosquitoes. Everyone agreed that the quicker a lake was filled up, the better. We've forgotten the lake's value when we severed our connection with the land.'

Lakshmi, who had helped Thangam wash up and come back into the room, met her father's eyes and smiled. The others were surprised, wondering what there was to smile about. 'That's the first social sign the book talks about,' chimed father and daughter in chorus.

'*We bite the hand that feeds us*
Tread on the Goddess's bountiful breast
We see ourselves as greater,
And not a part of all the rest.
Stepping out of balance
Taking more than our share
Not realizing when the maw opens,
And the Goddess begins to glare,
We're vulnerable as we stand apart,
On a land that we have made bare.
We pay the price, we must pay the price
Deluge and drought our fare.'

Rajan said, 'Throughout most of recorded history, every religion has celebrated nature. Taught us to respect boundaries. To give thanks for the bounty, and realize that we are a part of nature, not apart from nature. The book seems to suggest that when we see ourselves as separate, as somehow superior, we tilt the balance, and the Bhoomi Devi will exact a price.'

Arjun sighed. 'The world is literally out of balance. Oxygen is what first comes to mind when we think of the atmosphere. Fair enough, we need it to live, but our civilization depends on large-scale agriculture. That took stable temperatures, for which we must thank the greenhouse gases.'

'But,' Lakshmi intervened, 'I thought greenhouse gases were bad. We were told...actually you told us,' she said, turning to Swati, 'that they have to be brought down to zero.'

Arjun chuckled. 'The key is balance, Lakshmi. Without some greenhouse gases in the air, too much of the Earth's warmth would escape into space, and the average temperature of the planet would be −18°C, close to the average daytime temperature on Mars. That's too cold! It's these greenhouse gases – like carbon dioxide – that allow the sun's rays to pass through them and warm the Earth, but trap some of the heat leaving the Earth, which makes the planet warm enough for us.'

Seeing his audience listening intently, he continued, 'But there is such a thing as too much of a good thing: in the past two hundred years, we have been burning fossil fuels. These are actually remnants of long-dead plants that have been buried underground and turned into coal, crude oil or gas – that's why they are called "fossil" fuels. When we burn them, we release carbon dioxide faster than our plants, soils or oceans can take them in. These gases collect in the atmosphere, blocking more of the Earth's heat from escaping into space.'

'It's like wrapping layers of thick but transparent blankets around ourselves,' said Lakshmi.

'Exactly, Lakshmi!' exclaimed Arjun. 'Even the clouds are changing and making the world less shiny, and the planet even hotter. In the last few years, the planet is trapping as much as heat as eight Hiroshima bombs going off a second. Every second.'

Horrified silence greeted his words.

'Look at this cyclone – it draws its power from the heat of the ocean. You know, it just struck me. The word "cyclone" comes from the Greek word, kyklos, referring to the coil of a snake; how funny is that? There are snakes everywhere we seem to be turning. Anyway, the cyclone would have never had this power if the oceans hadn't been so hot. Then we make the hit worse, because we have built over all the places where water could collect. All this is because we are increasingly looking at Nature as something that exists only to service us and does not have rights of its own.'

Then, Thangam turned to Swati and asked, 'Paapa, do you remember the story of Pari Vallal?'

Swati and Arjun smiled – this was a story the old man had told them many times when they were children. The story of a proud king with a glittering chariot that he had taken into the forest for a hunting expedition. He had stepped out to get some water from a stream, and when he returned, he found that a tender *mullai* creeper had used the chariot for scaffolding. Unwilling to disturb it, he left his chariot and came back to his kingdom, a wiser man and a better king. His compassion was praised by all poets, and his fame outlasted his more narrow-minded rivals.

'Ancient wisdom – across all faiths – is rooted in balance. And that balance means respecting the needs of both Nature and ourselves,' continued Arjun. 'But when we begin to see Nature as less than us, the balance shifts. We think this imbalance is not a big deal. But look at what is happening in our bodies and in the world – we could not have been more wrong. Every complex system works on feedbacks – forces that try to bring us back to balance. And that's what we are seeing now – the effects of Nature reasserting itself.'

'But some of us are trying to fight alongside Nature,' said Swati. 'Those who live closest to it are often, though not always, aware of its worth. There is a tribe called Bishnoi in Rajasthan. A few hundred years ago, a king wanted to clear their forest to build something, I forget what. His guards went to clear out the tribe. They refused to move. The guards threatened them. They still refused to move. They hugged the trees the king wanted to cut. And so, the guards cut them down – men, women, children. When the news of their slaughter reached the king, he broke down and left the forest standing.'

Swati continued, 'It's not just the tribes. Some companies are trying make a difference. There are also legal teams trying to launch a defence for those who cannot speak for themselves – animals, but also children and our future generations. The laws that exist are quite strong – but because so many don't care…'

Thangam snorted. 'Today, some tribes hunt the animals and cut down the trees they once protected. They have lost touch with the old ways.'

Arjun interjected, 'You know, I learnt something very interesting when I was in Greece recently. The word "idiot" comes from the Greek word "*idiotes*", meaning private person – or someone who does not involve himself with public affairs. My guide told me that ancient democracy only worked when each citizen held leaders accountable. Nature is showing us what idiots we are when our homes are submerged and our crops wilt in the heat and our children starve.'

Swati looked puzzled, 'Something doesn't add up. If people are losing their homes, and food, why aren't they voting to make a difference? Look at the recent elections in Delhi. It's a gas chamber, but air pollution wasn't something any party was talking about.'

Rajan smiled grimly. 'That's when the second and third social signs begin to play their part. The second sign is about inequality. And when inequality keeps rising, as is happening in many parts of the world right now, people lose faith in the system and stop trying to engage with it. This creates a perfect condition for the crooked few to work the system for their own ends, making the inequality worse.'

Arjun's lips were pressed together in a thin line. He was

pulling at his wispy beard in a manner Lakshmi had come to recognize was a sign that he was deep in thought.

'And the third social sign seals the deal, doesn't it?' he quipped.

'An intelligent mind without a soul
Like a ship with thousand sails but no captain
Leads the world deeper into Maya
And away from the Paramatman.

'That's AI and virtual reality, isn't it? More jobs will go because of this, making everything worse. And because the social media algorithms exploit the differences between us and make money from it, they want us to be different. They *need* us to be different. This is a new demon, fed by our hate. And when we retreat into this false virtual world, we move further away from Nature, and from the realization that we are all connected. Balance doesn't matter, because balance will starve this demon of his food.'

29

The Siddhars

THREE WEEKS INTO THEIR ROUTINE, EVEN ARJUN WAS ABLE to complete a dozen sets of the Surya Namaskar, while the others finished twenty-seven sets each. Thangam had left them for a couple of days, and now, after his return, he pushed them to get started on breathing. Here, Rajan's father's journal proved helpful. 'Begin with the *Mooladhara*,' his father had written, in his neat and well-formed hand. 'You cannot fly before you run. And you should not attempt to run before you are well grounded. Mooladhara provides grounding.'

They moved to the forest adjoining the cabin, as his father had advised exercising on bare earth. 'When the whole point is about grounding, sitting on a rubber mat indoors isn't going to help much,' explained Rajan. So, they sat cross-legged on the forest floor and began to breathe – long, gentle inhalations, focusing on bringing the forest's energy to the base of the spine, followed by an exhale making an 'ah' sound like an ocean was being released from within. Then, Rajan showed them how to bring their heels to the crotch – legs forming the wings of a butterfly, both palms cupped over the feet pushing them towards the crotch, while bringing one's legs as close to the ground as possible. Thangam and Lakshmi both accomplished this easily. Swati did too, Rajan noted with interest, but without surprise; he had experienced her flexibility earlier. But both Rajan and Arjun struggled. Arjun had problems sitting on the ground, and then with bringing his heels to his crotch. And Rajan's knees stayed up.

Then, Rajan asked them to gently rock their legs, holding the feet in place, to further open the Mooladhara chakra. Finally, he asked them to spread their legs and bend from the spine forward, placing the crown of their head on the earth while stretching their palms forward and spreading the fingers gently on the earth. 'From earth to earth, through us,' he explained.

Swati found herself relaxing under the dappled sunlight that filtered through the forest canopy. She felt light and content. The cold air caressed her cheeks. The mist smoothed over her hair. Her body seemed to draw warmth from the earth itself. Because she did not care for the leeches that infested the forest, she had spread a bedsheet over the forest litter. There had been a slight tussle of wills over this point, which she had won. The others sat on the floor itself, and emerged a little damp, often with a leech or two clinging to their skin. Lakshmi told Swati how light she felt afterward.

After breakfast, they would sit on the stone benches, listening to the birds chirp, while reading or chatting. There were tiny birds, hardly bigger than an adult's forefinger, jumping from branch to branch in the cabin's garden. Swati insisted Lakshmi sit with her for her studies – in the off-chance the world didn't end, she would need an education. After lunch, she and Arjun headed to the club and the library.

The club, as Swati thought of the Kodaikanal Club, was a relic of India's colonial past. Indeed, a few decades earlier, Indians were not even permitted to enter the club. It was a low, stone building, painted white, with bright flowers at its entrance to greet visitors. Soon after entering, one came face to face with a Nilghai head mounted on the wall, a nod to both the hunting proclivities of the past membership and the grasslands that once graced the Palani Hills. On one's left, hung the boards with the names of the past presidents and secretaries of the club – mostly whites until Independence slowly gave way to Indian names. But even today, colonial practices persisted. Formal areas were clearly marked out, where men were expected to wear full-sleeved, collared shirts and covered shoes – no chappals and lungis allowed here. Several august persons found themselves evicted when they did not comply.

Walking a little way in, one came to the library, an open space filled with books, some older than a century. Arjun sank in with the latest copy of the *New Yorker*, while Swati browsed through the latest *Cosmo*, a guilty pleasure.

After an hour or so, both cousins began going through the shelves because Arjun remembered a book he'd read about the Kundalini and Kodaikanal. Suddenly, Swati called out, 'Hey, look what I found!'

Arjun shushed her – club rules were inflexible about maintaining silence in the library – as he came to her. She was holding a handsome leather-bound book on Poombarai, a small farming village eighteen kilometres from the main town. The book was titled *Kundalini and Poombarai – The Power of the Siddhars* by Colonel Weston. The slip in the back of the book showed that no one had checked it out in over a hundred years.

Just then, the librarian came upon them, drawn by Swati's voice. She looked over Arjun's shoulder at the book Swati was holding and noiselessly beckoned them with her finger. Next to her desk, in a couple of cardboard boxes were books that the library regularly disposed of to make room for newer books. Colonel Weston was well represented in those boxes. Swati crouched down.

Siddhars – Magical Mendicants
Sattaimuni and Bhogar
Kuzhandai Velappar – The Patron God of Siddhars
Sketches of Palani Hills
Beyond Devil's Kitchen and Neptune's Pool – Precolonial Kodaikanal
Siddhars of Poombarai
The Students of Agastya

It seemed like Col. Weston was a Kundalini buff. Swati looked up with a grin to see Arjun's eyes gleaming with pleasure. This was a treasure trove, and a sheer stroke of luck that they were able to get these before they were scrapped forever. They paid a princely sum of ₹700 for the books and left.

Once they were home, they shared the books with a thrilled Rajan and Lakshmi. Soon, each took a book and curled up in front of the fire. Swati chose *Siddhars – Magical Mendicants*.

The Siddhars, according to Col. Weston, were spiritual adepts who had awakened their Kundalini shakti to gain *siddhi*s, or powers. But the powers themselves were considered a mere by-product; the main goal was union with the divine. The Siddhar tradition within Tamil Nadu was ancient – believed to be thousands of years old. Agastya – one of the most venerated sages of the ancient world – the preceptor of Tamil, whose wife was the river Kaveri, was considered the first Siddhar. Popular belief had it that there were at least eighteen Siddhars – almost all of them in Tamil Nadu (though two had spent considerable time in China) – Agastya, Nandi Devar (sometimes considered Shiva's bull), Korakkar and Bhogar were some of the more distinguished of the lot.

The last was an interesting figure. Rajan, who was reading *Sattaimuni and Bhogar*, was entranced to find that their little group was walking in the steps of the great men in these books. Bhogar, if the book was to be believed, lived around the 3rd century BCE. He was born near Poombarai, a village not too far from Kodi, into a lineage of spiritual adepts. As a child, he showed great promise in both scientific and spiritual enquiry while possessing an abiding interest in nature. Seeing his potential, Kalangi Nathar, another Siddhar, initiated him onto the Siddha path, where the boy studied yoga, alchemy and ayurveda.

Soon, Bhogar had awakened the Kundalini. Alongside, he developed powerful herbal and mineral formulations to help the body bear the stress from the rising Kundalini. People said he could fly – an ability he used to travel the world. Weston wrote that Bhogar visited China, where he propagated Siddha. Some legends associated him with Taoist figures, suggesting he may have influenced the development of traditional Chinese medicine.

Bhogar became renowned for his expertise in *navapashanam* – a mystical alchemical compound made from nine poisons which, when combined in the correct proportions, was believed to confer immortality. With this compound, he crafted an idol of Lord Murugan, which was enshrined at the Palani Temple.

Bhogar crafted another idol – believed to have been made from ten poisons – the *dashapashanam*. He had to work fast because the formulation was temperamental. Because of this haste, the body of the idol remained a little rough. He installed the idol in a temple in Poombarai. The devout believed that only divine grace allowed someone to visit the temple, and that the *prasad* protected the body in its journey to awaken the Kundalini. Weston hinted at a secret tunnel leading from both the Palani and Poombarai Temples to a cave where Bhogar's body was still in a state of meditation.

'They sound like Jedi,' Swati said, after she finished her book.

Rajan looked lost for a moment, then illumination struck, as he remembered his lessons. 'Are you talking about the heroes of the Star Wars movies?' he asked.

'Have you seen *Star Wars*?' Arjun asked Lakshmi.

'No, Uncle.'

Arjun laughed. 'Sorry, you can't go through life without seeing *Star Wars*,' he said, pulling out a DVD compilation.

That night, Rajan's sleep was filled with dreams. He dreamt of Lakshmi foaming at the mouth. Of a tree tied with a thousand yellow charms. Of a smiling idol covered in ash. Of a thin man with matted hair and luminous eyes. Of a temple in the midst of snow-capped peaks and golden eyes opening in the dark.

They stuck with the Mooladhara routine for five days. Despite the gravity of their situation, they felt more grounded and relaxed. Rajan felt they were ready for the next step, and so, following his father's instructions, asked them to bring one heel to their groin, and then turn around, sitting on one heel, with the other leg stretched behind them. This opened the chakra, he said. They repeated it on both sides. Rajan asked them to focus on their *ishta devata*. 'What if one is a non-believer?' asked Arjun.

'Focus on the space behind your lungs,' answered Rajan.

He then asked them to sit back on their haunches, keeping their spine straight, in Vajrasana. 'Now, open your knees a little bit, bend from your spine and stretch your arms and palms forward as far as they will go and embrace the earth, placing your forehead on the ground. Breathe in to channel the energy from the earth to your Mooladhara chakra and hold your breath.'

Rajan felt a tingling in his spine. His father had written that when the Kundalini is activated, such signs were to be expected. He had not said anything to the others, because he did not want his instructions to influence their experience. His father had given a recipe for a *churanam* that they were supposed to be taking as well. Rajan had searched for the ingredients to make the churanam, but could not find all of them, and so had decided to incorporate it from the next day. But then he heard Swati cry out. He straightened to find Lakshmi and Thangam had both collapsed on the ground in what seemed to be epileptic fits. He jumped up and pulled his daughter's thin body into his arms. She continued to shake and was foaming from her mouth. In the corner of his eye, he noted that Swati had taken Thangam's body onto her lap and was trying to smoothen the old man's forehead. Arjun had fallen forward and looked to be unconscious. Rajan felt helpless. They were just trying to open the first chakra, and already their bodies seemed too weak.

'Help,' he chanted mentally. 'Please help.'

The shaking began to slow and, after a minute, stopped. The relief on Swati's face suggested that the old man had stopped shaking too. Swati laid Thangam down and moved to her cousin. When she tried lifting him, she found that he was burning hot to the touch. How could a fever come on so fast? Rajan carried his daughter to the bed and came out and helped Swati carry Thangam and Arjun inside. They gave them some water and applied the prasad from the local temple on their foreheads. In a bit, both Thangam and Lakshmi were able to sit up, but Arjun remained unconscious.

'Leave him,' said Thangam.

Rajan's father's journal had said to expect tingling and fits, but the fever was new. Once the others seemed to drop off, Swati and Rajan left them to rest and stepped out. Swati sensed Rajan's worry and frustration with not being able to help. She took his hand. He squeezed it, smiling down his thanks as they sat on the bench. Suddenly, he turned and buried his face in her body. She felt him breathing hard, his arms holding her tight. She held him close with one hand, the other hand stroking his hair.

After a while, they broke apart.

Swati looked at him and said, 'I have a thought. The Poombarai Temple – the idol there is made by Bhogar. It's supposed to have special properties – most devotees think the prasad has healing powers. But, when I read Weston's book, the prasad seems to be made for those who want their

Kundalini to ascend, to strengthen their body somehow. We could go there this afternoon; it could help them.'

Rajan stared at this woman who had become so central to his life. Why had he been so stubborn, almost churlish, earlier? He and Lakshmi would have failed at their quest – they may have very well died – if he had continued to be an idiot.

30

Poombarai

THAT AFTERNOON, THEY LEFT FOR POOMBARAI. ARJUN WAS barely conscious, so they put him in the back of the jeep, along with Rajan and Lakshmi to watch him. Thangam offered to drive, but after a long look at him, Swati took the wheel. It was cold in early January (although much warmer than usual, noted Swati), meaning the tourist hordes were absent, allowing her to step on the gas. They passed Pillar Rocks – three tall granite boulders, each several hundred feet high, that stood out from the rest of the emerald hills – as they wound their way up the wattle forest.

'These used to be grassland and shola, you know,' said Swati over her shoulder. 'The British wanted more "useful" forests, so they planted wattle, pine and eucalyptus, destroying the landscape. After Independence, the practice continued. We are now understanding what it did to wildlife, and how much it changed the water flowing to the plains. Last year, the forest department cleared a patch of wattle and planted grasses; this year, the range officer told me, elephants are coming back and the water in the streams flowing down to the plains in the summer has gone up.'

The road wound up the steep hills and they were soon passing through pine forests – Swati knew they were alien to their landscape, but she had always loved the contrast of the dark green waxy pine leaves against the chocolatey brown forest floor thickly carpeted with dried leaves. This had been Arjun and Swati's favourite picnic spot when they were children. At Moir Point – a popular sightseeing viewpoint named after the engineer who built the road they were on – they turned right, and the road began to weave downhill. A couple of kilometres down, they turned left and passed through roads that cut through more pine forests. The rain had carved out potholes in the road, making the drive especially bumpy. After twenty minutes, the vegetation changed, and the vista opened up to their right, revealing breathtaking views of the Palani Hills, and in the distance, they could see the terraced fields of Poombarai. Around them, the forests thinned to fields, and in minutes, the jeep pulled up in front of the temple, and Swati and Thangam stepped out.

Suddenly, Arjun began to stir. He sat up, rubbed his eyes and began trying to open the door. Rajan tried to hold him back, but Arjun, lost in a trance, proved too strong for Rajan. He began banging on the door. The temple seemed deserted, but as the banging grew more insistent, Swati, worried about the attention the banging would attract, opened the door.

'What's the matter with you, Arjun?' she began, but stopped, seeing the glazed look in Arjun's eyes. Arjun stumbled out and began walking to the main shrine. Swati ran after him.

Lakshmi, who had been sitting silently until then, jumped out too. 'Lakshmi!' Rajan shouted, but Thangam banged the door shut on him. Rajan, locked inside the jeep, could have screamed with frustration. He had caught a glimpse of his daughter's eyes before she had jumped out – they had that same otherworldly look that Arjun's had had. He wanted to bang on the door of the jeep but did not want to draw further attention to themselves.

He watched helplessly as his daughter and Thangam caught up with and then overtook Swati into the temple. Swati turned back – and saw Rajan's anxious face. She knew it was risky, but she ran back to the jeep and opened the door. Rajan gratefully jumped out, donning a monkey cap as an attempt at a disguise, and together, they rushed into the temple.

The sanctum itself was small and dark, and the deity was a little boy with a big smile. The other three were waiting there. The priest did the arati and then gave them the *rachandan* – a sandal paste that had been applied on the idol and was believed to possess healing power. Rajan and Swati applied it on their foreheads, but Thangam, Arjun and Lakshmi ate theirs, bowed once more to the idol, and stepped out. They paid no attention to Rajan and Swati. Swati placed the *dakshina* on the priest's plate and was about to rush after them, when the priest said, 'You are very lucky. Today is Margazhi Sashti. I would have expected huge crowds, but no one else is there. The Lord must really want you – no one can visit this temple unless the Lord wants them to. The prasad is very powerful today – it will protect you.'

Rajan bowed in thanks and asked, 'Sir, can we have some more?'

The priest smiled and went back to the shrine to get the sandal paste, a small bottle holding some *abhisheka* theertham and some *panchamritam*.

'All will be well, Thambi,' he said and blessed them.

Swati and Rajan bowed again to the idol and stepped out. They found the others next to a short wide tree with hundreds of yellow threads tied around it. *This is the tree I dreamed about*, Rajan mused. There was a very tall man with matted hair standing beside them. The man had a long beard, piercing, dark, luminous eyes, a beak of a nose, and was wearing only a white dhoti even on this cold January afternoon. It was the man from his dream. They saw him embrace a seated Thangam, before rising and patting Lakshmi's head and putting an arm around Arjun's shoulder. He looked at them and said, 'You are brave to open the chakra without the churanam. Don't you know that's why Bhogar invented his medicines? So many died after opening the first two chakras. Think! It's a different reality. To be present, to be content. It's a different path than everything your body and your mind have been trained to do. Most cannot survive such a jolt. It's good you came today. The rachandan will help rebalance their bodies to withstand the rise.'

Rajan listened quietly. His father's journal had mentioned the churanam. He had discounted its importance and nearly lost his daughter. How could he have been so foolish?

The man continued.

'Bhogar made three idols, you know. You will come to the third someday; I will meet you then. For now, go to the Kaatu Narasimhar Temple in Srirangam. Help will be given.'

Without waiting for a response, he walked away.

31

Svadhishthana

SWATI DROVE FAST, WHILE RAJAN SAT WITH THE OTHER three at the back. They were fast asleep. Rajan was numb with relief that his daughter was safe. Her breathing was even and she looked peaceful.

Swati's mind, on the other hand, was unsettled, with thoughts chasing one another like dolphins in her head.

What had they gotten into? Being tracked by a powerful foe? Now a danger rising within their own bodies? How much could they fight? Who was that man at the temple? Was he a friend…or not?

By nature, she was a sceptic. Her mother had always told her to leave everything to God. But Swati would point to the children in a landfill, poisonous fumes their birthright, or to a newborn fawn being hunted by a leopard, and she would ask what the fairness in that was. She never believed in astrology or blind faith, thinking it was a charlatan's trick. Now their very lives might depend on faith and astrology. She did not like it one bit.

Finally, Swati asked, 'Who was that man?'

Rajan started from his reverie but didn't answer.

'How did he know? Why did they all go to him? How does he know we are going to Srirangam? What's going on?'

Rajan looked out of the window – they were passing through shola now, and the dappled sunlight through those majestic trees calmed his mind somewhat.

'I don't know,' he said, and he reached out and squeezed her shoulder.

She smiled at him through the rear-view mirror. They were together. She trusted him. That made the journey – this dangerous plunge into the unknown – easier.

'You know I don't trust easily. But something tells me that man was not dangerous to us.'

'Hmmm.'

Swati was frustrated that Rajan was so uncommunicative.

Sensing her frustration, he squeezed her shoulder again but kept looking out of the window. His inner voice agreed with Swati, but he didn't trust it enough to openly agree with her.

It was dark when they reached home. The others were out cold, and had to be carried in. That night, they clung to each other, expressing through touch what words could not – fear, trust, need, solace. Rajan's sleep was unbroken that night, with no dreams to disturb the peace.

The next morning, Swati woke up as sunlight hit her face.

In a second, she sat up with a start. *What would the others think? What about the maid who came to clean?*

She shook Rajan, and he shuffled off to his room. But they need not have worried. The others were still sound asleep, not waking even when shaken.

Later that morning, after the maid had left, they settled down to read about the second chakra.

The second chakra, the *Svadhishthana*, read Rajan, was located a few finger widths below the navel. Called the 'embodiment or the establishment of the self', this chakra was often popular in the hippie movement for its link with sexual pleasure. The purpose of the chakra was to unblock creative urges, which could manifest as a desire to procreate, or indeed to create in other forms – art, music, ideas, energy, or even new worlds.

The writer of the text Rajan was reading sounded a caution: because of the beguiling nature of sexual pleasures, many aspirants got waylaid after the partial activation of this chakra, sinking deeper into *samsara* rather than walking further along the spiritual path. For some, sexual pleasure was the destination. True seekers considered this the most dangerous chakra because it was where most slipped up. He looked up to see Swati smiling at him. Clearly this was not going to be easy. He smiled back and, resisting temptation, continued reading.

Opening the chakra, his father had written, involved focusing on the pelvic region, suffusing it with a bright orange light, thinking of waves of water washing through the body and chanting the sacred mantra while sitting in the butterfly pose.

'Shall we try it at twilight?' asked Swati.

So, in the brilliant orange pink of the sunset, the two of them tried to activate their Svadhishthana chakra.

After thirty minutes, Swati felt light, free. She felt like singing, something she had not done for a long time. Yes, they had problems, but who didn't? And they were discovering magic! And she was making another, more personal, discovery: so much of the joy she craved lay within. She looked over at Rajan. He was so different from…why spoil the moment with the other's name. He grounded her. That he was handsome was just an added bonus.

When they were done, she said she would cook – again, something she hadn't done properly for a long time. The others were still fast asleep, but rather than worry about them (they looked peaceful like they were regenerating), Swati merely said, 'Sleep and fasting are the best medicines. Let's not disturb them.' She saw the frown lines ease on Rajan's forehead; he had bought her argument.

She put on some music and was humming and dancing while she cooked some old favourites of hers – a hearty tomato soup, some baba ganoush, tzatziki and rotis. Her energy was infectious, and Rajan, despite his anxiety over Lakshmi, found himself unwinding. For just one night, they were not two people on a desperate quest, but a couple enjoying each other's company.

The next morning, Rajan had set the alarm for 5. When he slipped into his room, he found Lakshmi stirring. He took a quick shower, and when he came out, his daughter was sitting up and rubbing her eyes.

'What happened, Appa? I remember being carried by you, and then I woke up here,' she asked.

'Don't you remember the temple, the man you met?'

'No, Appa. You're scaring me…what temple?'

'It's okay, Kanna. Get ready – we will finish the meditation and then speak.'

In ten minutes, when father and daughter stepped outside, they saw Thangam approach them with warm jeera water. He wore a slightly stony look every time he glanced at Rajan.

What does the old man suspect? Rajan wondered silently.

Arjun was sitting down on the sofa with a curiously intent look on his face. Swati gave a spoon of panchamritam to Arjun, Thangam and Lakshmi, and then applied a drop of the rachandan on their foreheads. At that, every trace of sleep vanished, and they each resembled nothing so much as a coiled spring.

Rajan was on alert, looking for anything out of the ordinary as they began their exercises and meditations, but all went off smoothly. So, he introduced them to the Svadhishthana meditation. They did the asanas just as the rising sun slid up the horizon, bathing the world in orange light.

After breakfast, they sat around the courtyard, Rajan sat

close to his daughter, noting silently that Thangam stood next to her, not next to Swati as he usually did. Swati and Arjun sat together. Arjun, like Lakshmi, did not seem to remember what had happened after their morning collapse. Swati briefly explained what they saw, ending with, 'We have so many questions about that man.'

'He recognizes others like him,' said Thangam. 'Others walking the path of the serpent, the pursuit of Kundalini. Our vibrations are different from everyone else.'

Rajan looked anxiously at Lakshmi. *She is too young*, he thought. When he looked up, he saw compassion in the old man's eyes.

'We have started walking along a path from which there is no going back. Not all those who walk that path are friends. But the one we met, he has walked far. I could feel his power,' said Thangam.

Rajan wasn't sure he bought this entirely. He wondered if there was something else going on when Swati voiced the doubt in all their minds. 'How do you know this?'

'I've met others who have walked this path.'

Arjun, who had been brooding until then, looked up and said, 'I feel this energy pulsing inside me – like a wave, like a serpent.'

'We seem to have activated the Mooladhara chakra – for ordinary people, this would mean a tingling or a warm near the base of their spine, and feeling calmer and more relaxed,' Rajan said. 'But for those with the ability to manifest their Kundalini energy, the results seem a little more...dramatic.'

'Always the master of understatement,' murmured Arjun.

Swati hugged her cousin. 'I couldn't bear to see you glassy-eyed, Arjun.'

'My father's journal spoke of a churanam to help the body withstand the rising. I ignored it. I'm truly very sorry,' Rajan said. Lakshmi squeezed her father's hand.

'Don't look so sad, Appa. We're fine now.'

'It is my mistake too. I saw the others I was with imbibe certain substances. I thought it was pure indulgence. I never realized there could be another reason,' said Thangam.

Over the next few days, as they worked on their Svadhishthana chakra, the group experienced a spurt in their creativity. Arjun found himself writing again, something he hadn't done in years. More than that, he found himself far more in tune with himself and others. The exercises and the abstinence cleared his mind, leaving him less jittery. This allowed him to actually listen to others without getting defensive or irritated, which made him a far better communicator. Swati was humming and dancing and cooking. Lakshmi found herself going into the garden amongst the herbs – they seemed to call out to her.

As for Rajan, he felt he had to cut off his hands to stop touching Swati. He was obsessed with her. He'd never thought he would fall in love again. But she made him less dour and more hopeful. And, to him, she was beautiful. The only problem was Thangam.

Swati understood this. Knowing that an accidental discovery could only have unpredictable outcomes, one afternoon, when Rajan and Lakshmi were out in the garden together and Arjun was writing in his room, she came to Thangam in the kitchen.

'I have something to say, and you may not like it…' she began.

Thangam smiled his grim smile.

'I…Rajan…'

'He is a good man, Paapa. Are you willing to accept the child as your own?'

Swati flung herself into Thangam's arms. In all these years, she had never done so. And for the first time, as his arms enfolded her, the old man felt tears running down his cheeks.

32

The Astrologer

THEIR MONTHLY MEETING ENDED, AND THE CHAIR CLOSED his computer, took off his mask and cowl. He had very thick lips, but in every other aspect, he had a totally forgettable appearance. Average height and weight, mid-60s, dressed unremarkably in the half-sleeved shirt and polywool slacks that constituted workwear for half the Indian male, white-collared workforce.

He was a professor in a government college. Years ago, he had made a speech in a select forum on how the powerful should unite to manage the chaotic forces of democracy. How, if representative democracy and unfettered intellectual enquiry were allowed to flourish, progressive taxation and higher competition would follow and hurt the ultra-rich. After his speech, an underling had approached him and requested his time to meet with another. No one else had approached, and the underling had been pretty, so he accepted. That night, he was flown out of the country and ushered into the presence of one of the most powerful men in the world, and over dinner that night, their Cabal was born.

Over the next few years, he had grown their group – selecting the effective, the ruthless, the ambitious and the discreet. This was an invitation that could have only one answer. His backer ensured his power, while maintaining his own anonymity. That was the advantage of real money – not getting one's own fingers dirty.

Their Cabal controlled the narrative – the pen was indeed mightier than the sword in shaping one's course, while the sword remained more effective at meting out punishment. And because they knew in advance what policies would be, modern financial tools did the rest.

For all his power, the professor's tastes remained simple. He stayed in the college campus in a government-provided three-bedroom flat – the only difference was a router and an antenna hidden behind the cable TV dish that allowed him to bypass the college network and log into the private network no government could hope to tap. He drove a budget car, and his wife wore no flashy jewellery. She had no idea what her husband did when he went into the third bedroom; she only knew that he was not to be disturbed then. He taught his classes, attended seminars, took her for a holiday every summer, where they visited popular tourist spots (although surprisingly, they never had to wait in line anywhere, and stayed in private luxurious guesthouses – he told her this was thanks to a client he consulted for, who had kindly offered them the use of their guesthouse). Only once a year he travelled without her to an academic conference; she visited family then, so it worked out well.

A week after the last meeting had ended, his phone rang. It was an untraceable number that only three people knew. A quick glance at the screen told him that it was the informant calling. He picked it up.

As usual, the man on the other end rambled. For every word of value that he spoke, the professor had to endure fifty words of diatribe and another fifty of unhinged self-aggrandisement. He remembered the moment, a few months ago, when he had first met this man. His wife had heard that he was a good astrologer and had forced her husband to get an appointment. The meeting was unremarkable – the man on the other side, in his 50s, with a face and body clearly showing a life spent in complaint and indulgence, said nothing of value. But when his wife stepped out to attend a phone call, the astrologer smirked and said, 'You lead a double life. In the other life, you are one of the most powerful men in the world. I should perhaps not have said this, because you can so easily have me eliminated, but I have access to another secret that can wreck all your plans.'

The professor acted as though he was shocked at even the mere insinuation, but the astrologer proceeded to outline the key dates and the steps on how their Cabal came to be. And then finally, told the professor a secret from his youth that no living soul could have known.

'What do you want? Speak quickly,' the professor muttered tersely.

Just then his wife returned. When they were leaving, the professor slipped in his phone number with the dakshina they left.

That evening, the astrologer called. He began by lamenting how his talent had never been recognized. How his family, who should have cherished him, had chucked him out. How he was destined for great things and great wealth. The professor listened patiently – he had met buffoons like this man many a time – men and women with talent, but not the discipline to hone their craft, or the character to make the necessary sacrifices. But for his hinting that he could foresee what threatened to ruin them, he would have had the man killed. More importantly, the professor's backer, when told of the astrologer's pronouncements, had instructed the professor to take his words seriously.

So, when the astrologer spoke of his family and the prophecy they possessed – of how balance could be restored to the world – the professor listened intently, thinking, *if this idiot was right, it was very bad news for the Cabal.*

And then the astrologer stopped.

'What do you want?'

'More money than I know what to do with.'

'In return for what?'

'I will share the location of my family, and the book that can wreck your plans.'

'I could…'

'Yes, you can torture me and get the information. But if you fail, you will still need me to tie up any loose ends.'

So, a deal was struck.

The temple and the priests' homes were bombed.

Then sixty days later, the astrologer had called again, warning of the break-in at the temple. That had turned out to be a common robbery.

And now, the man was calling again.

'They have escaped.'

'Impossible.'

'I am telling you. I see a *gandam* averted. I cast the shells. The signs are clear. They have escaped.'

'We checked the break-in at the temple. It was a simple robbery. For weeks now, nothing out of the ordinary has happened at any of the temples on the list you gave me.'

'I am sure of this. My family never believed I had any gifts. But I do. No one else can read the *prashnam* like I can. If I had received my just recognition, presidents would be queuing up for an appointment. I'm telling you now, they have escaped, and my shells show that you will suffer failure, unless you act now.'

The professor sat silently; he was not a man given to hasty action. C had been thorough. It looked like a robbery, but what if it wasn't? Every circuit in his brain hoped that the astrologer was wrong, but, *what if that braggart was right*?

He went to his study and read through the report from the temple blast. The room had been destroyed. But what if the book had been removed? He looked at those of the priest's house. The head priest's house had been destroyed. No remains. Then he looked at the report from the former head priest's house. Human remains found. Indicative of at least one body.

One body. The astrologer had told him that the former head priest had a drunkard of a son and a young granddaughter. He had assumed that the human remains referred to them.

What if the child escaped? Impossible.

But *what if*?

He whistled softly – a habit he had picked up as a child to defuse tension. Only one in their Cabal could pick up such a cold trail. And she would use any gains to make a run on his position. But if indeed someone had escaped, and that person succeeded in their mission, his position would be worthless. That evening he was preoccupied as he ate his dinner – a simple roti with sabzi. After dinner, he'd made his decision.

He picked up the phone.

33

Manipura

THE NEXT STEP IN THEIR JOURNEY, RAJAN'S FATHER HAD written, was opening the *Manipura* chakra. Within the body, this chakra's centre lay between the sternum and the navel, just above the solar plexus, and activating it would unleash the body's true power.

They started on the *kapalbhati* – a rapid breathing technique involving forced exhalations – an hour before lunch, when the sun was at its zenith. As their bodies grew warm, they began strengthening the core, using the Dhanurasana (bow pose) and Phalakasana (plank). Arjun, as expected, lasted a mere thirty seconds in the plank position before collapsing. Swati lasted twenty seconds more, Rajan could maintain it for about a couple of minutes before his quivering torso collapsed, Lakshmi could hold up for ten seconds more, and Thangam maintained it for a full three minutes.

While the others continued with the chanting and

meditation, Swati began cooking their lunch. Rajan's father's journal had indicated that activating the Manipura took a lot of energy, and so nourishing food was critical. Swati cooked by instinct – a rich dal, tempered with a dollop of ghee and scented with cinnamon and pepper, accompanied by some unpolished rice, a spinach and a ginger *pachadi*, and hung curd drizzled with honey from the garden to end their meal.

After lunch, they slept, allowing their bodies to use the energy gained from their food to become more powerful. Then they rose, read and finished the Svadhishthana practice at sunset and turned in early. That night, Rajan's sleep was broken. Thoughts of Swati during the Svadhishthana practice had pushed out every other consideration, but now with a new chakra activating, unsought dreams began intruding his sleep. He saw himself with a topknot, Lakshmi in a burqa. He dreamt of fleeing in fear, of Narasimha roaring, of golden eyes and silvery water underneath a black sky. He woke up shouting in a sweat.

His shouting woke Lakshmi up. 'What is it, Appa?'

'Nothing, Lakshmi, I just had a bad dream. Go back to sleep.'

'Let me massage your head like I used to do for Thaatha when he had trouble sleeping.'

Rajan lay down and Lakshmi began massaging her father's head, running gentle fingers across his forehead and ending each stroke by applying mild pressure at the pulse point at either side of the forehead. In a minute, Rajan felt peace wash over him, in another he was asleep. Lakshmi smiled as she lay down. Her grandfather had always said she had the healing touch.

A week later, in the late afternoon, Rajan and Lakshmi had gotten up from their nap. Rajan looked at his daughter. His task was not going to be easy. 'Lakshmi…' he began hesitantly.

'Yes, Appa?'

He did not know how to begin. He and Swati had discussed this. They had to tell Lakshmi, but what if she did not take to it?

'Umm…there is something I have to tell you.'

'Is it about you and Swati-ma'am?' Lakshmi asked, with a mischievous grin, which broadened as she saw the shock on her father's face.

'I…'

'It's obvious, Appa.'

'Lakshmi, I want you to know this. You come first. Always.'

Interlude

THE MAN STUDIED THE LATEST DATA FROM CERES – *Clouds and the Earth's Radiant Energy System* – with growing unease. These instruments, mounted on satellites, measured how much energy the Earth released into space, and the readings were grim. Outgoing radiation and cloud patterns showed that an El Niño far stronger than the monster of 2015–16 was underway.

The planet had been heating for more than a century now, with most of the heat trapped within the ocean. But now, the ocean was belching some of it out, sending temperatures soaring. January was far from over, and yet, already the month was easily the hottest January on record.

He then turned to the data from the buoys in the Niño 3.4 region (the part right along the equator, roughly halfway between Peru and Indonesia). Niño 3.4 temperatures showed how warm the central tropical Pacific Ocean was. When this region stayed more than about 0.5°C warmer than normal for several months, it signalled the flipping of the Pacific's heat engine, marking the onset of an El

Niño. The buoy data showed that the three-month average temperature of the Niño 3.4 region was 3°C hotter than normal – unprecedented in the records.

His lips thinned to a line and he took a deep breath. He pitied the poor devils growing wheat near the tropics. They were done for. But what worried him was the coming summer. This El Niño was just a few months in, if it persisted for a few more months, there was no telling what could happen.

34

Anahata

AFTER TWO WEEKS OF THE MANIPURA MEDITATION, THEY all felt much stronger and less anxious – after all, they'd survived and even thrived. The Svadhishthana meditation had lit the creative spark, but Manipura fed it energy, and each felt truly comfortable with their physical selves – and all the potential they held. With the days being packed with meditation, the few hours they had to spare were spent planning their trip to Srirangam. They would drive down to Trichy early on 3 February, lie low in a safe house, and then enter the temple at night, with Rajan and Swati going to the Dhanvantari Shrine, and Thangam and Arjun going to the Mettu Azhagiyasingar Shrine. The question was who Lakshmi would accompany. Rajan wanted his daughter with him. As did Swati. Arjun said that since Lakshmi clearly walked a different path, she should come with Thangam and him. Rajan countered him by saying she was not of age.

Lakshmi herself said nothing while she crushed her herbs – the eucalyptus that the British had introduced into the Palani Hills shed seeds and leaves that released an oil. A few drops of this oil placed in boiling water and inhaled cleared the sinuses. She also made cinnamon oil by boiling cinnamon sticks in sesame oil for a few hours. For the past few days, she had been massaging the solar plexus of each member of the group with a combination of these oils to ease their pain and strengthen their core. Swati had managed to borrow a few books on herb lore and Ayurveda from the club, which Lakshmi devoured. She'd always been interested in herbs, but the past month had unlocked something within her, opening a world she never knew existed and giving her a power she never knew she had. And in her gentle way, she wanted more.

With ten days left to go, they started on the Anahata practice. This was the heart chakra – Rajan's father had called it the lynchpin – the chakra that united the three lower chakras, those concerned with the body and samsara, with the three higher chakras, those that pulled the *jeevatma*, or the individual soul towards the paramatma, the universal soul. The Matsyasana (fish pose) and the Cobra pose were both helpful to open the chakra when maintained whilst chanting the root mantra. The Anahata practice responded to smells, his father's journal said, jasmine being one such.

Thangam bought some jasmine from the santhai, which they used during their sessions.

As the days slipped by, they found that it was getting hotter, even in the mountains. The time to leave was drawing nearer – they began packing their things, even as their practices continued; Manipura and Anahata left them stronger and more hopeful as January made way for February.

On the morning of the 2nd, Rajan and Lakshmi had lain hidden in the shed for an hour or so when they heard a scream. Swati and Thangam came running from the kitchen. The maid, who had finished her work and was leaving, had tripped and fallen from the steps onto a tree branch. The branch had gone through her abdomen, and she was bleeding profusely. They tried staunching the bleeding – but it was gushing out too fast. The woman continued screaming. Lakshmi stood up and darted out of the shed – Rajan tried holding her back, but she shook him off with a mysterious strength. In a minute, she had come upon the maid. Calmly, she asked Thangam to cut the branch and lift the woman and lay her on the ground. Swati noticed Thangam obey without hesitation – it was as if Thangam and Lakshmi were operating on a different frequency.

Lakshmi grasped the stump with one hand, keeping her other hand hovering over the woman's abdomen. With a deft movement, she pulled it out, ignoring the woman's scream, while pressing her other palm tightly on the wound. She seemed to glow for a moment before swooning to the ground. Thangam caught her before she hit the ground. Rajan, who had run after his daughter, sank down beside her.

'What were you thinking, Lakshmi?' he cried. But Lakshmi had fainted.

The wound looked as though it was a several-days-old scratch. The woman stood and bowed to Lakshmi.

'She healed me. She healed me. May God protect her, she healed me.'

The woman had left. Lakshmi was sleeping while the others sat in the garden.

'She will talk, that one,' began Thangam. 'We should leave soon, before everyone who wants a bit of healing shows up at our doorstep.'

Their idyll was at an end. Rajan realized how much he would miss this place. The cold, the beauty, and yes, the peace. But there was no doubt about it, they had to leave. In a couple of hours, their modest belongings were in the jeep, when Thangam called the maid. She came eagerly, but her face fell when she saw the house locked up, the child nowhere to be seen, and Thangam handing over the key to her, asking her to clean up.

35

The Huntress – Part 2

SHE RARELY SMILED. REALITY OFTEN FELL SHORT OF HER ambition, but now, the Chair had asked for her help, creating an opening that could mean much. She smiled therefore – her smile was the snarl of a predator. A restrained curl of the lips, a baring of the teeth even while the eyes gleamed at the thought of impending bloodshed.

She logged into the data room where the video files and the notes from the investigation after the bomb blasts rested. It took her a few minutes to go through the notes – they had hoped to eliminate a single male adult and a female child. But the post-bombing investigation identified human remains consistent with a single individual, sex indeterminate. This was a possible loose end.

She opened the video footage. These were files from six cameras around the temple and one from an ATM in the corner of the two streets near the house of the priest, and one more from an ATM three streets from the house.

She began going through the footage frame by frame. Her ability to maintain deep focus for long periods of time was exceptional, as was her ability to turn off her emotions at will. There were very few who had seen her transform from an ice queen to a snarling leopard – and none of those remained to tell of the tale. It took her well over three hours to go through the feed of a single camera before she turned off the computer.

She knew she needed peak focus to solve this puzzle, if indeed a solution existed. That meant sleep, exercise and a little chemical supplementation. She pressed a button and walked to the small room set beside her bathroom and slipped off her clothes and got onto a massage table. She sighed as she felt two powerful hands begin to knead the muscles of her neck and back, while breathing in the lavender perfume that mildly scented the air to promote relaxation. After fifteen minutes, she had almost dozed off and was carried to her bed and eased into silken sheets.

The next morning, she woke up to the smell of lemon in the air. A cup of warm water with a curl of lemon rested on her bedside table. She sipped and began her morning routine of meditation and exercise. A couple of hours later, she had showered, eaten and stood ready to tackle the day.

That day meant combing carefully through the footage frame-by-frame looking for a shadow that may be a man they were looking for – the only reference image she had seen was that of a tall man with dark skin, stubble, sunken eyes, swathed in a white dhoti, slouched next to a thin girl with a long plait and tear-stained cheeks. Going through the temple footage took up the full day. There were several dark-skinned tall men – slouched and otherwise – in there and it took both the assistance of her image-recognition software and her own eagle-eye to find that Rajan had entered the temple shortly after the blast. He had not visited the underground room, but had rushed to the sanctum and then, later, after the uncle's house was bombed, rushed out, alone – his daughter had not been with him. The idiots had missed that.

The child could have entered the house before, alone. Possible but unlikely. The child was of an age to be in school. School would have ended around the time the bomb went off in the temple. Rajan, even if he was the drunk he was reputed to be, would have never allowed the child to walk alone to the house. That was a loose end that would need to be tied up. On that thought she went to bed.

The next day, she had commitments during the day. So, she began going through the video from the ATM close to Rajan's house at night, after dinner. The footage began shortly before the bombing of the temple, which showed a quiet street with very few people walking nearby. Children had not yet begun to return from school. Then came the explosion. People were running out of their houses now. There was panic, mayhem. She kept going.

Now people came running from the temple. Children and their parents were coming in from school. The bomb went off in the head priest's house. She slowed down, moving forward microsecond by microsecond; she forwarded to the scene where Rajan was entering the house, alone, when there was a gentle tap on the door.

She started.

It was 1 a.m. He had been instructed only to knock if she had not come in by that time. She noted that Rajan was alone and, checking by the time stamp on the video, he had run in from the temple. He was alone then; he was alone now. The child was not with him and had not entered the house. The loose thread existed.

Part of her would have liked to keep going, but the other part, the part that made her fearsome, knew that she was more lethal if she rested now and started with a fresh mind the next morning. But first, she would need to calm down. She lay down on the table and this time slipped on a mask. In no time, the hands began kneading, and they kept going further and longer until the video was a distant memory, and she was sound asleep.

The next morning, after her usual routine, she moved the footage forward slowly to see if Rajan left the house; he had not, at least as far as she could tell from that video feed. The bomb in his house went off. She now moved to the feed from the last camera. Had the child entered from another way into the house? But when she began moving slowly forward in the feed, that did not seem to be the case. *But wait*, she said to herself, *what was that shadow*? There it was, at the edge of the screen moving away after the first bomb, about ten minutes after Rajan had entered his house. *Was this Rajan escaping?* She used another software to zoom into the image and clean it up, but the person had a cowl around their head. *Why would they do that?* That was suspicious – but there was a lot of smoke after the two bombings, so maybe not. But this was now yet another loose thread.

In a few minutes, the feed showed, the bomb had gone off in the priest's house. *Where was the child?* She asked herself. *Was that shadow Rajan? Had he escaped?* All other videos in that town would have had their feeds erased – it would be a waste of time even trying to look for them. *No,* she told herself, *this needed an in-person visit.*

Few could have recognized her. She sported a single oily plait, thick glasses, wore a synthetic salwar suit, a simple bindi, small gold earrings, her manicured fingernails had transformed into cleanly but not evenly clipped nails, a black thread was wound around her right wrist, and she had imperfectly covered up her body odour with cheap body spray. She had visited the school that morning, as a representative of a national talent scout ed-tech company, on a visit to meet and interview the most talented students in each class in middle school, with the intention of offering a scholarship. Had anyone bothered going through her laptop (no one did), they would have found files relating to her cover, right down to videos of interviews with other children. She was nothing if not thorough, and AI made the job so much easier.

The principal, to whom she had given a gift hamper by way of welcome, was eager to cooperate, and had given her a list of toppers from classes sixth to eighth. As she scanned the names, Lakshmi's name was there, as she had expected and hoped it would be. Then began the boring job of actually doing the interviews – half a day had passed, before she casually asked the teacher assigned to her about Lakshmi. The teacher's face fell, and she mumbled that the child had died in the bombing of her house.

Oh, how tragic.

Yes, she was very well-liked.

She would have been a great candidate for us.

Yes.

Usually, gifted children group together. Tell me, are her friends gifted as well?

Well, she had no particular friends…

Oh, she was a loner?

No, she moved well with all the children, but…

The huntress waited.

If I had to say who she was closest to, probably, one of the teachers.

Oh. Who is this teacher?

She's left the school.

Every muscle in the huntress's body was taut. She had caught a whiff of her prey, and she was completely alert but completely outwardly motionless, like a tigress lying hidden in tall grass.

Oh.

Can we see the next student?

It was only at the end of the day, when all the students had been interviewed, and they had 'shortlisted' two of them, that the huntress nonchalantly asked her last question.

Are there any other students of this, what's her name, that we can interview?

Oh, Swati Ganesan had no favourites except Lakshmi.

I see. Okay, thank you very much.

A quick web search about Swati Ganesan was very revealing. A highly trained lawyer from a well-respected family in Madurai who had come to teach in this small village. The huntress's instincts told her that the trail led to Madurai. After all, the break-in at Narasingam was near there. The drive to Madurai took a few hours, and by the time she and her assistant had checked into a hotel, it was night.

Later that night, she sent him to the tea shops and bars to enquire about Swati's family.

Yes, they were well-known.

The daughter – yes, she had returned, but there had been a fight.

No, I don't know more. Oh, thank you, that was very generous. But no, I really don't know more. Thank you. But the driver that worked in the family sometimes visited the bar down the street.

The assistant smiled to himself as he returned to his mistress.

A visit to the bar drew a blank for two days.

But on the third night, the bartender, who grew fond of his new free-spending patron, pointed to the driver. Two rounds loosened the driver's tongue.

Swati-ma, yes, that was a sad story. All he knew is that father and daughter had fought, and the daughter had left to teach in some remote village. With all her talent, to become a teacher. Pshaw!

Yes, very sad. How do her parents cope. Does she ever visit?

What a question! Yes, she came down a month ago. But they fought again and she left in tears.

The assistant said nothing but noiselessly filled up the man's drink.

What a father! Could he have not accepted his daughter!

The assistant pushed the pakora closer to the man.

He took a bite, a sip, and was silent.

Still, the assistant said nothing.

The two men sipped again.

Then the driver said, 'Thankfully, Thangam is with Swati-ma; he loves her like his own daughter and will protect her.'

The assistant refilled the driver's drink again and ordered some more chicken fry.

And she has Arjun-thambi.

Who is that?

Her chittappa's son, he stays nearby.

A web search of Arjun together with Swati's father revealed his full name. A more surreptitious search gave the huntress his address. A recon of the house showed clear signs that it had been locked up. They kept a vigil on the house for twenty-four hours and saw a man who came and went periodically, and who probably stayed in the house. Time was flying, and the huntress's thirst for blood was rising.

They lay in wait until the man entered the house. Her assistant had already deactivated the cameras covering the road. The huntress followed him in. He hadn't even locked the gate. She was excited, salivating slightly as she always did before bloodshed. He did not see her coming – they never did. Soon, he was tied to the chair, blindfolded.

What did his employer do?

Nothing.

When did Swati visit him?

About two months ago.

Was she alone?

No. Her man, Thangam, was with her.

Anyone else?

No.

Really? Think again.

Not with her, but the same night, a father and son from America came to stay.

Are you sure?

Yes, a tall man with a beard and a thin boy – about ten or so.

And when did they leave?

The man and the boy left two days later. And the same day, Arjun sir and Swati-ma left for Kodaikanal.

Where do they stay in Kodaikanal?

Arjun-sir has a house at the edge of the town. Shola-view, it is called. Everyone knows where it is.

Thank you.

She pulled a gag over Senthil's mouth and then taped over that. For what she had in mind, he would scream a great deal.

The next morning, they drove to Kodaikanal. The forests that had captivated Swati bored the huntress. In a few hours, they had reached the town. The map software showed Shola-view lay beyond the edge of town. As they drove, the huntress found herself salivating again. As they pulled up to the entrance, they saw a smiling woman walking down the long driveway leading to the house.

36

The Journey

THANGAM WAS DRIVING FASTER THAN HE USUALLY DID. Swati sat next to him, Arjun was in the back seat, while Rajan and his daughter crouched at the back. The rocking motion in the back lulled Rajan to sleep. Half an hour later, when they were slowing down at Silver Cascade, he shouted. The jeep swerved as Thangam hurriedly pulled over to the side.

'What happened?' Swati asked.

Fully awake now, Rajan realized he'd been dreaming. Of rivulets of blood running on the road.

'I think someone is following us,' said Rajan. 'I'm sorry, I can't be clearer than this, but I feel there is a great danger if we go by this path.'

They didn't know how to react for a moment, until Thangam said, 'We're not going to escape by standing still,' and turned on the ignition. He drove faster, faster than was safe on these curvy roads. Thankfully, this was a weekday in February, so there was very little oncoming traffic. In ten minutes, they came to a small settlement, deserted this wintery morning, and a fork in the road. The road to Madurai lay straight ahead, but Thangam made a sharp turn and went the other way.

'What are you doing?' snapped Arjun.

'If we are being followed, they know about us. Which means, they'd expect us to take the road to Madurai. We can get to Srirangam on this road too, it'll just take longer.'

This road was bendier than the other, but it had been re-laid recently and so was relatively free of potholes. It began drizzling and in no time, mist had covered the road, cutting visibility dramatically. Thangam was forced to slow down to a crawl and turn on the lights. They inched forward for half an hour, the mist creating an eerie, unearthly feel around them. And then it cleared, although the drizzle continued.

Now, the difference between the paths was apparent. In the other path, shola forests thrived on either side of the road for almost the entire stretch of the hill road, but in this one, the shola had mostly been cleared for plantations: eucalyptus, banana, with only a few, pitiable patches remaining.

With very little oncoming traffic, they were able to make good time. As they reached the plains, they saw a small temple dedicated to Ayyanar, a guardian deity, with its trademark large painted terracotta horses. Thangam turned the jeep into a little lane that ran next to the temple, but before they could enter the temple, he stopped them.

'Let's get our things. We need to move with caution. It should not have been possible for them to track us, and yet they have. We must split into two groups and proceed by bus. The child will come with me. Paapa, you go with the men.'

As he said this, he reached into his bag and brought out three burqas. 'We have to break the trail once again,' he said by way of explanation. He gave one to Swati, one to Lakshmi and the last to Arjun. Arjun looked puzzled for a minute, and then, when it dawned on him what Thangam intended, he looked like he would like to punch the old man. First, he was being asked to abandon his child, the jeep. And now, to dress in a burqa.

Rajan smiled. Even in such uncertain times, with their lives on the line, how precious was the gift of humour.

'It's perfect, Thangam.'

'Easy for you to say, you're not wearing a burqa.'

'With my height, it's a dead giveaway that it's a disguise.'

'Fine, mock me for my height. Add insult to injury, why don't you!'

When it was clear the old man would brook no opposition, Arjun donned the burqa, grumbling all the while. It was hot in the plains, almost as though summer were upon them. Thangam and Rajan split their possessions into two piles. Rajan hugged his daughter. It almost broke his heart to be parted from her, but she could not be in safer hands. Safer with Thangam than with him, if he was honest with himself. Finally, the old man gave Rajan three old-fashioned mobile phones.

'Use these judiciously. After you use it, throw the phone away. I will call you if you don't reach the safe house by midnight tonight. The child and I will travel to Dindigul and board the bus to Trichy from there. You take the direct bus from Palani to Trichy. It leaves later. Here, wear the cap and take off your glasses.'

Thangam disappeared behind a tree and when he reappeared, he was barely recognizable. He had donned dark glasses, a kurta, a lungi and a skull cap. He had a lush white beard around cheeks that were much fuller than his own and a nose that looked quite different. He tossed a bag with prosthetics and a disguise to Rajan, gesturing to him to dress similarly. In a few minutes, Rajan too looked unrecognizable.

'We will leave first. Do not miss the bus and be at the safe house by midnight. At Palani, keep your head down to avoid the cameras. Don't get down anywhere. You can be sure that the stops will have cameras. Take an auto from the bus stand to Kalyani Lodge in Srirangam. From there take another auto to Subham Lodge. Finally, take an auto to this address. Stop three streets away and walk. Be watchful always.'

Rajan hugged his daughter as though he could not bear to let her go, and soon, Swati joined in, and the three of them clung to each other. Then, Thangam took Lakshmi's hand and disappeared.

In the lust of the hunt, the huntress had not called the Chair to update him. Now, as they drove away from the house, the maid's tattered corpse hidden in the woods behind them, the huntress decided it was well past time to call.

The Chair answered on the first ring. He was clearly waiting for her call.

'They did escape.'

There was silence at the other end.

She continued. 'They have gathered a group around them. A woman. Two more men. They were hiding in the hills and have left this morning. To where, I don't know yet.'

'When did you learn they had escaped?'

Trust the Chair. If she had a hunter's instincts, he had sharpened antenna to sense any threat to his position. And an inhuman ability to neutralise that threat. Still, there was no point hiding.

'I knew for sure yesterday night, but I had my suspicions a couple of days prior.'

'And you did not feel the need to share your suspicions. My, my, one might almost infer that you are not a team player.'

She said nothing but bit her lip. Her bloodlust had overpowered both caution and logic.

'In our last meeting, you had announced nothing out of the ordinary. Now, when you spring this on the group, you need not share my role. That can be my punishment. But you may need to track them again. Will you trust your own tools, or do you think you still need me?'

It was a bold move, but he admired her chutzpah. He laughed.

'We meet in one hour.'

Such was the discipline of the Cabal that, even with short notice, the meeting started exactly one hour hence. One of the members had his daughter's engagement ceremony going on, but managed to step out, noting that two of his guests stepped out as well.

The Chair spoke.

'Our quarry has escaped. We are activating the Vishkanya plan. Kindly make the necessary transfers within the next hour.'

There was a silent groan – expressed as a slumping of shoulders, or indrawn breaths. No one dared to protest aloud. The Vishkanya plan would hurt financially, even for them.

The Vishkanyas – contrary to popular belief – were not poisonous beautiful female killers. No, they were efficient deadly operatives – of any sex – tasked with accomplishing a given task over a large area – physical or electronic. Kidnapping? Done. Raising protests? Done. Hacking? Of course. Murder? Yes. Taking down a competitor's factory? Easy. There was no job they would refuse. And they almost always succeeded. They had different names in different countries. The Indian branch was called the Vishkanyas. A coup in a neighbouring country had their fingerprints all over it, if one knew how to read the signs.

The only con was their price. Higher than the GDP of a state, payable in advance. With an even higher success fee on completion. Only a very few knew of their existence, and even fewer could afford to engage their services.

An hour later, when the professor joined the meeting room, a representative of the Vishkanyas was waiting – after all, they had been the ones who had set up the video conferencing platform for the Cabal.

'Payment received. What do you want?'

He filled them in. Giving the names of the temples that were on the pilgrimage route and the photographs of everyone in Rajan's group.

'Would kidnapping and torturing of any remaining family members work?'

'Unlikely,' replied the professor. Even if the woman wanted to, the rest of the group would likely overrule her. And the others had no family left.

'Would taking a large number of hostages help? Or large-scale casualties?'

The professor gulped. He was a squeamish man, his current role notwithstanding.

'Again, unlikely. How would the group know that the hostage situation was linked to their quest? How would we reach them? Then too, however much they may feel for hostages or casualties, they are unlikely to give up their quest. No, the only way is to hunt and eliminate them.'

'Do you know when they will visit the temple?'

'No, but the last time they travelled, they visited a temple on the pilgrimage route within two days of such travel.'

'Do you want them captured alive or dead? Do you need their physical remains? Of the entire group or will remains of some of the members be sufficient? Will you need their possessions?'

The professor gulped again. Then, with an attempt at calmness, responded, 'Kill them only when they are all together. If you eliminate some but not all, the problem remains. And we will need proof of their remains and their possessions.'

'Very well. I will call when I have an update.'

37

The Journey – Part 2

THANGAM AND LAKSHMI WALKED DOWN THE LANE TOWARD the main road and then towards a bus stand a kilometre away. In fifteen minutes, they came to the stop, just as a local bus to the Palani bus terminal was pulling up. From Palani, they had to catch a bus to Dindigul, and thence to Srirangam. Thangam bought two tickets, and they boarded the bus.

The journey to Srirangam was hassle-free, but, underneath his dark glasses, the old man's eyes were watchful, scanning his surroundings for any sign of trouble. There were plenty of vagrants in both terminals, they were easy to spot and steer clear of. He also kept an eye for the less obvious, but more deadly hunters – those were harder to find; the good ones were veritable chameleons.

They did not have a long wait in Dindigul – the bus to Trichy came within minutes. They found two seats together at the back of the bus – uncomfortable but all things considered, a boon. Lakshmi slept, tired after the excitement of the day, while the old man stayed awake and alert, guarding her rest.

Meanwhile, Rajan, as Thangam had instructed, took a share auto, a larger auto that carried ten to twelve people along a prescribed route. They had to wait for half hour before one with enough space for the three of them and their luggage pulled up. The driver quoted an exorbitant rate, which they were forced to accept. Rajan, conscious of his Tamil that was clearly accented with the brogue common in southern Tamil Nadu and not wanting to leave any identifying trace, did not bargain. They squeezed in and were jolted as the share auto trundled along.

It was past four when they pulled into the Palani bus terminal. The only bus to Srirangam that day left at 4.35 and they had to scramble to catch it. The bus driver wanted to see IDs – Rajan showed him their fake IDs, with a ₹500 note folded in to prevent the driver asking any questions. Because they were the last ones to board, they could not find seats together. Rajan took a window seat at the back while the two 'women' found seats together in the middle of the bus. It was an air-conditioned bus, with shaded windows. Rajan had placed the bags containing their food and clothes in the overhead compartment but kept the book, his father's journal and the prasad under the seat in front of him. Then, he leaned against the window and gazed outside as the bus left the terminal. They soon pulled onto a highway, and in the swaying of the bus, despite all the will in the world to remain watchful, he fell asleep.

He was running down a street, but the concrete was not solid – his feet felt like they were sinking in, and so, he couldn't run away, no matter how hard he tried, from the shadowy person hunting him. He knew, without a doubt, if that person caught up with him, he was finished. Then, he was looking down at a beautiful woman – tall, with short, straight hair and full lips – she was lying down while another massaged her back. She had a dangerous aura about her. The scene shifted in his dream. He was in a temple. It looked like a hallway in any one of the Nayak temples, with majestic pillars on either side. He was running again, but because the corridor had grown very steep, he kept slipping. Now he was looking down, but this time, at a thin woman with a single, oily plait, wearing a cheap polyester saree and no jewellery, just a dirty yellow thread around her neck with a safety pin on it. She was selling flowers in front of a temple. She looked perfectly ordinary, except for the foot bent behind her, with its narrow, pointed, very dark toenails. The scene shifted again in his dream. He was sitting next to a man, short, plump and dark, who was seated in a bus like the one they were travelling on. The same aura of deadliness that surrounded the beautiful woman hung about him as well. Then he was looking down at a very ordinary-looking man with very thick lips working on a computer, again with an aura though not quite as sharp as the others. And finally, a middle-aged man with a long, flowing beard, dressed in saffron with beads and amulets about his neck and a prominent *naamam* on his forehead, with a dissatisfied expression on his lined face and in his darting eyes.

Rajan awoke with a start. He knew the last man; indeed, he was related to him. His father had always spoken of him with scorn; indeed, his father's nickname for the man – his father had always come up with very apt nicknames for people – was 'Empty rice pot'. He was considered gifted in astrology, especially in prashnam, but his character was not deemed suitable by the elders in Rajan's family. So, after his upanayana, the elders had decreed that he could not be taken on the full pilgrimage. Upon his return from a truncated pilgrimage, he was forbidden access to the book. He'd flown into a rage then and had tried to steal it. That's when his own father had disowned him.

Was my dream a warning? Rajan asked himself. Were these the people after them? Was his cousin somehow mixed up in this – was that how they knew who to hunt? He looked for Swati and Arjun, but both seemed fast asleep. The short, plump man from his dream was travelling on a bus. From his seat at the back, he could not see if one of the people on the bus was that man. He pulled his cap lower on his forehead and gazed out of the window.

The sun had set long ago, the sky was black, and it was raining, very unusual for this time of year, with lightning streaking across the sky. A glance at his watch through the passing lights of oncoming vehicles (he had not wanted to turn on the overhead light) showed that it was past nine. He had been asleep for several hours. They would soon be arriving to Trichy.

Is Lakshmi safe? he wondered. She probably was. But that didn't prevent the pit of his stomach from tightening. Soon, the bus pulled into the Trichy bus terminus and the three of them got off.

'My bladder is bloody bursting,' exclaimed Arjun.

'So is mine,' said Swati, shuffling from foot to foot.

'We can't stop. Any lingering gives a greater chance that the cameras can spot us, and alert the hunters,' replied Rajan, shepherding his flock towards the auto stand.

It was past ten, yet the terminus was bustling – providing a welcome cover, letting them blend into the crowd and avoid detection. It had stopped drizzling, and it was hot and humid. But there were autos everywhere. They engaged one and set off, following the route Thangam had laid down. An hour later, just as the rains picked up again, they reached what looked to be a respectable neighbourhood at the edge of the city. Boxy two-storey houses painted in sober hues stood in small plots, some with a tiny garage in front of them, others with trees around them. Others were even smaller, holding just a single-storey building with a motorcycle standing in front. All looked relatively new – no peeling paint or grimy windows here. If someone had asked Swati, she would have said this looked like a neighbourhood of rising professionals – houses proudly built by first-generation doctors or managers. The only oddity was that the street was relatively dark – there were no streetlights, perhaps this makeshift neighbourhood had sprung up beyond the reach or interest of the municipality.

They stopped three streets away from their destination, paid off the auto and continued on foot in the now-ferocious rain, with Arjun grumbling about the heat and his bladder the whole time. In ten minutes, they were standing in front of a nondescript house, built much like its neighbours, except that it had mango and banana trees all around it.

Rajan knocked on the door.

In a few seconds, he heard footsteps. The door opened and Thangam stood there with a smile.

'Where is she?' Rajan asked, pushing past Thangam and running to find Lakshmi. Arjun and Swati followed, both in a rush to head straight to the nearest bathroom.

Later, as they ate, Rajan told the rest of the group about his dream.

'I read about dreams becoming more vivid as the Kundalini rises,' Swati said, working her way through the curd rice. 'Even prophetic for some.'

'You seem to have the gift of foresight: your dreams, your warning,' added Arjun, before quipping, 'pity you can't crack all the clues.'

Rajan munched on a banana and said, 'What I am worried about is my cousin. He would know about the pilgrimage, which temples we visited, and also about the outlines of the book, of its power to restore balance. If he is working with others in the dream – who I think are the people hunting us – it explains why they attacked us and perhaps why they were able to track us.'

Arjun shook his head.

'I can understand why they attacked you and bombed the temple in the first place, and maybe even why they killed that poor father and daughter. But how did they track us to Kodi? That has nothing to do with your family.'

Thangam spoke up.

'You mentioned your relative was gifted in astrology. Could he have seen that you had escaped? And then the group hunting us did the rest. Clearly someone there has excellent tracking instincts.'

Swati's mind went to her mother. But if something had happened to her mother, news would have reached Kodaikanal. She forced herself to stay calm. But her face mirrored her disquiet.

Rajan, ever watchful of that face, noticed and squeezed her hand. 'Your parents are well so far. You would have certainly got the news in the club if something had happened.'

So far.

Thangam sensed the worry around the table. It was time to intervene.

'Fear will help us – it makes us careful, more watchful – but only up to a point, after which, it becomes an enemy.

Worry doesn't help at all – it gives an illusion of action but only eats away our energy and clarity. We have an important day coming up. Let us rest while we can. No one will disturb us here. We have each other. Our cause is righteous. The Lord will surely help. Let us get some sleep.'

38

The Vishkanyas

THE MAN ON THE BUS BARELY THOUGHT OF HIS FAMILY anymore. It had been three years since he had seen them. When he had finished his final exams, it had caused a sensation: a child from the slums topping the country. The newspapermen had all descended on his family's shack and the celebrities had publicly cooed over his success.

But no one came to help his little sister, born with a deadly disease. She had been a laughing baby – the only spot of brightness in his grey life – much younger than him, born after his father married another. But when the baby couldn't walk at a year, they took her to the nearest public health centre. Surprisingly, the doctor there was sympathetic, noting how anxiously the boy hung over his baby sister.

But his kindness did not ease the blow. The baby had a mutation in a gene that caused certain muscles to waste. She did not have the worst form, but it was still a death sentence without the cure. A cure that came with a seventeen-crore bill. His father, when he worked, worked as a loadman. His stepmother did not work, nor was she likely to. Even if he sold his organs, he could not raise this amount, and after he died, his stepmother would just let her daughter die and use the money for herself.

He moved back into his small home from his fancy dorm in one of the country's leading engineering colleges. His grades began to suffer. And then one day, he was asked by his professor to report to an interview room, where he found a woman waiting. Once the door closed behind him, she wasted no time in laying out her proposition. His sister's medication would be paid for, along with a lifetime annuity so she would always be comfortable. In return, they would need his services. For life, however long that was, no questions asked, no instruction disobeyed. And he could never see his family again.

He thought of his sister's gummy smile, and how cheerfully she accepted not being able to walk. But he had read about the condition, it would get worse, and without him in her life, that smile would disappear and bitterness would creep into its place.

There was no decision to make. He just wanted a month with her before wishing her farewell.

The woman accepted. The next day, he carried the baby to a fancy hospital, where she was given an intravenous injection. The doctors said she would need to be brought in a few times for check-ups, but they were confident she would be well – the woman who had interviewed him assured them she would bring the child in regularly.

The following month, the siblings spent every waking moment together. At the end of the month, when the baby took her first faltering steps alone, the boy felt his heart would burst with bittersweet joy.

The next day, he hugged the baby, kissed her and left her with his father.

He was taken in a car to a private aircraft. No one stopped them or checked for ID. He was given two tablets to swallow and a bitter-tasting black tea to drink. He obeyed without question. The tablets contained substances, he was told, that not only enhanced his senses but also memory, emotional regulation, synaptic function, neural connectivity, and increased hormone levels. They contained, amongst other compounds, Ayurvedic herbs such as Brahmi and Bhallataka. The tea came from a rare, black-blossomed herb that grew only where lightning struck in the high mountains of Sikkim. A small cup of that tea would bring piercing clarity, strength, emotional control and superhuman focus. But with each use, his soul's grip on his body would grow thinner, until the final dose removed any attachment from the world. Everything had a price – he would become a superhuman automaton for a few years before being consumed by darkness.

Maybe the tablets were working already, because he felt no sadness. His month with his sister and the knowledge that she would be cared for were his reward, and an early death, in his reckoning, was a small price to pay.

He became one of the foot-soldiers who had entered into

a Faustian bargain with an organization with many names in as many countries. In India, they were the Vishkanyas. Each soldier, and there were not many, was naturally gifted but came from a humble background – the kind that created desperate needs that could not be fulfilled through available channels. The Vishkanyas met those needs and then some, and in return bought the soldier – body and soul. The drugs and the training did the rest. The drugs gave the soldiers superhuman abilities and a focus that distinguished them from other mercenaries. They could not be bought. They could not be bargained with. They could not be distracted.

Their natural brilliance was honed and burnished in an intense training and conditioning period for six months, which made them priceless for the remaining period of their short lives.

Only ten Vishkanyas had convened on the evening of the 2nd – the strict parameters of their talent recruitment along with the burgeoning demand for their services meant they did not have too many soldiers free at any given time. But the astrologer had shared twenty-five temples where Rajan and Co. could have gone to. Given the parameters, the Vishkanyas ruled out the northern and the eastern temples – it was unlikely that the group would be able to travel to those in such a short period of time. They also ruled out temples in and around Madurai and the priest's hometown – this was a more calculated risk, but one they believed was worth taking. After these eliminations, they were still left with thirteen temples to cover, ten of them well-known. The

Vishkanyas had no way to narrow the list further given the available data.

'What about checking with the astrologer?' one operative had asked.

They had reached out to the professor and connected with the astrologer to see if they could narrow down the list. The man had begun with his usual litany of complaints and then laid down the places within each of the temples that his father had taken him.

The Vishkanyas' representative kept asking probing questions: Which times had they gone on the pilgrimage? Was it on sacred days? Was it crowded when they visited? Did others join them then? Did his father say some temples were more important than others?

Despite the astrologer's boasting, the Vishkanyas' representative gauged that there was no way to eliminate any temple. This left gaps in their net, but that could not be helped. He ended the call with the astrologer and informed the professor of this weakness.

The operatives began fanning out to each temple dressed as pilgrims. By the morning of the 3rd, they had established a safe room near each temple and had hacked into the security systems of the camera feeds. By afternoon, each operative had completed a full round of the temple, established or activated local sources and understood which cameras showed them entry and exit points.

At 4 p.m., all ten operatives logged into a secured channel. Six operatives stationed at the smaller temples said they would not have any problems detecting any entry and neutralizing the quarry. Two of the smaller temples were located within the Kaveri delta and had been deluged in heavy rains from the previous night. The deluge had broken several of the cameras, but the operatives were confident that they could still manage to track and neutralize the quarry. But another operative, who was stationed at possibly one of the largest temples in the world, said that it would be very difficult to contain the quarry, especially if members of the quarry split up. Also, several of the cameras near the northern entrance of the temple were not working, probably ruined in the rain. The last operative, posted at what was considered the wealthiest temple in the world, also said the restrictions on movements placed therein made neutralizing the quarry harder, especially if the quarry visited sites outside the main temple.

At the end of the discussion, it was decided that central command would supplement digital monitoring at these two sites. With this dispassionate assessment of their odds, they began setting their trap in motion.

39

The Safe House

IT RAINED CATS AND DOGS THAT NIGHT. WHEN THEY WOKE at dawn and went up to the balcony, they noticed that the branches of several trees had fallen down, and countless mango flowers lay strewn over the balcony floor. Thangam told them not to clear the debris in the dark as that ran the risk of being bitten by some insect or snake.

After breakfast they sat around the table laying their plans. They knew they would be watched. No hunter would ignore Srirangam. The only advantage they had, if at all, was the enormous size of the temple. Thangam asked Rajan, 'What path did you follow with your father?'

Rajan had his elbows on the table with his head down, sunken into his palms. The risks they were running, the risks he was subjecting his little daughter to, were getting to him. He looked up at that and said, 'We entered from the north in the evening. We prayed to the Goddess Ranganayaki first and then climbed up the steps of the Mettu Azhagiyasingar shrine and meditated in the antechamber for a couple of hours. After that, we visited the Dhanvantari shrine, where again, we meditated for a while and watched the arati. Then we walked clockwise, past the 1000-pillared hall, bowed to the Vellai Gopuram, came out, prayed to Chakrathalwar and the Ramanuja shrine, before coming in, bowing to Garuda, and ending with the Lord. We exited the temple through the north.'

Arjun, who had a sketch of the temple in front of him, sighed. 'We need to be near the north entrance. If our hunters know what you know, they will be watching that entrance like a hawk.'

Lakshmi, who had been following the conversation intently, frowned and then hesitantly spoke up, 'I remember *Periya-thaatha* talking to Thaatha. I should not have been listening, but…anyway, I did. He was crying about his son and asking what sins he had committed to have given birth to a wastrel like that. He said he could not bear to take him in front of Mettu Azhagiyasingar – he was too ferocious and would have torn the son apart, and he was a father, after all. So, he said they entered the temple through the main entrance from the south, prayed for a long time in front of Ramanuja, visited the Lord, and left.'

The silence that followed Lakshmi's speech could have been cut by a knife. The adults sat up straighter in their chairs, hope blossoming in their chests.

'Are you sure, Kanna?' Swati asked, unable to believe what they were hearing.

'I'm sure. I remember looking for a picture of the Narasimha after that and saw that he was tearing Hiranyakashipu's abdomen with his nails, so I felt Periya-thaatha's fears were well-founded.'

Thangam gave a tight smile. 'This gives us a chance. A very slim chance, but still a chance. Let's assume that they have access to every feed from every camera. If the astrologer is working with them, they would be watching the south entrance and the Ramanuja shrine closely.'

He fell silent and was immersed in thought. No one interrupted him. They could almost hear the wheels in the old man's brain whirring.

'Thambi,' he said to Rajan. 'You and Paapa go to the Dhanvantari Shrine. You will shave your head and beard and sport a *kudumi*. You will also wear a mask. Paapa,' he said, turning to Swati. 'You must dress in traditional attire. With any luck, there will be hundreds like you in the crowd tomorrow night, and with your head down, you can escape.'

'Arjun-thambi, Kutti and I will go to the Mettu Azhagiyasingar Shrine together,' he added, and then turning to Arjun, said, 'Arjun-thambi, you dress as a woman.'

Arjun had had enough. 'Why me? Why is it always me? Why can't Rajan dress as a woman?'

Lakshmi was giggling.

'Because he's too tall, Arjun. And it's bad enough that he's losing his hair,' said Swati. 'Can't he wear a cap of some sort, you know the one that makes you look bald?'

'No, Paapa,' responded Thangam. 'He needs to have a kudumi that looks real. I'm sorry, Arjun-thambi, but this is really a life-or-death situation. You will have to shave your beard, wear a wig, flowers and a salwar kameez.'

Arjun looked like he was going to explode. Thangam ignored him and continued, 'I'll shave my head and dress like Thambi here, and Kutti is tall, we will disguise her as an old woman. Can you pretend to walk with a limp, Kutti? I'll give you prosthesis to wear as well.'

'Yes, of course I can. I would love to be an old woman!' Lakshmi said brightly, excited more than scared about their coming adventure.

Rajan could not bear to be parted from his daughter again. And this time, quite literally when they were walking into an active battlefield against a cunning and merciless foe. 'I want Lakshmi with us. She can easily pretend to be an old woman with us as with you,' he said to Thangam. 'I don't doubt your ability or your desire to protect her. Not a bit. But I cannot be parted from her again.'

'Come on, Rajan,' snapped Arjun. 'You know as well as I do that Lakshmi is on the same path as Thangam and me. We need to be at whatever this "key" is. And from everything we can gather, that seems to be the Narasimha shrine.'

Despite the meditation, despite the faith, the tension finally got to Rajan.

'She's twelve years old! She's too young! No one in my family was expected to do this before fifteen. She is a child. I am her father. And I say no!' Rajan shouted, standing up.

Thangam had also stood up. He put an encouraging hand on Rajan's shoulder. 'Lakshmi is our child. Not just yours. All of ours. Yes, she is too young. But sometimes, fate doesn't care. And in these times, you can keep walking, doing your best and leaving the rest to the Lord. Have faith in her. She is a smart child. Have faith in us. I would rather die than let her come to harm. Have faith in Him. Do you really think He will let harm come to her? And Narasimha too – the form of Vishnu who protects children above all else, even from their own parents. Have faith. He will guard His own.'

The rest of the day passed quietly. They did not step out of the house. They knew that they were being hunted. The very fact that they were undisturbed meant that their escape from Kodaikanal had not yet been discovered. That made this day and the time they had a luxury. And they wallowed in it, and each other.

But Arjun's mind was always restless.

'Whose house is this?' he asked.

'Mine,' answered Thangam. 'My family is from Srirangam. This was our ancestral land, next to the Kattu Narasimhar Temple. But many decades ago, the family fell on hard times, and we had to sell most of the land. I kept this piece, and with what share of money I got from my family, and whatever I earned over the years, I built this house.'

But Arjun's mind was not silenced.

'What about the food? And the place is so clean.'

'Once I knew we were coming to Srirangam, I figured we would use this place. So, in the short time I was away from Kodaikanal, I came here, bought supplies to store. Lakshmi and I arrived a few hours before you. I bought more supplies, and we cleaned the house together.'

That evening, Swati made an elaborate meal, and tried not to think of it like a last meal before an execution. But no one knew when they would get a chance like this again.

One or two mangoes in the garden had grown big – they became part of a pachadi with jaggery and chillies. She would have liked to add neem flowers, but those had not blossomed yet. And then yams for the child, who loved them roasted with ghee. She made a pumpkin dish for Arjun, a hot, peppery rasam (having drizzled all day, it was cold outside) and a warm *payasam* with dal, coconut and bananas.

After dinner, they sang together – Rajan had a lovely voice – rich and deep. Arjun's voice was higher, with a slightly nasal quality, but he had a peculiar genius in creating harmonies. The others listened, drowning their cares in the lilting melodies, living in the present for that one evening.

Swati looked around the group, smiling. *How little was needed for joy*, she thought. *Love. A little humour. Good food. Some music.* She hugged Lakshmi, as the men cleared up. Then, they turned in early. Tomorrow would be a long day.

Interlude

THE MAN DISCONNECTED THE CALL. THE EL NIÑO WAS NOT weakening – the data from the buoys, the satellites and the Argo floats made that clear.

He, usually so calm and restrained, banged his desk in frustration.

So many were suffering from a chaos they had not created.

If only he could show the world the message from the buoys.

If only he could show them how out of whack the oceans were.

If only he was as eloquent as some of the glib talkers his daughter showed him on her feed.

But he wasn't.

He turned back to his screen and watched the colours overlaid on the world map – yellow, orange, scarlet.

The next few weeks would be critical – would the El Niño weaken or not?

40

The Safe House – Part 2

IT WAS THE DAY OF THE *THAI PURAPPADU*, WHEN THE processional deity would circumambulate the temple in a palanquin. By 7.30 p.m., there would be thousands milling about, making it an ideal time to enter the temple. The phrase from the book was vague about when exactly they had to be in the Dhanvantari Sannidhi, but Rajan knew that the idol, set deep inside, was not directly exposed to the moonlight, except during one ancient ritual that used mirrors to shine the reflected moonlight on the idol. That ritual took place around 8, which was probably when they would need to be close to the sanctum, a tough ask given the crowds.

The plan was for Swati and Rajan, dressed as a traditional couple, to enter via the northern entrance by 7.30, pray to the goddess and wait near the Dhanvantari Shrine, taking care to stand amidst the crowds. This would give them enough time to get to the shrine, but not so much to give cameras too many opportunities to spot them.

The other three would enter an hour later, again through the northern entrance, go to the Narasimha shrine, find and take the key and leave through the Vellai Gopuram.

The Vellai Gopuram, or the white tower, had a tragic past. In the fourteenth century, when the temple was sacked by the forces of the Delhi Sultanate, one of their commanders established his household within the temple. He was a cruel man, the story went, who enjoyed tormenting devotees. A beautiful dancer, Vellayi, could not bear this. She captivated the commander and lured him up to the tower. With lust overcoming prudence, the commander followed her up the steep steps. She pushed him from the top of the tower, before jumping to her own death. The tower remained white to honour her memory.

'Will we not see the Lord?' asked Lakshmi.

'We can't, Lakshmi,' replied Rajan, his heart sinking as he said it. Visiting Srirangam without seeing Ranganatha was like eating a mango without savouring its juice. One of Rajan's favourite places to sit had always been the northeast corner, near the painting of Bibi Natchiar.

'At least, tell me about Bibi Natchiar again, Appa,' said Lakshmi, as though she read his mind.

'In the fourteenth century, after the Sultanate sacked the temple, their forces carried back an enormous bounty back to Delhi, along with the processional deity called Azhagiya Manavalan, or the handsome bridegroom. The Sultan ordered the idol to be placed along with the other treasure in the treasury, but his daughter took a fancy to it and asked for the idol to be placed in her chamber. But ardent devotees followed the idol and, dressed as dancers, performed for the Sultan. Their performance pleased him so much that he offered them any reward they chose. They asked for the return of Azhagiya Manavalan. He agreed, but he had not taken his daughter's inclinations in mind.

'On hearing the idol's fate, the princess was inconsolable and begged her father to send an army for its recapture. An army was duly sent, with the princess in tow. But when the devotees got a whiff of what was happening, a smaller group left post-haste for Srirangam, carrying the idol through forests. The distraught princess followed them to the temple. But when she reached, she found the sanctum bricked up with the idol inside. Heartbroken, she died. Her painting hangs in the inner courtyard of the temple. The Lord accepted her as his wife,' said Rajan, 'and even today, the deity is offered rotis cooked in ghee as a nod to the preferences of his wife from the north.'

It would be a wrench not to see the deity, but they could not take the risk.

'What is this key?' Arjun asked.

'I don't know, Arjun Uncle. But we will need to look for it by Narasimha's toes. The statue is not very big, so it may not be very difficult to find.'

'What will you do if you go into a trance or are incapacitated like you were in Kodaikanal?' asked Rajan.

'We will sit down if we feel we are going into a trance or Kutti can wait behind us; we will get the key first,' replied Thangam.

Rajan did not like it.

'Lakshmi, why don't you wait in the lower level of the Narasimha shrine? Let the two men get the key.'

But Lakshmi's lips clenched together, and her nostrils flared – a sign her father recognized as her way of digging her heels in. She was usually an easy-going child; but as he had learned, she knew her own mind and once she took a position – usually, a well-thought-out position – she could not be easily budged.

'Appa, I want this. I know it's right for me. Yes, it's dangerous, but what path to power isn't? And in danger, who can protect better than Narasimha? I will stand behind Thangam-thaatha and Arjun Uncle, but I won't wait below.'

Swati spoke up then, 'Lakshmi, it's more than just about your safety. If something happens to the men, then we need one person to get them to sit, so we can rescue you all.'

'That's too much to ask of me,' Lakshmi replied simply.

'The rising Kundalini seems to be activating a different power for each of us,' said Arjun. 'From what we saw in Kodi, Lakshmi has the gift of healing. That's a powerful gift, and it's not something we should ignore, especially if she needs the key to take it to the next level.'

But still Rajan did not like it. Neither did Swati. But they could not convince the others.

'Rajan-thambi, what if the key is needed to restore balance? And Kutti is central in that effort?' Thangam added. 'All our efforts – the effort of every person in your family over the centuries – have been for this moment. Be honest with yourself. You know what I am saying is true. This is not the moment for caution. Yes, there is danger, but sometimes risks have to be taken.'

'What about the two of you?' Arjun asked.

'What do you mean?' Swati replied.

'Well, when and how will you leave?'

'The ritual takes about half an hour. No one can enter or exit the Dhanvantari shrine at that time. After that, we will leave with the crowds and be near the Narasimha shrine by about 8.45 p.m. or so.'

'What if you are attacked?' asked Thangam.

'It's unlikely that the attack will happen inside the Dhanvantari shrine. We'll be packed in very tightly. And our plan is to stand next to the deity. But we will stand apart, so that we can see around one another. To attack us, the assassin would have to recognize us, get close to us and then attack us. I think that's unlikely.'

'These people don't seem to care how many people they have to kill to get to us,' Thangam said. 'But they cannot keep bombing all the temples on the pilgrimage route. That would mean closing the temples, leading to uncomfortable questions, and maybe an enquiry into the origins of such a group. More importantly, they will also not be sure that they got rid of us. Our only hope is that unless we are all together, they will not try and kill us because they will want to get all of us. Stay away from each other, but in such a way that you can keep the deity and each other and your surroundings in view.

'An assassin will most likely use a chemical poison to weaken you – that will be noiseless and easy to do in a crowd. In your costume, we can't protect against that. If you have been attacked and are conscious, then type * and send a message to 4544 on your phone. The rest of us will try and come to you. Same goes for us.

'If all goes well, we will meet in the safe house tonight.'

After sunset, they were ready to leave. Rajan wore diamond drops in his ears, his forehead was shaved in the front, and he sported a kudumi at the back. He also wore a mask that made his cheeks heavier and gave him shaggy eyebrows. He wore an elaborate naamam and was wearing a traditional dhoti with a broad angavastram covering his upper body. Swati was dressed in a dark blue *madisaar.* Thangam had managed to procure a pre-stitched one, because she would have never managed the folds herself. Her hair was oiled, with a fake plait attached to the end, with the joint covered with flowers. She had traditional jewellery on and was wearing glasses resting on a prosthetic nose and had padding that made her look rounder.

Lakshmi wore a madisaar too, and a grey-haired wig in a bun. She had a full prosthetic mask that gave her a wrinkled face. Thangam asked her to cover her arms with her saree because they looked too smooth for an old woman.

Arjun had tweezed his eyebrows and was clean-shaven. He had been given a single braid and was wearing a salwar kameez, with large earrings and flowers. Rajan was amazed at how feminine he looked.

Thangam also had shaved the top of his head and was wearing a kudumi. He too sported glasses, a naamam, and was wearing the same costume as Rajan along with a prosthetic on his chin and nose. They had applied their makeup, and it had stopped raining, which meant it would hopefully last all evening.

Thangam and Rajan had split their possessions into two backpacks with false bottoms. The book, the journal and his other things were with Rajan, the prasad with Thangam. Their backpacks also held a change of clothes for each of them, prosthetics, IDs and cash. Lakshmi's precious herbs were packed into Thangam's backpack. A phone was strapped on to their calves, along with a small knife. They were ready. Rajan hugged his daughter for as long as he could. Swati joined in, and then, it was time to leave.

41

The Temple

AS THEY HAD EXPECTED, THERE WAS A HEAVY RUSH WHEN they entered the temple and the x-ray machine was jam-packed with bags. But their backpack had no metal in it, and no one cared about their sundry possessions. The harassed temple guards passed it through. Every person passing through the metal detector had set it beeping, so they passed through the metal screener without being stopped. As Thangam had predicted, the perfunctory swipe over their bodies did not pick up the knife or the phone. They kept their heads down and walked in. Out of the corner of his eye, Rajan noted a flower-seller who looked vaguely like one in his dream – he swiftly turned away.

The rush to get into the shrine of the goddess was immense. They were literally pushed in and pushed out quickly by the teeming masses. It was well that they had used strong glue to stick on the prosthetics – otherwise, in the crush, those would have come loose.

It was almost 8 when they passed through the narrow passageway leading to the inner alleyway of temple in which the Dhanvantari shrine stood. The moon had ascended high in the sky, full and luscious, a yellow orb shining in the inky black sky.

There was a rush around that shrine as well, and they joined the masses pressing to get in. Just then, the crowds picked up, and they could hear the sounds of the *naadaswaram* and *mridangam* in the distance. Then, as the music came closer, they heard the chanting, even as the crowd swelled. Rajan felt tears trickling down his cheeks. And he stood with his palms folded as Azhagiya Manavalan passed him. He had been unable to visit, but the deity had graced them with a visit. He stood spellbound, hope blossoming in his chest, until he felt Swati tugging at his waist. They had to go in, or they would miss the ritual. They pushed through, ignoring the exclamations of irritation and indignation from the crowd. Soon, they faced the deity, and each other, just as the priests brought the mirrors out. The lights were switched off and the arati began, not with a flame but with moonlight, cleverly manipulated by mirrors in a pattern that had been passed down through the centuries.

Rajan, who was standing closer to the deity, squinted his eyes to see where the light hit. There were no inscriptions near the deity as far as he could tell, only carvings of symbols along the base, so he was not sure what to look for. The arati continued – and Rajan became desperate; without a sign, they had no idea where to go to next. He didn't dare glance at Swati – a moment's distraction could well ruin centuries of preparation.

Then the music stopped, the mirrors stopped moving, and the light steadied onto the feet of Dhanvantari. And there, Rajan could see a five-headed serpent with its hood spread over a *lingam*, and a conch entwined in its coils. The light shone for a few seconds, and then the priests drew the screens shut.

The man had been waiting near the Ramanuja shrine, following the astrologer's advice, ever since the temple opened that afternoon. He was dressed as a priest, blending into his surroundings. Now, the moon was rising above his head but still, the quarry had not appeared in any of the cameras. His well-honed instincts told him something was off. Every other temple the quarry had visited had featured the lion-god prominently – why not in this one? There was a shrine to the lion-god in the north of the temple, why hadn't the astrologer mentioned that? His colleague had called the astrologer a vain weakling and had flagged any input from him as unreliable.

He checked the data from the camera feeds again. Almost one in five cameras was not working – mostly in the northern half of the temple, which had flooded the day before. What if the quarry had come in through that entrance? He made a call. He would go to the lion-god shrine.

He chose to walk anticlockwise around the temple, to better see faces coming his way. He scanned the crowds systematically. But either the quarry was not present or they had hidden themselves very well. He kept walking.

Thangam's group entered the temple at 8.30. The old man was proud of Lakshmi, who had hobbled her way through, bent and shaky. No one could tell she was not the old woman she pretended to be. Arjun, in contrast, was exasperating. His strides were too wide, and he had tried going through the male queue when entering the temple.

Upon entering, they found most of the crowd clustered around the shrine of the goddess. Elsewhere, the crowd was beginning to thin. They passed a small, square, pillared courtyard as they moved towards the Narasimha shrine. The courtyard was empty but for a short, plump priest leaning against one of the pillars and gazing at the moon.

Arjun wanted to visit the *jeevasamadhi* of Sattaimuni, the disciple of Bhogar, who wrote so eloquently about imbalance and climate change. But there wasn't enough time to visit, and so, ignoring Arjun's protests, the trio began climbing the steps of the shrine. Arjun pretended to help Lakshmi up the steps, while the old man followed, keeping a watchful eye all around. They passed an antechamber, decorated with beautiful Nayaka-period paintings, as they climbed up to the sanctum. Here they found, as Lakshmi had said, that the copper-coloured idol was indeed quite small, with the lion-god ripping out the intestines from the demon, Hiranyakashipu, who was resting on his lap. The idol's right hand was raised with the palm facing forward – some saw the palm coming to smite them, others saw it as a sign of grace in the most desperate times. The priest at the shrine performed the arati eagerly, seeing the largesse in Arjun's hand, and was rewarded instead by three fingers unerringly pressed on his neck. He fell down, unconscious.

Thangam laid him to rest on the floor inside the shrine. Then, he and Arjun began probing the base of the statue, as Lakshmi stood behind a small pillar inside the sanctum. But the base, small as it was, did not yield its secrets easily. The men pushed and pressed, but nothing budged. In desperation, they asked Lakshmi to try, but she did not make any headway either. Then, Arjun saw moonlight streaking through the ventilator and falling on the feet of Prahlada, the devotee whose call the deity had answered. He pushed at that point, applying force along the path of the moonlight. The base opened, and something golden came out. Arjun felt intense pain as a pair of fangs pierced his hand. He could not see what it was that bit him, but he felt his grip on reality fading. He heard the old man scream, 'Kutti, go away!' as he fell.

Swati and Rajan were walking to the Narasimha shrine when they heard Thangam's scream. Fear unleashed adrenaline, and they ran. Out of the corner of his eye, Rajan noted that the area had emptied and the lights around the passageway were not working. Only the moonlight, bouncing off the granite, bathed the area with a pale, ghostly light.

Rajan ran up the steps and soon came to the antechamber with the murals. He could not see Lakshmi, but Thangam and Arjun were stretched out on the floor, unconscious and foaming at the mouth. Golden bite marks on their hand sparkled where the light from the lamp in the sanctum and the pale moonlight hit them. Rajan also saw a short, plump priest kneeling next to them, rummaging through Thangam's backpack. The priest must have had supernatural hearing and reflexes because he turned before Rajan had reached the top step and shot a dart at him. Rajan felt it sing past his cheek. It was the man from his dream, Rajan mused. But, already, the priest was loading another.

There was nowhere to hide in the antechamber. Rajan leapt down onto a small parapet that lay below. His heart was beating hard; he felt like it might burst – the assassin was right there, and he didn't know what had happened to his daughter. Suddenly, there was a loud noise, something metallic being flung against stone. At the same time, there was a clattering in the sanctum. The plump priest stopped, weighing his options. Should he neutralize the person in the sanctum – most likely the child? Or should he go after the other two? He decided: *I'll catch the child and use her as bait.*

He turned towards the sanctum, just as the mighty doors closed. He heard a bolt being drawn across them. The child had locked herself in. He could not break in, but she was contained. The two men seemed neutralized. He considered killing them, but his instructions had been clear – kill all only when they are together. On the off-chance that the other two escaped, these two could be tortured to extract information. He contented himself by placing restraints on their feet and hands.

Rajan also heard the doors slamming shut and deadbolt being pulled across them. From his perch, he could see the priest's feet. So, Lakshmi was alive, and had locked herself in. His heart swelled with relief. He jumped down from the parapet, and seconds later, heard the priest follow him. He turned and ran into a small corridor, just as another dart sang past his ear. He ran faster and clambered into the hall and began dashing down a corridor with pillars all about him. Silently, his brain noted that this was the corridor from his dream. Swati was nowhere to be seen. Another dart flew and caught up in his angavastram. He tossed it aside and darted to the side, hiding behind a large pillar. He could hear footsteps coming closer. His heart was beating so fast. He knew, despite his training, he could not run much further. Then, he heard a shout and the thud of a body hitting granite. He could no longer hear the footsteps and warily looked around the pillar to see the priest lying on the granite floor, blood welling up next to his head. The flower-seller he had seen earlier was standing over him, holding a stout stick in her hand. Swati was standing beside her.

Rajan came up to them and looked down at the priest. He was a very young man, with a face that seemed peaceful in death. *What had made him hound them with such ferocity?* Rajan asked himself. *How had he tracked them? And who was this flower-seller?* Looking closely at the woman, he saw she had a similar aura as the man they had met in Poombarai, though far more muddied. So, Rajan was not surprised when she said, 'I'm here to help you. This one will not trouble you anymore.'

Swati hugged Rajan and asked, 'What do we do with the body?'

'Leave it – there is nothing we can do.'

They ran back to the Narasimha shrine. There was hardly anyone in their path. They found the two men lying in the antechamber. As Swati cut through their restraints, Rajan banged at the door.

'Lakshmi? Lakshmi? It's Appa. It's safe to come out.'

In a minute, the bolt pulled back. An old priest stood there. Lakshmi was unconscious like the men, foaming at the mouth, with gold bite marks on her palm. Rajan swayed. His world seemed to end as he took her limp body into his arms.

The priest had applied prasad on the wound and on her forehead. 'Only He can save her now,' he said sadly, gesturing towards Narasimha.

'Come, we must go,' said the woman.

Rajan swung Thangam and both backpacks over his shoulder; Swati carried Lakshmi and the woman surprisingly hoisted Arjun's limp body over her shoulder, and the three of them made their way to the Vellai Gopuram. Once they were inside the tower, the woman laid Arjun's body on the parapet, made her way to a small antechamber, and approached a pillar of a dancer holding a mirror. The woman pushed the mirror and a large stone slid back on the floor, revealing steps leading down. The woman hoisted Arjun's body back onto her shoulder, lit an old-fashioned fire torch, held it up and led the way into the passage. Swati followed her, with Rajan bringing up the rear. The moment Rajan was in the passage, the woman pressed a mirror in a matching statue inside with her elbow, and the stone slab slid back into place. They were in complete darkness, save for the light supplied by the torch held by their guide.

'Follow me. We don't have to go far,' she said.

The path, paved with uneven granite slabs, was narrow and low. Rajan and Swati kept as close as they could to their guide. Swati found the going hard. Though their exercise regimen had made her stronger, and Lakshmi was skinny, it was still hard to carry her while being bent over in the dark. Her back, arms and legs ached. After a few hundred metres, they stopped in front of another pillar with a dancer holding a lotus. The woman set Arjun down and pushed the lotus, and a slab opened above them. As they climbed up the steps, they found themselves in a pillared room. Their guide switched on a light and a fan, and they laid their charges gently on the floor. Swati and Rajan sat down panting, but the woman showed no signs of fatigue. She fetched them some water, which they drank gratefully.

She unfurled reed mats and said, 'Rest. We will discuss how to move forward tomorrow.'

'Where are we?'

'You are in the Kattu Narasimhar Temple grounds. This is a room that no one comes to. You are safe here from those who pursue you. At least for tonight. Rest.'

Rajan had many questions. But first, he took the bottle containing the theertham from Thangam's backpack and poured a few drops carefully into Lakshmi's and the men's mouths. He then applied a little of the rachandan on the bite marks. In a few minutes, the foaming stopped and the three of them appeared to breathe easier.

42

The Vishkanyas – Part 2

AT 10 P.M., NINE OPERATIVES DIALLED INTO THE SECURE connection. They were not entirely surprised by the tenth operative's absence. About an hour earlier, they had each received a message saying his chip had transmitted a 'No heartbeat' code, suggesting he had been overcome. The central command had pored over the CCTV coverage at the Srirangam temple, where he had been posted. But the evidence emerging was mixed. There had been some activity near the 1000-pillared hall of the temple, but the cameras caught only a blurred feed, maybe because of rain damage, showing six figures, three of whom appeared incapacitated, entering the Vellai Gopuram. A quick scan of the outside cameras showed nothing useful, just teeming masses even at that late hour. The quarry was not seen. It appeared that they had not exited the temple.

A small team was despatched to the Srirangam Temple, while the Vishkanyas representative called the professor, apprising him of the situation. The quarry had once again slipped through their fingers. But they had been in Srirangam. The input from the astrologer was patchy – he had been right that they were alive and had escaped, but he was not privy to the plans to the extent he thought he was.

They decided to scrape the data from all the cameras of that city, prioritizing those closest to the east entrance to the temple, analysing the data using artificial intelligence and machine learning tools. They would begin with Srirangam and fan out across the state.

The professor sighed. This would be expensive. The raw computing power needed would entail, at a minimum, a multi-crore outlay. And that was for one city alone. State- or country-wide continuous surveillance would exponentially raise costs.

But the alternative was worse.

'Proceed.'

43

The Choultry

SWATI WOKE FIRST AND SAT UP WITH A WHIMPER – HER body still sore from the rigours of their escape. Dawn had come and gone. She saw sunlight pouring in through windows. The woman who had helped them was nowhere to be seen. The room appeared to be part of an ancient choultry. There wasn't a kitchen, but she found some fruit and a mud pot with water in a small antechamber.

She was just pouring herself some water when she heard someone stirring in the next room. She went back and saw Thangam stirring. She knelt by his side and placed a hand on his forehead. He was warmer than normal, but not quite feverish. The old man opened his eyes and smiled to see Swati. Was it her imagination, or were his eyes lighter?

'I'm okay, Paapa,' he smiled. 'I'm not leaving you yet.'

Swati teared up, and took the old man's hand, the one with the bite marks, and pressed it to her lips.

They sat there for a while, when they heard Rajan say, 'I'm

glad you are awake,' – even their quiet whispering had woken him up. Rajan turned to his daughter. She was fast asleep. He ever-so-gently placed his palm on her forehead. She was feverish and did not stir when Rajan's palm touched her.

Rajan's lips thinned. He fetched some more of the theertham from Poombarai – he noted with concern that it was running low – and placed a few drops carefully into Lakshmi's and Arjun's mouths and applied the rachandan again on their wounds. He offered both to Thangam, but the old man waved him away.

The three of them freshened up. Rajan wanted to discuss next steps, but Thangam was insistent they continue their exercises. He said, 'We cannot pause. Every ounce of strength – mental, physical, spiritual – will make a difference.' Afterwards they sat down together in a veranda overlooking a small, unkempt forest.

'What happened?' Swati asked.

The old man spoke slowly, 'We probed the base of the Narasimha statue, looking for a key of some form when something golden came out. Kutti was hiding behind us, and I heard Arjun scream before I lost consciousness. I had hoped to save Kutti, Thambi. I'm sorry I failed.' The old man sounded heartbroken. Swati squeezed his shoulder reassuringly.

Rajan shared no details. When Swati said, 'But what about…' Rajan squeezed her hand meaningfully to stop her, raising his eyebrows to convey to the old man that he did not feel comfortable sharing more at present. After all, they were in a strange place, and he did not quite trust their rescuer. Swati looked indignant. Thangam, however, smiled his agreement.

They had been resting for an hour or so, when the woman entered, bringing food with her. Rajan noted that she had very distinct toenails – narrow, pointed and dark, almost black, just like in his dream.

'You can stay as long as you like. I am here to help you in whatever way I can.'

'We couldn't have escaped without you. Thank you,' said Swati.

'It was my duty. My guru told me to expect followers of the serpent path in Srirangam. I took on a job as a flower-seller to that end.'

'How can you recognize initiates?' Rajan asked.

'Oh, it's very simple – your auras are different. Yours,' she said, pointing to Rajan, 'is strong while she,' pointing to Swati, 'doesn't have one. His,' pointing to Thangam, 'aura shines brighter than any I have seen before.' There was open greed in the look she gave Thangam.

'How many of you are there?'

'I don't know. I only know my guru. He told me that earlier there used to be many, but nowadays very few try to walk this path. If I see one person with an aura in five years, I would say that was lucky.'

Then looking at Lakshmi and Arjun sleeping on the mats, she asked, 'Can I help them? Or get someone to help them?'

'No, they will be all right. Thank you,' said Thangam.

The woman smiled, saying she would return that evening, and left.

There was something about her which made Rajan feel uneasy. Thangam must have sensed it because he looked out of the window at the thick forest outside and said, 'I will be back,' and left. He returned half an hour later but said nothing further.

Both Rajan and Swati forbore to question him, even though Swati very much wanted to. The rest of the day passed quietly. It was far too hot to exercise. Lakshmi and Arjun continued sleeping. Lakshmi's fever did not rise but did not fall either. Arjun was more feverish, and Swati sponged him with wet rags placed on his forehead and arms to bring down the temperature. The woman visited them, as promised, in the late afternoon, bringing more food with her. She extended her offer of help again, which they declined.

Then, sometime after sunset, Thangam came up to Rajan and whispered, 'We're leaving.'

Rajan said nothing. It was a mark of how much he had grown to trust and rely on the old man that he obeyed without question. Their minimal possessions were already packed. They had not changed out of their disguises from their previous day. Thangam switched off the lights and hoisted Arjun onto his shoulders, while Rajan took Lakshmi into his arms. They quietly walked into the forest.

The moon, though not full, was still bright, and they used its light to edge their way through the forest.

They had walked for about 200 metres, when they came to a boundary wall. Thangam signalled that they should cross it. It was not very high, but it was still hard climbing over it with two unconscious persons in tow. Once over it, they found themselves in a small, dark lane with high-walled compounds on either side of the road. The lane had no streetlights. They walked a short way down it, to where a small van was parked. Thangam signalled for them to get in. They obeyed without question. Once they were all in, the van left.

Rajan could not see who was driving – as they were all crouched in the back. But, from the start–stop nature of driving, he guessed they were running into a lot of traffic. Then, the rhythmic thud of the tyres told him they were on a bridge and were leaving Srirangam. In an hour or so, the vehicle picked up speed, but did not go too fast, as the road was quite bumpy. He guessed that they were not on a highway. They drove for another hour before the van stopped. Thangam got out and shut the van door behind him.

The rest of them waited for about five minutes, before the door opened again, and the old man asked them to get out. Swati saw they were parked inside what looked to be a very big garage. They walked out, shaking the stiffness out of their legs, with the men carrying Arjun and Lakshmi. They entered an ornately decorated room – paintings graced the walls, thick curtains covered the windows, carved, sumptuous silk sofas sat on a large oriental carpet and there was a very tall, very fat man with a disarming smile waiting for them.

'Welcome, welcome. When Thangam-bhai called me, I was so happy. He has saved my life so many times. The one regret in my life is that I have never been able to help him in any way. But I promise by Rahmatullah Shuttari and Bhura Samy, that my life and all that is mine is yours.' Without waiting for them to respond, he lifted Arjun with ease and walked up the stairs, talking all the time.

'You must be so tired. Thangam-bhai would not let me bring a nicer vehicle. Is this your mother?' he asked, pointing to Lakshmi, who had still not come out of her disguise. 'Come, let us take her to a bedroom to lie down. Why is he feverish? I have some sugar from the *dargah* that can help.'

The big man's affability was immense – he even hugged Thangam, enveloping the old man with his bear-like arms and lifting him clean off the ground. Swati couldn't help warming up to this man. Rajan characteristically stayed more aloof, but followed the man into a richly appointed bedroom, where he placed his daughter on the bed. Despite multiple attempts to dislodge him from her side, Rajan insisted on staying with her, while the rest of them had their dinner. He said that he would eat later.

The man protested. He could not, would not eat without his guests eating first. But Rajan held firm. Finally, the man brought some rotis with hot sabzi for Rajan, along with a glass of buttermilk, begged him to tell him if there was anything he wanted, apologized for the fare, pointed to a fresh change of clothes laid out in the cupboard for him, and left.

Rajan had a long bath. The water washed off his fatigue but not his anxiety. His daughter had not regained consciousness. But as each mug of water cascaded down his face and shoulders, he found himself becoming more hopeful. After all, their experience when activating the Mooladhara suggested that this prolonged sleep was transient. A little refreshed, he dried himself and changed into the kurta pyjama the man had left for him, and ate the rotis, delicious sabzi and drank the buttermilk. He was bringing out the plate when he ran into Swati and Thangam, who had come up with the man.

The man almost grabbed the plate from Rajan, expressing a hope that he had enjoyed the meal. He then said he would leave them to rest, touched Thangam's feet and left. Rajan found that they were in some sort of a sitting room on the first floor of the mansion, as richly appointed as the living room downstairs. To one side was the staircase leading down to the living room. Across it was a door leading, as Rajan later learned, to a balcony. The four bedrooms they had for themselves were set on two remaining sides of this room. Swati wanted to shower, so she left the two men alone. Rajan had a million questions running through his head, but waited for the old man to speak.

'He worked with me in my younger days,' Thangam began. 'We called ourselves ethical smugglers. Many farmers around here were forced to sell their coconuts to local merchants at throwaway prices because of the loans they had taken. It was almost a form of slavery maintained with a cage of debt – one they could never break out of because the low prices and high interest rates. Then Bhura here told me it was the same with fishermen too. So, we decided to provide an alternative. They could not sell their produce in local markets because those were tightly controlled by the merchants. So, we began to smuggle their produce to faraway markets, which helped them fetch better prices. As our expertise grew, we also began smuggling in branded medicines, to save lives. Bhura loves animals of every form – we will be tripping over his pets during our stay here. We soon began working with the wildlife department to catch wildlife smugglers. And then, idol thieves too. I've known Bhura for decades. I trust him with my life.'

Rajan had heard enough to feel comfortable to share what he and Swati had seen in Srirangam.

'We have a problem. All we could see highlighted by the moonlight was a symbol. We don't know when to go, and we don't know where.'

Thangam did not react. 'We have come this far. Let us sleep and hope the morning brings answers.'

44

Vishuddha

THE NEXT MORNING, RAJAN FOUND THAT LAKSHMI'S forehead had become cool to the touch although she still did not stir when he placed his hand on her forehead. He applied the tiniest touch of rachandan, as they were running very low and stepped out to find Swati and Thangam waiting in the hall. Together, they moved to the balcony, where the morning air was not yet hot, to begin exercising. The stretches cleared Rajan's mind, but by the time they were done, the sun had risen and the heat had begun to set in. From the gaps of the shrubbery, they could see rice fields stretched out like a green tablecloth laid on the flat earth, with a river snaking in the distance, its waters shimmering with reflected sunlight. Coconut and mango groves added texture and shade to the tableau. Swati could see solar panels but no electrical wires, and she later learned from Thangam that there were no electronics or electric connections within several miles of the house. They were completely alone.

Swati said she would check up on Lakshmi and Arjun as the two men went down for breakfast. She found Arjun was still out, although his fever had come down. When she entered Rajan's room, she saw Lakshmi stirring. She sat beside her and stroked the child's forehead. Lakshmi woke up and Swati, sagging with relief, hugged and kissed her.

'What happened?' Lakshmi asked.

Swati gave her a brief account of what had happened over the last two days. Maybe it was a trick of light, but the child's eyes seemed different.

Rajan entered the room just then; he had been worried when Swati hadn't come down. His face lit up with a smile when he saw his daughter sitting up, and he ran to her.

'How do you feel?'

'I feel fine, Appa. Quite energetic actually. How are Thaatha and Arjun Uncle?'

'Thaatha is fine; he's waiting for you downstairs – he will be so happy that you are okay. Arjun Uncle has not woken up yet.'

'Can I try healing him?' she asked.

But Rajan did not want her risking her health – this was an unknown path and they had to tread with care.

'No, he will be better soon.'

They went down together.

Thangam's dour face cracked into a smile when he saw Lakshmi. He took her palm and placed it on his cheek.

'Forgive me, Kutti,' he said.

'Please don't say that, Thaatha. I would have been very upset if I had missed out on this.'

Swati and Rajan exchanged a glance. In the bright sunlit room, the change in the child's eye colour was apparent. Even Thangam's eyes, black as they were, showed signs of lightening.

Just then Bhura walked in. 'Thank Rahmatullah, you are awake. I said a prayer for you this morning. It worked. But you are too skinny – you are the boy I made the passport for. Your parents should feed you better. What will you eat?'

Lakshmi smiled. She looked mischievously at Rajan.

'Can I have anything I want?'

'Just for today.'

'Can I have a jam sandwich?'

'You can have a hundred,' he said, signalling to his attendant to bring sandwiches for the child.

Soon a plate piled high with sandwiches – jam, butter, cheese, tomatoes – appeared. Lakshmi eagerly reached for the food, as did Swati. Rajan frowned but said nothing. They had earned the break. But Lakshmi found that after one bite, she couldn't eat anymore, and she apologetically asked for idlis.

'Was the jam bad, child?' asked Bhura.

'No, not at all, Uncle. It was delicious. Only, my body can't seem to take it anymore,' sighed Lakshmi, looking longingly at the sandwiches.

After breakfast, they gathered in the hall. The weather had grown much hotter this past week, and February felt like May. 'We never used the fan before; now we need it, even during the winter,' Bhura complained. 'Look at the poor mango trees. This week's rains have pulled down the baby fruit, and the heat has brought on killing humidity. Every form of insect is thriving, while the mangoes and their farmers suffer.'

An attendant entered. Bhura excused himself after checking his guests had all they needed. As they walked back upstairs, Lakshmi asked, 'Can we look through the book or Thaatha's journal for your symbol?'

It was a great suggestion, and Rajan mentally kicked himself for not thinking of it himself. He took out the book and started reading, while Lakshmi pored over her grandfather's journal. But they did not find the symbol or anything related to it. But seeing his father's diary reminded Rajan of the remaining chakras.

The next chakra was *Vishuddha*, or the throat chakra. Once activated, it was held to bring about an ability to speak the truth, to sing, to persuade, to communicate. But Rajan was nervous. Every step deeper into the Kundalini was taking a toll on them. They had very little theertham and rachandan left. He suggested they wait a few days.

Lakshmi and Thangam, however, were adamant. They had taken a step into another realm, and they wanted to go further. Lakshmi said she would make a churanam to increase their resilience. After trying in vain to preach caution, Rajan relented when he saw his daughter getting very worked up.

That afternoon, they began work on the Vishuddha chakra. Rajan's father had suggested a *kashayam* made with cinnamon, dried ginger, pepper, citron and a little jaggery. Lakshmi brewed it, adding the herb she had collected from Kodaikanal, stirring meditatively for nearly an hour. As they sipped on the drink, they felt their throats warm up. They no longer needed Rajan's prompting to imagine a blue light suffusing their throats – their throats felt blue. And the mantra Rajan asked them to chant came effortlessly, with all of them stretching out the vowels, making the chant seem almost like plainsong. They began swaying to their own music, when a door opened, and Arjun came out. In the bright light, everyone could see that his eyes were much lighter.

'Don't stop,' he said.

They continued as Arjun added harmonies. While the melody of the mantra was simple, almost basic, the harmonies added majesty and mystery, and when they finally stopped, they felt a pang for the music's loss.

'How are you feeling, Arjun Uncle?'

'Hungry.'

A week passed. They added the shoulder stand to their evening exercises. Thangam, Arjun and Lakshmi were voracious – they ate like their lives depended on it and their eyes were unmistakably lighter – as though a new energy was burning inside of them. They slept more as well. Their energy, however, left Rajan untouched; he worried that they were making no headway on their next step.

But that puzzle was solved one afternoon when Lakshmi was flipping through the book idly with Rajan next to her.

'This chapter looks different, Appa,' she said, squinting at the eighth chapter. 'The words have changed,' she said, pointing to the book. 'This was not what was there before.'

Rajan looked to where Lakshmi was pointing. He did not see anything different. He read out one line: 'The dwarf places his foot on the king's head.' And then looked at Lakshmi and asked, 'What do you read?'

'The bite is a blessing and a curse.'

Rajan did not like the sound of that.

Then Lakshmi asked, 'Appa, can you describe the symbol again?' He described what he had seen. Then Lakshmi pointed to an empty page and said, 'But it's right here.'

Rajan couldn't see anything and asked Lakshmi to explain. Lakshmi pointed to a blank spot on the book and read out:

'An ancient poison quenched
By waters white and cold
Hara's throat upheld
In the Goddess's slender hold
When a cloudy snake girds around
Bhoomi's mighty waist
Hara and Hari lie entwined
'Neath a sky a full moon graced
On serpent-fashioned bed

On a tank by glacial waters fed
Water within
Water below
Water around
Under the ancient mountain's gaze

'Here is the symbol,' Lakshmi said, pointing again to an empty space on the page, 'and what I read out was the verse following that.' But all Rajan could see was,

'They lie together
Balance above, Destruction below.
When balance fails, destruction will follow.'

This was a breakthrough.

'Let's tell the others,' Rajan said, and the two of them went down.

The others waited patiently to hear Lakshmi's tale. Arjun took the book from Lakshmi, saying, 'Let me see.' He read the page and affirmed what she had said.

'Where do we need to go?' asked Thangam.

'We need to go to a place where Shiva (Hara) and Vishnu (Hari) are together,' said Lakshmi. 'One option is Trivandrum; another is Chidambaram, but there is no mountain, ancient or otherwise, there.'

'What about Kashi?' Arjun asked. 'Varanasi holds both Vishnu and Shiva, and Ganga could mean water that is around them.'

'There is no mountain there,' said Swati.

Rajan was smiling quietly. He was thinking about the time his father took him to the north. They had stopped at Kashi, but as Swati had pointed out, there was no mountain there. Back then, father and son had taken a bus into Nepal, jolting over the bad roads. They had been to Muktinath, where the Vishnu shrine hovered above an ancient river in the heart of the Himalayas. But Rajan felt this was not the temple the verse was referring to, although the Gandaki could be the water and Muktinath did have an ancient mountain above it. But Shiva and Vishnu did not coexist as they did in another temple in Nepal.

But before he could say anything, Thangam spoke up, 'Don't tell us, Thambi. Try not to even think of it.'

Rajan was puzzled but remained silent.

Arjun, however, could not stay silent.

'Why?'

'My father always said walls have ears. And I don't much care for this group that tracks us so well, nor the group that seems to know what we are thinking. Better to keep our thoughts controlled.'

Arjun rolled his eyes, not quite buying into the old man's argument, 'Okay. Then I won't share my secrets either.'

They gathered, the huntress joining mere seconds before the Chair's image appeared on the screens.

The Chair got straight to the point.

'The quarry had escaped. The Vishkanyas are in pursuit.'

Silence met his announcement. The others knew that this would put further demands on their purses, but they dared not refuse.

'The wheat harvests this year look poor. Our field agents are saying that between the unseasonal rain and the heatwaves, the crop will fail. Our friends in the oil-producing countries are unlikely to increase production quotas, which means oil prices will rise. Between these two predictions, commodities will make good investments. Ensure that we stir up our farmer friends to prevent any grain imports.'

The silence seemed smugger now. Their returns on these forward bets would more than recoup their spend on the Vishkanyas.

'Ensure that we keep drumming up cautionary stories against genetic engineering. We cannot afford to have heat-resilient varieties coming up in rice or wheat. You have your tasks. We meet in two weeks.'

That night, Rajan's sleep was disturbed. He dreamt of golden eyes. Of pointed toenails walking away from a pool of blood. Of funeral corteges and women weeping. Of white snow melting into a pool of serpents. He woke up, sweating.

The next morning, the exercises calmed him down as they always did. But, as the morning sun rose, he noticed how much lighter Arjun's eyes had become. His strengths – brilliance, music, writing – had all become accentuated, and while his weaknesses – impatience and flippancy – had improved somewhat, his physical strength appeared to be giving way. Worried, Rajan looked at Lakshmi's and Thangam's eyes – they too had lightened though not as much as Arjun's had.

That afternoon, Rajan approached Thangam, who was sitting with Bhura in the muttram. Bhura tried excusing himself, but Thangam waved him down. The old man was radiating serenity, more than he usually did, dispelling Rajan's fears.

'With friends, sometimes one can ask without sharing,' Thangam quipped.

Rajan's face broke into a reluctant smile.

'We need to go to Nepal.'

Bhura's usual smile had been replaced by an intent look of concentration. Looking at him, Rajan became very conscious of how his arms bulged with muscle, and how his powerful thigh muscles were barely concealed by his loose kurta pajama.

'By when do we need to be there?' asked the old man.

'I don't know. I have no idea what the cloudy belt around Bhoomi's waist means.'

Bhura spoke up, 'Forgive me, but there are others in the group. Would any of them know?'

Rajan remained silent, but Thangam spoke.

'We think Arjun may know but he's not sharing.'

Swati came running down.

'Come quickly!' she said. Then noticing how pale Rajan had gone, added, 'It's not Lakshmi.'

They ran up to find that Arjun had fallen down and was foaming at the mouth. The veins about his throat stood out prominently. His throat appeared blue. Lakshmi was sitting next to him. She had her hands on him, and a look of strain on her face.

Rajan brought out the small bottle of theertham. There was very little left, but he placed a few drops into Arjun's mouth and applied a little rachandan on his neck.

Slowly, Arjun stopped shaking. After a few minutes, he sat up.

Time was running out.

'Sorry, Arjun, but I need to ask. Do you know what "a cloudy snake girding Bhoomi's waist" is?' asked Rajan.

Arjun turned his light-eyed gaze on Rajan, who felt something otherworldly was connecting with him. Arjun smiled and said, in a slightly mocking voice, 'Bhoomi's waist is the equator. A cloudy snake is the ITCZ.'

Lakshmi, who had kept her hands on Arjun, was puzzled like the rest of them. 'Sorry, Arjun Uncle, what is an eye-tee-see-zee?'

Arjun smiled. 'Lakshmi, you know the sun's rays heat up the Earth's surface. Now, as the surface heats up, it heats the air above it. What is the place where the most heating takes place?' All trace of mockery had vanished from his manner. He was a teacher now, patient and encouraging.

'The equator!' Lakshmi replied triumphantly.

'Correct,' Arjun continued. 'Now, as we know, hot air rises, and as it does, it creates a kind of hole near the equator. Winds from the north and south rush in, carrying moisture, to fill this hole. There, they rise again, creating clouds and releasing their burden as rain. This is seen as a band of clouds called the Intertropical Convergence Zone, or the ITCZ. You can almost picture it as the Earth blushing at the sun's gaze.'

'But when?' pushed Swati.

Arjun waved her aside. 'This band of clouds keeps moving with the sun, but with a lag. In mid-to-late March, the band will be above the equator, and full moon will be when we celebrate Vasant Purnima, a day of renewals and awakenings. In some years, this coincides with Panguni Uthiram, a day about divine unions – Parvati with Shiva, or Murugan with Devasena, or Rama with Sita. But what is more divine than the union of the soul, the jeevatma, with the universal soul, the paramatma? That's when we will need to be wherever you are being so secretive about.'

This long speech drained the last of his strength and he fainted.

Vasant Purnima was about a month away. In one sense, Rajan was relieved. They could rest in this place that appeared cut off from the world and build up their strength. But he wasn't sure if some of them – Arjun, in particular – would last that long.

Thangam and Bhura exchanged a look.

Bhura spoke, 'Good, I will start making preparations.'

45

Bhura Salim Rahmatullah Sheikh

BHURA SALIM RAHMATULLAH SHEIKH WALKED DOWN THE stairs with purpose. He whistled, and a golden labrador, his dear love, came towards him slowly. Noor, beauty, he called her. They had been together for fifteen years – and finally, age was catching up. Her hips were giving way, and her eyesight was failing. But still she came slowly to his whistle – she had not liked the restrictions placed on her these past few days.

He sat down at his large desk, the same desk at which generations of his family had sat. He came from a family of zamindars who had farmed this part of the Kaveri delta for centuries. They had always been known for their generosity and their tenants had loved them. But that meant their house was not as big as the other zamindars, their jewellery not as fine, their parties not as raucous, but Bhura's family had always felt that this was a small price to pay.

Once, his ancestor had been very ill. Every doctor from

near and far had thrown up their hands. In desperation, his ancestor had heeded his wazir's advice and approached the temple of Srimushnam, promising to honour the deity if he got better. And he did. And he kept his promise.

Later, a Sufi saint came to their neighbourhood. Unlike the meanness and bloodshed that characterized relations elsewhere, here, the saint and the temple decided to coexist peacefully. Even today, when the processional deity took his annual procession in March, he would stop in front of the dargah where the imam would bring out dried fruits and would receive a silk shawl and some tulsi in return. Bhura's family had always played a prominent part in that festival.

But as they say, no good deed goes unpunished. His family's generosity saw their once grand zamindari estate being chipped away. The new landowners began to treat their tenants poorly. When Bhura had tried to protest, they laughed at him. That was when he met Thangam, whose family had lost their lands. Together, the older and younger man hatched an audacious plan to help the small farmers.

His double-life left little room for a family, and so Bhura, who loved animals, grew his menagerie instead. Birds, dogs, deer – he welcomed them all. A couple of years ago, Thangam had left. Then, a few months ago, he had come back, wanting some help creating new identification papers for a man, woman and child. Bhura knew all about Swati, but the man and child were new. Then, a week ago, Thangam had reached out for help again. Bhura had responded as he always had, and the family had come to stay.

Bhura thought of Lakshmi, smiling, as he sketched the plan for their transport. They had been spending a lot of time together, the big man and the thin girl. He introduced her to his animals, and she loved them, especially his pigeon coop with thousands of pigeons. She walked him through her herbs. She was a special child, he smiled to himself, as his pen flew across the sheets, and soon, a completed sketch of what he needed to build appeared on the page.

A container truck for mangoes with a temperature-controlled interior. From the back, three-fourths of the way in, it would appear like any other container vehicle, but the last quarter, which could be accessed through a hidden hatch in the driver's cabin would house living quarters with bunk beds, a kitchenette, a folding table and a tiny toilet.

Thangam walked in and Bhura looked up.

'This will be dangerous.'

'Oh, really. I would have never imagined,' Bhura replied, smiling.

'I'm serious. I cannot guarantee your safety. I came because I had no choice. And the world hangs in balance.'

'Then you honour me,' Bhura replied. He showed Thangam his plan, and the old man nodded his approval.

'Some of these things are not available here. I will go buy them. I will be back in a week.'

46

Ajna

THEY MISSED BHURA TREMENDOUSLY WHILE HE WAS AWAY. His warmth and positivity had acted like a blanket that kept their cold anxieties at bay. His faith – in himself and in the divine – was rock-solid, giving him a shimmering confidence in their quest. They could not fail, he believed, and in doing so, made them believe too. His good humour had washed over any griping like an unguent, smoothing away sharp corners. Now, his absence, like a receding tide, had exposed their fears like jagged rocks under the sea.

Rajan, on Thangam's advice and his own instincts, had not shared their next destination with the others, which irritated Arjun. This irritation showed up as mean jibes, which both Thangam and Swati put down savagely. He also kept pointing out all the ways they were likely to fail. Here, Lakshmi intervened, with a maturity belying her years, saying gently, 'But we have come so far, Arjun Uncle.' Rajan noted that this usually stopped him. He always seemed to heed Lakshmi.

Both of them were spending more and more time on the book. Every day, they shared new insights on Kundalini theory; advanced exercises to activate chakras; signs to check if one could become an adept.

Lakshmi was very excited, her now-much-lighter eyes shining as she said, 'Healing is so much more than sorting out infection and injury, Appa. It's about removing any blockages on your soul's journey. As the blockages are removed, we have more energy and joy.' She tripped over words in her excitement. 'It's a change of focus, when one's journey is outside – studies, job, money, relationships, power – there are always more steps one can climb, and every step is an uphill journey. But when one's journey goes within, each step becomes a discovery and wonderous, and after a point, there is a pull from within, making each step easier.'

Lakshmi found herself literally rippling with energy after breakfast in the mornings and began placing her palms on either side of someone's head. This evoked a different sensation in each person: Arjun found that it brought him calm, Thangam joy, Rajan wonder, and Swati comfort.

Arjun spoke eloquently of how Kundalini could restore balance. After all, he said, only material power – money or armament – was valued today. And humanity made its choices on this basis. But when alternate paths, alternate values, emerged, the tilt towards material power would be counterbalanced.

Swati had never seen her cousin so lucid or, indeed, so persuasive. He had always been articulate but often did not bother to tailor his message to his audience. Most discussions had him storming out in a huff. Now, he made so much sense that she found herself in sync with him. She was mentioning this to Rajan, on what had become their evening walk, when he stopped her and asked, 'Have you ever thought that this lucidity could be the result of whatever key they unlocked in Srirangam and that Vishuddha is Arjun's special chakra? It is the chakra of communication, after all.'

They were walking through the garden, with coconut trees along its periphery, a fecund vegetable patch behind the house and a mango orchard that lay further beyond. Several overfed strays accompanied them on their walk. Bhura picked up any stray, vaccinated them, and adopted them. But he fed them far too much, meaning each sprouted a rounded tummy. Rajan was nervous around dogs – he had been chased and bitten as a child, but Swati cooed over them all and they loved her for it. Noor, in particular, found that Swati made an acceptable replacement for Bhura while he was away.

'Let me get this straight. Each of us has a special chakra?' she asked.

'Well, each of us have different strengths, right? Some of us are good with numbers, other with our hands. Some bring joy with their attitude; others are good at managing people. In the same way, different people naturally have different chakras stronger, I think. It's part of their soul's journey.'

'So, what's my chakra?'

Rajan looked at this woman who had come to mean so much to him and asked himself, '*What was her chakra?*' He thought of her chart. Mars, the lord of speech, was strong in his own house. But her *lagnaadhipathi*, the planet that represented her, was present in the 5th house, the house of creativity. He was her Aatmakaraka too – the planet that signified her soul's desires in this lifetime.

'I think it is Svadhishthana.'

'Yeah, of course, you would give me the sex chakra,' Swati smirked.

'No, it's more than that – it is about creativity,' Rajan stammered, blushing.

Swati walked on, thinking. After they had worked on that chakra, she had become more herself, reverting to things that had made her joyful when she was a child.

'Maybe a little of Vishuddha too…'

'Hmmm…And what do you think is Lakshmi's?'

There was no hesitation.

'Anahata. She has always been compassionate, and the power she showed while healing the maid left no doubt.'

'And Thangam?'

'I think it is Mooladhara. He's always been the foundation of our group. He calms any situation down. But maybe Manipura too, because he is so strong and energetic.'

'And you?'

Rajan fell silent. What *was* his gift? He sighed. And then thought of his own chart. His Aatmakaraka was Mercury, so something with the mind.

'Something to do with my brain...'

'What about your dreams?'

Dreams were a form of insight, Rajan thought. A type of sixth sense. And Mercury was placed in his Lagna, in his own sign. This could mean his strength came from looking within. Insight, he realized in a flash. That would then mean his chakra was Ajna – the chakra they had not begun to work on yet.

That night, Rajan got them working on their Ajna. The meditation, his father had written, was relatively simple. Breathing in through one nostril, while holding the other closed. Holding the breath for eight seconds and then breathing out for ten through the other nostril. Repeating this on the other side completed a cycle. That night, they each completed five cycles. By the third cycle, Rajan's head had begun to experience a prickling of pins and needles.

That night Rajan's dreams were more vivid than they ever had been. He saw nine strangers he had never met before, all enveloped in the same aura of deadliness as the assassin from Srirangam. He was in a forest, sitting on the steps of a small hut by a lake, while butterflies hovered over Swati's head. He dreamt of laying Lakshmi's unconscious body in front of a white Narasimha. He saw golden eyes everywhere. He looked into a mirror and found his own eyes turning gold. He saw the blue of a lake in snowy mountains reflecting the cerulean blue of a cloudless sky. He saw golden fangs in the dark. Along with dark toenails standing next to him. Though he did not wake as he had in the past, in the morning, he seemed to understand what his dreams were trying to convey.

'I think there are nine people hunting us,' he explained to the others as they sat around the table, briefly sketching out the appearance of those nine. 'I see golden eyes everywhere, and my own eyes turning gold – I think that is a sign of the Kundalini energy rising.'

'Is that why our eyes are lightening, Appa?' asked Lakshmi, between bites of idli. 'Does that mean they will soon turn gold?'

'I'm not sure, Lakshmi. Maybe,' Rajan replied. He paused, took a deep breath and continued, 'I think the golden fangs at Srirangam probably belonged to the manifest Kundalini – and the bite gave you a supercharge.'

'I think we were wise to escape from the choultry. I'm not sure the woman means us well, and I think we will see her, or someone like her, again.'

He did not mention the lake or the toenails. A voice within seemed to be telling him not to, and he listened. The others listened to him with mixed feelings. They enjoyed their routine, and they didn't want it to end.

Their mornings started with a salutation to the sun, followed by a grounding with the Mooladhara, spurring their creativity through the Svadhishthana before opening themselves up with the Anahata. Then came breakfast, sometimes discussing the book, other times just being present in the moment and with each other. Afterward, they used the kapalbhati and the plank for activating their

Manipura chakra. Before Lakshmi's healing touch, they could only hold the plank for a few minutes, but now they found they were able to hold it for ten minutes – even Arjun did not collapse. Swati made lunch with the help of Bhura's staff, which Thangam, Lakshmi and Arjun wolfed down. After lunch, they slept, finding renewal in their rest.

They woke a couple of hours before sunset. Lakshmi put her kashayam to brew on the stove. While it brewed, Arjun and Lakshmi played cards, and the others joined in, carving out a precious island of lightness and laughter in their disciplined day. Then came Vishuddha with sunset, and finally Ajna in the dark, before a light dinner and bed.

This routine kept up for a week – it was an idyllic time; one Rajan would always remember with gratitude. Then Bhura returned, bringing with him the parts needed to build their transport. He also came bearing gifts for Lakshmi. Books that he knew she would love, but also beautiful clothes, which she was less enthusiastic about, and tools and containers for her herbs. He excused himself from joining in their exercises, 'You said yourself each of us has different strengths,' but joined them for their cards, where he shrewdly caught Swati cheating.

'I keep losing!' she screamed, blushing.

'And you are a teacher! Lakshmi, tell me truly, did she also do this in school?' Bhura asked laughingly as Swati hid behind Rajan. Lakshmi shook her head, giggling helplessly. Bhura also joined in their songs in the evening as Vishuddha ended, adding a rich baritone to their harmonies.

Two weeks after he had returned, he had almost finished building their transport. Bhura had built a hidden hatch behind the driver's seat that could be opened by the press of a lever. It opened into a room about ten feet in length and eight feet in width, with a tiny bathroom in one corner. Two walls of the room had berths that could be let down or folded up, like those in a railway compartment. There was a stove on a counter in the corner opposite the toilet, with built-in storage around it. The cabin was air-conditioned and had a little pull-back window built on its ceiling to let sunlight in, if they chose. Bhura had provided a hatch in the floor of the room to get out. He had also added solar panels to the top of the vehicle, which charged a set of batteries. In a pinch, the stored energy could keep the little room refrigerated for a few hours.

Lakshmi, Rajan and Thangam were admiring Bhura's handiwork when they heard Swati shout. They quickly ran to the room to find Arjun on the ground, his throat blue, shaking with fits, foaming in the mouth.

'What happened?' asked the old man, even as Lakshmi placed her healing hands on his chest.

'He said he was going to try one of the exercises in the coded chapters in the book. He was a few minutes in, when this happened,' Swati said.

It was typical Arjun, Rajan thought. *To try and fly, when one was struggling to walk*. But it was in Arjun's nature, and there was little they could do to change that. Lakshmi was unable to wake him, and so Swati fetched the theertham and the rachandan. There was very little left of either. She applied the tiniest dab of the rachandan on Arjun and poured a few drops into his mouth. The shaking and foaming stopped, but he did not wake.

'I think he is meant to be resting, Appa,' Lakshmi told Rajan. 'I think this is his body's way of coping.' They let him be.

Two more days passed, and Arjun remained unconscious. They were down to a few drops of the theertham and a small dab of rachandan, which Rajan wanted to keep it for emergencies.

Swati asked, 'If this isn't an emergency, what is?' They argued and descended into their first real fight – with Swati accusing Rajan of being prejudiced against Arjun. Well, he was not the only person who got to choose. Rajan was stung – there was a fair bit of truth in what Swati was saying. He did want to save the last bit if anything happened to his daughter. But he wasn't about to admit that, resorting instead to biting meanly at her and saying how spoilt the cousins were, well, they were in the real world now, before retreating into silence. Perhaps it was the heat, but they were both too wrought up to listen to the other's point of view.

When Thangam later found Swati in tears, his lips tightened to a thin line, and he cunningly intervened by setting Lakshmi on Rajan.

The old man's stratagem worked. Rajan apologized – rather half-heartedly – to Swati.

Bhura was listening, holding Lakshmi's hand, as the child did not like the tension in the room. He spoke up, offering to get some prasad from the dargah and the temple, saying both had healing properties. They agreed, and the big man left.

Lunch was a subdued meal. Swati and Rajan were still glowering at each other – there had been enough truth in each allegation, delivered with bite and malice, to sting painfully. Lakshmi, caught between the two and missing Arjun's flippancy, kept her head down and ate sparingly. Thangam's world revolved around Swati, and whether or not he agreed with Rajan's decision, his loyalty lay with her, and he ate in stony silence.

After the meal, Lakshmi and the old man fell asleep quickly, but Rajan tossed about. After a while, when he realised he wasn't going to fall asleep, he went to Swati's room and knocked at her door.

He entered and found her sitting down with dried tear stains on her pale cheeks.

He went to the sofa, knelt on the floor, and taking her hands in his, said, 'I'm so sorry. You were right. I did want to save the prasad for Lakshmi. And I'm not that fond of Arjun and was worried about him compromising our quest.'

'How?'

'I'm not sure. I just think he broadcasts his thoughts to whoever is listening. It's a hunch. How else could the man at Poombarai have guessed we were going to Srirangam?'

Swati felt her anger dissolving, but pointed out, 'Without him, we would not have cracked the clue.'

'Agreed. If I felt his life was in danger, I would have yielded.'

At that, she pulled away.

'Rajan, it's not only your decision; it's all of ours. Don't you get that?'

'Fair enough. Vishuddha is not my strong suit – but still, from now on, I will try to convince you.'

While Bhura put the finishing touches on the truck, Lakshmi taught them a thought-shielding exercise from the book. Rajan then tested them on how powerful their mental shields were. He smiled when he broke through Lakshmi's thoughts. Thangam, of course, was predictably impenetrable. So were Bhura's thoughts. And surprisingly, so were Swati's. Rajan felt his pins and needles getting steadily worse, until he fainted after the Ajna practice one night. When he woke, he noticed the sun was setting out of his window. *Have I slept a full day?* he wondered. He walked down to hear the clattering in the kitchen; Lakshmi was probably brewing her kashayam. He saw Thangam and Bhura seated at the table with Swati, who turned around and ran towards him, giving him a giant hug.

'What happened?' he asked her.

'You fainted last night, clutching your head. Lakshmi placed her hands on your head, and you seemed to calm into a sleep. There was no fever or foaming, so we let you rest. I was just about to come upstairs to check on you when you came down.'

Just then, he heard Lakshmi shouting out to Bhura's assistant to get her some more jaggery from the store. Rajan walked into the kitchen and saw the bashful young man fetching the jaggery and begin to knock the mounds into a powder. The boy turned around and gave him a shy smile. As their eyes met, he noticed a very faint reddish hue around the boy. He blinked to see if he was imagining it. He was not – when he opened his eyes again and made contact with the boy's eyes, there it was, a pale reddish hue, almost like a glowing mist around the body of the young man. He turned and looked at Swati, who had walked into the kitchen, but there was nothing around her. He called out to Lakshmi, who had just added the jaggery to the pot and was wiping her hands; she turned. He saw a bright red aura around her – not faint like the boy's, but a thick red fluidic aura, streaked through with gold, shimmering and alive.

'Appa! You are okay! I'm so happy!' said Lakshmi, coming to her father with a beaming smile, that died on seeing the obvious shock on his face. 'What is it, Appa? What's wrong?'

He found he could not speak. Lakshmi and Swati were worried now, and they took him to the next room, sat him down, and gave him some water to drink. Rajan kept looking at Lakshmi with so much concern on his face that the girl was rattled.

Just then Thangam and Bhura walked in. Rajan looked up – there was no aura around Bhura, but he was not surprised at the thick, fluidic, golden-brown aura flashing around Thangam. He gulped down the rest of his water and sank his head into his hands.

Swati was really concerned. She put her arm around him. 'What is it, Rajan? Is it your head again? Is something else wrong? Come on, tell us.'

Lakshmi was kneeling in front of her father. 'Appa, tell us. Whatever it is, we can face it together.'

Thangam came to the younger man and pulled him to his feet. 'Thambi, you are scaring your daughter. Pull yourself together.'

His touch, more than his words, calmed Rajan. And after eating some of the prasad that Bhura had fetched, he calmed down further. He told them about the auras he was seeing. On hearing this, Lakshmi said she remembered something from the book and ran up and came back carrying it with an intense look upon her face.

She opened a page in the ninth chapter, which appeared to be blank to Rajan, and read:

'As within so without
As the serpent climbs, your aura grows
But the body a heavy price then owes
Precious life blood, its chosen coin

It burns, it burns
Shadows flee as the flame ascends
And the soul, its many cracks, it mends
But without the waters that cooled Halahala's breath
The rising snake brings certain death.'

Rajan felt his world collapse. What use was saving the world if the price was his sweet daughter's life? His anguish was palpable. They had a week before they needed to get to Nepal, but who knew now if Arjun would last that long?

At last, Bhura spoke, 'We leave tonight.'

Interlude

THE MAN WATCHED THE NEWS ON HIS COMPUTER WITH horror, a feeling of helplessness and of growing anger. The innocent always suffered the most.

Australia was burning.

Asia was beginning to burn.

The vulnerable were forced to choose between life and livelihood.

India's wheat harvest was shrivelling up.

The Europeans were seeing a surge in migration – they had a choice to make: shoot at the unarmed masses on the boats, people desperate to flee their dying fields, or watch their society remade.

And the El Niño was still not weakening…

47

Kalakada

THEY WERE ON THE ROAD IN LESS THAN TWO HOURS. Bhura wanted to take his assistant, but Thangam pointed out that the mild aura around the boy might give them away. It was a stretch, the others felt, but a plausible one. So, they decided Bhura and Swati, the two persons without auras, would drive.

The cabinets of the truck were stocked with enough food and supplies for a couple of weeks. The cargo was loaded. They lifted Arjun carefully into a berth, as the rest of them boarded into the small room. Lakshmi was excited, but her father, holding her hand firmly, had a tight knot in his stomach.

As the truck swung into the road, a gloom settled over the group. The idyll was over. No more card games, no more evening walks in the orchard. Just a race into the unknown while being hunted. They had discussed their journey – their first stop was to be near Kalakada, a small village in

Andhra Pradesh, which was a seven-hour drive away. Bhura would drive until they crossed the state boundary between Tamil Nadu and Andhra Pradesh, after which Swati would take over.

The sun had set by the time the truck pulled onto the highway. Bhura, who had made this trip countless times, knew the road like the back of his hand. The truck was new; he had run through the pre-journey checklist himself, even packing a full set of spare tyres as an added precaution. But in a nod to the preciousness of his cargo, he kept his eyes firmly on the road, not even turning back when Swati re-entered the driver's cabin after a brief visit to the room at the back.

An hour later, they were passing through Gingee (or Senji), a historic town whose once-impregnable fort had held immense strategic importance for controlling access to the fertile Kaveri delta. Bhura, who had hiked up the fort many a time, told Swati about its history. Over the centuries, the fort had been held by the Vijayanagar empire, the Marathas, the Mughals and the English. It was so formidable that it took a Mughal general eight years to break the Maratha hold on the fort. Swati could not see the fort at night, only the giant boulder it sat on. They were leaving the Kaveri Delta behind, and the landscape was getting rockier, with granite hillocks sprouting irregularly through the plains, like pimples on a teenager's face.

In another hour, they had crossed into Andhra Pradesh, passing a check post just beyond the town of Vellore, home to a famous medical college. Bhura's paperwork was flawless, and the largesse enclosed within made their passage even quicker.

Bhura and Swati (who was disguised as a swarthy, spectacled man) changed places in a teashop just after the check post. Even at night, the weather was clammy, the hot air hitting them like a blast as they left the air-conditioned cabin. They walked into a teashop (with a bar behind it), noting that several men appeared to be passed out near the entrance. It was too hot for tea; they opted for cool buttermilk instead. As Bhura chatted with some of the drivers, he discovered that there was a heatwave warning in effect in the states of Andhra, Telangana and Maharashtra. That explained the unconscious drivers in the shop. Alcohol and dehydrating heat made for bad bedfellows. He learned that many drivers were either planning to drive only at night or remain off the road entirely if the climate didn't cool down. They finished their buttermilk, wiped the sweat off their foreheads and necks, and got back into their truck.

The truck began climbing now, and Swati found she needed every scrap of concentration to maintain control. For one, the truck was much larger than any vehicle she had driven before, and while the power steering was featherlight, the vehicle was fully loaded, giving it a drag that reduced manoeuvrability. The highway was dark and empty; only the red lights from the reflectors and the white glow from the lane separators provided any relief from the inky blackness. Once, they passed what seemed to be a funeral procession, and Swati had to take extra care to weave the truck through it.

Around midnight, Swati gratefully turned the truck into the farm of Bhura's friend, one of the largest tomato farmers of the district. A security guard let them in and the truck drove straight down a narrow mud road. Swati could see the outlines of rows and rows of plants, before turning into a clearing within a grove of mango trees, where a small cottage stood. She saw a white SUV parked there, with a man standing next to it. Bhura and Swati got down from the truck and the men embraced. The refrigerated truck needed to be plugged in to keep the cold chain going, and Bhura's friend showed him where the plug point was. The men settled down on the porch to chat while Swati stepped into the cottage.

Bhura's keen eyes swept the compound as he listened to his friend. There appeared to be no cameras about, at least not next to the cottage. He casually brought up the topic, complaining how he had put cameras in his farm to check for theft. Surprisingly, his friend began lamenting. What was the point of trying to prevent theft, when the climate was killing him. He could not afford cameras. The climate had been terrible this past decade, but, even so, this year was unprecedented. The heat had ruined much of the stored tomato crop. The farmers had been hoping that bumper prices for their April harvest would make up for the losses, but the heatwave was causing the tomato plants to wilt and the pests to make merry. Just today, he was battling tomato fruitworms. What camera would protect against that? This past week, in the Annamayya district alone, ten farmers had taken their lives, and a shroud of despair hung over the area. Bhura, listening silently, recalled the funeral procession they had passed that evening.

Finally, Bhura's friend left, and the big man waved as he watched the car drive away. When the headlights were no longer visible, he got back into the truck and opened the bottom hatch. Arjun still hadn't woken up, but the others came out of the truck, grateful to stretch their legs for a while before returning to their little room to sleep. Swati went into the cottage, while Bhura stretched out on the charpoy on the veranda. It should have been cold that night – typical nighttime temperatures in that area in mid-March hovered between 15 and 18°C, but it was much warmer than that, and he found himself sweating.

They got up at dawn. With Bhura keeping a lookout, the rest completed their exercises – Thangam said it was their only hope to bear the rising Kundalini shakti – and breakfast before getting on the road, with Swati at the wheel. She was getting the hang of the truck, and it was easier driving in the day. She relaxed enough to take in the beauty of the Penna River, when they passed Kadapa, as it gurgled beneath the bridge, fringed by low, dark emerald hills all around.

An hour later, they were driving past Ahobilam, believed by many Hindus to be the site of the Narasimha avatar. They had stopped to swap places in a teashop, and Swati used the opportunity to scootch into the small room. When

Rajan heard where they were, he desperately wanted to visit the temple. He knew, deep within and with perfect certainty, that the prasad from that temple would help his daughter. But Thangam poured cold water on the idea, saying that since the shrine was on their pilgrimage and was dedicated entirely to Narasimha, it would no doubt be under surveillance. They could not afford to visit. It caused a sharp pang to skip it, but Rajan had to admit that the old man's logic was sound.

They set off, with Bhura driving, hoping to make it to Kurnool by noon. They made a left at a town called Nandyala, onto a four-lane highway that passed through dry plains before cutting through shallow, brush-forest-covered hillocks. The sun had risen high in the sky and as the heat mounted, the road surface ahead of the truck rippled in a mirage. There was no sign of life – no animal would risk being shrivelled in the midday heat. Swati spied a spire of smoke in the distance – she asked Bhura if it was from a forest fire. He replied that it was quite possible, given how dry and hot it was. By lunchtime, they reached their destination.

Kurnool, on the southern bank of the Tungabhadra, had gained prominence under the Vijayanagara kingdom for its diamonds. They had made good time thanks to the very light traffic, but Bhura was surprised to find that they had used so much fuel. Clearly, the refrigeration equipment was guzzling far more diesel than he had budgeted. As he stopped to fill gas, he saw the station attendant nearly fainting. The truck's temperature dial indicated an outside temperature of 44°C, several notches above normal. He had believed that the dial was malfunctioning, but the blast of heat as he stepped out proved him wrong. Now, Bhura was worried: in this heat, tyre failure was a real possibility, and he needed them to last a few more days. This wretched heat! He checked the tyre pressure and saw that it was dangerously high. They had no choice: they had to halt, and stay in the shade for a few hours, if they didn't want to get into an accident. Panting in the heat, he poured water on the tyres to cool them off, then on himself for good measure, adjusted the tyre pressure and started the truck.

He slowed the vehicle dramatically and, after crossing the mighty river, which in the dry season resembled pitiful puddles scattered amid mighty boulders, turned the truck into a grove. He bribed the grove's watchman with cash and two crates of mangoes. The sun was now directly overhead and it was boiling outside, but at least they were in the shade, where the tyres would not be under extra pressure. Bhura turned off the refrigeration, leaving it on only for their small room. When Swati conveyed the news of their slower pace, Rajan's panic rose. *We can't afford this!* he thought. He could see auras intensifying; the noose around his daughter's neck was already tightening, and now this.

He explained this to Bhura, who had entered the room. The big man saw the desperation on the Rajan's face, and understood all too well his fears, but said, 'We cannot risk driving during the day. We will drive at night when the roads are somewhat cooler. Our journey may be slower, but if we don't slow down, we will fail to reach the destination.'

Rajan had no choice but accept the painful logic of his argument.

The minutes trickled past. Arjun was still out. Bhura, tired out by the heat, crashed. Thangam and Lakshmi also slept. But Rajan was too distraught to sleep, and Swati stayed next to him, offering what comfort she could. After the sun had set and the stars came out, they hit the road again.

Bhura deliberately drove slowly, taking five-minute breaks every half-hour. Traffic on the road remained light, but still they passed an unusual number of accidents – *were they caused by tyre blowouts or drivers suffering from heat exhaustion*, wondered Swati. It was well after midnight when they arrived at a farmhouse that belonged to Bhura's cousin on the outskirts of Hyderabad. They had hoped to cover more ground that day, but at least they were safe.

48

The Cabal

THEY MET AS THEY ALWAYS DID, WITH THE HUNTRESS joining mere moments before the Chair. The Chair spoke: 'Our bets are working out and our outlays have been more than compensated. But now we have a problem. You would have no doubt seen the news of the farmer suicides across central India. There are protests breaking out – no, not by our supporters, but by others. This could result in a pushback.'

The huntress spoke – sleek and soft, 'Can you please elaborate?'

The Chair continued, 'For one, the government could place price controls. But worse still, they could set off investigations against speculators and hoarders, who buy cheap from farmers and sell dear. In six months, several states head for elections – sending a rich cat feeding off the farmers to prison could be just what the government needs.'

He imagined the blood draining from her face as the import of his words sunk in. He knew she would have bet heavily on food prices, and while she would have taken care to cover her tracks, the fact that he knew and could betray her would no doubt be playing on her mind. He smiled behind his mask. Maybe he should explore that option.

Another hand rose.

'Yes?'

'In a recent meeting with the agricultural minister, I heard they were planning to liberalize agricultural markets selectively, using smaller startups and farmer producer organizations. This would increase competition, which would reduce our spread.' The spread between the prices the farmer received for their crops and those at which speculators sold to wholesalers existed largely because of a lack of competition. If farmers had more options, that spread, and the profits of the Cabal would fall.

Another hand rose.

'I was at a meeting at the Institute today, where many of these start-ups were sharing their experiences in a conclave. They bring better seeds, technical know-how and handhold the farmers, even offering them funding, to help them improve their operations. If that happens, productivity would go up, prices could fall, even as farmer incomes are protected. Our profits would evaporate.'

Silence followed these comments. Competition, lifeblood of capitalism, was poison to the Cabal.

One more hand rose.

'Yes?'

The voice was female and accented.

'There is more than one way to catch a cat. Let us sympathize with the deaths and urge for action. But let us blame the climate. And what can these small measures – slow and dispersed – do against such a big thing as that? There is something that the UK government is investing in, a form of technology to change the climate itself, to cool it. It's called geoengineering.'

Geoengineering came in many forms, she explained. One was to inject a stream of reflective particles into the stratosphere, where they could reflect and thus prevent a fraction of the sun's rays from reaching and warming the Earth. This was not a new idea – no, it was based on a phenomenon that predated humanity, and indeed, life itself – a volcanic eruption. Powerful volcanic eruptions sent out large amounts of ash and sulphur high into the sky, cooling the planet rapidly by blocking out sunlight. One of the most powerful eruptions in recent times had been Tambora's eruption in 1815. The ensuing global fallout created a year without summer, and had inspired Byron to pen his poem 'Darkness'.

The bright sun was extinguish'd,

...

Famine had written Fiend. The world was void,
The populous and the powerful was a lump,
Seasonless, herbless, treeless, manless, lifeless—
A lump of death—a chaos of hard clay.

For years, geoengineering had been a taboo topic in climate conversations. It was seen as unknown, untested, and one that could have potentially devastating impacts. There was also the question of moral hazard – why would anyone take the trouble to cut emissions, scientists asked, when one could cool down the planet in other ways? Also, once begun, like an opioid addiction, one could not withdraw from the particulate injections – they would need to continue indefinitely, risking conflict between countries that supported the global technological intervention and those who opposed it.

Indian scientists pointed out a troubling side effect of this cooling: drying the Indian monsoon. They pointed to data that monsoons tended to fail for two years after a large volcanic eruption. Monster El Niños could become more common in the future, they said, with aerosols adding fodder to their fire. The safest way to bring down temperatures, they argued, was to cut emissions.

The woman continued, seeing her audience intrigued, 'We can say that today, with wars breaking out, and the potential of AI to leave millions jobless, climate action should not be abandoned; indeed it should be accelerated. But because conventional action takes so long, we should act fast and cool the Earth in months, not decades.'

A pregnant silence followed her speech. The others, especially those within the fossil fuel industry, were quick to spot how they could have their cake and eat it too. With geoengineering, their sales would not be hurt, but the Earth's temperatures would come down.

'How would we keep grain prices high?' This was the huntress.

'Because in India, models suggest that rainfall will come down and extremes could increase.'

The chairman could imagine her purring.

'All those in favour of promoting this…this geoengineering.'

All hands rose.

'Very well. Our colleague will share a note on the technology and talking points. We will share those through our networks. We meet in two weeks.'

49

Nagpur

BHURA PULLED THE TRUCK OUT OF THE FARMHOUSE WELL before dawn. Temperatures were forecast to be in the 40s that day, several notches above normal for this time of year, and they needed to cover as much distance as they could in the dark. Thangam tried to get them started on their exercises, but it was difficult in the cramped confines of the cabin, and they soon gave up.

After several hours, they crossed the second-longest river in India, the mighty Godavari, and were soon driving through a forest at the periphery of the Kawal Tiger Reserve. Bhura knew this area well – his mother's family was from the area, and as a boy, he had spent many of his summers walking and even camping in these forests. So apparent was the boy's love for animals and so warm his family's hospitality that many in the forest department had grown close to him.

He had called one such, a range officer in these parts – they had played as boys together – and on his direction, turned off the highway and drove the truck deeper into the forest. They were in the buffer zone of the reserve, and in a few minutes, came up to a *machan* next to a large lake, where a man in uniform was waiting by the side of the road. Bhura got down and the men embraced. Swati got down too and shook hands with the ranger. It was much cooler within the forest, especially by the lake.

There was no electricity here, and Swati knew that there was not enough power in the batteries to keep the room refrigerated for more than an hour. She hoped her nervousness did not show as she listened to what Bhura's friend was saying. Three tigers had been poached in the last month. Bhura was shaken. This was an old reserve, an erstwhile hunting ground of the Nizam and his colonial guests, whose trees helped ensure that the Godavari flowed strongly in the summer. After it was declared a tiger reserve, cases of poaching and hunting had fallen, which made the news of three tigers poached in a month shocking.

'What happened?' Swati asked, making her voice as hoarse as she could, seeing her friend's face crumple in sorrow.

'It's the drought,' the ranger replied.

'The drought?' Bhura asked, roused from his shock.

'Most farms around here have seen their harvests fail this year. In some parts of some districts, the harvests have been poor for three years in a row. Either it's too hot or it rains too little or it rains all at once and floods the poor farmer's fields.

'Some families have taken to hunting for bushmeat for

survival. Others do it because they can get away with it. We are chronically understaffed, we cannot patrol all of the area, especially when the hunting happens outside the protected areas. But their hunting brings them into conflict with the tigers. Just last month, a young man was mauled.

'Some villagers attack the tiger out of revenge. Others know that a single tiger can fetch a year's income, especially if they sell it in parts. The trafficking syndicates are well-oiled and funded. It's too much money. And the temptation is too high, especially now.'

Bhura said nothing. One felt for the villagers but without the tigers, the forest would soon disappear, falling prey to encroachment and special interests, and without the forest, the millions who depended on the river would perish. The forests birthed the river, if only people understood that. He couldn't intervene, and he wasn't the kind of man to bandy idle words, so he stayed silent.

The range officer told them they could rest for a few hours before resuming their journey in the evening. He would let the guards know. Then he left. When they could no longer hear the sound of his motorcycle, Swati gratefully snuck into the little room. Bhura had parked the truck as close as he could to the machan, and soon, the others came out through the hatch in the floor.

They could not have chosen a more idyllic spot to halt. The small hut, built on stilts, perched above the waters of the lake under a giant tree – Lakshmi wasn't sure of the species – that had spread its branches over the hut, cocooning it in shade. Birdsong surrounded them. The forest and the giant tree conspired to keep the inside the hut cool, even in the midday heat, with the gentle breeze wafting in from the lake making it even cooler from time to time. Thangam and Bhura managed to move Arjun into the machan with difficulty. Both men were panting as they laid him gently on the floor.

After being cooped up in the little room, being in the forest was heavenly. Even though the sun was high in the sky, they started on their morning exercises. Thangam and Lakshmi almost seemed to pass out after the Mooladhara; they told a frantic Rajan that it was just that the energy within the forest was incredible – a thing alive, similar to the shola in Kodaikanal, but because they were able to reach so much deeper, it was exhilarating. Swati felt her Svadhishthana set her free like the butterflies fluttering overhead. Lakshmi felt like the tree roots were growing from her, connecting her with the forest. They continued with their exercises and Rajan believed he could almost hear the thoughts of every living thing in the forest. *No wonder the ancient seers lived within the forests*, he thought, *the energy the forest was giving out was unreal.* Bhura, who came to watch after finishing his prayers, smiled to see their beaming faces. Their afternoon meal seemed sweeter than it had ever been, and they fell asleep almost at once, with Swati reluctantly staying up to guard.

She roused them as the sun began to set. Going by the changing nature of the calls, the predators were waking up, and she would feel safer with everyone conscious and in the vehicle. By the time the sun had set, they were out of the forest and on their way to Nagpur. Bhura's maternal great-grandfather's family hailed from there, and the family still had a lovely property just north of the city. His great-grandfather had passed away decades ago, and the property was involved in a family dispute, but an old aunt lived on in the main bungalow these days and she was fond of him in her own batty way.

It was well past midnight when they finally reached because they had run into a protest where people, gripped by both rage and sorrow, were holding up pictures of their families. Bhura, who had stopped at a teashop to switch places with Swati, learned that an entire hamlet of farmers had killed themselves because they saw no way to escape the burden of their debt after yet another failed harvest. Maharashtra had the highest number of farmer suicides in the country, he told Swati, but even so, an entire village ending their lives was a new form of horror. He thought of the tigers and realized there were few winners in the changing climate.

Bhura had asked for a guest house at the far end of the estate to be prepared, and he now parked the truck near the guest house, plugged in his vehicle, and went into the house. The house was graceful in the way of buildings from another era, with arched verandas, cutglass chandeliers and beautiful mosaic floors. But, while the surfaces were sparkling, the damp showed on the walls, and the carpets and the fabrics on the sofas were threadbare. There were photographs of family gracing the walls, and Lakshmi, who along with the others, had snuck in once the caretaker had left, was enormously tickled by a photograph of a plump young Bhura with a big toothy smile on his face cradling a baby hedgehog, while trying to hold up his shorts which appeared to be slipping off.

They fell asleep quickly – the tension and the drive had taken a toll, and it was good to sleep on a bed again.

50

The Narmada

THEY HAD BARELY SLEPT FOR A COUPLE OF HOURS WHEN Bhura roused them. They set off shortly, reaching the national highway in minutes. It was eerily quiet – just the hum as rubber met road – and dark, with only the reflectors, red and white, and the yellow turning signs providing any relief. Bhura was on full alert – they were passing through forest – an animal could dart across at any time, and they could not afford an accident.

He heaved a sigh of relief when they finally ascended an elevated highway. After a while, they seemed to be surrounded by mist. He would have thought it was too hot for fog, but the visibility had fallen, so he pushed down a window and discovered that the 'mist' was, in fact, smoke.

'What is it?' mumbled Swati, roused from slumber by the blast of the wind through the open window. Then the smell hit her, and she sat up, 'What's burning?'

'The forest,' Bhura replied grimly.

'Where are we?'

'We are passing through Pench National Park.'

Swati looked around, a bit puzzled. It looked like they were on a highway with green tarp on either side of the road. It didn't look like a forest, let alone a national park.

Bhura, even without looking at her, sensed her puzzlement. 'It's an elevated highway. The first of its kind – with underpasses for the animals to move without danger of being run over.'

'That's cool,' Swati said. 'But why the smoke?'

'It's forest fire season. From the amount of smoke, I would say it's a big one.'

Swati said nothing. The last few days she had had little sleep and was groggy – she had remained on guard at the forest yesterday and stayed awake with Rajan the day before that. But as she grew more wakeful, she could see the orange licks of fire faintly in the distance with giant plumes of smoke discernible even in the dark. As Bhura had said, it did look like a big fire. Their sealed, air-conditioned cabin cocooned them from the harsh reality, but just outside, just below, she imagined animals fleeing in terror; trees, ancient and young, burning as the merciless fire bore down on them.

She sighed. 'Why is this the season?'

'The dry weather. It mostly doesn't rain after November, which means the forest floor is bone-dry. The unusual heat this year only made that worse. And this is when the Mahua blossoms.'

'The Mahua?' asked Swati.

Bhura's smile was twisted. The Mahua was one of India's iconic trees – the Gond tribe considered it the tree of life – and yet, even well-educated Indians like his new friend did not know of its existence.

'The Mahua is a tree that flowers around this time. Villagers gather the blossoms to make it into oil, sweets, but mostly, they brew it into alcohol. They light small crescent-shaped fires at the base of the tree to clear the litter, to easily gather flowers that fall.'

'Sounds risky.'

'It is.'

'Why do they do it?'

'Because selling Mahua gets them cash. And in today's world, cash is king, right?'

Swati caught the bitterness in his voice.

'There has to be a better way.'

Bhura stayed silent for a while and finally answered.

'In one forest, north of here, one group is working with communities to design nets to collect the flowers. I'd actually heard that the department had been working with local communities to make the forest here fire-free. My friend told me it was working well, but even a small accident in this weather can undo years of hard work.'

Day was dawning, and even though sunrise was still some time away, the sky was turning blue-gold, and they could see clearly that they had left the forest behind. They were also gaining altitude, and a signboard told her that they were passing a town called Seoni. They were driving steadily, not too fast, and the gentle swaying of the truck lulled her back to sleep.

After an hour, Bhura heard a small scratching sound near the hatch and saw it opening.

'Is Swati okay?' Rajan whispered. 'She usually visits.'

'Just tired out.'

He looked briefly, longingly, at the outside, where the sky was turning orange and gold as the sun rose over the Wainganga River at Chhapara. He didn't need Thangam's counsel to know the dangers they faced if discovered and regretfully went back to the little room. The others were still sleeping, and Rajan decided not to wake them, judging sleep to be the best medicine.

Bhura drove for another hour before turning off the highway and driving for a short distance and parking the truck. Swati woke up and together they walked the little way to the Narmada River. The air was not quite cool, but not yet hot. It was a lazy morning – there were no festivals on that day, it was too early for tourists, so it was just the local children splashing in the water while colourful boats stood moored haphazardly at the edge of the river. Bhura filled the water bottle he carried with water from the river, while Swati splashed some of the deliciously cold water over her face, arms and neck. She looked longingly at the water – how much she wished she could jump in as well. She saw three bridges across the river – two were part of the highway they had been on but the third appeared to be a far older stone bridge. No vehicle appeared on it, but as she squinted, she saw a woman walking over it.

She turned to Bhura and asked, 'What's that?' pointing to the stone bridge.

'That's the old British bridge. When Thangam and I came here long ago, a guide told us that the bridge was submerged by the swollen river in the monsoon season.'

She looked up again at the bridge. It stood several metres off the ground – she could not imagine this tame, placid river swelling so much. What a mighty river it must have been. No wonder people revered it so!

As she splashed the river's water on her face, Swati felt stronger than she had felt in a long time. No, that was not the right word. She felt...purer, even though she did not like the shades of meaning that had gathered on the word. It was as though her soul was shining through clearly, without the grime of samsara to occlude its vision. She wished the others could come too, but she knew that was too risky. Looking around, she could see sadhus near the temple. The chance of discovery was too high.

They walked back to the vehicle, and Bhura continued to drive. Swati snuck into the small room in the back and woke the others, and gave them some of the Narmada's water, which they drank, each feeling that their soul could see more clearly. Lakshmi's body seemed to shake slightly, but the fit passed before Rajan could even ask her what it was.

As they ate their breakfast, Thangam, unusually, began talking to them about a trip he had taken with Bhura ten years ago. They had been working with the forest department to help trap poachers killing tigers and leopards in the region. Once, he had gone to the Tala Zone in the Bandhavgarh National Park to visit Seshasayee, a giant statue of a reclining Vishnu in the middle of the forest, with a tiny spring welling up near his feet. The waters of that stream were the sweetest he'd ever tasted.

'Did you feel like how we did now?' asked Rajan.

'Even better,' replied the old man.

'I wonder why that is,' mused Swati.

'I think the forests and the mountains and places of nature have a renewing power that rivers carry with them,' ventured Lakshmi.

Thangam continued, 'The Narmada is considered so holy that even looking at her is supposed to cleanse a person, and we have drunk her waters. Maybe the holiness has to do with the energy. A woman from Jabalpur told me that they believe the Narmada was a princess who was besotted with a prince of neighbouring kingdom called Sonbhadra. Too shy to approach him directly, she sent her maid Johilla to convey her feelings to the prince. Johilla, with her own schemes in mind, got her mistress to deck her with jewels so that the messenger would be taken seriously. Narmada waited and waited, and finally, when her impatient heart could wait no more, she went to Sonbhadra only to find Johilla and Sonbhadra in each other's arms. Heartbroken, she turned and stalked off in the opposite direction.'

'She should have just found someone else,' said Swati. 'Why be wimpy like that?'

Thangam smiled and continued, 'Our stories help us understand reality. Don't take them so literally. While the Johilla joins the Sone, which flows northward to join the Ganga, the Narmada flows in the opposite direction. So, you see, the story mirrors geography and explains why the Narmada, unlike most rivers in peninsular India, flows east to west, emptying into the Arabian Sea. And when we understand how the grand forests of central India have nurtured some of India's mightiest rivers, maybe we will protect them better.'

The old man had never spoken so much at a stretch before. *Maybe the Narmada did have magic powers*, Swati thought.

She went back to the driver's cabin to relieve Bhura, who had decided that it was cool enough for them to push on. They had left river and forest behind and were passing through farmland. Swati saw irregularly shaped plots, with large earthen bunds separating them, and lone trees scattered about. They passed mud huts painted a bright blue, topped by tiled roofs. From the many threshing machines and straw bales she could see, she guessed wheat was being harvested. Her guess was confirmed at every tea shop they stopped at, where they heard the same tragic story. The crop was wilting in the heat and the farmers were in despair. Wheat was particularly sensitive to heat, any disturbance hitting hard at yields. In village after village, they saw detritus – flags, discarded placards, posters – from processions and protests over the failed harvest.

Two hours later, they passed a village where the harvests were going on peacefully, where there were no signs of any unrest. The reason was revealed by a teashop owner, who told them, 'Our babu is a son of a farmer. And our MP also. And the MLA's wife is from here. Two years ago, they got the local Krishi Vigyan Kendra, the government organization responsible for farmer outreach, to give good-quality seeds to the farmers. They also had a person from the university to stay here all year working with our farmers. One company came and put small machines into the soil. The machines helped farmers give just the right amount of water exactly when the plants needed it. Earlier, they had been over-watering the plants, and watering them at the wrong times. The company also helped them understand how much fertilizer to apply and when. They also added a lot of compost made from the village leftovers and cow dung. Our farmers have had a bumper harvest this year. With the high prices, every farmer here will buy a two-wheeler.'

Swati was listening to him with a smile on her face when Bhura came back. He was not smiling. The reason for that became clear the moment they got back on the truck.

'A herd of elephants have come to the farm where we were supposed to stay tonight.'

'Why is that a problem for us staying there?'

'You don't understand. There haven't been elephants in this area for decades. They came a few years ago, but now, my friend tells me, they have started staying here all the time. Possibly because of the deforestation in their old haunts. Last year, a bunch of elephants died. There was a huge enquiry and now the forest department…well, they are not taking any chances. They've placed a full contingent of guards in this area, and we can't afford any questions.'

They had been on the road for seven hours that day already – the sun was overhead, and it was hot. Bhura's plan of staying in a safe house was dashed. As Swati drove, she glanced to the side and saw they were passing a place called Katni. She also noticed that her friend's brow was knitted in concentration, trying to figure out where they could stop. After a few minutes of silence, his brow cleared, and he dialled a number on his phone and spoke animatedly in a dialect that Swati did not quite follow. He ended the call and told Swati to keep driving straight. They would stop in another couple of hours. After two hours, they stopped at a petrol pump about half an hour past Rewa. It was clear from Bhura's body language that he was not very comfortable with the people who owned it. But he had managed to get them a plug-in point, and they stayed in the cabin, vehicle plugged in. It was too open a space for Swati to try and sneak to their little room, so she took a cue from Bhura, who had locked his door and was snoring loudly, to get some shuteye herself.

When they woke, the sun was beginning to set. Swati's watch told her that they had slept for three hours. Bhura and she swapped places, and as soon as they were enroute again, Swati took the opportunity to head back into the little room and, to her surprise, found them all sleeping. She shook Rajan and Thangam; Rajan, sleeping on a middle berth, woke after a bit of shaking, surprised to even find himself sleeping. Thangam, sleeping on the top berth, was a little harder to awaken, but a little more urgent shaking did the job.

But Arjun would not wake up. And, now, neither would Lakshmi.

51

Kashi

RAJAN TOOK HIS DAUGHTER'S UNCONSCIOUS BODY INTO his arms and rocked her. She seemed so young, her face calm, and her chest gently rising and falling with each breath. To all appearances, she was peacefully sleeping, except no amount of shaking could wake her up. They had exhausted the theertham from Poombarai, but there was the tiniest bit of rachandan left. They applied that on her, but to no avail.

'What about the water from the river?' asked Swati.

'I don't think so; I think that may have brought this on,' said Rajan.

Swati's face fell – she was the one who had brought the water.

'Paapa, don't blame yourself,' said Thangam, watching his chick. 'This is part of the journey we are all on. The river's water added more energy. My body has been preparing for this for a long time, so it could handle that energy. Arjun's body was the least prepared. Kutti is too young, else she could have withstood this.'

Rajan cradled his daughter in his arms, continuing to rock her back and forth, while softly chanting the Vishnu Sahasranama. That had always been his bedrock. And as he finished it, the pace of the rocking slowed, and Rajan's face had lost some of its manic despair.

'I had a dream,' he said to Thangam and Swati.

'I dreamt of this. Of Lakshmi not waking up. I was laying her body in front of a small white Narasimha idol with Goddess Lakshmi on his lap. There were marigold flowers strewn about. Then, we were travelling on a boat across a black river, and I could see bodies burning. A priest gave me some sandal paste, and when I applied it on her forehead, she woke up.'

'Where was this, you think?' Swati asked him.

'Kashi,' it was Thangam who answered.

Kashi, or Varanasi, was considered a city older than time, the site of a, some say, *the* Jyotirlinga, an endless, flaming form of Shiva. The paste, the old man explained, was most likely the prasad from the *Mangla Arati* when the lingam was bathed and worshipped with many offerings. The tickets to this ceremony sold out weeks in advance.

'Let me ask Bhura,' said Swati, darting back to the driver's cabin.

Rajan continued to rock his daughter gently, as though she was a little baby. Thangam sat opposite, looking down, with his palms placed on his knees. After a while, he looked up at Rajan, and spoke, 'Most problems have a solution, Thambi. We just need to break this one down. First, we need the prasad from the Mangla Arati at Kashi. This means, we need to be at the temple by 4 a.m. tomorrow, when the puja ends.' He smiled grimly to see Rajan's surprise. 'Yes, I have been there for the puja,' he said, and continued, 'Second, we have to evade detection at the temple, not just from our hunters but from others, tantrics, who can see our auras, like that woman from Srirangam. And every tantric worth his salt will be there. Lastly, we have to carry the prasad back to Kutti and Arjun-thambi and apply it.'

Just then Swati came back.

'Bhura said we could be in Varanasi in four hours.'

Thangam smiled. 'So that is one piece of the puzzle solved.'

Rajan then spoke, 'I know the priest, Krishna, at the Adi Keshava Temple in Varanasi. We studied together in the Patashala. He spoke no Tamil and the other boys made fun of him, so I was his only friend.'

'Was the Adi Keshava Temple part of your pilgrimage?'

'No, we stopped there because he was my friend, and we stayed for a couple of weeks because our fathers got along.'

'Is he still the priest there?'

'I'm not sure, but from a message I got from him a year ago, I think he was.'

'Can he be trusted?'

'I don't know, but I think so. We took a boat from the ghat next to the Adi Keshava Temple to another ghat, and then we walked to Kashi Vishwanath, and the priest took all of us in.'

'So, if your friend helps us, we will have cracked another piece of the puzzle.'

The old man's calm was infectious. Rajan stopped rocking Lakshmi and laid her down on a berth. He sat down next to Thangam and sighed. 'How do we evade the tantrics?'

Thangam turned his face away from Rajan and asked, 'Can you see my aura now?'

Rajan looked at the back of the old man's head and was surprised – he could no longer see the brown and gold thick pulsing aura.

Thangam turned towards Rajan again and asked, 'What about now?'

As soon as their eyes connected, there it was, that almost-liquid brown aura flashing gold in places. 'It's there now.'

Then it struck him. 'It needs eye-contact.'

'It needs eye-contact,' repeated the old man, nodding and smiling. 'Our eyes are the windows to our soul, and they need to connect with others to see certain truths. If your friend can be trusted, you and I will dress as blind, old priests and go with him to the temple. If that doesn't work, as a backup we can use my contact – an old constable in the Varanasi police – Bhura and I helped him recover a stolen idol from the Annapurna Temple once. He can help.'

Thangam laid out their plan. 'We drive to the Adi Keshava temple at Kashi. You will brief your friend and ask for his help. We will leave Kutti and Arjun-thambi in the truck, with Bhura and Paapa to watch over them, while you and I and your friend catch a boat by 3.30 a.m. We get the prasad, take the boat back and apply it on the others. All should be well.'

'All going well,' repeated Rajan grimly.

The drive to Kashi took just under four hours. They crossed into Uttar Pradesh, leaving the forests of the highlands behind and entered the Indo-Gangetic plain. Now, the traffic was high, and the going slow. When Swati and Bhura stopped for tea just after they crossed Mirzapur, the blast of heat that hit them when they got out showed them how much the highland forests of Madhya Pradesh had shielded them from the heat. With that cover gone, they could barely stand outside for a minute, even at night – and the tepid sherbet on offer was far too luridly orange to be either appetizing or safe. They beat a hasty retreat to the truck. Bhura, worried for his tyres, was driving very slowly, but, by 9 p.m., they were crossing the Ganga. Swati, who had never seen the Ganga before, felt a frisson pass through her. In the dark, all she could see was its inky-black surface – soft, rippling, alive, about half-a-kilometre wide, tranquilly flowing under the bridge. *This is the lifeline for hundreds of millions*, she thought.

Having crossed it, they turned right and trundled down a quiet leafy lane, coming to a stop in a parking lot in front of a group of unevenly built houses, with a small red shikhara rising above them all. Swati opened the hatch and Rajan and Thangam clambered out. Swati saw that he had removed any trace of makeup or disguise from his face, but had a towel wrapped around his head. Bhura said, 'There doesn't seem to be anywhere to plug the truck, and I don't know how long you'll take. It's very hot, so Swati and I will take the truck to the petrol bunk we just passed.' As Rajan and Thangam stepped out into the open, they reeled in the heat, their throats clenching for something cool to drink.

Rajan squinted in the dark, trying to recall the house he'd stayed in all those years ago. But when they walked closer, he found that the houses hadn't changed much with time, and the small Narasimha his father had given his hosts was still hanging above the small white house's doorway. He walked up to that house, took a deep breath, prayed to the Narasimha hanging above the doorway, and pressed the doorbell. In a few seconds, they heard footsteps followed by a male voice asking in Hindi, 'Who is it?'

Rajan answered.

The door flung open and a middle-aged (*when had Krishna grown so old?* Rajan asked himself), paunchy man stood there smiling.

'You shaved your head! You – who were so vain about your hair!' Krishna laughed, pulling Rajan into a hug. 'Come in, come in.'

Thangam and Rajan stepped in. 'Is your father with you?'

Rajan hung his head. His gentle father who, even after death, had been guiding them steadily on their journey. He missed him.

Krishna, interpreting Rajan's expression correctly, asked, 'When?'

'Almost a year ago.'

'I'm very sorry.'

'Thank you.'

'Have you eaten?'

'Yes.'

'Then have some buttermilk,' and then looking at Thangam, 'both of you.'

He drew them into a small living room, whose sea-green walls and beige tiled floor were lit by naked blue tube lights. A modest TV set within a shelf dominated one wall, while a brown sofa stood against another, with a couple of biscuit-coloured plastic chairs set beside it. A fan was moving hot air about without cooling them in any way. An old, erudite-looking man sat in one of the plastic chairs, propped with cushions, immersed in a book in his hand. Rajan, recognizing Krishna's father, Keshavan, touched his feet, but the man did not look up from his book, as he gave Rajan a perfunctory blessing. Krishna called out to his wife, and a tiny woman with very long hair came in with two glasses of buttermilk. They drank it gratefully.

'What brings you to Kashi?' asked Krishna.

Rajan looked at Thangam, before telling his audience the broad outlines of their predicament: Lakshmi had become unconscious when they were trying to raise their Kundalini shakti. He believed that the prasad from the Mangla Arati at Kashi Vishwanath could help. But there were people chasing them, possibly tantrics.

'And you dreamt that the prasad would help you?'

Rajan started. Keshavan had spoken, and now, for the first time, when he looked him in the eye, he saw a purple haze around the old man. Realization washed over him like a cold shower. *He knew. Oh God. He knew.*

Keshavan, seeing the shock on Rajan's face, laughed.

'Don't worry about me. I taught your father half the things he knew about Kundalini.' Rajan buried his face in his hands. His father was with him in so many ways. He found his eyes getting wet. Thangam placed a hand on his shoulder, and he felt calm flowing through him.

Krishna's father spoke again, 'You have the same gift as me – the gift of Ajna. And your aura is the strongest I have seen,' he paused and looked at Thangam. For a few seconds, he was silent and then continued, 'But your companion… I have never seen, nor ever imagined an aura like that.' There was wonder, and a touch, the faintest touch, of envy in that statement, noted Rajan.

'Sir, can you help my daughter?' he asked.

'How old is she?'

'She is twelve.'

'What were you about, starting her on that journey so early? The earliest that one should start is fifteen.'

'We did not have a choice.'

'What churanam are you taking daily?'

Rajan explained the churanam Lakshmi had made and that she brewed her own kashayam.

'So, she has the gift of Anahata. Those ones are usually

stubborn by nature. Think that their compassion makes them superior to the rest of us,' the old man mumbled. 'It is the same with my sister as well.'

He then asked Krishna to get a box from the shelf and took out a jar from within it. 'Take this with you. My sister prepares it. Each of you have a spoonful a day. It will make your body stronger. Also have your friend place his hands on your daughter's head or hold her palms. He has the gift of Mooladhara, and maybe Manipura as well. That will also help her. Since you dreamt that you need Vishwanath's prasad, you will have to go to the temple. Krishna will take you. Go and come back. I sense danger swirling around you. Be careful. You are not telling me everything, and I'm not asking you to, but be careful.'

'Sir…'

Thangam stood up. He had heard the truck pulling up outside.

'Sir…' Rajan continued. 'Can I bring my daughter here? Can you help her?'

The old man smiled. The mockery in his eyes vanished and only kindness shone through. 'Not here… carry her to the temple. The Narasimha shrine is known for its healing power.'

In a short while, they were climbing up the steep steps to the tiny temple, with both the old men leading the way. Rajan was carrying Lakshmi, Bhura carried Arjun, and Swati and Krishna followed. After ten or so steps, they passed between two buildings to enter a pillared hall, with a vaulted white ceiling and a chessboard black-and-white flooring. They could see the Ganga lapping away in the distance, almost gurgling as the River Varuna flowed into it. Many considered the Adi Keshava Temple to be the oldest temple of Varanasi, older than the Vishwanath Temple itself. Vishnu himself had fashioned the idol and bathed in the ghat, at the confluence of the two rivers.

Keshavan opened the door to the shrine, smiling. 'He's asleep, but he won't mind. So few come to see him, anyway.' He lit the small lamp on his plate and performed a small arati for the idol. Then he went to another chamber nearby, opened it and switched on the light. This was the Narasimha shrine that had appeared in Rajan's dream. Rajan laid his daughter on the floor and prayed fervently as the old man placed a little prasad into her mouth, and into Arjun's mouth as well.

They did not wake up.

'It seems your dream was right after all. Only Vishwanath can help you. Sleep here tonight. Krishna will take you and your friend to the temple in a few hours. Dress yourself as priests. Bandage your eyes. Some will be suspicious, but it can't be helped. Come back as quickly as you can.'

They stretched out in the pillared hall, with the cool breeze from the Ganga blowing over them. They had barely closed their eyes, before Krishna was shaking them to wake them.

Thangam and Rajan bathed and got into costume, with prosthetics attached to their cheeks and noses to match the IDs Thangam had arranged for them. As they were preparing to leave, Rajan had a disquieting feeling every time he looked at Thangam, a feeling he could not quite interpret.

The old man sensed his unease and asked him, but Rajan couldn't explain it. Just as they were about to descend the flight of steps leading to the ghat, they saw Keshavan rushing towards them. He looked anxious. 'Krishna and you go, I get the sense that if your friend goes with you, things will not work out well.'

So, his premonitions had basis, Rajan thought. But he was now torn as he realized how much he leaned on Thangam for strength, counsel, and even comfort. He was their safe port in a storm. And they were headed into a storm, no doubt about it. Swati and Bhura, with whom Rajan had not shared his thoughts, were surprised. Rajan and Krishna needed backup and it would take too long to get their disguises and matching IDs sorted out. Finally, Thangam himself came up with a compromise. 'Bhura and I will come with you, but only up to the ghat and will wait there, in case you need help. Will that work?'

Keshavan repeated, 'I still think it would be better if Rajan and Krishna went alone.'

As he saw Rajan wavering, Krishna said, 'We have to leave now. Decide what you wish but decide quickly.'

'Come,' he asked Thangam.

The four of them got into the boat and set off. At this time of night, there was very little traffic on the river; only the lights from the various ghats were reflected in the dark waters. Some of the ghats had music playing. The boatman, Bhura and Thangam chatted quietly at the back. Krishna dozed off, while Rajan sat at the prow of the boat, watching the boat cleave through the dark water. He couldn't shake off that unsettled feeling.

After twenty minutes of cruising, they saw pyres burning next to the river – this was the Manikarnika Ghat, where the flames of cremation reputedly never stopped. Rajan found watching the flames lick the air strangely meditative. After all, this was the one destination they were all headed to – the one great certainty of life. The boat slowed and drew to the edge of Dashashwamedh Ghat, and the boatman jumped out and moored the boat. Rajan shook himself out of his reverie, Krishna woke up, and the two of them walked towards the temple, Rajan taking care to keep his eyes down so as to not make eye contact with anyone. It should have been cool at this time of night, but it wasn't. Riding on the boat had made it seem cooler than it was, but now Rajan found sticky sweat running down his back. A ten-minute walk brought them to the temple, where the Mangla Arati had already begun and the crowds for the regular darshan were waiting to get in. Rajan donned his father's dark glasses – Swati had stuck plain paper on the inside, which meant that while he could not see through them, no one else would be able to see his aura.

Krishna knew this temple well – he had been coming to it since childhood – and easily took them into the temple enclosure, where the Mangla Arati was just finishing. Krishna spoke to another priest, a friend of his father's, and managed to get them both a place in the line. Soon, they were kneeling to touch the lingam, and as he did so, Rajan felt a frisson run through him and a jolt of electricity pass through the space between his brows. He got enough of the prasad to fill a small jar and moved with Krishna to the Dattatreya shrine. They were about to leave when they heard shouting. Thangam was standing in the temple entrance, his eyes sporting that glazed look Rajan had seen in Poombarai. Then, he was running at superhuman speed, dodging policemen and priests, before dropping on his knees before the lingam and embracing it. As the prasad touched him, he swooned and fell. The police, who had been chasing Thangam, lifted and hauled him off. Rajan and Krishna followed them unobtrusively, but it was hard given the crowd that had gathered around the cops and the fact that Rajan was pretending to be blind. Krishna saw the cops trying to lift Thangam onto a vehicle at the street entrance to the temple, when a group of men with matted hair came rushing towards the policemen, attacked them, and carried Thangam off in a small car.

As he told Rajan what was happening, Rajan was in a quandary: he knew he was not strong enough to take on the cops or the men who had kidnapped Thangam. He was pretending to be a blind man. If he tried mounting any kind of rescue, he would be caught, and where would that leave them? He should have listened to his own intuition, even if he had chosen not to trust Krishna's father. He was feeling wretched when Krishna said he had spied a familiar large figure following the car in a two-wheeler.

That gave Rajan some hope, and he and Krishna returned to the ghat and caught a boat. The sky was growing lighter, and soon they saw the white and red shikharas of the Adi Keshava Temple rise out of the Ganga in the distance. Rajan jumped off the boat, while Krishna paid the boatman, and ran up the steps. Swati was waiting with Krishna's father in the pillared hall. Neither had slept and both looked anxiously as the men entered. Swati noticed Thangam and Bhura's absence and asked, 'Where are they?'

Rajan quickly related what had happened. Swati broke down. Thangam was more of a father to her than her own father had ever been.

'Have you got the prasad?' asked Keshavan.

Rajan gave him the jar. The old man took the paste and applied it in the shape of a serpent on the foreheads of Lakshmi and Arjun. Their eyes fluttered and opened. In the rising sun's light, their irises looked almost ochre in colour.

'What happened?' asked Arjun. Then, looking around, 'Where are we?' and at the old man bending down over him, 'Who is he?'

Lakshmi and Arjun were ravenous. Krishna and his wife did not have children of their own, and they fussed over Lakshmi, feeding her whatever she wanted. Arjun chatted with Krishna's father while Rajan held Swati, comforting her. Swati wanted to use the burner phone to call Bhura. Rajan advised caution; they needed that phone. It was better to wait, however agonizing that was.

Keshavan looked at Arjun and Lakshmi as though they were made of gold. He saw a pulsing aura of deep red around the child, streaked with gold, as though *Sesha* himself swirled protectively around her. Arjun too had a thick aura, almost like a coat around him – mostly blue, but with red and purple winking at the edges. *This should not be possible*, he thought to himself. In the recesses of his mind, an old memory stirred. Something his grandfather had told him long ago. Something about restoring balance and how the path of Kundalini would show the way. That story had inspired his lifelong quest into understanding the serpent power, and even now, his practice deepened every day. His son's friend's aura was the strongest he had ever seen, but even so, it was a matchstick held against the wildfire of the auras of the other three. Keshavan was old and his knees ached, even with his meticulous exercise regimen and his sister's unguents. But maybe it was the Kundalini, or maybe it was the mischievousness that had made him the despair of many a teacher, but he decided he would join this motley group.

Just then the phone in Swati's hand rang. She picked it up and listened to the voice at the other end give her precise instructions, before ending the call and breaking the phone. 'He's safe. We need to pick them up from the petrol pump just before Ghazipur in three hours.'

52

The Vishkanyas – Part 3

THE SUN HAD RISEN WHEN AN ALERT APPEARED ON THE Vishkanyas network. An operative watched an old man running, with more grace and speed than a twenty-year-old Olympian, through the corridors leading to the Kashi Vishwanath Temple. Policemen tried to stop him, but they only succeeded in loosening his prosthetic disguise. The Vishkanyas operative sat up. It was their quarry. At least one was alive and in Varanasi. Within minutes, they put out a general alert on the city, tapping into every CCTV stream from next to the Vishwanath shrine. It took two hours for the most sophisticated image recognition software in the world to find that the old man had been captured by six men and carted away. It took a few more hours to find the registration details of the car. That had led to a small choultry where a bunch of chillum-smoking tantrics were lolling about. The quarry had long since escaped.

53

The Journey – Part 3

IT TOOK OVER AN HOUR TO PACK UP AND LEAVE. KESHAVAN had fifty books he wanted to bring. Any suggestion of leaving them sparked veiled threats. Arjun, who was lost in one of them, backed Keshavan. Then, there were his churanams and churanam-making ingredients. Those took up three large boxes. When Rajan protested, Keshavan retorted, 'You are travelling in a truck!'

Krishna and his wife packed more food into their pantry, before locking up their house and leaving for a pilgrimage. Rajan had told them what kind of people hunted them, and while Keshavan sensed no immediate danger, leaving appeared to be a wise choice.

Finally, they were on the road. Without a smartphone, Swati would have struggled to find their way, but Keshavan sat beside and guided her, keeping his eyes down as much he could. The streets were empty, and in a few minutes, they were on the highway, and Swati stepped on the gas. It was getting hot, but the tyres had been unused for hours, and besides, she missed Thangam and Bhura.

The sun rose, and the flat road stretched before her, with fields as far as the eye could see on either side of the road. Keshavan talked endlessly – he clicked his tongue in disapproval while gazing out – the wheat crop was shrivelling up – 'See,' he said, pointing to it, even though Swati could not take her eyes off the road. 'The plant is stunted. It can't take the heat. It was never meant to be grown here. We broke the balance long ago; now we pay.'

The highway was wide, several lanes across, and well-laid. There was some traffic – the two-wheelers had stayed off the road because of the heat, but other trucks were still plying. The small trees planted on the side of the road could have done with watering. Periodically, they saw cows wandering across the highway. Swati nearly hit one, and the truck swerved as she turned to avoid it. She had been distracted by Keshavan, who had been pontificating on the consequences of climate-negligent crop choice, and nearly hit the cow. She bluntly told him to shut up, but he was impervious to criticism. So, she slyly suggested he check up on Lakshmi, knowing his fascination with the others would get him out of her hair. It worked. He opened the hatch and disappeared into the room.

He found Lakshmi munching on the *kachori* sabzi made by Krishna's wife. The woman had also left them a large earthen pot of cool *thandai* to enjoy. Keshavan smiled and sat next to Arjun. Rajan had been trying to get them started on the meditations, but with little success. The old man, however, tried a different tack.

'You're stupid for someone with a well-activated Vishuddha,' he said to Arjun.

Stung, Arjun asked, 'What makes you say that?'

'If I had your power, I would want to use it, not lie flat on my back like a tired-out tapeworm.'

Lakshmi giggled and even Rajan smiled. The old man was certainly adopting some unusual tactics.

'It's really hard to stretch in this little room.'

'But you can still work on your breathing.'

It was very difficult to argue with him. Rajan noticed a little blue mixed in with the violet in Keshavan's aura. He had his Vishuddha activated as well. That cleared things up a bit.

The breathing techniques that Keshavan taught them were far more complex than those in Rajan's father's journal. They involved opening and closing different nostrils, specific loci to focus upon during inhalations and others during exhalations, and these practices varied in count and intensity.

After an hour, they felt like they had run a marathon, and lay back on the berths. The old man smiled sweetly and pityingly said he never imagined they would be such weaklings, which left Arjun seething. Before he could retort, Keshavan returned to the driver's cabin.

Swati spied a petrol bunk coming up, and she began to slow down. She could not wait to pick up Bhura and

Thangam – she missed them so – and Keshavan was getting on her nerves. As she neared the station, she saw two burqa-clad figures walking next to the road – the shorter of the two looked up at them in the truck, and the old man laughed, 'Why is your friend dressed like that?'

She pulled the truck to the side of the road, and the two men clambered up. Swati hugged Thangam. Leaving Bhura to Keshavan's tender mercies, she and Thangam entered the little room.

But Keshavan soon followed them – the temptation to hear Thangam's story was too strong. He saw Thangam sitting between Lakshmi and Swati, holding both their hands. 'I'm very sorry, Thambi,' he said to Rajan. 'I seem to be saying this a lot nowadays. I don't know what it was – we were waiting for you – Bhura and I – at the boat. Then the bells tolled. Something changed inside me. Something else took over. I don't remember anything until I woke up on a stone floor. It seemed like a temple, but the vibe was wrong. Almost like a buzzing in my ears. I got up, and opened a door, and there were people in red robes sitting there. When they saw me, they tried to stop me – using weapons, both physical and mental. But I overpowered them and came out. I was in an old building – like the choultry in Srirangam – with a path leading out. I ran down that path and came to a gate when Bhura came out of hiding and met me. We drove to Ghazipur, picking up the burqas on the way.'

'How many people were there?' asked Arjun.

'Maybe ten.'

'How did you overpower so many?' Swati asked.

It was Keshavan who answered.

'It's his Manipura. I first thought it was only your Mooladhara which was activated, because of your aura's colour, but now that I look closely, I can see the fine orange woven into the brown. Your Manipura's fully active. I would wager that no one can beat you in combat. Maybe that's why you stayed conscious through Rajan's clumsy attempts to activate your chakras.'

Rajan folded his lips but did not rise to the bait.

Arjun was about to say something, but Thangam continued, 'But with the disturbance I caused, I think it is very likely that our hunters will know where we are. And given how cunningly they track, they will connect us with this truck.'

Silence followed as the group thought hard. They had two groups after them, possibly working together. The group that bombed Rajan's house and temple, the man with the deadly aura in Srirangam – were they connected? And what about the men with matted hair at Varanasi? Had they wanted only Thangam?

Keshavan's eyes lit up as his mercurial mind tried to connect the threads.

'And with all your gifts, I suppose no one bothered to tell you about the gift of delving that Ajna gives?'

The confusion on their faces answered his question.

'What you would have done if I hadn't been there, I shudder to think,' he said as he took out a betel leaf. Then he turned to them and asked, 'Do you have anything that these people touched, or did they touch any of you?'

Thangam answered, 'The young priest in Srirangam touched this backpack, and possibly me and Arjun-thambi. The young tantric woman who rescued us carried Arjun. The men with matted hair in Varanasi carried me.'

Rajan added, 'I think one of my family members, a cousin, could also be caught up in this.'

Keshavan held a wick soaked in ghee over a plate and then lit it with a match. It burned, leaving a black sooty residue on the plate. He took the soot, and applied it on the fingertips of Thangam, Arjun and Rajan, and asked them to touch the betel leaf. Feeling remarkably foolish, Rajan obeyed, while Arjun mumbled, 'I didn't sign up for this mumbo-jumbo.'

Keshavan then touched the leaf and gazed intently at it, seemingly concentrating on it, while the rest of them remained silent. After a minute or so, he opened his eyes and said, 'Nothing. I can't sense anything.'

'Big surprise,' Arjun mumbled.

'Is there another way, Thaatha?' asked Lakshmi.

'Maybe, child.'

'Let us join hands, all of us, and think a simple question: Is there anyone following us right now?' He turned to Rajan and said, 'Then, you and I need to tap into the universe and see what it throws up.'

'What universe?' Arjun asked, not bothering to keep his sarcasm hidden.

'The one within, that connects us all,' answered Keshavan.

They did as he asked and were soon seated holding hands in a circle.

'Keep your doubts out; that clouds the query,' warned Keshavan.

'I honestly don't think I can,' Arjun replied.

'That's a pity. We could have used your power, but if you can't, then it's better you stay out,' the old man replied.

Arjun sat apart, while the rest of them joined hands.

'Now remember,' said Keshavan. 'Focus only on this question: Is there anyone following us right now? Close your eyes. I will guide your breathing and speak this question. Focus and ask the universe to help us.' He turned to Rajan. 'Look for the images that pop up in your mind; note them, but don't analyse them, just let them come, we will discuss later.'

He then turned to the group and said, 'Close your eyes.'

They obeyed.

'Take a deep breath and now let it out. Another. Now focus on my voice. Is there anyone following us right now?'

The only sounds were the hum of the AC, the buzz of rubber on road, and their breathing. They stayed in the circle for five minutes.

Rajan found the old man's voice hypnotic. He was holding hands with Keshavan and Lakshmi. At first there was nothing, and then as his anxiety fell away and he became fully immersed in the moment, he saw figures appear in the periphery of his mind's eye, but none stood out clearly before he heard the old man say, 'Now open your eyes.'

He turned to Rajan, and asked, 'Well?'

'I saw figures appearing in the periphery, nothing more.'

Keshavan smiled. 'With this much power feeding into our circle, we can be confident that, while our enemies are in pursuit, they have not yet caught our scent.'

A sigh of relief passed around the group.

54

Gorakhpur

THEY REACHED GORAKHPUR WELL PAST LUNCHTIME. Arjun was awake, which made the little room far less peaceful. He felt the need to share everything that he learned. He was reading from a book he had found in Keshavan's library, and exclaimed, 'Hey, this Gorakhnath is one of the eighteen Siddhars – they call them *mahayogis* here. He also said awakening the Kundalini was critical in attaining balance. Shows that once you go within, everything seems the same. In Tamil Nadu, he's called Korakkar. He is another of Bhogar's disciples, like Sattaimuni, whose samadhi you,' he pointed to Thangam, 'stopped me from visiting. Gorakhpur was named after him.'

To keep him quiet, Keshavan gave him a book on the deeper powers of Mooladhara and Manipura. As Arjun disappeared behind the book, the others heaved a sigh of relief.

They parked their truck near a small Durga temple that stood within the Kushmi forest, where Keshavan's cousin worked as a priest. Keshavan trusted his cousin; Rajan did not. But after Thangam's outburst in Kashi, their hunters had likely picked up their scent and the container truck was a dead giveaway. They packed disguises, fake IDs, food, two bags of Keshavan's books and supplies, and Rajan's backpack with his father's journal, the book, and a few keepsakes, before boarding a tempo van to the India–Nepal border.

The ride to Sonauli took three hours – the most uncomfortable three hours that they had experienced in their journey. The heat. The soul-sapping heat! The air-conditioning in the van was dodgy. Plus they did not drink too much water, because the driver had warned them that they would not be stopping for bio breaks. This combo left them dangerously dehydrated in the heat. Rajan looked at his daughter with concern – she had briefly brightened up after Kashi, but she seemed to be wilting as the day progressed. He doubted it was just the heat because even as her body weakened, he saw that her aura strengthened. It was the same with Arjun, except that he became more sarcastic. Tempers frayed in the heat, and his gibes became grating, leading to a lot of bickering in the van. Thangam's aura also strengthened, but he did not show signs of weakening.

The crossing went smoothly – their fake IDs were flawless, and Keshavan's was genuine. They found themselves in a Nepali border town, with money-changers, SIM card providers, touts, food stalls, and buses headed to every part of Nepal. Heat and dehydration had left them weak. Keshavan had stomach problems, which prompted an extended stop in the bathroom. The others guzzled water, dousing themselves with it to cool down. That was when they saw some of the coolies, who helped people with their luggage, passed out in the heat.

Arjun was sitting next to a food stall where a bunch of college kids, obviously on an excursion, were milling about. They were loud, which set his teeth on edge. He saw that they were tossing their snack packets to the ground, even though a perfectly usable dustbin (and a segregated dustbin at that) stood nearby. The straw that broke Arjun's silence was a kid wearing a 'Net Zero by 2050' T-shirt tossing a soda bottle onto the ground right next to where a coolie had fallen in the heat.

Swati, sitting next to Arjun, expected him to blow up. Instead, Arjun merely said, 'Hey, nice T-shirt.'

The kid smiled and thanked him.

Arjun persisted, 'Gosh, this heat. That soda,' he said, pointing to the bottle on the ground, 'must have been so refreshing.'

'It was,' the kid answered.

Arjun rose, bought a cold bottle of water and gave it to the barely conscious coolie, who smiled his thanks. Then he deliberately picked up the soda bottle and dropped it into the dustbin. The other kids had seen this entire episode. Some of them began mocking the kid wearing the T-shirt. Arjun stopped them. 'Mocking her is easy. But there are twenty bottles on the ground, and countless packets. This is on all of us. It will take less than ten minutes to clean it up, if we work together. Who's with me?'

Three kids came forward. They and Arjun, who drew from unknown reserves of strength to keep going, began cleaning. When their eyes met briefly, Rajan could see his aura swell and swirl, where the blue of Vishuddha was tinged with the red of Anahata and the orange of Svadhishthana. His earlier conjecture had been right: the activation of the other chakras was helping, increasing the resonance somehow.

One coolie struggled to stand up and help. Seeing him, more kids began to pitch in. Swati and Rajan joined them. Lakshmi got up, but Thangam pulled her down again – he did not want her to exert herself. In less than ten minutes, the entire ground next to the food stalls became litter-free. The food stall owners brought out several big sacks to hold the litter. Soon everyone in the bus stand area was cleaning, and in another fifteen minutes, the entire area was spotless. Others had dragged the coolies inside and plied them with water and glucose.

The kids glowed with a sense of achievement. Arjun smiled at them. 'Don't you feel better? Once you see yourself as part of the solution – and we all are part of the problem and the solution – it becomes easy.'

Bhura, who had gone to buy tickets, tugged at Arjun's sleeve. He had managed to get tickets for all of them on an overnight bus to Kathmandu and it was about to leave. Rajan dragged Keshavan from the bathroom, threatening to leave him behind if he did not come now.

The college kids were waving to them as their bus left the station. The bus – an air-conditioned luxury bus – was decorated in tropical themes of blue, and had a kitschy blue ceiling, brown fans, polyester curtains across its windows, and even a plug point next to the seats.

They began climbing the emerald mountains, which slid into one another like interlocking fingers, with a river cutting through the centre. The roads had been tolerable thus far, but upon entering the mountains, they became terrible – almost non-existent muddy affairs, clinging perilously to the mountain's edge.

The bus crossed a metal suspension bridge over a gleaming river; Swati saw mountains stretch out indefinitely in every direction. They were deep in the Himalaya, they could feel their souls became more conspicuous, making them feel lighter and yet more grounded in the present. After a couple of hours, they stopped at a roadside dhaba for an early dinner. They had not gained too much altitude, but the forests that surrounded them in every direction made it seem much cooler. The heat was nowhere as oppressive as in Sonauli or Varanasi. They opted for a surprisingly tasty dal and rice, which they washed down with some buttermilk, and Keshavan gave them all some of his churanam. He also taught Thangam to calm them through his Mooladhara energy, so that they could get a good night's rest.

'It's very easy. Just hold their hands and think of making them peaceful by visualizing your energy flowing through your hands into theirs.'

Thangam repeated the exercise with each of them, and they fell asleep effortlessly. Rajan, although he too had fallen asleep quickly, found himself turning in his seat after a few hours, because his dreams were especially vivid that night. He dreamt of blood, of the same dark and pointed toenails standing next to him, of taking a friend's hand and falling into a ravine, of steel-blue mountains with snow-capped peaks, of an azure lake underneath a cobalt sky, of golden eyes. He woke with a start to find Lakshmi sleeping peacefully next to him. A quick glance around the bus showed that all his companions were asleep, except Keshavan, who was gazing at his phone.

Something felt off, but before he could unpack what it was, Rajan dozed off again, and woke up hours later to see a beautiful Himalayan tableau, with orange sunlight glinting off snow-capped peaks in the distance. His daughter was stirring; he woke her up and excitedly pointed to the peaks. Lakshmi was thrilled, as he knew she would be. She saw the sun rise over the curl of the grey river flowing in a ravine by the side of the road. A band of bright green terraced fields lay further beyond the ravine, with swathes of deep emerald forests above them, and then further back, at the edge of the horizon, a jagged line of snow-covered mountains with a yellow-blue sky above. She felt her soul laughing – it was a wonderful feeling.

Rajan saw her aura pulse bright red, and his joy evaporated, leaving a sticky residue of anxiety behind. 'What were you thinking just now, Lakshmi?' he asked with concern.

'The beauty made my soul laugh, Appa.'

Even in paradise, fear gnawed at him as he remembered the lines from the book:

'But without the waters that cooled Halahala's breath
The rising snake brings certain death.'

As though in response to these words, Lakshmi slumped down into her seat. Suddenly, he couldn't wait to be done with this journey. A signboard said they were forty kilometres from Kathmandu. Vasant Purnima was tonight. Tonight, they would get to the waters that could save his daughter.

But just then, the bus had a puncture.

55

The Vishkanyas – Part 4

BY AFTERNOON, FOUR VISHKANYA OPERATIVES HAD reached Varanasi. Two operatives went to the choultry with the tantrics. Another group went through the camera feed from the Dashashwamedh Ghat. A close inspection suggested that at least two were from the group they were tracking. They continued examining the camera feeds from that location and discovered that Rajan and another man had returned to the ghat, catching another boat and speeding away.

That evening, an operative visited the boatman, who told him that he had taken the two men to the Adi Keshava Ghat in the morning. The operative called his partner, who hacked into the CCTV feeds near that temple. There were just two feeds, one near the ghat itself and one near the parking lot next the temple. That data did not take too much time to parse. All members of the quarry were present, along with a large man with a beard, an older, smaller man and a middle-aged couple. The operative saw the group, except for the middle-aged couple, leave in a container truck. She noted down the registration plate of the truck. The middle-aged couple left a little later, on a two-wheeler. She noted the registration plate of that vehicle too.

The Vishkanyas representative called the professor.

'Varanasi!' he said. 'That far north! How did they get so far without discovery?'

'We are on to them.'

'Do you know where they are headed next?'

'We have the registration details of the vehicles. We know the truck is headed further north. It has reached Gorakhpur. We are tracking the two-wheeler. We are also interrogating some tantrics who captured the old man. We believe we have them.'

'Understood. But given the developments, someone from our side will be joining your operations.'

'Understood.'

Interlude

THE MAN'S MEETING WITH THE HEADS OF THE OTHER meteorological organizations of the world was later that day. The El Niño showed no signs of fading away, though it should typically have by now.

Data from the Argo floats exposed sustained deep ocean temperature anomalies, even as the buoys showed that temperatures in the Niño 3.4 region remained elevated. There was no telling when this beast would weaken.

The Indians were reporting that the TEJ (the Tropical Easterly Jet) was weak and delayed, boding ill for their monsoon. His friend there told him that the nights in the north were so hot that people were dying. One or two cities had implemented their heat action plans, keeping their citizens safe, but many had not, and the vulnerable were suffering. The wheat crop was lost in most places, and the unrest was growing.

If things did not change soon, India was staring down the barrel of a failed monsoon.

Action on mitigating the climate had been uneven –

some rushing ahead, others pointing fingers, and still others trying to stall action altogether – and now, they were paying the price.

He was not a religious man, but he bent his head and prayed.

The world needed a miracle. And soon.

56

Vasant Purnima

IT WAS COOLER BY FAR IN KATHMANDU, AND THE companions finally poured out of the bus in relief. Arjun and Lakshmi were too weak to walk alone, but something told Rajan not to ply them with more churanam. He applied a little of the prasad from Varanasi on their foreheads and tried to bottle up his anxiety while Bhura expertly negotiated their transport and stay and efficiently organized their transfer to a homestay in a suburb of Kathmandu called Gokarna.

Rajan managed to get himself and Thangam alone in a smaller cab with the luggage, leaving the others in a larger cab. He asked Thangam to repeat their delving exercise, cuing himself to breathe as Keshavan had taught him. This time, there were more figures coming out of the shadows, their outlines clearly visible – one was travelling by bus, four by plane. Once again, he saw dark and pointed toenails outside a shining bronze door, and a pool of blood. Then the figures opened their eyes; Rajan looked up and told Thangam, 'They are after us.'

Thangam remained silent for a few minutes. Like Lakshmi, his aura had grown in the Himalayas, and in the old man's case, that just made him stronger and even more grounded. 'Let's not share this with the others for now. Especially not in front of Arjun-thambi,' he said.

Rajan was puzzled, and asked himself: *Why did Thangam suspect Arjun?*

The old man continued as though he had read Rajan's thoughts. 'Arjun-thambi is strong with Vishuddha – perhaps too strong. Which means he can transmit to those who have their antennas up. Paapa told me that you think that that's how the man we met at Poombarai was able to guess that we were headed to Srirangam. I too think that's what happened. But, no matter what we say, Arjun-thambi won't shield his thoughts.'

He paused. And then continued, 'Tell me now, Thambi, where do we have to be tonight?'

Rajan whispered it to him.

The old man smiled. 'We will be there. By God's grace, we have come so far. We will make it to the next step. But we have to be careful. Here is my plan for this evening.'

She looked out of the window, and noted, without excitement, that the peaks were tall enough to poke through the clouds. She could hear the gasps around her, as her fellow passengers took photos of Everest. She went back to her notes.

How did they slip through our net, across the length of India? she asked herself. Clearly the quarry had skills, which only made them worthy prey.

Her notes showed pictures that the team had collated: A tall man, a thin child, a tall woman, an old man, and a short and flabby man. But the grainy images from the latest CCTV camera capture in Varanasi showed that they had all become far fitter. The flabby man had shaved while the tall man and the old man had grown beards but shaved part of their heads.

She watched the video from Varanasi again. The old man moved with a speed that no human could have possessed and shook off those trying to restrain him with an inhuman strength. The Vishkanyas had made a note of that and had resolved to discover the secret behind that strength.

She looked through the notes from the team who had visited the tantrics. The tantrics were after the same secret but had failed to get it.

Her instructions had changed: capture, but don't kill the tall man or the child. The reasoning was that those two were the most likely to know the secret of this power. Capture the woman alive, if possible. She could prove useful; torturing her could motivate the others to reveal the secrets.

In her earlier life, the Vishkanya had been a passionate defender of women's rights. She had been hurt badly as a woman. But there was nary a wrinkle in her mind at this instruction – the Vishkanyas' training was nothing if not thorough.

Their homestay turned out to be a small cottage next to a forest with a riotous explosion of flowers to greet them at the entrance. After freshening up, they regrouped in a cool living room from where they could see the mountains.

'Where do we need to go, O Great One?' quizzed Arjun, peeling and eating a banana. 'You have been so cagey until now.'

Swati marvelled at how Arjun changed from persuasive and thoughtful when he spoke about issues he cared about to sarcastic and blasé at other times.

Rajan took a deep breath. The time for disclosure had come.

'The Changu Narayan Temple lies a short way from here. A devotee severed Vishnu's head by accident, but the Lord forgave him and blessed him. Our destination, however, is a smaller shrine within the complex – it is a rare form of the Mother Goddess – where she is holding her own severed head in her hand, and drinking her own blood, while standing on an entwined human couple. We have to drink the blood from that shrine to gain power.'

'Charming,' said Arjun.

Lakshmi was about to speak, but Rajan, who was sitting next to her, squeezed her shoulder before continuing, 'It makes sense, Arjun – think about it – the severed head is about cutting off your ego and opening yourself to the universal consciousness – the seventh chakra. The entwined couple is a nod to Svadhishthana – the creativity that powers all life. And the blood represents both the spirit of sacrifice required in this journey, and the power needed to ascend to the next level.'

Arjun looked unconvinced. But Keshavan, for some reason, looked positively gleeful.

With a few hours left before they had to leave, Thangam, Arjun, Lakshmi and Bhura embarked on a raucous game of cards. Keshavan said he would visit a small temple next door. Rajan and Swati snatched a quiet moment together.

Rajan looked at the woman lying down next to him, the woman who had changed his life. He thought back to the moment they had met, when she had called him out for his care of Lakshmi – how long ago that seemed. He had been stubborn. If he had remained that way, the quest would have never succeeded. He owed her everything, he realized, pulling her closer.

'Ow! What was that for?' Swati said, as Rajan's hold grew too tight.

'For being you.'

She looked at him – this quiet, awkward man, who loved so deeply. Then she saw Rajan's face grow serious.

'I have to tell you something. But before that, I want you

to shield your thoughts with extra care.' And then, as they snuggled even closer, he whispered Thangam's plan into her ears.

A little later, they came out to find Bhura and Thangam sipping tea. Swati took them aside to prepare for the evening while Rajan rechecked his backpack. The book, his father's journal, the album, Radha's jewellery set, some cash, IDs, disguises and the remaining prasad from Kashi were all there. That was the sum total of his material possessions. He had no room for more baggage.

There was an hour until sunset. Rajan went into the room he shared with his daughter to find her stirring. As he looked down at her, his heart swelled with pride – she was gentle, intelligent, self-sufficient, compassionate. How she had blossomed – she would change the world. But, and his heart constricted at the thought, only if she survived the night. He sat at her side and stroked her hair. She woke up. He hugged her before carrying her to the sofa.

Outside, he found Thangam and Swati helping Arjun out of his room. As they began their exercises, Swati felt there was an air of solemnity to it, almost as if this was the last time they would do it together. Bhura was just completing his Asr prayer, when Keshavan entered the room. The old man looked surprisingly grim, but when asked about it, replied he had been making arrangements: it was a full moon night, when the crowds would be immense and they would not be able to enter the temple without help. He had been speaking to a priest, who knew a priest in the Changu Narayan Temple. That man would be waiting for them near the car park to help them.

They watched the sunset from the garden. It was a clear day and they could see Kathmandu stretched below them, with green hills encircling it, and the mighty Himalaya stretching across the horizon, their snow-capped peaks turning peach in the twilight. Then they left the house, with Rajan, Lakshmi, Swati and Thangam in one minivan, while Bhura, Arjun and Keshavan following them in another.

Rajan felt like he was in a trance. *Can we actually change anything?* he asked himself. Against a planet in disorder. Imbalanced. Forces exploiting the chaos, growing in it, feeding off it. A planet in flames, where life-giving rain came late, or became a scourge, a deluge. All they had behind them were centuries of effort, of secrets and rituals, passing from father to son, leading to this moment. The immensity of it weighed on him. Thangam sensed some of this. The old man said, 'Remember your truth. As within, so without. An ocean in a drop. The drop becomes the ocean.' His words, almost identical to what his father had told him all those years ago, infused Rajan's heart with hope. The old man was holding Lakshmi's hands, his eyes closed. He squeezed, and Rajan saw his aura glow like luminous sunlight, while Lakshmi's pulsed as well, not her usual red, but more orange. She sat up straighter, stronger, while the old man slumped a little. Rajan understood. Thangam was infusing her with his power.

The cars drove up the short distance to the temple and dropped them off a hundred meters from the temple. It was as Keshavan had said – packed. A thin man was waiting for them in the car park; he had an aura, Rajan saw, although the colour was rather muddy and weak. They got down and began inching forward. Pushing through was hard, given how weak Arjun was – he seemed to be sinking with each passing minute. Lakshmi, thanks to Thangam's boost, was able to walk without assistance, but Rajan and Thangam had to support Arjun, while Keshavan led the way with the guide. It took them half an hour to reach the temple. The crowds were so great; it would have been impossible to enter without their guide.

The Changu Narayan Temple was considered one of the oldest temples in Nepal, dating back to at least the fourth century AD. The main structure had a two-storey pagoda-type tiled roof covered with sheets of copper and gold, supported by lavishly carved wooden supports. Sculptures from the Licchavi period, including one that appeared in the currency notes of the country, were strewn around the temple compound. The main pagoda rested on a stone pedestal within a courtyard that contained smaller shrines dedicated to other deities.

The courtyard was so crowded that they were literally pushed around the temple. As the moon rose, they found themselves close to a smaller structure, more wide than tall, with three bronze doors and a wide metal roof. It was the building from his dream, Rajan realized. An unfinished statue of a stone elephant stood nearby. Rajan noted that the number of people with auras swelled near the shrine. Clearly, this was a magnet for those walking on the path of the Kundalini. He had asked Thangam, Lakshmi and Arjun to keep their eyes down, but was not surprised to see Arjun looking around. He clicked his tongue in annoyance; with their auras, their group would be shining like a beacon.

As they drew closer, Rajan tripped, and would have surely fallen, had Thangam not grabbed on to him. The power emanating from that place! Of all the forms of the Goddess, Chhinnamasta was considered to be one of the fiercest. And here, her power was palpable. Thangam glowed. Arjun was almost able to stand without support. Lakshmi shivered. Her father looked at her with concern, but she smiled at him reassuringly. There was no weakness now, her smile seemed to say, only strength.

A man entered the shrine holding a flaming torch. The light fell strongly on all of them, and when Rajan cast his eyes down to avoid the glare, he saw the flame illuminate their guide's feet. The toenails were very dark and very pointed.

Rajan stiffened.

Keeping a mental shield in place, he gestured to the guide to enter the shrine after the man carrying the flame. The guide obeyed and entered, followed by Keshavan, and the crowd pushed after them, but Rajan held back. Instead, he stretched his hand over his head – this was the signal Thangam and Swati had been waiting for. They turned and ran. Thangam had flung Arjun over his shoulder, ignoring his protests, and was parting the crowds with ease, moving steadily towards the exit; Swati followed him, grabbing Lakshmi's hand. Lakshmi was surprised for a moment but did not protest, as she saw the urgency on her father's face when he turned and took her other hand. As he did, he felt an energy course from her little palm to his and felt her stumble. His head began tingling like it was being pricked by a thousand pins and needles.

Ahead of them, Thangam had clearly told Arjun what was happening, because Arjun began to shout, asking people to make way, and the people complied, obeying him without question. Rajan saw a blue glow envelop Arjun and realized his Vishuddha was at work.

Then, in the recesses of his mind, Rajan felt like he was being hunted. He turned and saw two young women and a young man, all enveloped with the same deadly aura of the young priest from Srirangam, step out from behind the Chhinnamasta Shrine and rush after them. Then, he saw, in the corner of the main shrine, standing on a platform, a little higher than the crowd, a beautiful woman. She did not chase them like the others did, but watched, much like a tiger hidden in the grass watches its prey, gauging the perfect time to pounce. She caught Rajan's eye, and she smiled. A slow smile that sent a cold trickle of sweat down Rajan's back. She was the woman from his dreams.

Something clicked and suddenly, it all made sense – *she* was the tracker, the huntress.

Rajan was unsurprised to feel the whoosh of a dart sing past his ear. What did surprise him was that he had sensed what would happen two seconds before it actually did and was thus able to move his head out of the way. *Lakshmi did this*, he realized, understanding the import of that energy transfer when he had taken her hand. Then, seizing this advantage, he grabbed an offering plate left near a shrine and began using it as a shield, facing his enemy now and shielding the others from their darts.

Aah!

He had stepped on a flame and fallen. The huntress smiled and slowly began moving in for the kill. But Lakshmi had stopped too and had bent to place her little hand over her father's foot. He shouted at her, asking her to save her strength, but she ignored him. There was a flash, Lakshmi glowed red, and his pain disappeared. More than that. He felt better and stronger than he had in days. The pins-and-needles sensation in his head had morphed into a resonant clarity. As he looked around, he could perceive a jumble of thoughts and emotions of those around him. Lakshmi had done more than heal, she had activated his Ajna. But as she slumped down, he saw the toll that had taken. The huntress drew closer. Rajan looked at her and could now clearly hear her thoughts – her single-minded purpose, yes, but also the bloodlust that consumed her. He recoiled from the violence of her intent and crouched over his daughter; he had no other shield but his body. Swati, who had stopped when she heard Rajan scream, ran back and now stood over him.

The huntress almost felt pity. Almost. *This was the fearsome family?*, she thought to herself, *they were pitiful – no power at all.* She took out her dagger. As much as she loved the tang and mouthfeel of blood, she found the scent of terror even more intoxicating. She slowed her pace, savouring the scent, feeling it grow, licking her lips.

Swati looked around frantically, but there was no sign of Thangam and Arjun. The other woman was closing in, pushing through the crowd with ease. The assassins approached as well; by some silent pact, they had let the huntress strike first. But they were ready – if she failed, they would not let the prey escape.

Swati took Rajan's hand – if this was the end, they would face it together – as they exchanged a smile of grim understanding while covering Lakshmi together.

Suddenly, at the edge of his consciousness, Rajan sensed a protective presence, like a cool cloth laid on the forehead on a hot day, and two monks – one with a long grey beard, wiry and tall, and the other younger and well-muscled – came running from behind one of the small shrines, emerging just behind the young assassins. As their eyes met, Rajan saw powerful auras swirl around them, purple, orange and brown, woven together. They pressed their fingers on the necks of two of the young assassins, who crumpled and were trampled by the crowd. The last assassin stopped, turning to face this new foe.

The huntress was surprised, Rajan could feel that, and she paused for a moment, gauging the importance of this new threat.

And in that moment, something charged at her. Something that was moving so fast, it did not appear human. Something that threw her so high up in the air that she landed on the platform with a thud and lay still.

Thangam stood protectively in front of Swati, his aura swirling around him, glowing orange and brown with threads of gold flashing through it.

In the distance, Rajan saw Keshavan and the other guide emerging from the temple, with blood dripping from their mouths – they had fallen for the bait of Chhinnamasta. With his activated Ajna, he sensed what was going to happen and shouted, 'Look out!' but his words were swallowed by the din. The guide shot a dart towards the monks, and the younger monk crumpled. The older monk pulled out his belt, which turned out to be a long flexible blade, an *urumi*, and began swirling it in a circle around him. This cleared the crowd around him and intercepted the darts the young assassin and the guide were shooting at him. People began to scream and run, but the old monk had checked the young female assassin, Keshavan and the guide.

Thangam lifted Rajan to his feet. Rajan grabbed Lakshmi and threw her over his shoulder. They began to run. They soon reached Arjun, who was seated near the exit, and Thangam threw him up over his shoulder.

The guide and the young assassin saw their prey escaping.

They exchanged a glance before pushing Keshavan onto the monk's blade. The blade wrapped itself around Keshavan's body, and the old man screamed in agony. The old monk was diverted, trying to loosen the blade from around Keshavan's body. In the confusion, the guide and the young female assassin got past him and continued their chase.

The crowd was immense, providing a mixed blessing. It slowed them down but also prevented their attackers from getting a clean shot. Rajan handed Lakshmi over to Swati as he turned around and faced his attackers, even as Arjun, barely conscious, hoarsely asked people to make way, clearing a path for their escape. But even so, the assassin was gaining on them.

Rajan looked at her, trying to read her mind. Her mental discipline was admirable; her mind was almost an impenetrable shield. Almost. He could read her confusion. *Why is she not attacking?* he asked himself.

The assassin saw the tall man turn around and stare at her. *Why is he doing that?* she thought. She could have lobbed a grenade and killed them all, but her new orders were clear: capture the man and child alive. She decided to get closer to them and capture them.

They reached the car. Thangam pushed Arjun into the very back. Swati got in next to Arjun and pulled Lakshmi next to her. As Thangam was getting into the car, the assassin lunged forward. At the same time, Rajan saw the guide release a dart towards them. He grabbed the assassin, pulling her towards him, almost into an embrace, so that the guide's dart embedded itself in her cheek. Bhura had started the car. Rajan was about to push the woman, when Thangam whispered, 'Pull her in.'

'Why?' asked Rajan.

'Let's find out who she works for.'

Bhura began threading the car through the gaps in the road. He knew every second mattered, and their destination, their *real* destination, was at least forty minutes away.

The woman's head had drooped forward onto her chest, her body slumped in the seat between Rajan and Thangam. She was moments from death. Rajan did not need his intuition to see that. If Lakshmi had been stronger, she would have tried healing her. He had no power of healing, and he wasn't sure if he would have helped her even if he had. He lifted her head roughly and stared into her eyes, forcing her with his mind to get her to reveal who she was and why she was trying to kill them.

The young woman felt the dart's venom cruise through her blood; as it did, her mental shield began to fray, and she answered.

'I come from a village near Dharamshala in Himachal Pradesh. I had studied well in school, and had passed my MBBS, the first in my village to do so. A year later, a local goonda raped me and my sister. I wanted revenge, but his gang covered it up. They even threatened to kill my parents. Then my family lost what little they had in the floods. The Vishkanyas offered revenge, protection and wealth for my family in return for my service. I accepted their offer. We have been tracking your family for months. No one else has evaded us for so long.'

'Why are you trying to kill us?'

'A group called the Cabal hired us to kill you.'

'But you did not kill us now.'

'We had strict instructions to kill you only when you were all together. We were asked to take your possessions and give it to them. But we sensed a power in you. We learned more about it when we visited the tantrics in Varanasi. We want this power for ourselves.'

'How many of you are there?'

The woman was fading fast. But she slurred, 'We are endless.'

'Are there others in Nepal?'

She did not answer, and as the light from the headlights of the oncoming vehicles fell on her face, Rajan saw that she was finally at peace.

The full moon rose higher in the sky, lighting their way as they crossed Kathmandu. They did not dare stop to drop off the woman's body – Lakshmi and Arjun were weakening too fast for that – and so she lay between them – a grim reminder of danger and mortality. Rajan looked out of the window. How many millions going home, visiting family, working. Completely unaware of what was happening. He still felt that they were being pursued. *Who else is after us*, he asked himself, *and will it ever stop*?

They had driven for half an hour when Swati, sitting between Lakshmi and Arjun, asked them to hurry as she felt their breathing slow down. Bhura sped up, weaving a little recklessly through the heavy traffic. Thangam turned around and took Arjun's hands in his. Rajan saw them glow for a second. He saw Thangam's aura weaken as Arjun breathed easier. Thangam released Arjun's hands, and then taking a deep breath, reached out over the assassin's body and further back to take Lakshmi's hands in his. As he did, he met Rajan's eyes.

They exchanged volumes in that glance. Rajan realized what Thangam was doing. What he was sacrificing. He also knew that nothing he could say would stop the old man. The old man smiled at Rajan, reading his thoughts and reassuring him, even as he took Lakshmi's hands into his. Rajan saw them both glow, and caught Thangam's body as it shook, and gently eased him back into his seat.

Arjun, awake now, though barely, grasped at Thangam. Rajan saw him glow blue. His Vishuddha was working strongly.

'I see you now,' Arjun whispered hoarsely. 'I see you. You can save us.'

'What are you saying, Arjun?' Swati asked. 'What do you see? How can Thangam save us?'

'At the end, look up at the sky, and into the air, and you will know what to do.'

His head lolled back, and the others realised there was no getting anything from him now.

The car sped on, and after a while, Bhura turned into what appeared to be a residential neighbourhood, where the traffic was much lighter. They drove for a couple of minutes before stopping in front of a red building with an arch over its entrance. There were no milling crowds here. They got down, Rajan and Swati holding onto Lakshmi. But Thangam stumbled, and Bhura took Arjun from him while simultaneously supporting his old friend. Lakshmi tried to put her hands on the old man, but he swatted her away. The assassin's body lay forgotten in the car.

They passed through the arch and stepped onto a flat courtyard, at the centre of which, a sandal-coloured metal fence enclosed another sunken courtyard. All around them, monks, priests and families went about their business, entering, praying and exiting quietly. But everyone who Rajan was able to connect eyes with seemed to have an aura of purple swirling around them – meaning their Ajna was in some state of openness. Rajan felt Lakshmi's breathing slow, and he ran forward, carrying her now, throwing caution to the winds. Bhura had tossed Arjun over his shoulder.

The moon had risen high in the sky as they descended into the inner courtyard. A small stone pathway, about three feet wide, snaked all around a giant tank of water, in the midst of the which lay an enormous statue of Vishnu. It was one of the most beautiful idols Rajan had ever seen: Budhanilkantha, he was called. Five metres in length, lying on his coiled serpent, Anantha, smiling serenely while savouring the Leela of existence.

Rajan remembered his father telling him the story of how the forces of light and dark churned the primordial ocean using the king of snakes wrapped around a divine mountain. Their churning drew out riches like the healing power of Dhanvantari and the wealth of Lakshmi. But to balance these out, the churning also spawned a deadly poison, Halahala. Rajan realized it was always about balance: light and dark; plenitude and poison. The universe quaked as the poison emerged, knowing its own end drew near. Then, Shiva gathered the poison from the celestial ocean and drank it. Shakti caught his throat, trapping the poison and turning his throat blue. And so, one of Shiva's names became Nilakantha, the blue-throated one. Rajan remembered that Shiva drank the waters of the Gosaikhund lake high up in the Himalayas to cool his throat afterward. That very lake that just happened to lie thirty-five kilometres above this temple. His father had told him that the waters from the lake fed this tank, giving it a potent healing power. Indeed, many believed that the hidden underside of this statue held the face of Shiva. He was Harihara – Vishnu and Shiva in one – as the prophecy had said.

On most days, the statue was shielded from the elements by a yellow cloth canopy, but tonight, that canopy was absent and the idol shone in the silver moonlight lying on waters that gleamed like molten silver. There was a narrow access platform to the tank itself for devotees to present their offerings. Rajan carried his daughter to the platform and laid her at the Lord's feet. He could see Bhura doing the same with Arjun next to him, while Thangam was kneeling on his other side, cupping the water in his hand. Swati stood behind them, looking out for pursuers.

Rajan watched as his daughter's aura glowed crimson, with swirls of gold pulsating up and down around her body. He realized that Thangam's gift of strength was the only thing that had kept her alive in the car. But now, as the boost of energy from Thangam's Manipura faded, he could feel her heartbeat slow right down. Desperation drove every other thought from his mind as he moved next to Arjun, with his daughter in his arms, and reached down to take some water from the tank to wash Lakshmi's face.

For a moment, there was just the sound of the lapping water and the chants of the devotees.

Then suddenly, out of nowhere, the huntress came flying at them, holding a glinting dagger in her hand. She had debated with herself on the weapon she would wield. A revolver or a dart would have been so much cleaner and far more efficient, but that was not who she was. She lived for the taste, the grist and the feel of tearing into blood and flesh, which only a dagger could offer.

She leapt at Lakshmi, seeing that the child was nearly unconscious and somewhat unprotected, with her father bent down toward the water. The old man, the one who had charged at her, seemed to have weakened too. But Thangam, seemingly drawing strength from the water, was too quick for her. He jumped up and deflected her away from the child. But, her dagger cut through his shoulder, leaving a deep gash behind. He staggered back, almost falling into the water. The huntress turned to Swati, who had rushed forward. Her dagger glittered in the moonlight. Swati screamed as it came down, expecting to be hit, but the dagger sliced through thin air. Thangam had pulled the huntress back and was holding onto her, while she, like a restrained tigress, thrashed about, slashing and hissing, trying to escape his hold.

Bhura jumped up but it was too late. The huntress plunged the dagger into Thangam's side. A dark red stain began spreading across Thangam's abdomen. His grip loosened, and the huntress broke free. She sprang at Swati, but Bhura lunged forward and pushed her. Caught unbalanced, she stumbled and tripped on the *paduka* and hit her back on a stone pillar and fell down.

The platform, built to hold two – maybe three at a stretch – was unable to handle the sudden chaos. When Bhura rushed forward, he knocked Rajan to the side, which caused Arjun and Lakshmi to slip into the pond. Rajan tried jumping in after his daughter, but he found his legs had turned to stone. He watched helplessly as she disappeared under the silver waters.

Monks came forward and formed a circle around the group, shielding them from any further attack. Swati had thrown herself on Thangam's chest. The old man was breathing raggedly, but he smiled as he stroked her hair.

'Don't cry, Paapa. I've lived a full life. For most of it, I thought it was pointless and cruel, but now I know that there is so much meaning inside, if we only look for it. I see you are not alone, and that's all I need.'

Then he looked around, and whispered, 'Now I see', and then looked up, 'Now I see'. He pushed Swati back gently and stretched out his hands, turning them and pressing his palms flat on the earth. The ground trembled – not shaking, but pulsing – as though something deep below had drawn a single long breath. The air around Thangam thinned and cooled. Monks felt the warmth drain upward, like invisible rivers of heat racing toward the sky. The clouds above the temple began twisting into a slow spiral even as a faint blue corona flared around Thangam's body. Instruments on distant weather towers would later record a sudden surge in outgoing longwave radiation – a single point of brightness over Nepal that spread outward through the upper troposphere.

For an instant, daylight seemed to return: with Thangam as the sun. Then his body sagged; the glow contracted to a heartbeat-sized spark, and went out.

Thangam's eyes closed. Bhura and Swati wept over his body as the moon disappeared behind a cloud, leaving the world in darkness, the face and the feet of the deity alone glowing in the light of oil lamps.

Rajan was distraught, seething in anger and impotence. He wanted to hurt someone, something, when he felt the huntress stirring. She appeared to have broken her spine in the fall for she did not move. But her eyes were open. He knew what Thangam would have counselled. As much as he wanted to hurt her, kill her, he needed information.

'Who are you? And why are you after us?' he asked intentionally.

The woman smiled but did not speak.

Rajan felt her mind fighting his. He asked again, this time from his mind, pushing her mercilessly to answer. Now, his mind sensed the tendrils of truth emerging from within hers.

'There have always been those of us who feast on chaos,' she seemed to say. 'And now, old bonds are fading, old practices dying, allowing chaos a free rein. But then, a year ago, we were warned of a threat to our rule. A return to balance. A warning that came from a member of your family,' her thoughts mocked him. 'It's always family who betrays you, isn't it?'

He said nothing, but she noted from the change in his expression that her mental barb had drawn blood. Her smile widened. 'He said that you have the power to restore balance. Balance is poison to chaos, which is the source of our power and profit. We couldn't have that. It may seem like you have won this bout, priest, but never underestimate the power of chaos.'

The huntress closed her eyes.

Rajan could feel her presence fade.

But there was no joy in his victory. Thangam was dead and his daughter and Arjun were gone.

'Is this it?' Rajan shouted at the stone idol. 'Is this it, death and more death? What's the point? Where is the balance?'

Rajan's sobs grew hoarser and hoarser as he slumped down.

Then, from nowhere and everywhere, came the sound of a flute, a single note, followed by another and then one more. The moon emerged from behind her cloudy veil, bright and silver now, and the waters glistened, making it seem like Narayana was almost sleeping on his milky ocean, with ancient mountains all around.

Rajan looked up. The music and the moonlight were like sweet rain on one's face, but how did it matter when his daughter was gone! But then he saw a ripple in the silver waters. He stopped and shook his head. Was he dreaming? But there it was again. And again. And again.

Lakshmi and Arjun rose from the waters.

He could move finally, and with tears running down his cheeks, he pulled his daughter into his arms, even as Bhura pulled Arjun out. Rajan tried to wipe his daughter's face, but he found her dry to the touch and breathing gently. Her face was blooming, and so was Arjun's.

He heard a cough and felt a touch on his shoulder. He turned and saw it was the old monk standing behind him, bearing Keshavan. Rajan found bile rise up in his throat. Right then, he could have strangled Keshavan where he lay dying. The old man said, 'They got Krishna after we left Sonauli. They sent me a video of him being tortured late last night. What would you do if someone threatened Lakshmi? Krishna is my Lakshmi.' And with that, he died.

Rajan found himself shaking in anger. The loss of

Thangam was too raw, and with that loss, his calm had vanished.

But the moonlight and the flute continued, working their magic. Lakshmi and Arjun were alive. The old monk sat down beside Rajan and placed a hand on his shoulder. In spite of himself, Rajan felt himself calming down.

The music from the flute continued, and Rajan looked up at the moon.

As he did, something told him that the water was key. As though in a trance, he set Lakshmi down and lifted Thangam's body and gently placed it in the water. Swati and Bhura shouted as the old man's body sank into the silvery waters.

Rajan could not explain why he had done this, except that it had seemed the right thing to do. They waited, but Thangam's body, unlike the others, did not rise again.

The flute's music stopped. The moon was directly overhead, and after one interminable moment, the water turned gold.

Everyone gasped.

The glow from the golden water and the silver moonlight united to form a halo around Budhanilkantha. Rajan felt tears running down his cheeks – on this most divine of nights, he felt Thangam's jeevatma merging with the paramatma.

No one moved. No one spoke until he heard the old monk cough gently, breaking the spell.

He turned and asked him, 'What's happening?'

The old monk smiled. 'Balance is returning.'

'How?'

'Do you think it is an accident that the two chakras to survive are Anahata and Vishuddha? He,' the monk said, pointing to Arjun, 'will have the power of speech, the power to know and speak the truth. He will persuade and show people that all they need, all they seek, lies within. Once they believe that, all the charlatans in the world will try in vain to shake them.

'But she, she carries the most precious gift. Anahata can heal, but in very rare cases, it can bestow the power of Kundalini on others.' He saw Rajan's expression change, and smiled. 'She can create an army to restore the balance.'

'And finally, there is the gift of Mooladhara, the foundational chakra, and Manipura, the chakra of strength. Your friend's Manipura saved countless lives. But his Mooladhara…With his sacrifice, your friend has given the world a fighting chance. Today is the day of union, of rebirth. And on this day, here, his sacrifice shifts the foundation within each of us, creating a need, almost an itch, in each of us to strive for balance, allowing the power of Vishuddha to work its magic.'

'Who are you?' Rajan asked. 'How do you know all of this?'

The monk was about to answer but stopped as he saw Lakshmi's eyelids flutter and Arjun stir with a groan. A hushed whisper passed through the crowd and then there was silence as everyone held their breath. Lakshmi and Arjun opened their eyes. Their irises were liquid gold. They sat up, and a sigh went through the crowd, as auras shimmered around them. Rajan looked towards Swati in enquiry, and she nodded. It wasn't just him; everyone could see the auras.

He thought he heard the monk whisper, 'It's beginning.'

Epilogue

THE MAN COULD NOT BELIEVE WHAT HIS EYES WERE telling him.

CERES had picked up an intense, short-lived flare of outgoing longwave radiation over Nepal, near Kathmandu. It was nothing like he'd ever seen or imagined. The upper atmosphere was changing.

This could pause the beast.

He allowed himself to smile. To hope.

But then the data from the Argo float popped up: the deep ocean was still far too warm. They had bought some time, but the battle was far from over.

Glossary

adharmic: acting against the code of behaviour

agraharam: the locality adjacent to a temple where priests and their families typically stay

amrit: the nectar of immortality

Amsam: 9th divisional chart, used to understand the strength of planets

angavastraman: upper cloth

Appa: father

arati: a ritual of light, where a lamp is circled before the deity in reverence

aruval: a deadly-looking scimitar

ashtakshara: eight-syllabled

Ashtashaktis: eight goddesses

atma: soul

Attangudi: a bright red tile from the Chettinad region in Tamil Nadu

Azhagiya Manavalan: handsome bridegroom

badusha: an Indian sweet, somewhat similar to a glazed donut

bhakti yoga: the path to salvation through love

bhashyam: an explanation

Chandra: moon

chellam: a term of endearment

chittappa: father's younger brother

churanam: medicinal paste

dabaras: a tumbler in a container, a traditional way to drink coffee in south India

dakshina: token

dargah: shrine built over the grave of a Sufi saint

Dashas: the periods into which one's life was divided in Indian astrology

dharma: a code of behaviour centred on righteousness

doshas: an Ayurvedic concept of metaphysical humours that govern the body, personality and mind

gandam: disaster

garbha griha: sanctum sanctorum

gopuram: temple tower

ishta devata: favourite deity

jeevasamadhi: final resting place for a saint

jeevatma: the individual soul

kachori: deep-fried Indian snack with a sweet or savoury filling

kadalai mittai: peanut candy

Kali muthipocchu: Kali has ripened

Kanna: a term of endearment

kapalbhati: rapid breathing technique

Karthikai: the Tamil month which falls between 15 November and 15 December

kashayam: decoction

kriya: practice

kudumi: topknot

kumkum: vermillion; a temple prasad

Kundalini: Kundalini is a spiritual energy, symbolized as a coiled serpent resting at the base of the spine. Through yoga and meditation, it can be awakened to ascend through the body's energy centers, or chakras, leading toward spiritual awakening or enlightenment.

Kurai ondrum illai, marai moorthy kanna: I lack nothing, Krishna. 'Marai' could mean hidden or the Vedas.

Kurai Ondrum Illai: a Tamil devotional song, about how a devotee sings, 'I lack nothing, because I have the Lord's grace.'

kutti: little one

Lagna: the first house

lagnaadhipathi: the planet that represents a person

lingam: a phallic-shaped representation of Shiva

machan: a raised hut in a forest, often used by the forest department to observe wildlife unobtrusively

madisaar: nine-yard saree

mahayogi: great saint

Mangla Arati: the first arati of the day

Mannikka: forgive me

Margazhi Sashti: Margazhi is the Tamil month that falls between December and January. Sashti is the 6th day of the lunar fortnight in the Hindu calendar.

Matsya: fish

maya: the illusory nature of the world that shields humans from understanding the true nature of the world.

milagai podi: a chilli powder leavened by roasted lentils and other spices, a traditional accompaniment in a south Indian breakfast

mitahara: nutritious diet

moksha: spiritual release

Mooladhara: the first chakra in the Kundalini practice, said to be located in the base of the spine

mridangam: traditional South Indian drum

mullai: Indian jasmine

muttram: central courtyard

naadaswaram: traditional South Indian trumpet

naamam: a Vaishnavite forehead mark

paapa: baby, in Tamil

pachadi: a South Indian side-dish with vegetables or fruits in a creamy or relish-like base of yoghurt or tamarind

paduka: a statue of the feet of the deity

panchamritam: sacred offering made with fruits and honey; literally, five elixirs

paramatma: universal soul

Patashala: a traditional school for young Brahmin boys

payasam: milk-based dessert

periya-thaatha: elder grandfather

podi: a spicy condiment made of chillies and lentils

prakaram: circular passageway that surrounds the sanctum sanctorum

prana: the breathing techniques

prasad: sacred offering

prashnam: question

Pulliyamaram Eri: tamarind lake

rachandan: sandal paste applied on the idol and believed to have healing powers

Ramanuja: Ramanuja is considered one of the greatest saints in Vaishnavism. His samadhi is a shrine within the Srirangam.

samsara: worldly life

santhai: the weekly farmer's market

Sesha: Adi Sesha, or Sesha, is the five-headed serpent on whom Vishnu sleeps in the milky ocean

shakti: energy

Shashtiamsa: 60th division of an astrological chart

shloka: a verse or couplet of Sanskrit verse

siddhis: supernatural powers

Sridevi: another name for Goddess Lakshmi, Vishnu's consort

Thaatha: grandfather

Thai Purappadu: a procession in the Tamil month of Thai, which falls between January and February

thailam: medicated oil

thambi: younger brother in Tamil; a term used by an older person to address a younger man

thandai: a South Asian beverage made with milk, nuts, seeds and spices

thayir saadam: curd rice

theertham: holy water

upanayana: thread ceremony

urumi: a long flexible blade

varada-hasta: boon-conferring pose

Vargottama: the state of a planet which occupies the same house in Rasi and 9th divisional chart

Vasant Purnima: Vasant Purnima is the full moon day falling in the month of Phalguna, or Panguni, the last month in the Tamil year. This sometimes coincides with the Tamil festival, Panguni Uthiram, where Uthiram is the name of a constellation. It's most popularly celebrated as Holi.

Vishnu Sahasranama: a hymn on the thousand names of Vishnu

A Note and an Acknowledgement

This is a risky bet. The driving impulse was to reach beyond the readership of climate non-fiction and op-eds, beyond documentaries and reels. We need greater climate action, and the more people drawn into this arena, the better.

I began writing this very early, before my first column in *The Hindu* was penned, but then the first few chapters lay in cold storage for nearly a decade. It needed a push from Namita Gokhale, who told me, 'Fiction goes to places that non-fiction never can.' And a growing sense that much of existing climate fiction either didn't speak to the good old-fashioned thriller reader, or wasn't rooted in our landscapes, in our ways of being.

Is the book fiction? Yes, indubitably. The places Rajan and his companions travel through are drawn from real terrain, however; the temples they visit and the shrines within are real, but as you will discover, there are elements that are imagined and used creatively within an entirely fictional narrative. Much of the climate science underlying the fictional climate events in the book holds true as well, with one very important exception.

Now, for the thanks. Namita, for pushing me – in more ways than one. Thomas, for believing in this book and backing it, and for his valuable input. Kanishka and team for their thoughtful comments; Meru and her team for theirs. Vanessa Sasson, for showing me that non-fiction writers can step into fiction. Sukumar Ranganathan, for his input. R. Srinithi and L. Ramakrishnan, for theirs. If only you all knew how nervous I was. Anupama Manral, for her careful reading and for shepherding this project to fruition.

And now, for my family – my daughter, who insisted the story needed a touch of magic (completely upending the plot in the process); my son for his patience; my parents, for immersing me in the world of temples early on; my mother, for her comments; and my husband, for his close reading and, as always, the inappropriate humour.

Mridula Ramesh is the award-winning author of *The Climate Solution* and *Watershed* and the founder of Sundaram Climate Institute, which focuses on waste and water solutions. She is an active climatetech angel investor with a portfolio of over thirty start-ups, and is involved with several initiatives to spur climatetech entrepreneurship. A graduate with distinction from Cornell University and an MBA from the Kellogg School of Management, she worked in McKinsey's Silicon Valley office and is the executive director of Sundaram Textiles – the company was amongst the first textile companies globally to win the coveted TPM Excellence Award. She is part of the board of trustees of World Wildlife Fund, India, the former Chairperson of the Board of Governors of the National Institute of Technology, Andhra Pradesh, and is part of the Global Future Councils of the World Economic Forum. She is a columnist with leading Indian newspapers, penning a monthly column in *The Hindustan Times*.

She lives and experiments in Madurai in a (nearly) net-zero-waste and water-secure home with her husband and two children.